MARRY ME, COWBOY!

When your lover is a cowboy…

You'll have a Stetson on the bedpost and boots
under the bed.
And you'll have a man who's hard-livin',
hard-lovin' and sexy as hell to keep you warm
all night…*every* night!

These are the pleasures Victoria Thornton,
Roishin Grant, Erin Taylor and Sara Jane Jones
are about to discover.

Watch it happen in these four delightful new
stories by your favorite authors!

ABOUT THE AUTHORS

Janet Dailey needs no introduction. This well-known author has been writing since 1975. Her first book, *No Quarter Asked*, was published in 1976 by Harlequin Books. She was the company's first American author. Over the next six years, Harlequin published 57 romance novels by Janet Dailey. She broke into mainstream fiction more than 15 years ago and is now the number one female writer in America and the third bestselling living author in the world. Janet and her husband, Bill, live in a spectacular plantation-style mansion on the shore of Lake Taneycomo in Branson, Missouri.

Margaret Way's passionate romances and her wonderfully lyrical descriptions of her homeland, Australia, have made her a longtime favorite with readers. Her writing career began in 1970 with the publication of her first romance. Prior to this, Margaret had a musical career—she was a pianist, teacher, vocal coach and accompanist. She still plays the piano seriously; she also collects art and antiques and is devoted to her garden. Born in Brisbane, Australia, Margaret now makes her home in beautiful Moreton Bay in the state of Queensland.

Susan Fox won two Romance Writers of America Golden Heart awards at the start of her writing career. She has been a lifelong fan of Westerns and cowboys—she thinks of romantic heroes in terms of Stetsons and boots and, in her own words, "may never do a story without a Western man." Readers will be happy to know she has plans to write many books in the future. Susan lives with her youngest son, Patrick, in Des Moines, Iowa.

Anne McAllister taught, copyedited, capped deodorant bottles and ghost-wrote sermons before publishing her first romance novel in 1985. Since then, she's written more than a dozen bestselling American Romance novels. She also writes for Harlequin Presents. In all her stories, Anne writes about relationships—how they develop and how they affect the people who share them. Born in Southern California, she spent much of her time on the beach and still considers herself a beach person even though she's lived in the Midwest—where she and her husband have raised four children—for more than twenty years.

MARRY ME, COWBOY!

JANET DAILEY
MARGARET WAY
SUSAN FOX
ANNE McALLISTER

Harlequin Books

TORONTO • NEW YORK • LONDON
AMSTERDAM • PARIS • SYDNEY • HAMBURG
STOCKHOLM • ATHENS • TOKYO • MILAN
MADRID • WARSAW • BUDAPEST • AUCKLAND

HARLEQUIN BOOKS

MARRY ME, COWBOY!
Copyright © 1995 by Harlequin Enterprises B.V.

ISBN 0-373-83299-0

MARRY ME, COWBOY! first printing April 1995
The publisher acknowledges the copyright holders
of the individual works as follows:

RIDING HIGH
Copyright © 1995 by Janet Dailey
THE MAN FROM SOUTHERN CROSS
Copyright © 1995 by Margaret Way
CHANCE FOR A LIFETIME
Copyright © 1995 by Susan Fox
HITCHED IN TIME
Copyright © 1995 by Anne McAllister

CONTENTS

RIDING HIGH

Janet Dailey

Acknowledgment:
Recognition is given to Lauback Literacy
.for its use of a short version of this work
to promote literacy.

Chapter One

"No way! Forget it, Martin. I'm not going to do it and that's final!" Deke Flanders leaned back in his well-worn cowhide chair and propped his muddy boots on top of his equally battered desk. A deep frown creased his rugged face as he spoke into the phone.

"Oh, come on, Deke," said the nasal voice on the other end of the line. "Do it for old times' sake. The two of us go back years now. I'd do *anything* for you, and you know it."

"But *I* wouldn't ask *you* to teach a bratty movie star how to ride a horse—in *one* weekend." Deke pushed back his Stetson with his thumb, a gesture he frequently used when he was irritated. Martin knew better than to ask him for something like this. Of all people, Martie was well aware of his reasons for leaving Hollywood and moving to Colorado. Every day Deke congratulated himself for leaving Tinseltown behind and making a "real" life for himself here among the mountains and aspen pines.

"But Victoria Thornton is gorgeous!" Martin argued. He certainly didn't give up easily. "Don't be an idiot, Flanders. Do you know how many men would kill for this chance?"

Oh, yeah, Deke knew. He'd seen the pictures, the articles, the television interviews. Like a billion other people, he'd been watching the night Victoria had received her Oscar, floating across the stage in a dress that flowed over her shapely body like liquid gold. So what if she was stunning? Stunning women were a plentiful commodity in Hollywood, and Deke had seen more than his share.

He had also seen the tabloid covers while waiting in line at the local grocery store. Victoria Thornton was as well-known for her fiery temper and arrogance as for her mane of brassy red curls and tourmaline green eyes.

"If other guys would kill for the chance to spend a weekend with her," Deke said, "they're welcome to it. Put the two of us together and we might wind up murdering each other. Then you'd have to find another star for your precious movie."

"No, you wouldn't," Martin replied in a singsong voice that perturbed Deke even more. "You're wrong about Victoria. She can be really nice." He paused, then added, "When she gets everything she wants."

"What a sweetheart," Deke muttered. This battle of wills and words had been going on for half an hour, and Deke was growing weary, not an uncommon occurrence when he argued with Martin.

"Come on, Deke," Martin whined. "She's my star, and we begin filming on Monday. She has to be able to ride a horse by then."

Oh, no, Deke thought. *He's graduated to whimpering. In a minute he'll slide over into full-scale blubbering.* Deke could feel himself starting to cave. He couldn't help himself. A highly successful director, Martin Conroy had helped Deke get into the movies years ago as a stunt cowboy and all-around wrangler. Between riding wild horses, roping getaway steers, breaking bottles and chairs over bad guys' heads and making more money than he had ever thought possible, Deke had to admit he'd loved being a Hollywood wrangler.

Best of all, the movie business had enabled him to buy this spread, a piece of land he loved more than anything on earth. Okay, he thought, maybe he *did* owe Martin this one last favor.

"Has she ever been on a horse before?" he asked, feeling defeated.

"She says she has." Martin was almost gleeful. "But to be honest, you wouldn't know it by watching her ride."

"Oh, wonderful," Deke said sarcastically as he shoved his Stetson farther back on his head. "I can see I have my work cut out for me."

"Great!" Martin replied. Deke hated how happy he sounded. Ol' Martie had won. Again. "She'll be there at your ranch first thing Friday morning."

"Goody," Deke said as he hung up the phone. "I can hardly wait."

Rising from his chair, he stretched his long lanky body, then reached for the magazine lying on his desk. He picked it up and flipped through the pages until he came to the article he'd seen earlier that morning.

Victoria Thornton stood in front of her Hollywood mansion, wearing an elegant sequined evening gown. She was about to step into a red Ferrari that must have cost as much as Deke's ranch house.

Deke sniffed contemptuously. Glitter and fluff, sparkle and phony baloney. That was what Hollywood and women like that were all about. She'd probably never done a real day's work in her life or even broken a sweat, except maybe in a sauna.

But when Deke looked past the designer gown, the fancy car, the mansion, and stared into the woman's pale green eyes, she gazed back at him with an intensity that went through him like a brush fire.

Okay, so maybe she wasn't all fluff. Come to think of it, she looked like a pretty strong-minded woman. Teaching her anything might prove quite a challenge. In fact, it would probably be a pain in the neck.

But Martin was right, Deke decided as he continued to study the picture. Victoria Thornton *was* gorgeous.

"NO, MARTIE. I'm not going to do it, and you can't make me!" Victoria knew she sounded like a petulant child, but she didn't care. When she was scared, she got angry. Fury had always been her best defense.

She and Martin Conroy were squaring off like a couple of bantamweights in the middle of a studio stage. Surrounding them was a country kitchen, one of the interior sets for her latest movie, *San Francisco Bride*. But Victoria didn't care about the set, the movie, or even her career at the moment. She had a higher priority—her life.

Martin walked closer and patted her shoulder. Cringing, she crossed her arms over her chest and leaned away from him.

"Deke is a great guy," he said. "Really, he'll make it easy for you. You'll see. He's just dying to do this."

"No, Martie, *no!* What part of that word don't you understand? I wish you would stop pushing this horse thing down my throat. It isn't part of my contract, and I don't have to do it."

She tossed her long red curls behind her shoulder and walked around one of the fake walls, made of two-by-four studs and thin plywood. Picking up her leather jacket from a stack of game-show props in the corner, she said, "I told you, I *hate* horses. I don't dislike them, I *despise* them. They smell bad. They're big and heavy, and they step on your feet. If you don't give them carrots or sugar or apples, they bite you. And they have flies, Martin. I hate flies, too."

Martin caught up with her, gently took her arm and guided her toward the back door. "Now, now, Deke knows how very important you are to me, Vickie. He won't let anything bad happen to you. I promise."

Victoria had been in the business long enough to know when she was being buttered up, and Martie was slathering it on even thicker than usual. She knew she was only important to Martin because of all the millions he had invested in *San Francisco Bride,* his first Western, a lifelong ambition of his.

"Please, sweetheart," he said. "If you'll do this for me, I'll owe you one."

She considered that for a minute or so. In the past she had found it most advantageous to have the director "owe you one" in the beginning of a movie. Somewhere along the line, you would certainly find an opportunity to cash in the marker.

"You'll owe me a *big* one," she said, giving him a sly sideways smile.

Grabbing her, he planted a big sloppy kiss on her cheek. "Vickie, you're a doll!" he said.

She clucked her tongue and shook her head. "Martie, Martie, when will you join the ranks of the politically correct? It's no longer considered appropriate to call a woman a doll."

Martin thought for a moment. "Okay...you're a heck of a broad."

"Gee, thanks. That's so much better, Martie," she said as she slipped on her jacket and headed out the door. "There's hope for the male gender, after all."

Once outside the building, she dropped her facade of casual confidence and leaned against the stucco wall to catch her breath. Her throat felt like it was about to close completely, and her heart pounded against her ribs.

Was she really going to do this? A cold, clammy, sick feeling stole over her at the thought. Some people were phobic about spiders, some about snakes. But she would rather invite a dozen black widows to meander across her naked body or play a game of crack the whip with an angry rattler than get on a horse.

You're being very dumb about this, Vickie, she told herself. *It's just a horse.*

Sure, a great big horse with biting teeth and kicking hooves and—

I can't do it, she thought as her anxiety escalated into a first-degree panic attack. *I can't!*

But she knew she had to. Maybe her contract didn't say so in black and white, but her ability to get on a horse and stay there was necessary for the movie. As an actress, she never skimped. If it made the picture better, she did it, whatever the cost. And she wasn't going to back down now.

Taking a couple of deep breaths, she forced herself to calm down. She didn't have to worry—at least not yet. Saturday was still two days away.

Two more days to live, to feel the sunshine on her face, to smell the roses and enjoy the sound of children's laughter, to get her affairs in order, to . . .

Oh, stop already, she thought as she headed for her red Ferrari, parked behind the studio in the slot stenciled with her name. She had to get her fear under control before she arrived at that ranch in Colorado. If she didn't, the horse wouldn't need to stomp her flat or eat her alive. She'd just die of heart failure the moment she saw it.

DEKE PROPPED one arm on top of the rusted pitchfork's handle and wiped the perspiration off his brow with the back of his hand, leaving muddy streaks across his forehead. He didn't care. If a guy wanted to raise horses, he couldn't worry about a little thing like getting dirty.

A lock of his black hair hung down into his sapphire blue eyes. Blowing upward, he tried to dislodge it, but the sweat-drenched curl didn't budge.

Ranch work was hard, no doubt about that, and there seemed to be no end to it. No matter how early he got up or how fast he tried to mow through his tasks, he was never finished before that last ray of sunlight dipped below the distant mountaintops. But Deke didn't mind; in fact, he thrived on it. The air was clean, clear and sweet up here in the Rockies, a definite contrast to Los Angeles, where he had lived for nearly ten years.

The thought of L.A. was quickly followed by a mental reminder that his weekend guest would be arriving soon. He glanced at his watch. Ten-thirty. Yep, she'd be along any minute now.

For a moment he studied the muck on his jeans and considered going into the house to change clothes in honor of the celebrated arrival. Then he decided not to. If Miss Victoria wanted to experience the authentic Old West, she might as well get the full treatment.

Peering across the green pasture, which was surrounded by freshly painted white fences and dotted with the occasional pine, Deke saw a cloud of dust coming down the road. Victoria Thornton—Oscar-winning actress, spoiled brat, worthless horsewoman—had arrived.

At least she was punctual; he had to give her that. But what the heck was she riding in?

As the automobile drew nearer, he realized it was a white limousine. An extremely long, stretched-to-the-maximum, Mercedes limousine. Deke shook his head and chuckled. When he had been on the rodeo circuit, he had lived in trailers smaller than that. He grinned broadly when he saw how much of his good ol' down-home dust was collecting on the pristine white finish.

"Might as well get used to eatin' a little dirt, lady," he mumbled.

The Mercedes pulled to a stop in front of the house. After propping the pitchfork against the side of the barn, Deke strolled across the field to meet his new student.

The driver's door opened and a chauffeur stepped out, wearing a tuxedo.

A penguin suit, Deke thought with an inward chuckle. The guy looked as though he had just stepped off the cover of a gentlemen's fashion magazine. In a perverse sort of way, Deke was glad he hadn't changed his mucky clothes.

As Deke neared the limo, the driver opened the rear door. A long pair of blue-jean-clad legs slid out, followed by the most breathtakingly beautiful woman Deke had ever seen. Most Hollywood stars had proved to be disappointing when he had seen them in person for the first time. They never lived up to the image created on the screen.

But Victoria was different. She was even *more* gorgeous.

Now he regretted his decision not to change. Instantly his clothes seemed more ragged, filthier and much more smelly than they had a minute ago.

On the other hand, she was decked out in full Western garb—or at least, Hollywood's version of Western garb. She wore a plaid shirt, designer jeans and snakeskin cowboy boots with silver-tipped toes. Everything was crisp and new.

Deke didn't know whether to laugh or be touched by the fact that she had bought this costume for the weekend here at Flanders' Folly. The outfit was totally impractical, as she would soon discover. The boots would kill her feet, and the seam on the inside of the jeans would rub her thighs raw when she rode.

Oh, well, he thought. What else could you expect from a city slicker?

He ran his fingers through his hair and wished he had combed it. Heck, if he'd known she was going to look this good, he might have even taken a shower.

"Hello," he called out. "Welcome to Flanders' Folly."

"Ah . . . thanks . . . I think," she said, choking on the dust that swirled around her.

Deke couldn't help noticing how her red hair shone in the morning sun like a polished copper kettle. He wished she would take off her dark sunglasses so he could see her eyes.

Gracefully she glided toward him and held out her hand. "You must be Deke," she said. "I'm Victoria Thornton."

"I know," he said, feeling awkward as one of his Arabian colts ten minutes after it was born. He took her hand in his and was surprised at the firmness of her handshake. "I recognize you. I'm a big fan of yours."

She took off her sunglasses and fixed him with that same intense green stare he had seen in the magazine. "Really?" she asked.

He laughed. "Well, I am now."

"That's good," she said offhandedly. "It'll help us get through this miserable weekend. I have to tell you, I'm not looking forward to this ordeal one bit."

Her bluntness surprised and irritated him. He hadn't exactly asked for this job or been counting the hours until Miss Fancy Pants arrived. But at least he was courteous enough not to say so the minute they met. His welcome smile vanished. Stepping back a bit, he crossed his arms over his broad chest.

"Okay," he said, drawling the word. "Then let's get this show on the road. The sooner we start, the sooner we'll be rid of each other."

There! With grim satisfaction he watched as her face registered her own shock and aggravation. She wasn't that all-fired secure herself or she wouldn't have been so easy to rattle.

"Fine," she snapped. She turned to the driver who was standing quietly beside the limo. At her curt nod, he hurried to the back of the Mercedes and withdrew four enormous suitcases from its cavernous trunk.

"If you'll just show Michael where to put those..." she said, sending the words in Deke's general direction but refusing to make eye contact with him.

Something about the airy wave of her hand caused the stubborn bull inside him to snort and paw the ground. She was even worse than he'd anticipated. But this Hollywood princess had waved her red petticoat in front of the wrong bull. Deke reminded himself that he didn't have to play these games the way Martie did. It wasn't *his* movie that was on the line here. In fact, he didn't give a hoot whether she learned to ride or not. She could sit on a horse backwards and ride it to straight to Hades for all he cared.

"I said," she repeated impatiently, "if you would just tell Michael where he can put my bags...."

Deke shook his head. No, it was just too tempting, and he prided himself on being a gentleman, whether he was in the presence of a lady or a spoiled brat.

But he couldn't resist one little dig. "Just drop them there where you stand, Mike," he said evenly.

Victoria's pretty face flushed as she looked down at the dusty dirt road. "Ex-cu-se me, Mr. Flanders," she said. "But that is Louis Vuitton luggage."

"Well, I reckon Mr. Vuitton is going to be pretty upset when he realizes you've got his suitcases. The airlines get my luggage mixed up sometimes, too."

She shot him a look filled with disdain, but he ignored it. He had recognized the expensive brand name, but apparently she had decided he was a hick. So be it.

Turning his back to her, he began to saunter toward the house. Once again his Southern upbringing came to the fore, reminding him of how rude it was to walk in front of a lady. But he silently congratulated himself for putting Miss Victoria Thornton in her place. If she knew who was boss from the start, this whole rigmarole would go more smoothly.

He continued toward the converted barn that served as his ranch house. Victoria followed a few steps behind, wearing a pout on her famous face, while Michael struggled with the four suitcases. Taking pity on him, Deke grabbed two of the bags and pushed open the front door with the toe of his boot.

"This way," he said as he hurried through the living room.

He braced himself for a sarcastic comment about his decor, but Victoria smiled and nodded approvingly as she looked around the enormous room. Deke had designed it himself. Not in fancy interior-decorator fashion, but sitting in the middle of the old barn with a stack of notebook paper and a couple of sharp yellow pencils. He liked to think the place had a "manly" feel about it, with its high ceiling supported with rough-hewn beams, the stone fireplace that reached to the roof, the redwood walls and rustic furniture.

Big, solid, masculine. That was the way Deke liked it. He was more than a little surprised that she seemed to like it, too.

"Very nice," she said. "Feels homey."

Deke was pleased but determined not to show it. With a nod toward the hall he said, "Your room is this way."

"My room?" she replied in a slightly sarcastic tone as she followed him, Michael in tow. "You mean, I get to sleep in the house? I thought you'd put me out in the barn—the unconverted one, that is."

"I wanted to," Deke said, "but Maggie didn't approve."

"Who's Maggie?"

"You'll meet her later."

He led them to a small bedroom at the end of the hall. "I washed the sheets," he said, pointing to the iron frame bed with its colorful red-and-blue quilt. He jerked a thumb toward the bathroom across the hall. "And I put out soap and towels and stuff in there."

"Gee, just like the Plaza," she said, running her perfectly manicured fingertip through the layer of dust that covered the antique dresser.

Deke noted the exaggeration in the gesture and knew she was trying to get his goat. "I don't dust," he said. "There's no point. A week later, you just have to do it all over again."

She walked to the mullioned window, pulled the curtain aside and looked out at the scenery. "No point in washing windows, either, I see," she said. "Come spring, they'd just be dirty again."

"You got it."

He tossed the two suitcases he had been holding onto the bed and motioned for Michael to do the same. The driver hesitated, glanced from Deke to Victoria, then carefully placed the two bags he carried beside the dresser.

"Will that be all, ma'am?" he asked with a slight bow.

"Yes, I suppose so." She gave Deke a look that made him wish he could apply his boot to her shapely fanny.

"Then I'll return on Sunday night," Michael said as he tipped his hat to her.

"Don't be late," she called after him. "I have a feeling that by then I will have enjoyed Flanders' Folly as much as I can stand."

That did it! Deke whirled on his heel and left the room. He told himself it was because he was afraid he might pop her one if he stayed, but he knew it was because he couldn't think of a good retort.

Hurrying after the chauffeur, he called, "Yeah, Michael, don't be late. In fact, why don't you come back early." He glanced toward the bedroom. Seeing her standing, arms akimbo, in the doorway, he added, "Make that *very* early. Say, in about ten minutes."

Chapter Two

"LESSON ONE—make friends with your horse," Deke said as he led Victoria across the backyard and down a winding path to the barn.

"I've never had a horse for a friend," she replied dryly. "I never really considered them friendship material."

"Then you don't know what you're missing." He swung the wide door open to reveal an immaculately kept series of stalls, inhabited by numerous horses. "A horse," he continued, "is a man's best friend."

"I thought that was a dog."

"Boy, you *do* need lessons," he said with a smug chuckle.

Victoria didn't get the idea that he was laughing because he considered her witty. She felt laughed *at,* and being ridiculed was one of her least favorite things in the world.

As a skinny, rather painfully plain adolescent, she had been subjected to more than her share of ill-natured teasing. But over the years—through the magic of growth, exercise, cosmetics and careful wardrobe choices—Victoria had managed to leave that image behind.

Deep inside, she still felt like a scrawny little freckle-faced kid; she certainly didn't feel beautiful. But the world constantly assured her that she was, and the public accolades were a passable substitute for self-acceptance.

Breathing in the earthy smells of the barn, she had to admit it wasn't an altogether unpleasant place to be—not as unpleasant as its owner. The sweet scent of the grain and hay blended with the animal smells to create a unique fragrance she found strangely soothing, in spite of her fear.

Rays of sunlight streamed into the barn from a row of small windows near the top of the roof, golden beams filled with glistening motes of dust. The tiny particles swirled like miniature constellations as Victoria passed through their path, momentarily disrupting their dance.

Deke walked toward the corner of the barn, where a large burlap bag stood against the wall. Victoria followed, aware that he was as uneasy with her as she was with him. Obviously they had gotten off on the wrong foot, but she wasn't sure how.

She wondered if he was always so somber, or if his moodiness was simply because he didn't like her.

If that was true, it was okay, she decided. She didn't like him, either, so what was the problem?

As he opened the burlap bag and reached inside, she scolded herself. *If you don't like him, why is it so important that he like you? Can't you live with the fact that someone somewhere on this planet doesn't think Victoria Thornton is a perfectly wonderful human being?*

Okay, so her ego was a little overblown. She admitted it. Surely she got Brownie points for being so honest, further proof that she was, indeed, an incredible person.

He held out a couple of gnarled orange things she recognized as carrots—definitely not supermarket quality.

"Here," he said. "You're going to need all the help you can get."

"Gee, thanks. How reassuring." She took the carrots from him, being careful not to let her fingers brush his. Just the thought of having to confront the flesh-and-blood embodiment of her phobia within minutes was stressful enough. Physical contact with this humorless cowboy would only add to her tension.

Why?

The word only crossed her brain once and lingered less than half a second. Some questions were best ignored, and Victoria had grown fairly adept at ignoring inquiries whose answers she might not like.

Deke walked through the barn and out a side door. Following, Victoria could feel her heart beginning to pound as a cold clammy sweat broke out on her forehead.

Horses. Big, heavy, mean, smelly, step-on-your-toes-and-squash-them-flat-just-for-the-fun-of-it horses.

She passed through the door and found herself in a corral. With, not one, but *two* of them.

At the far end of the pen a spirited black gelding paced, pausing occasionally to snort and paw the dirt. An old brown mare stood quietly at the fence to Victoria's right, pulling niblets of succulent grass from the other side—with *very* big, *very* yellow teeth, Victoria noted.

"This is Black Fury," Deke said as he walked toward the gelding. "He's yours for the day, so you'd better make friends with him."

"Black Fury!" She almost screamed the words. "You expect me to get on a horse named Black Fury? You must be out of your mind!"

"He's the best choice for you," Deke replied calmly. "Trust me."

"Yeah, right." Her stomach felt like it was doing a double back flip as she watched Black Fury shake his head and fix her with what she was sure was the evil eye. His muscles bulged beneath his sleek ebony hide, which twitched as his long tail swept from side to side. He was enormous! At least nine feet tall, she estimated. Maybe twelve. She'd have to use a ladder just to climb on him.

A quiet voice inside told her he couldn't possibly be twelve feet tall, that perhaps she was overreacting just a wee bit.

Shut up! she told the voice. *I'm not going to do it! I can't!*

"Mr. Flanders," she said, lifting her chin and attempting to look haughty and indignant rather than scared to death, "I am *not* going to get on that animal. Surely you have something a little more...more tame."

She pointed to the old mare in the corner, who had finished with the grass and appeared to be dozing. "Like that one?"

"Who?" he asked. "Maggie?" He shook his head. "Believe me, you don't want to ride her."

Victoria watched as the ancient horse's sides gently rose and fell. She could almost hear her snoring. "She's exactly what I want." Holding out one of the carrots, she headed toward the mare. "Here, horsey, horsey. Nice horsey, horsey."

"Hey!" Deke shouted. "Don't do that!" He ran to her and grabbed her hand.

His fingers closed around hers, strong and warm—another fact that didn't bear thinking about at the moment, she decided.

"Do what?" she snapped.

"Don't hold a carrot out like that to a horse. You'll get your fingers bitten off."

Her fingers bitten off! Bitten off, chewed into a bloody cud and spit onto the ground. That was exactly what had happened in her latest nightmare.

"Horses don't see very well," he said, "especially old Maggie. They can't tell the difference between a carrot and a finger."

He placed the carrot in the palm of her hand and wrapped her fingers around it. "When you offer it to a horse, you hold it so that it's sticking out of your fist. Like this."

Victoria was mad. She was scared silly. But she was also acutely aware of the pleasantly masculine roughness of his fingers against hers. Most of the men she knew had soft hands, some softer than hers. She had to admit that she rather liked the contrast.

For a moment she looked up into his sapphire blue eyes. Something she saw there told her that maybe he was equally aware of the contact.

Another unsettling thought to push away.

"You really will do much better with Black Fury," he said quietly. "Trust me."

Trust him? She didn't trust anyone on earth enough to get on that prancing, snorting, pawing bundle of muscles.

She pulled her hand away from his and turned her back to him in defiance. "No, I'll take Maggie. Here,

Maggie," she said, holding out the carrot to the mare in the manner she'd just been shown. "Come get the nice carrot, Maggie."

Maggie perked up right away. Ears twitching, she began to walk toward Victoria.

"Oh, no," she whispered. She fought the urge to run, to scream, to cry hysterically. To do all three at once. The horse was coming straight to her. She could see its mangy hide—dull, tawny, dusty and dotted with fly bites. She could feel its breath on her face, moist, warm and smelling like . . . like the barn had smelled. She could sense, the vibrations in the ground with every step of its heavy solid hooves.

Her hand began to shake so badly she nearly dropped the carrot.

Stop it! she told herself. *It's just a tired, old horse. It probably doesn't have the energy to even . . .*

Lifting its head to her, the horse showed its long yellow teeth and curled back its upper lip. Victoria closed her eyes and steeled herself for the worst. A second later, the carrot was gone.

As she opened her eyes and looked at her empty palm she could hardly believe her good fortune. Four fingers and a thumb. No munched, crunched, bloody stubs. Excellent.

"See there. That wasn't so bad," she heard Deke say. "Now you've got a friend for life."

Victoria was just getting used to the idea that she wasn't permanently mutilated. Having a faithful companion for life was beyond her comprehension. "Does that mean she won't bite me, step on me or throw me off?" she asked hopefully.

"Well . . . I wouldn't go that far," he drawled. "Maggie may be old, but she still has a few tricks up her sleeve. Wait until you try to bridle her."

Bridle a horse? The thrill of her recent victory evaporated. "Me?" Maybe she'd heard wrong. "Did you say *I* have to do it?"

"Of course. Martin told me not to skimp, to give you the full course."

"I'll have to thank him the next time I see him," she said through gritted teeth.

Deke took two bridles from hooks on the barn wall, tossed one to her and walked over to Black Fury. The giant horse stood, as gentle as an oversized Labrador puppy, while Deke slipped the bridle on him.

As Deke explained the steps to her, Victoria began to relax a little. The procedure seemed simple enough. Maybe it wouldn't be so difficult, after all.

But as she began to walk toward Maggie, the old horse suddenly seemed to resurrect from the dead. Her ears perked. She snorted and took off, trotting gleefully across the corral.

"Oh, yeah," Deke said with a grin. "I forgot to tell you, Maggie's lazy. She'll do anything to get out of being ridden."

Victoria watched, totally disheartened, as her mount scampered around the pen, neck arched proudly, tail high in the air. She appeared to be thoroughly enjoying herself, playing games with a silly woman foolish enough to think she might slip a bridle on her.

From the corner of her eye, Victoria could see Deke leaning against the fence, one leg propped up, chewing on a piece of straw. He, too, seemed to enjoy watching her run around after the mischievous animal until her tongue was almost hanging out.

After ten minutes of the chase, Victoria stood in the middle of the corral, panting, with copious amounts of sweat rolling down her face. "Well, Mr. Flanders," she said, struggling to catch her breath, "if you have any words of wisdom, now would be a great time to offer them."

"Nope." He spit the straw onto the ground. "You're doing just dandy, Miss Thornton," he said. "Keep running around like that, and you'll wear her down pretty soon."

Victoria looked at the horse, who seemed friskier.

"Gee, thanks," she said, giving him a dirty look. "What a great teacher you are!"

He shrugged his broad shoulders and laughed at her. Victoria's temper soared. It didn't matter if he was handsome and looked incredible in his tight jeans. So what if he was easy on the eyes and particularly pleasant to follow around? He was a jerk—a hick cowboy and a first-rate jerk—and she'd had just about enough of his darned horse, too.

She was never going to catch the old nag this way. The horse had four legs; she had only two. It just wasn't going to work.

Better try something else, she told herself, *before you fall flat on your face and die of a heat stroke. When her time came to depart the earth, she didn't want to make her final exit with her nose buried in a pile of horse manure.*

Maggie might be faster, but she was smarter than a dumb old horse. At least she hoped so.

She had won an Oscar for her acting. Maybe now was the time to plumb the depths of whatever talents she possessed. This was war.

Slowly she walked to the center of the corral, picked a clean spot and sat down in the dirt. In her periphery she could see Deke watching her closely, looking mildly puzzled. Good, she thought with satisfaction, *let him wonder.*

She drew her knees up and rested her forearms across them, then buried her face in her arms and began to make soft crying sounds. She thought she heard footsteps—*boot* steps—walking in her direction. Peeking through the cascade of her hair, she saw Deke sauntering toward her.

"Stop!" she whispered angrily. "Go away!"

He gave her a look that clearly said he thought she'd lost her mind, then resumed his position at the fence.

Victoria began to cry again, even louder than before. Through the crook of her elbow, she watched as Maggie paused and stood still, studying her suspiciously. Victoria could see that she was wary of coming closer.

Smart horse, she thought. *But she's female, and that means she's curious.*

Victoria continued to sob, and eventually the mare began to stroll toward her.

It was working.

The horse came closer and closer. Finally Victoria felt a thrill of gratification as the mare's velvety nose nuzzled her neck and cheek.

Slowly she reached up and stroked the soft nose. "That's a girl," she said. "That's my pretty girl. What a beautiful horse you are."

Rising to her feet, she gently slipped the bit into the horse's mouth and drew the leather straps up and over its ears as Deke had shown her.

The whole time she whispered sweet nothings to the old mare in a soft soothing voice. "That's my pretty Maggie," she said, her mouth close to the horse's ear. "What a lovely horse you are."

At last, she fastened the buckle and realized with a wave of elation that she'd done it. She was finished. She, Victoria Thornton, had bridled a horse all by herself.

"There!" she said, turning to Deke, feeling obnoxiously proud of herself. "How did I do, Mr. Flanders?"

"Great," he said as he left his position on the fence and walked over to stroke the mare's nose. He gave Victoria a warm smile that went through her even more sharply than her victory with the horse. He might be a hick cowboy, she thought, but he was certainly a gorgeous one.

"Yep, you did just fine, Miss Thornton." His attractive smile twisted into a sarcastic smirk. "But then," he added, "Maggie never did mind the bridle all that much. Just wait till you try to saddle her."

"Now, NEVER PUT a blanket or a saddle on a horse without showing it to her first," Deke said ten minutes later as they continued with the lesson.

To demonstrate, he presented the blanket to Black Fury, then spread it across the gelding's glossy back. Deke watched, amused, as Victoria awkwardly followed his lead and did the same to Maggie. This was turning out to be a lot more fun than he had expected, and it was only going to get better.

Maggie wasn't finished with Victoria yet. Deke had come to know the old mare well over the years, and she was the most stubborn horse he'd ever met. She obeyed Deke out of love, but Maggie didn't love very many people. By the gleam in the horse's eyes, Deke could tell that she didn't like this hoity-toity actress at all.

Deke picked up his saddle and presented it to Black Fury. "And you show them the saddle, too…like this," he told her. "Then they know they're about to feel something on their back and it doesn't startle them."

With a groan of exertion Victoria lifted her saddle and held it briefly under Maggie's nose. Then she grunted as she swung the heavy thing up onto the horse's back. For a delicious moment, Deke thought she was going to put it on backwards, but at the last minute she corrected it and, after a bit of adjustment, got it right.

Deke watched Maggie lay her ears back, snort and shake her head. *Yep,* he thought, *this is gonna be good.*

"Now you grab the girth like this," he said, "and cinch it good and tight."

She did as he instructed. "Done," she said.

He shook his head. "Tighter, or else the saddle will slip and you'll fall off."

She pulled the girth tighter, but Deke smiled, knowing it would do no good. Maggie was an old pro at a trick called bloating. She would inhale, puff out her ribs, and hold her breath while being cinched, causing the girth to be too loose. Soon after the rider got into the saddle, the whole thing would slip to the side, dumping the rider into the dirt. Maggie had fed Deke more than one mouthful of corral dust before he had broken her of doing it to him.

"There, that's as tight as I can get it," she said as she gave the girth one last jerk.

She turned and looked up at him, her face flushed. He couldn't help noticing how pretty she was with the sun in her copper hair and a delicate peach blush in her cheeks. Her green eyes sparkling and her mouth curved in a grin, she looked more like a little girl who was very pleased with herself than a conceited, self-centered movie star.

"All right," he said. "Now, I just want to know one thing, and you'd better tell me the truth."

"What's that?"

"Have you ever been on a horse before? Really?"

She flushed even more and looked away. "Yes," she said, but her eyes didn't meet his.

"Come on, be honest. This is important," he said. "I hate it when people lie to me."

"Okay, okay," she replied with a sigh. "I'm not lying. I *was* on a horse—for about one and a half seconds."

He digested this information, then frowned. "In other words, you got on one side and fell off the other," he said.

"That may be true. But for a second there, I was *on* a horse." She stuck out her lower lip in a pout and looked so cute that Deke thought how nice it might be to kiss those full lips. With a start, he yanked his mind back to the business at hand.

"Okay, here's how you mount a horse," he said.

He showed her how to turn the stirrup toward her and grab the saddle horn. Swinging himself up onto Black Fury, he told her to do the same with Maggie.

Her green eyes widened with fear as she stood beside the mare. Although she had her fists clenched tightly at her sides, he thought he could see her trembling. She really *was* scared; her reaction went far beyond the natural apprehension he'd seen in other novices.

"I always forget how big horses are," she said, "until I'm about to get on one."

"Just hop on up there," Deke said gently. Chuckling, he added, "With those famous long legs of yours, you shouldn't have any trouble."

She shot him an irritated glance, but her anger seemed to give her courage. Grabbing the bridle and horn, she pulled herself up into the saddle with far more grace than he'd expected.

"All right," she snapped, giving him a challenging look. "Now what, Mr. Flanders?"

Deke nodded and smiled, satisfied with himself. So, the way to get Miss Fancy Pants to do something was to make her mad. He'd have to remember that.

Besides, she was gorgeous when she was angry. Her emerald eyes turned two shades darker, and her cheeks flushed bright red. Yes, he decided, it was certainly worth getting her dander up.

"Now, you just give her a nudge in the ribs with your heels like this," he said, demonstrating, "and off you go."

He rode Black Fury around the corral, and Victoria followed, clinging desperately to Maggie.

"When you want to turn the horse to the left, you just lay the reins against the right side of her neck, like this," he said, demonstrating with his own reins.

"On the *right* if I want her to go *left?*" she said. "That doesn't make any sense. Are you sure?"

The condescending tone of her voice irked him; she really was a know-it-all.

"It makes sense to the horse," he shot back. "But then, some people don't even have horse sense."

She laid the reins on the right side of Maggie's neck, and Deke grinned. This was when it usually happened. He rode up beside her just in case.

Sure enough. Maggie went one way. Victoria, the saddle and blanket went the other.

She screamed, but he was there to catch her by the arm as she fell. Gently he allowed her to slide to the ground.

Maggie pranced away, her tail high in the air, nose pointed to the sky.

"What . . . what happened?" Victoria said from her seat in the dirt.

Deke swallowed the laughter that bubbled up inside him. He had a feeling this wasn't the time to tease her any further. The color of her face had long gone beyond the pretty-peach stage and was now an undeniable passionate purple. Her blood pressure must be over the top.

He could just see the tabloid headlines now and hear the television news teasers. "Beautiful and talented Victoria Thornton dies of stroke in Colorado horse corral. Film at eleven." Martin would have his hide drying on the side of the barn by morning.

"I asked you, what happened?" she repeated with a huff of impatience.

"I don't know," he said between stifled chuckles. "I reckon you just didn't get that girth tight enough."

"Then I reckon," she said, imitating his drawl, "that you aren't much of a teacher."

"And you, my dear Miss Thornton—" he swept his hat from his head and bowed low "—are no Annie Oakley."

Chapter Three

VICTORIA STOOD at the window of her appointed bedroom, drinking in the Colorado mountain scenery. Snow still covered the peaks that glowed blue-white in the distance, but closer to the house, grass was springing up in green tufts here and there, where the snow had melted. On a nearby hill, cattle plucked at the bales of hay Deke had dropped for them. A tiny black-and-white calf trotted after its mother, bawling at the top of its lungs.

Victoria breathed in the fresh clean air, so different from Los Angeles. Yes, spring had arrived in the Rockies.

Some other time, she might have found a weekend like this enjoyable. After all, she was in one of the most beautiful places in the world, and Deke Flanders was one of the sexiest men she had ever met.

Too bad he's such a pain in the rear, she thought. He could be quite sarcastic, bordering on nasty, when he wanted to be. So what if he had shining black hair and eyes as blue as the Colorado sky, and filled out his jeans and Western shirt in a way that set her heart to pounding? And he did have a breathtaking smile—when he wasn't smirking at her.

But looks weren't everything. Right?

She remembered how his back and shoulder muscles had flexed when he had swung the saddle up onto Black

Fury. Most of the men she knew worked out in gyms to maintain their physiques. But Deke's muscles had been developed from hard work, not lifting weights. Victoria decided she liked the difference.

Last night, after their lessons, they had shared a simple dinner of steak and potatoes in his dining room. Usually she didn't eat meat, but she hadn't wanted to insult him by refusing. There was enough animosity between them without adding to it unnecessarily.

The meal had been much better than she'd expected. He was a good cook, as well as being handsome.

Their conversation had been light, almost pleasant, until he had teased her about falling off Maggie. Furious, she'd stormed off to her room without finishing her apple pie.

Now, looking back, she was afraid she'd acted like a child. She couldn't exactly blame him for laughing; she must have looked pretty ridiculous—a grown woman sliding sideways off a horse in slow motion.

Well, she thought with a sigh, *better get on with it.*

Sitting on the side of the bed, she pulled her boots onto her sore feet and groaned. Even her blisters had blisters. The insides of her thighs could feel every stitch in the jeans seams, and her arms and shoulders ached from the unaccustomed effort of hanging on to the saddle.

Darn Martin for getting her into this. She was already plotting how she was going to make him pay.

Okay, so, she wasn't Annie Oakley. She could live with that.

But she was going to *ride* that horse today, if she had to glue herself to the saddle. Before the day was over, she would show that smart-mouthed cowboy a thing or two.

No man got the last laugh on her.

Especially a hick cowboy—with bright blue eyes and great buns!

VICTORIA WAS PROUD of her new record; she had stayed on Maggie for almost half an hour now. Before saddling her, Victoria had given the mare three carrots, instead of one. Maybe that was the trick—bribery. She filed the information away for future use.

"So, how does it feel to sit in a saddle—longer than thirty seconds, that is?" Deke asked. He grinned at her, his blue eyes sparkling with mischief as he rode beside her on Black Fury.

"To be honest," she replied, "my bottom is sore, and my tailbone feels like it's taken root to the saddle. Other than that, I'm just ducky. Thanks for asking."

He glanced down at her shapely rear for a second, then back to her face. The light in his eyes warmed her and kindled a blaze that spread throughout her body, whether she wanted it to or not. Why did he have to be so handsome? And why did he have to be a stubborn Rocky Mountain cowboy with dirt under his fingernails and only marginally adequate table manners?

Perhaps most importantly, she thought, why did she care one way or the other? He was just her riding teacher for a weekend. Sunday she would climb into the limo with Michael and that would be it.

As always when confronted with an unpleasant thought, she pushed it aside.

They had come to a fork in the road. To their right lay a picturesque green meadow, dotted with wildflowers and bisected by a bubbling creek. A dark forest of pine loomed to the left.

She laid the reins against the side of Maggie's neck, signaling her to go toward the meadow, but the horse snorted and obstinately turned left.

"Hey, what's going on here?" Victoria shouted as the horse broke into a brisk trot. "Slow down! What do you think you're doing?"

"Oh, no," Deke said, shaking his head. "Darned horse. I was afraid she'd do that."

"Do what?" Victoria called over her shoulder as she pulled back on the reins with all her strength. "Whoa! Whoa, horse. Stop!"

But Maggie ignored her rider and galloped headlong toward the nearest pine tree with low limbs.

Deke rode after them, grabbed his rope and began to circle it over his head.

"Deke!" Victoria screamed. "De-e-k-e! Make her stop!"

Too late, she realized what Maggie had planned. The limb seemed to be rushing at her, getting bigger by the moment and filling her vision. She ducked as low as she could, but she knew she would still hit it.

A second before her face made contact with the bristly needles, Victoria heard a whoosh in the air over her head. Something circled her waist and yanked hard.

The next thing she knew, she was sitting on the ground, instead of the horse, and her bottom was hurting almost as much as her pride.

Glancing over at Deke, she wasn't surprised to see him laughing himself silly. In one hand he held the rope he had used to lasso her. The other hand gripped the saddle horn. He was laughing so hard he was about to fall off. She heartily wished he would.

"I'm glad you're enjoying yourself so much, Mr. Flanders," she said, dragging herself to her feet. Groaning, she rubbed her rear, which was aching far more now than before, if that was possible. With an angry huff, she pulled the rope from around her waist and threw it to the ground.

She watched as Maggie whirled around and trotted past her, tail floating in the air. The horse was heading back to the barn and, more importantly, her food.

"Bad horse," Victoria called out to her. "B-a-a-ad horse. Somebody should make glue out of you."

"Are you..." Deke gasped between guffaws, "are you...okay?"

"No, of course I'm not okay!" She dusted the dirt from the seat of her jeans. "You just lassoed me like a heifer and yanked me off a horse. How do you suppose I am?"

He wiped the tears from his eyes with the sleeve of his shirt. "Would you have preferred to hit that limb with your face?" he asked.

"My butt hit the ground—*hard*," she said. "Is that the best a champion stunt rider could do?"

"Sorry," he said with that irritating smirk. "I didn't have a lot of time to plan it out."

"Obviously."

He rode his horse closer to her. Leaning down, he held out his hand. "Want a boost up?" he asked. "Black Fury and I will give you a ride home—since you seem to have misplaced your horse."

Instead of taking his hand, she slapped it away. "No, thank you, Mr. Flanders. I'd rather walk fifty miles than ride on a horse behind you." She thought for a moment, then added, "On hot coals, that is, barefoot."

He laughed and shrugged. "Well, I can see you feel strongly about it, so I won't argue with you. See you back at the ranch."

She ignored him, refusing to answer.

Glancing up at the sun, which was straight overhead, he said, "It's about noon. Try to make it back before dinner, okay? I start getting hungry by six."

Victoria fumed as she watched him gallop away. She took a couple of steps and realized that her feet hurt more than her rear. New boots. Whose great idea was that?

Oh, yeah. Hers. She had only herself to blame for that one.

"Cowboys!" she said, tossing her red hair over her shoulders as she began the painful journey back to the ranch. "I just decided…I hate them even more than flies and horses!"

DEKE SAT UP in bed and peered at the old alarm clock whose numbers and hands glowed phosphorous blue in the darkness. It was three-thirty in the morning. No wonder he still felt tired.

He searched his sleep-drugged mind, trying to remember what had woken him. When the soft sounds of a woman's voice drifted into the room, he remembered. A woman was in his house, and she was conversing with someone.

As consciousness returned, he quickly recalled that he had a houseguest. And quite a houseguest she was, too. The evening before, she had returned from her trek back to the house, stomped down the hall to her bedroom and slammed the door behind her.

He had been both relieved that he hadn't been required to entertain her and disappointed that he hadn't had the dubious pleasure of her company.

From the sound of the conversation that seemed to be coming from his living room, it appeared she was entertaining someone on her own. The thought upset him more than he would have anticipated. He wanted to believe he was angry because she had taken the liberty of inviting a guest into his home without asking permission. But he knew that he would be a lot less agitated if he found out that her visitor was female.

He pulled on a pair of jeans and crept quietly down the hall to the living room, straining to determine the gender of the speaker. It was Victoria, no doubt at all. After spending this weekend with her, he would never be able to forget that low sexy voice of hers.

As he was about to enter the living room, he heard her say, "I do love you, Jonathan. Why won't you believe me?"

Apparently this Jonathan character—who was about to get tossed out on his ear—was very soft-spoken, because Deke couldn't hear his reply. But Victoria's response stopped him cold, and for some reason he couldn't explain, Deke wished he'd never heard her words.

"Of course I'll become your wife. That's what I want, too."

Wife! She was going to marry some guy named Jonathan, and Deke didn't even know she had a steady boyfriend!

Before he could stop himself, he charged into the room, determined to tell Mr. Jonathan What's-His-Face to do his courting on his own turf.

He froze when he saw there was no one in the room but Victoria. Curled in a wing-back chair, wearing a cobalt blue silk robe, she held a script in one hand and a steaming mug in the other. From the aroma he realized she had made fresh coffee. He also realized he had just made a fool of himself.

Victoria was giving him a quizzical look, but he didn't have to be told she was acting—in more ways than one. She knew darn well why he had rushed into the room like an idiot. She knew what he'd heard and what he'd been thinking. And, of course, egotistic brat that she was, he could tell she was quite pleased.

"I'm sorry if I woke you," she said too sweetly. "I couldn't sleep, so I decided to go over my lines."

"Did you have to do it out here?" he snapped. "What's the matter with your room? Was the dust bothering you?"

"No-o-o." She raised one eyebrow and gave him a condescending smile. "If I'd been trying to escape the dust, I wouldn't have bothered to come out here," she added as she trailed one fingertip across the small table beside her chair, drawing a distinct line in the layer of dust that had accumulated there.

She flipped the script closed and stood. He noticed that she winced with the movement, probably some residual discomfort from her long walk back. Oh, well, he decided, she deserved it.

"I'm sorry," she said. "I didn't realize I was confined to my room. And I'm sorry I woke you."

Suddenly he felt rather petty. She hadn't really done anything wrong, and he had jumped down her throat. Close personal contact with this woman didn't seem to bring out the best in his character.

"Don't go," he said. "I'm awake now. You might as well stick around and finish your coffee."

She hesitated, and he found himself hoping fervently that she would stay. Of course, he didn't particularly like her, but Flanders' Folly did get a bit lonely from time to time. Any company was better than none.

"Okay, thank you," she said, slowly sitting down and crossing her long legs. As the blue silk slipped to the side, exposing her shapely calves and ankles, Deke tried his best to avert his eyes but couldn't. He'd always hated guys who shot those stupid covert looks at a woman's body parts. But he had always been a dyed-in-the-wool leg man, and she had the most graceful, elegant pair he'd ever seen.

"What's the movie about?" he said, searching for any conversational gambit.

"Are you really interested or are you just being polite?" she asked.

Nonplussed, he shrugged, then said, "A little of both, I guess."

She nodded, apparently pleased with his honesty. "It's based on the true story of Sylvia Berkley, the woman who opened the first school for blind children on the West Coast in the mid 1800s."

"Sounds like a great character, self-sacrificing and all that."

She laughed. "Actually, Sylvia was an arrogant pain in the butt. She was raised in the highest levels of St. Louis society by wealthy parents, and she never gave a thought for anyone else—until her father arranged a marriage for her to an older gentleman in San Francisco. She was defying all the rules of polite society, and he wanted to get her out of the area before she ruined the family name."

"My kind of girl," he said with a chuckle. He watched Victoria's face as she related the details of the story, and he realized how much she loved her work. No wonder she was so good at it.

"Sylvia had to travel west by wagon train," she continued. "She made life pretty miserable for everyone else, demanding special treatment. Mostly she was worried that she'd sunburn and ruin her perfect complexion. She wanted to look her beautiful best for her new husband. But when she arrived in San Francisco, she was shocked to find out that it didn't matter how she looked. Her husband-to-be was blind—a small detail her father had forgotten to mention."

"Let me guess. She refused to marry him."

"At first, yes. She wanted a man who could fully appreciate her beauty." Victoria paused and smiled. "Humility was never one of Sylvia's greatest virtues. But eventually he convinced her that it was better to be loved for the person she truly was inside than to simply be adored. Together they opened the Berkley School for the Blind in San Francisco."

Better loved than adored. Deke turned the concept over in his mind as he studied this woman before him, who had certainly received more than her share of adoration.

"And how about you, Victoria?" he asked. "Which do you prefer, to be loved or adored?"

She returned his steady gaze without flinching, but she stood and picked up her mug from the side table. Clutching her script to the front of her robe, she said, "I think . . . Mr. Flanders . . . that you and I don't know each other well enough for you to ask me a question like that."

Limping slightly, she walked away, her chin in the air, her back stiff. A second later Deke found himself sitting in a room that felt more empty and lonely than ever before.

Even though she had dismissed both him and his question, the answer had been written all over her pretty face. Victoria Thornton had received a lot more adoration than love. That was too bad, he thought. Because, like the hero in her story, when Deke saw her with his heart, not just his eyes, he could see a lot in Victoria Thornton that was lovable. For all of her vanity and egocentricity, she was also smart, courageous, witty and occasionally—when she thought no one was looking—vulnerable.

Yes, someone could fall for a woman like Victoria. Someone else, that was. Another movie star, a producer, maybe an oil tycoon. Certainly not a plain old Colorado rancher.

LATER IN THE MORNING, Deke walked into the kitchen, ready to make a breakfast of hotcakes and sausages. But Victoria was already having hers—a bowl of cold cereal.

That didn't surprise him as much as the fact that she was eating it sitting on the radiator.

A surge of guilt washed over him. After all, he had been pretty hard on her since her arrival.

"I'll make you pancakes, if you like," he offered.

"No, thank you," she said. She avoided his eyes. It seemed the question he had asked her last night had disturbed her even more than he'd thought.

Hobbling over to the sink, she rinsed her bowl and stuck it into the dishwasher.

Her feet must be killing her, he thought as he watched her limp. Apparently her muscles had stiffened during the night. He should have insisted that she ride back with him yesterday. Blisters could be a serious matter, and he hadn't given it a second thought when he'd ridden away from her. No, he hadn't been particularly chivalrous.

After all, Martin had asked him to teach her how to ride a horse—not cripple her.

"You really are doing well," he said. He walked over to her and placed his hand on her shoulder. To his surprise, she didn't push him away as she had before. "You're a quick study—just like Sylvia Berkley."

"Yeah, sure." She appeared to be about to cry. "Today is my last day here, and I can't even stay on a horse. I'd say I flunked riding school. Completely."

With his hands on her shoulder, he turned her around to face him. "No, that isn't true. It isn't your fault. It's Maggie. She's a really difficult horse."

Suddenly Deke realized that he was standing face-to-face with *the* Victoria Thornton. Her green eyes gazed up into his, tears shining on her long lashes. She looked like a sad little girl who'd just gotten a bad report card. He had to admit she wasn't really all that bratty or conceited like he'd thought before.

Oh, she had a temper, to be sure. But he'd never held that against anyone. He could get riled pretty easily himself from time to time.

It was all he could do not to lower his head and press his lips to hers. More than anything, he just wanted to kiss her hurt away and make everything better.

He leaned closer to her. For a moment he thought he saw desire in her eyes, too, but he decided he must be mistaken. He was a beat-up cowboy; she was a world-famous movie star. Who did he think he was kidding?

"I . . . I just feel like I've let everybody down. Martin, myself . . . even you," she said.

"But that isn't true. I'm telling you, it's Maggie. She pulls those tricks on everybody. When you try to saddle her, she sucks in her breath, then, once you're on, she exhales and dumps you."

"Oh, really?" Victoria stopped sniffling and raised one perfectly shaped eyebrow.

"Yeah. And Maggie loves to go under a low-hanging limb and sweep her rider off."

"I see," she said slowly. "She does this all the time, huh?"

"All the time."

"Thank you for telling me," she said. "I feel *so* much better now."

Deke wondered at the strange look on her face. Her mouth was smiling, but her eyes weren't. They bored into his, until he looked away.

"Well, do you want to go out again?" he asked, releasing her shoulders.

"Not right now. I'm still pretty stiff and sore," she replied, closing the dishwasher. "How about later this afternoon?"

"Whatever you say. Make it easy on yourself."

"I'll do that," she said. Again she gave him a smile that didn't reach her green eyes. "See you later."

She turned and walked down the hall toward her bedroom. Deke had an uneasy feeling. She had acted like everything was fine, but he knew it wasn't.

Something was wrong. He just didn't know what, and that made Deke Flanders very nervous.

THAT JERK! He'd known all along, Victoria thought as she led Black Fury out of the barn. Bridling and saddling him had been no problem, and she didn't know whether to be angry or grateful. Okay, so she should have taken Deke's advice and ridden the gelding in the first place, although it irritated her to have to admit it, even to herself. But that didn't get him off the hook with her. Not by a long shot.

Deke had let her think it was her fault that the saddle had slipped, instead of telling her about Maggie's trick. He had known the old mare would run her under a tree, but he had let her ride the cantankerous beast, anyway.

He had made a fool of her, and even worse, he had enjoyed it. Victoria Thornton wasn't a woman to let something like that just slide by without retaliation. No way. She'd get even with him. Oh, yes.

As she pulled herself up into the saddle, she realized that she wasn't so scared this time. Her anger took the edge off her fear. Gingerly she nudged Black Fury forward with her heels, and to her relief he obeyed perfectly.

As they trotted down the winding dirt road in the direction of the pine forest, Victoria smiled to herself.

Ah, revenge was sweet, and she could hardly wait to taste it.

DEKE HAD LOOKED everywhere for her without success. Her bedroom was empty, though the bed was neatly made—a definite point in her favor. The door to the bathroom was open, the room dark. After glancing around the yard and not finding her, he decided she must be in the kitchen helping herself to a late-afternoon snack. But when he walked into the room, it was as empty as the others.

His anxiety level rose several notches. Where was she? He had felt that something was wrong earlier, and he cursed himself for not pursuing the matter with her.

Turning to leave the room, he saw the piece of pink notepaper taped to the front of the refrigerator. Pink, with silly frilly edges. He shook his head in disgust. How predictable.

Ripping it off the door, he read the large ornate handwriting, which he considered equally silly and frilly.

Dear Deke,

I'm so ashamed of my horrible riding that I decided to go out alone. I hope you don't mind. I didn't want you to have to bother with me anymore.

Thanks for everything,
Victoria

Bother with her? he thought. Why did she think she was a bother?

His conscience gave him a serious pang. He really had treated her like she was a fly in his ice cream. Maybe she hadn't been the easiest person to deal with, but he hadn't exactly been a knight in shining armor, either.

He thought of how clumsy she'd been in the saddle, and his pulse quickened. She was the worst rider he'd ever seen, and she certainly wasn't ready to go out alone. For a novice, there were all kinds of ways to get hurt—badly.

He shuddered. If anything happened to her . . .

It wouldn't. He wouldn't let anything bad happen to her. He'd find her, and when he did, he'd give her a piece of his mind.

Who did she think she was, anyway? This wasn't Hollywood; this was reality, and in the real world, not every episode had a happy ending.

Yes, when he found her, she was going to be told a thing or two about risking her life just to salve her wounded ego.

As he hurried out the back door and headed for the barn, he admitted that she was as courageous as she was conceited. Not everyone he knew, himself included,

could face one of their greatest fears as bravely as she
had. But that didn't matter. Not now.

It was one thing to be brave; it was quite another to be
foolish!

VICTORIA RODE Black Fury along the narrow path that
wound through the woods, searching for the place. The
perfect place.

She was surprised at how pleasant the experience
could be when seated on a well-behaved mount.
Breathing in the sweet fragrance of the pines mixed with
the musty scent of the forest loam, she compared it to the
acrid smell and metallic taste of L.A. smog.

The soft sounds of the forest animals surrounded
them: the singing of a mockingbird, the cawing of a
crow, the rustling of rabbits and other small animals in
the brush on either side of the path. She could see why
Deke enjoyed this rural life. Maybe he wasn't such a
hick, after all.

No, she wouldn't allow herself to think positive
thoughts about him. Not now. She needed the momentum her anger supplied to pull this off. This wasn't the
time to forgive and forget—not until she had reaped her
full measure of revenge.

Rounding a sharp curve, she saw it—the place she had
been looking for. The perfect stage where she could
conduct her little play.

The path widened slightly, and brambles grew thickly
on either side. She had to duck as they passed beneath
some low-hanging branches.

Yes. It was ideal.

Reaching inside her jacket pocket, she pulled out the small plastic bag she had prepared earlier. It was filled with a liquid she'd discreetly mixed in Deke's kitchen before leaving.

She was brilliant, no doubt about it, she thought as she climbed down from the horse.

Stroking his satiny neck, she said, "I'm sure you can find your way home without me, Black Fury." As she opened the plastic bag she gave him a sympathetic look. He seemed so docile, so trusting and innocent, that she felt a little guilty. "I hate to do this to you, old buddy, but we're in this together."

Carefully she smeared some of the sticky red liquid on the saddle and the horse's neck. Then she gave him an affectionate pat on the rear. "Run along home," she said, "and do me a favor, would you? When you get there, try to look worried."

As though he understood every word, the horse galloped back down the path they had just traveled. "Good boy," she whispered as she watched him disappear around the bend. "Go-o-o-d horse. I'll have to remember to give you some extra carrots later."

Searching the ground at her feet, she found a comfortable place to lie. After tossing a few offending rocks aside, she stretched out on the soft bed of decaying pine needles.

"Now," she said as she placed her arms and legs one direction, then the other, and twisted her arm behind her head at an awkward angle, "I wonder... which position looks the most dead?"

DEKE RODE Maggie fast and hard through the forest. He had been searching for almost an hour but had found no sign of Victoria. Long ago, he had given up the hope of finding her safe and sound. Instinctively he knew she was in trouble. All he wanted now was to find her and offer her whatever help he could.

He couldn't stop thinking about the blood on Black Fury's saddle. At first he'd thought the horse was hurt, then he had realized the animal wasn't the one who had been bleeding. That meant only one thing. It was *Victoria's* blood.

God only knew how badly she was hurt. He *had* to find her, and soon, before it was too late.

Rounding a corner, he saw a familiar shape sprawled in the middle of the path, and his heart sank. It was her.

She was lying on her side, her arm twisted at a horrible angle, and worst of all she wasn't moving.

"Victoria!" he shouted as he jumped off the horse. He ran to her and dropped to his knees beside her still form. "It's Deke, Victoria. Are you all right? Say something to me, please."

He shook her shoulder gently, but she didn't respond.

Carefully he checked for broken limbs, but everything seemed okay. There were no bumps on her head, in spite of all the blood in her hair. The horrible red stuff was all over the front of her white blouse, but he couldn't find the awful wound that had caused so much bleeding.

He had to get her back to the house and to a doctor as soon as possible. Cradling her in his arms, he climbed back on the horse.

"Easy does it, Maggie," he said. "We have to give her a smooth ride back."

For once, the horse seemed to understand, and she behaved, picking her way carefully through the forest, which was growing darker by the moment. Soon they would have no light at all.

Deke clasped her tightly against his chest. "Victoria," he whispered. "Can you hear me? Open your eyes if you can."

She said nothing, and her eyes remained closed. But he could feel her warm breath on his cheek, and that was a good sign.

"I shouldn't have made fun of you. That was a rotten thing to do," he said, feeling more miserably guilty than he ever had in his life. "You weren't all that bad a rider," he added, blackening his soul with the blatant lie. "You were just scared, that's all. And now . . ."

He placed a quick soft kiss on her forehead. "I'm so sorry this happened. I wanted . . . to tell you something. I wanted . . ."

He couldn't bring himself to say the words, even if she was unconscious.

"Tell me . . ." she mumbled, her eyes still closed, ". . . tell me what?"

Relief flooded over him. Drawing a deep breath, he dared to say the words that were in his heart. "I wanted to tell you that you aren't a spoiled brat. You're really a pretty gutsy lady. You faced one of your greatest fears, and most people never do that. I admire you."

She sighed and snuggled closer into his arms.

"And," he said, "I like you. A lot. You have to pull through this. I couldn't stand it if anything happened to you because of me."

He held the reins with one hand. With the other he brushed her hair back from her bloodstained face. "We have to get you to a doctor," he said. "You're bleeding really badly, and I can't find where it's coming from. Where does it hurt?"

For a moment she said nothing, then murmured, "Hurt? Umm…mm…all over." She moaned and rolled her head from side to side. "I didn't think…you… cared," she said. Her words were weak, barely a whisper. "You said…you said…"

He bent his head low to hear her. "I said what?"

"You said…you had…never seen—" she fought for breath "—so much…sky between a woman's rear end…and a saddle."

He felt his face grow hot. "I'm sorry, Victoria. That was a lousy thing to say. I'm so sorry."

Her eyelids fluttered open, and she looked up at him. "Then…I'm a good rider?"

"Except for falling off the horse, you're great!"

She smiled faintly. "Good. How long do you think it will take me to learn?"

His arms closed around her more tightly as he pressed a kiss to her cheek and another to her upturned lips. Her response was soft, but passionate, stealing his breath away.

"Well…" He could see the lights of the ranch glowing golden in the distance. "I really want to get to know you better. I want the chance to convince you that cowboys aren't all bad."

She grinned up at him, then gave him a kiss. "And how long do think that will take?"

"I want to take my time and do a really good job."

"Yes, that's very important," she said, nuzzling his neck. "I want you to take all the time you need."

"Horseback riding isn't easy," he said. "And neither is learning how to love a cowboy."

He looked puzzled and licked his lower lip. Some of her blood had gotten on his mouth when they had kissed. "Tastes like syrup," he said, confused. "Maple syrup."

"Gee, imagine that!" She laughed. "Maybe maple syrup with red food coloring?"

Looking down at her, seeing the wicked grin on her pretty face, he felt like turning her over the saddle and swatting her cute little rear. But his relief was stronger than his anger. "You mean you faked it?" he said. "The whole thing? You're not even hurt?"

"It's called acting, not faking." She wrapped her arms around his waist and held him close. "I think *I* can learn to love a cowboy," she said. "The question is, can *you* learn to love an actress?"

"I don't know," he said. "Are you intending to do any more acting for me?"

"If you deserve it."

He laughed. "Well, that's going to take some getting used to. You'd have to stick around for quite a while."

"How long?"

He leaned down and licked a drop of the syrup off her forehead. "A long time. A long, long time."

Epilogue

SPRING HAD COME again to the Rockies, and Victoria thought it even more beautiful than the year before. As she sat on the bluff overlooking Flanders' Folly, she breathed in the sweet crisp air and felt a rush of gratitude that this wonderful spot on earth would soon be her home.

Turning to Deke, who sat beside her, she said, "It didn't take all that long."

He looked puzzled. "What do you mean?"

"You said it would take a long time for you to teach me how to love a cowboy."

Laughing, he shook his head. "I said it would take me a long time to teach you how to ride a horse, and I was right. You still haven't got it."

"Oh, well," she sighed, "if we do what we intend to tomorrow, you'll have the rest of your life to teach me."

Reaching for her hand, he leaned closer to her and kissed her. His lips felt as warm and natural on hers as the first time he'd kissed her a year before.

"Are you sure, Vickie?" he asked. "Are you absolutely sure you want to marry a beat-up old cowboy?"

She could hear the vulnerability in his voice, the fear that somehow this was too good to be real. She understood completely. Her own fear surfaced frequently, the old feelings of inadequacy, the doubts that this could be real love and not simply a misguided infatuation.

But over the past twelve months, Deke had shown her, as no other man ever had, that he loved her. Truly loved *her*, not the image on the screen.

He didn't always tell her that she was the most breathtakingly beautiful woman on the face of the earth. He didn't grovel at her feet and beg for her attention, like some of the men in her life. But he frequently told her how important she was to him, how much he respected and admired her, how much he enjoyed her wit and sense of humor.

Most important Deke had taught her the difference in being adored and being loved. She found that she much preferred the latter.

"I do love you, Deke," she said, squeezing his hand between both of hers. "Of course I want to become your wife. That's what I've always wanted."

He smiled and kissed her forehead. "And those are the words I've always wanted to hear—ever since I heard you say them to Jonathan What's-His-Face in my living room that night."

"Jonathan?" she asked, puzzled.

"Don't worry about it," he said as he rose and pulled her to her feet. "He's one of those men you cast aside along the way. I'm just glad I'm not piled on top of the heap with the rest of them."

She laughed and socked him in the shoulder. "Come on," she said, taking his hand and leading him toward the path where Maggie and Black Fury were grazing, patiently awaiting their return. "We've got a wedding to go to."

"I KNEW you'd like her!" Martin Conroy whispered as he stood beside Deke at the front of the chapel. Deke shushed him, then returned his attention to the door in the back of the room. His bride was going to appear any moment now, and he couldn't wait to see her.

"But I had no idea that you'd like her *this* much!" Martin leaned closer and poked Deke in the ribs with his elbow. "I guess you owe me big time for this one, huh?"

Deke looked out across the sea of people, only a few of whom he knew. It seemed that the entire world had come to see Victoria Thornton marry this unknown cowboy.

He guessed he would just have to get used to the fact that he would have to share a part of his wife with her adoring fans and the press. But there was a soft, warm and loving side of Victoria Thornton they would never know, a side that was his alone.

The organ music swelled, and even Martin was quiet as a hush descended on the crowd.

Deke's heart pounded as he waited. This was it. No turning back.

The moment she stepped into the doorway, dressed in a gown that was as shimmering and white as Aspen Mountain on a spring morning, Deke knew he would never want to go back.

And from this moment on, the word "bride" would have a whole new meaning for him. From this day forward he would hear the word and remember the way she had looked, walking down the aisle to him, forever a part of his heart, his life.

A Note from Janet Dailey

Who was the first man you ever truly loved? (Your dad, your handsome big brother and that cute kid in first grade don't count.) Chances are, when you call to mind those days of yesteryear, you'll remember that your heartstrings were first twanged by some swaggering, gun-totin', bronco-wranglin', guitar-pickin' cowboy.

Whether it was Gene Autry, Roy Rogers, Rowdy Yates, Little Joe Cartwright, Bret Maverick or Marshal Matt Dillon, we lived for the moment when we could sit in front of a screen—be it a theater matinee or an old black-and-white television set with a defective vertical hold—and swoon over their every drawled word and marvel at every noble deed.

Our pulses raced when our hero faced the bad guy in the middle of Main Street at high noon, though we knew he would win the gun battle. Back then, the good guys *always* won. You could count on it; just as you could rely on the fact that your favorite Cartwright would always be eligible to marry you when you finally grew up. Every female who fell in love with a Cartwright on screen was destined to die within an hour, thank God!

Where are they now, these gorgeous, confident, capable men, who smelled of freshly soaped leather, horseflesh, whiskey and tobacco? (Why did we ever think that was a winning combination?) Where are the good guys who always shot straight, with their guns and their mouths, and treated a lady with respect?

Occasionally, you can find them on independent television stations on Saturday afternoons, or at your local video stores under "Classic Westerns," or...once in a while, between the covers of a book, written by women who still remember what it was like to fall in love with a cowboy.

Here's hoping that, as you read these stories, you'll remember, too.

THE MAN FROM
SOUTHERN CROSS

Margaret Way

Chapter One

HE LEFT the mustering camp late afternoon, when the still-blazing sun was slipping down the sky in a glory of red, gold and amethyst.

Every bone, every muscle in his body was throbbing with fatigue. It had been a long hard day made doubly frustrating because he and a handful of the men had to fight yet another brushfire at the old "dancing grounds."

The aboriginals claimed, perhaps with perfect truth, that the grounds were sacred and the brushfires, which had gone on for as long as anyone could remember, were the work of Jumboona, one of the more mischievous of the ancient gods. Sometimes when he was tired, like now, he accepted that possibility with a laconic shrug. Unless the fires were lit deliberately—and no one had ever found any evidence of it—there seemed to be no easy explanation. As his father used to say, "Old Jumboona strikes again!" Charlie Eaglehawk, their best tracker, claimed to have seen Jumboona through the flames, but then Charlie specialized in stories that made the hair on the back of one's neck prickle.

He rode on, allowing the splendor of the sunset to revive him. The muster would resume at dawn the next day, but there was a tension in the men and in the cattle he didn't much like. The hot winds had a bearing on it. As well, for the aboriginal stockmen, Jandra Crossing was the site of an old ritual killing by one of the dreaded *kurdaitcha* men, dispensers of justice since the Dreamtime. Stories about the ritual *kurdaitcha* killings were interwoven with the legends of Southern Cross; so were the stories about Jumboona and his hostile cavortings. Jumboona certainly liked to keep them all busy, he thought now with a sort of rueful humor.

A wallaby jumped out in front of his big stallion, The Brigadier, who executed a high-stepping dance. He reined the horse in, then pushed his akubra farther back on his head, looking up at the sky. It was pearlescent with smoke, the smell of burned bush land hot in his nostrils. Even the birds seemed disturbed, sending up spine-tingling shrieks as they flew home to the billabongs and swamps. The *kurdaitcha* man's victims, transgressors of the tribal laws, were said to wander the lignum swamps at night. Many a stockman over the long years had claimed to see their spirits setting up camp near the water. He had never seen anything paranormal himself, and he didn't expect to. But even his so-called iron nerves had been tested now and again in the hill country, where the extensive network of caves served as immensely old galleries for images of love magic and sorcery.

Southern Cross, the Mountford desert stronghold since the 1860s, was also a mythical place for the Jurra Jurra tribe. So the legends had begun and were allowed to grow. This was his country and he loved it with a passion. No woman could ever hold him in the same way. At thirty, with half a dozen affairs behind him, he had reason to know. He'd come close to marriage once—it was expected that at some stage he would provide the historic Mountford station with an heir—but he'd found himself unable to take the final step. No woman had ever fired his blood.

Dusk saw him riding through the main compound on his way to the huge complex of stables at the rear of the homestead. He dismounted in the circular courtyard, looking around. Where the hell was Manny? Probably whittling away at one of his little wooden sculptures; they were so good, he thought it was about time he encouraged the boy to do something with his skill. He summoned him with a loud whistle and Manny came running, his face split in a wide grin.

"Old Jumboona get yah again, Boss?"

Tired as he was, he couldn't help returning Manny's infectious grin. "The worst thing, Manny, is that you seem to enjoy it."

"No, Boss." Manny shook his curly head. "You'll cut 'im down to size and that's a fact. I'm beginnin' to wonder if the old boy ain't losin' his powers."

His laugh rasped in his dry throat. "You should have spent the day with me. And I wouldn't speak too loudly, either. The old boy might hear you."

"Wouldn't bother about the likes o' me." Manny took charge of The Brigadier's saddle. "Saw Miss Annabel a while ago. She was all excited about her friend."

Her friend! God, he didn't know whether to laugh or bang his head against the stone wall. He'd clean forgotten about Annabel's friend. She would be up at the homestead right now.

"Everything okay, Boss?" Manny asked anxiously.

"I just need an ice-cold beer, Manny. And a hot tub. In that order." He didn't say the thought of having to make small talk with a strange woman intensified his feelings of tiredness and irritation. He swept off his akubra and ran an impatient hand through his hair, black and shiny as a magpie's wing. It was too thick and too long at the back and, he supposed, that together with the marks of grime and smoke gave him the appearance of a wild man. Not exactly what Miss Roishin—what kind of name was that?—Grant would expect to see. He laughed out loud remembering how some women's magazine had voted him one of the sexiest men in the country. Eligible and rich. The *rich* surely helped; the *sexy* bit amazed him. He knew he was attractive to women, but he didn't flatter himself unduly. Most women were very frivolous, he'd found. They had this big ongoing affair with glamour and glitz.

His thoughts inevitably shifted to the wedding. In a few days' time, Annabel, his stepsister—the elder, by fully five minutes, of identical twins—was to be married in the homestead's ballroom, with the reception in the Great Hall. The whole thing had gotten a little out of hand as far as he was concerned. And he was footing the bill.

To be fair, as a leading "landed" family, their guest list had to be long. The extended Mountford family was spread over three states, with Southern Cross the ancestral home. They all expected to be represented, along with close friends, business friends, the usual socialites, assorted politicians and a fair sprinkling of the legal profession to which the groom, Michael Courtney, belonged. It sometimes seemed to him that half the country had been invited, but Annabel assured him 250 guests was the lowest possible count. Roishin—was it

Gallic for rose?—was one of the four bridesmaids. She had been a close friend of the twins at university, yet strangely enough he had never met her. The one time she'd visited the station he'd been on a business trip to Texas, seeing a fellow rancher. The girls, Annabel and Vanessa, spent a lot of time with her in Sydney where she lived and he maintained an apartment as a family pied-à-terre. When he'd had time to listen, he'd learned that her father was a merchant banker, her mother a divorce lawyer. Roishin probably arranged flowers. The twins, "the Mountford heiresses" as they were usually referred to in the press, didn't work much, either. He, as head of the Mountford clan since the untimely death of his father, worked like a dog and always had.

His stepmother, Sasha, of whom he was very fond, had taken to spending a good deal of her time traveling. In fact, Sasha's travels had become something of a family joke. His own mother, Charlotte, had walked out on him and his father after a grueling seven years of marital war. His father had applied for custody of their only child, with the considerable weight of the family's power and influence behind him, and had emerged triumphant, just as everyone had known he would. *He* had been the heir, the helpless six-year-old victim who'd never been prepared for the emotional devastation. Even now, sometimes, in some deep place inside him, it hurt like hell. He'd had such love for his mother. Enormous love. He'd worshiped her. For years he just couldn't take in her treachery. She had left them both for a man she hadn't even bothered to marry.

His father had engineered it so that he rarely saw his mother. On those few occasions, he'd been full of hurt and hostility, very difficult to handle. He hadn't seen his mother in many years now, though Sasha persisted in trying to shove photographs in the glossies under his nose. She was Lady Vandenberg now, wife of Eric Vandenberg, the industrialist. His mother had tried to make contact with him after his father's death, but feeling as he did, he couldn't bring himself to see her. *She* was the one who had made an art form of rejection.

He decided to enter the house through the front door. It was the quickest route upstairs, where he had the entire west wing to himself. Sasha and the twins shared the east wing. The house was so big they could all rattle around in it without even seeing each other. The Hon. George Clifford Mountford had begun work in the early 1860s on what was to become a thirty-five room mansion. The complex of surrounding buildings included a picturesque old stone church built for the master, his family and servants. No way could it accommodate 250 wedding guests, but the big reception rooms at the homestead could.

He had barely moved across the threshold when the sound of footsteps along the gallery made him look up. A young woman was descending the staircase at a rush.

His first thought was she had strayed out of a painting. Something by John Singer Sargent. Her image stamped itself indelibly on his mind. She was a waking dream, a creature of incredible light and grace. She kept moving…floating…. Colors shimmered. She had long dark hair with a burnish of purple, luminous white skin, large faintly slanted blue or green eyes. He couldn't be sure. Her full mouth, so fresh and tender, was smiling in some kind of pleasurable anticipation. She was wearing what had to be her bridesmaid's gown. A sumptuous champagne silk creation with a neckline cut to reveal bare sloping shoulders. The rich material gleamed. The beading and embroidery on the bodice and the full sleeves flickered and flashed in the light from the chandelier. She was tantalizing . . . tantalizing. . . .

Something like a wave of heat broke over him. It was as though his skin caught fire. Just as he thought no woman could move him, he felt a shock of desire so powerful his fists clenched instinctively until the knuckles showed white. For an instant he was the helpless male again. Bitter and powerless in the face of a woman's sheer magic. He was no match for her. The thought appalled him, influencing his attitude drastically.

She looked down. Saw him. Became arrested, unsure of her next movement. She'd been hurrying down the staircase, one hand holding up the skirt of her long billowing gown, the other trailing along the banister. Now she stood immobilized.

Adrenaline pumped through him, energizing his tired body and keying up his senses. Experience had taught him to be a very careful man. But here she was! Out of nowhere, a crisis in his life. And more than anything he wanted her away. Back to the city and the hothouse where she belonged. Such women couldn't bloom in the desert. They only brought heartbreak and trouble.

He saw her make a visible effort to speak. A soft ripple moved her throat. "You must be David. We've never met, have we? How do you do? I'm Roishin."

She had a lovely voice, warmly pitched, self-possessed. Or it would have been except for the faintest tremor. Perhaps his appearance frightened her? The wild hair, the dark stubble of beard, his stained clothes. She pronounced her name Roh-sheen with the accent on the second syllable. Appropriately, it sounded like a name from myth and legend.

Any civilized man would have moved to greet her, but he stood perfectly still, making her come to him. No one had ever called him David except his mother. He'd been Mont to his father, as he was to Sasha and the twins. Mountford to just about everyone else, including family.

She went to give him her slender white hand, but he evinced cool surprise. "Welcome to Southern Cross," he said, aware his voice sounded curt and formal. "I won't take your hand. I'm covered in grime and it's important not to mark your beautiful gown."

There was a fraught little silence as if she realized he didn't want to touch her. Her iridescent eyes darkened, glistened as though stung by tears.

I want her, he thought. *This is the woman who will change my life.*

Chapter Two

HE KNEW he was quiet at dinner. Once or twice he caught Sasha and the twins looking at him, obviously wondering why he wasn't making his usual contribution to the conversation, especially when a guest was present. But Roishin Grant was having a strange effect on him. She might have been a creature from another planet, beguiling his eye but stilling his tongue. Her presence undermined his control, dredging up some part of him he'd thought long buried—a need and a longing that seemed to possess him although he was reluctant to experience such emotions again. Remembered love burned in him. For an instant he had a clear recollection of his mother sitting where Sasha was sitting now. He wasn't aware of it, but his eyes turned stormy. The pain had dulled, but not the anger. The anger was a permanent scar.

His mother had been beautiful in just the way this woman was beautiful. Dark-haired, jewel-eyed, pale-skinned. Bewitching, where Sasha and the twins with their fair pretty faces and rounded curves had the freshness of apples. Tonight she wore something silky in a swirl of blues, greens and purples, the V neckline allowing tantalizing glimpses of the shadowy cleft between her breasts. Her features in the rose gold lighting had the perfection of sculpture, but the eyes and the mouth were ravishingly female. That he could do without. He could even understand why a man might want to marry a sensible plain-faced woman. A *dull* woman, who wouldn't have the capacity to inflict mortal wounds.

From time to time, because he couldn't resist it, he inserted a probing question, which she parried without fluster. She had a charming candid way about her, but he was determined to remain unimpressed—far from easy when his every sense was being seduced. By the time coffee arrived, the realization suddenly hit him that *she* had been drawing *him* out. And she'd done it with considerable tact and skill, leaving him in no doubt that as a lawyer she'd be a very deft operator. In a whispered aside, Annabel had told him about Roishin's qualification in law. Another shock. Not a flower-arranging dilettante, after all. At least she had a career to take her straight back home. She wouldn't be lingering here to finish what she'd started—the oldest story in the world. Seduction.

He excused himself fairly early, saying he had correspondence to attend to; it was true, but had their guest been almost anyone else, the job would have kept. Later, when he was drafting a letter to the chairman of a government committee of which he was a member, he heard them fooling around the piano. Both his sisters played, Annabel extremely well, and he smiled to himself as she launched into a spirited and highly embellished version of Mendelssohn's "Wedding March." It was so entertaining he got up to open his door. From "The Wedding March," Annabel began to work her way through a number of songs, old and new, love songs, wedding songs, with Vanessa singing snatches as her twin played. Sasha, who wasn't terribly accurate with her pitching, called for an old wedding song that had probably been all the rage in her day and began singing it almost before Annabel had finished the introduction.

He put down his pen, listening to the words.

His own lips formed the words ironically. *Promise me.* Promises. Love and togetherness . . .

His mother had made sacred promises she had never kept. She had scorned the husband she'd married in the sight of God, abandoned her small son. So much for promises and dazzling women. He had a sure instinct in these matters.

Sasha was having difficulties with her vocalizing, and another voice took over. At first happily, slightly exaggerating the sentimental lyrics, then as though with a sudden change of heart, seriously, in a voice that held him spellbound.

His hands on the huge mahogany partner's desk, his father's desk, clenched and unclenched. He'd *liked* Vanessa's version of some Whitney Houston song, but this was unbearably sweet, a naturally beautiful female voice singing an old song with great tenderness, sincerity and purity. Annabel's accompaniment moved into a matching mode, became stirring, full of feeling. The extreme top note soared with ease and absolute certainty. As a performance it was unique in his experience, invading caverns in his heart he had thought sealed.

Annabel called a spontaneous "Bravo!", clapping like a devotee at a classical concert.

Vanessa, as always, seconded her, barely a heartbeat later, sounding the least bit tearful. Then Sasha's astonished, "That was *lovely*, Roishin!"

Now he heard *her* laugh. A melodious ripple, with a music all its own. He should have known from the cadences of her speaking voice that she could sing. Roishin Grant was becoming more disturbing by the minute.

Later he came to stand in the doorway to say goodnight. "I enjoyed the concert, ladies!" He gave a slight bow, contemplating the charming tableau, faces turned toward him. "Roishin was the soloist?" As though he didn't know.

"Yes, isn't she brilliant?" Pleasure and animation was all over Annabel's sunny open face. "She even made us cry."

"Dare I admit to a tear myself?" His eyes singled out Roishin briefly. He meant his tone to be pleasant, but even then an edge crept in. "Would you care to go riding in the morning, Roishin?" he asked, to make amends. What in sweet hell was making him say her name like that? It was rolling off his tongue like honey.

"Yes, go!" the others urged.

"You *do* ride?" Again the degree of challenge.

The twins exchanged glances, but Roishin was perfectly poised, looking at him with her iridescent eyes. Blue, green, he wasn't sure. They seemed to change dramatically with different flashes of color from her dress.

"I do, but I think as a renowned horseman and polo player you might judge me harshly."

"Mont's always kind to beginners," Van, his faithful disciple, said.

"Roishin doesn't look terribly convinced," Annabel laughed.

"I'd love to come with you, David." She smiled, softening his mood and charming him. "If it makes you feel happier, I belonged to a pony club as a child."

Her voice was actually connecting with his nerve ends, vastly unsettling him. "Well, that's something, I'm sure. Until the morning, then. Just around daybreak is perfect, but I suppose that's too early for you?" Did he have to make everything sound like a rebuke?

"Dawn sounds perfect." She continued to smile gently, humoring his abrasiveness. Her mouth was full, soft, with a pronounced cupid's bow. Was that supposed to mean sensuality? Vulnerability? All he knew was that he wanted to crush it with his own.

"We'll have breakfast waiting when you come home," Sasha promised, her smile registering a certain roguishness.

Don't try your matchmaking on me, Sasha, he thought. Fond as he was of his stepmother, he was the master of his own fate. And he had rejected Roishin Grant on sight.

HE AWOKE at first light from long habit, finding in himself an excitement he wanted to shut out. Damn and blast, what was the matter with him? He wasn't a callow adolescent. If he wanted to brag, he could have said he was immensely successful with women. But this Roishin Grant was affecting him sharply, bringing out something almost primitive in his nature. He felt threatened, hostile, enslaved. All at the same time. He couldn't help feeling a certain contempt for himself, as well. No woman was going to dominate his life ever again. He'd decided that long ago.

Still, the coming of Sasha, then the twins, had made Southern Cross cheerful. When he married—and he *would* have to—he'd have the sense to find an honest openhearted woman like Sasha. She'd brought peace, but no drama. His father's experience, and he remembered his beloved father in all his moods, had warned him off drama for life.

Yet here he was, showering and dressing at full speed. It was a spell of sorts, and he despised it. He scooped up his akubra and went out the door, hoping she'd have the sense to bring a hat. The sun would be up soon enough, and he found himself hating the thought of any burning to her skin. No wonder they described a woman's skin as "magnolia." Hers had the same flawless, creamy, stroke-me quality.

Miracle of miracles, she was waiting for him in the hallway, as straight as a boy except for the soft, high thrust of her breasts. She actually jumped when he came up behind her saying, "Hello, there," then swung to face him, her long hair, very thick and straight, brushed back from her face and caught in some kind of knot on her nape. As a hairstyle it couldn't have been more severe, but she carried it beautifully. In fact, he saw more this way—the lovely line of her jaw, the way it merged with the graceful column of her neck, the almost flower-like set of her ears.

"David, you startled me!" she gasped. "You have a very quiet tread."

"So I've been told." He could see a trace of something—near-fright?—in her eyes. "I'm sorry. I had no intention of alarming you." But she *knew* there was a hardness in him; a hardness that might make a sensitive woman shrink. "I'm glad you thought to bring a hat."

"One of Van's."

"Then put it on. The sun's strong even this early, and your skin is very white." He couldn't seem to keep his eyes off her, although that wasn't what he wanted at all. Her hair, her face, the feminine slope of her shoulders. She, too, stood staring up at him, like a creature trying to struggle out of a trap.

"I'm not arguing with you, David," she said finally, putting the hat on and adjusting the chin strap. "It's very obvious that you're right—and it's equally obvious that you're accustomed to command."

His gaze raked her, trying to decipher her expression. "I *do* run Southern Cross. And I know that any other way wouldn't work." He extended his arm, indicating she should precede him out the door.

Manny was already up and about, parading his infectious grin. "Mornin' Boss. Mornin' Miss."

"Miss Grant," he told the boy briefly.

"Miss Grant, o'course!" Manny studied Roishin with immense approval.

"Good morning, Manny," she smiled. "We've met before. Don't you remember?"

"Sure do, ma'am. Are you gonna take the same horse?"

"And which horse was that?" Mountford asked, deceptively quiet.

"Miss Grant's a plenty good rider," Manny told him warmly. "She really knows how to treat horses."

"That doesn't exactly answer my question, Manny."

"She took The Brigadier!" Manny whooped.

He looked and felt thoroughly jolted. "The Brigadier is much too strong for a woman."

Manny sobered abruptly, doing a little mime with his hands.

"Please don't blame Manny," Roishin begged. "I . . . rather insisted."

"Manny should know better. You won't be riding The Brigadier today." He couldn't control the curtness and he saw her flush. Damn! He didn't really want to upset her.

He gave an order to Manny and the boy moved away, returning a few moments later leading Star Lady, a small but beautifully proportioned silver gray mare with a sweet temper and a surprisingly long stride.

"Oh, isn't she lovely? Is she for me?" Roishin must have forgiven him, because she looked up at him with a smile that would have melted a stonier heart than his.

"She is. You'll find her a pleasant ride. I'll take The Brigadier . . . if you don't mind."

It didn't take long to saddle up the horses, and soon they were on their way. He rode the big, dashing jet black stallion that stood a good seventeen hands high. If she could hold The Brigadier as she must have done, she was an excellent horsewoman.

As he soon found out. The talk of the pony club had been no more than a tease. She was an experienced rider, with considerable style. A feeling of great contentment welled up in him, calming his inner conflicts. It was an incomparable feeling, riding together in the pearly dawn. The air was blissfully pure and cool, laden with the sweet scents of the bush. Bird song poured from the trees that scattered blossom like confetti as they rode beneath them and out onto the open plain. Her face beneath his sister's white akubra was alive with quick feelings. She looked entranced, as though the magic he always felt was getting to her, too. It pleased him more than he would ever have believed.

Not everyone understood the outback, its vastness and savage majesty. Some found it eerie, others intimidating, and many professed to a kind of atavistic fear that raised the short hairs on the backs of their necks. It had something to do with the enormous empty distances, the great silence, the play of color, light and shadow on the monumental primeval rocks. The outback had an incredible mystique. It was the wild beating heart of the most ancient continent on earth.

At one of the crystal-clear gullies overhung by the weeping casuarinas they came upon a small party of aboriginal women and children gathering herbs, and they exchanged greetings before moving on. After a long and agonizing drought, Southern Cross had experienced its first good season in years, and the wildflowers were prodigious, running in a marvelous multicolored embroidered carpet to the curiously domed hillocks that rose like Persian minarets on the station's western border.

At this time of day the hills were a soft pink, but like many of the great rocks of the interior they changed color with weather conditions, aspect and time of day. Mountford had seen them run the gamut from salmon pink to rose to glowing furnace red, then back to deep purple and misty mauve. There were aboriginal legends connected to every natural feature on the station, and as they slowed their exhilarating gallop to a comfortable walk, he began to point out different places of geographical interest, outlining the Dreamtime legends that went along with them.

The sun was up now in full splendor, dispersing the strange mists that hung like clouds along the ancient watercourses. The aborigines looked on them as guardian spirits, and to an imaginative eye they appeared to be just that, lying in milky circlets and ribbons only a few inches above the green canopy of trees. One could expect mists when a chill hung over the bush, but the mists moved in faithfully even when the weather was brilliantly clear and hot.

"Magic!" she said, listening to him. "And why not, in such a place?"

Her answer delighted him, but he tried to hide it. "Time to go back," he announced matter-of-factly, unwilling to prolong his joy in her company. "As Manny said, you know how to treat horses."

"Because they're such beautiful creatures!" She leaned forward to stroke the mare's neck. The wind had torn at her hair, releasing a few strands, which she casually brushed away. She turned her head to him, using one hand to shield her eyes from the strong slanting sunlight. "I *can* ride The Brigadier, you know."

"I'm sure you can, but I'd rather you didn't." He heard his own voice, deep, smooth, vaguely taunting. "I wouldn't care to see you break your lovely neck."

For all her poise, she flushed, a soft peach bloom on her cheeks. "You don't like me, do you, David?"

"What am I supposed to say to that?" He was surprised by her directness.

"Perhaps what you've got against me?"

"What idiotic nonsense!"

"Don't you realize how hostile you are?"

"Hostile, possibly," he agreed. "You disturb me, Miss Grant. You're...extremely direct. Anyway, it's nothing personal." Despite himself, he tried to explain. "Something about exotic creatures makes me tense inside."

"How? In what way?"

He glanced at her briefly, a silver sparkle in his eyes. "One can see you're a lawyer from all the practiced questioning. Surely you're not attempting to *analyze* me?"

"Forgive me. I'm just trying to understand what I've done. Annabel and Vanessa are my dear friends. I want you to like me."

"Presumably every man you meet *likes* you?" His tone was cool to the point of cutting—and there was nothing he could do about it.

"Well, I don't go around blazing out challenge."

"Don't you?"

"I want to be your friend, David. Please believe me."

"I'm sorry, Roishin." He smiled at her. "That may never happen."

FOR THE REST of the day he lost himself in backbreaking work, only returning to the house as the sun was setting in a blaze of varied reds and golds. He went straight to his room. Suite of rooms really—a bedroom the size of a football field, as Van described it, bathroom, dressing room, a sitting room large enough to accommodate some excellent pieces he had appropriated from other parts of the house. He was entirely self-contained and private, which was the way he liked it. One of these days he would have his wing of the house refurbished, but it all cost money. Big money. Much as he loved his ancestral home, he had to admit that its maintenance had created a few problems over the years. As well, he had outlaid an astonishing amount of money to have decorators flown in to pretty up the main reception rooms for the wedding. He intended to do Annabel proud. Vanessa, too, when it came her turn to be married. Whatever his fears of the femme fatales of this world, he understood that Sasha and his sisters were the sort of women who would work at making their marriages happy.

The actual wedding ceremony was to be performed by a longtime family friend, an Anglican bishop. It would take place in the old ballroom, which could easily accommodate the guests. The reception was being held in the Great Hall in the main compound. Ironically the Great Hall had been erected for his late father's wedding to the beautiful Charlotte Sheffield, the current Lady Vandenberg.

Sasha had met his mother many times over the years when she was socializing in Sydney or Melbourne and always returned home saying what a "lovely person" Lady Vandenberg was. She had even suggested Lady Vandenberg might be sent an invitation to the wedding; the twins had met her, as well, and found her "fabulous." But as ever, Sasha's efforts at reconciling mother and son had met with total failure. As far as he was concerned, marriage meant one mate forever. Even the *brolgas* that danced on the river flats knew all about that.

When he went downstairs, showered and changed, he found the women setting out wedding gifts in what the family called the Sistine Chapel. It was really the original drawing room in the east wing, a very large room, cedar-paneled. A bit dark and dingy now, but it had a remarkable plaster ceiling that his father had had restored by a master painter and then insured for many thousands of dollars.

Mountford surveyed the room carefully. The furniture, also high Victorian, had been rearranged for the occasion, and he'd had the station's carpenters make long trestle tables to line three sides of the room. Sasha had hunted up the most beautiful of the old lace-appliquéd linen tablecloths to cover them, and they skimmed the parquet floor. The trestles groaned with their magnificent freight of wedding gifts. It all meant a lot of extra work, but Annabel had been determined that her guests be able to see and enjoy all the lovely things she and Michael had been given.

He called a greeting, acknowledged with sweet smiles, and Annabel ran to him eagerly. "What do you think, Mont?"

He realized his approval was important to his sister, so he backed off into the double doorway, making a frame with his hands.

"Splendid!" he announced. "A marvelous display. Not too many people make the gesture these days. The Austins didn't, remember?"

"A pity, but the custom is disappearing. Too much work, I suppose," Annabel thrust her hand through her short blond curls. "It was Roishin's idea to create all the different levels, and she wants to use those big white porcelain swans for a table decoration."

"Very effective." He let his eyes rest on Roishin's face, marveling that it could appear both sensual and wonderfully tender. "What sort of flowers would you use?"

"Perhaps sprays of white Singapore orchids if I could get them. A little greenery."

"Why don't you get on to the fellow who's doing all the floral arrangements?" he suggested. "I'm sure he could run to a few more orchids." All the flower arrangements and bouquets were being flown in from Melbourne, along with the country's most fashionable floral designer and his assistants. Whatever it took, he would see that Roishin had her porcelain swans carrying masses of white orchids on their backs. "All practice for your own wedding, Roishin," he added lightly.

"Roishin hasn't got any wedding plans," Vanessa told him, glancing at her friend with a smile. "But she could have her pick of at least a dozen eligible men."

Roishin shook her head, obviously wishing Vanessa hadn't said it, but he finished for his sister, "Drawn like moths to the flame!" Idly he moved down the line, reading the cards attached to the wedding gifts. There was tableware of every make, design and color, quietly elegant, which he preferred, or richly embellished. Limoges, Lenox, Wedgwood, Royal Doulton, Royal Copenhagen, Mikasa. Crystal galore, Waterford patterns, Baccarat champagne flutes, wine, sherry, liqueur glasses, brandy balloons. A magnificent ruby decanter and a dozen matching goblets decorated with gold. Silver of all kinds, wine carafes, tureens, trays, an antique silver tea service, candlesticks and candelabra by the score. There were antique clocks, Lalique vases, ceramic vases and paintings. Furniture in one corner—six antique dining chairs, an embroidered screen, a very beautiful French *secretaire* that had belonged to his grandmother for as long as he could remember. Linen occupied the entire length of one trestle, from tablecloths to napkins, through bath towels to satin-bound blankets and the finest American-cotton sheets. All in all, there was just about everything a very fortunate and popular young woman could desire.

He transferred his attention to the sections of wall above the cedar paneling. "I don't know why someone didn't point this out. The room needs freshening up."

"We weren't going to use it, remember?" Sasha said, looking up. "Besides, you've spent so much already, Mont."

"A coat of paint should do it." Roishin came to stand near him, her particular fragrance entering his nostrils. "What about a lovely blue, instead of the ivory? The same blue as the plasterwork in the ceiling. And maybe we could take that gorgeous Persian rug out of the library just for the occasion. The guests won't be going in there, and the rug has such marvelous rich blues, pinks and reds. Annabel, what about a few gilt-framed mirrors, instead of paintings? There's so much in the attic. Van showed me. Turn on the chandeliers and voilà! It'll look much lighter in mood and tone."

"Why, of course! How delightful!" Annabel exclaimed. "May we have that done, Mont?"

"Whatever you want," he said with gentle indulgence. He ran his hand down her cheek. "I'll have someone mix the paint in the morning. Roishin will have to stand by to ensure it's just the shade she wants. Raid the attic, too, by all means, Roishin. You have carte blanche.'' He moved toward the door. "I'll be in my study until dinnertime. Call me if there's any lifting to be done.''

IN THE MORNING he detailed two of his best maintenance men to take some white interior paint and a couple of tubes of tint from the station store and present themselves to Miss Grant at the homestead for further instructions. He himself had a meeting with one of the big meat buyers flying in from Bahloo Springs, a Mountford property some one thousand kilometers to the northwest. He expected the usual haggling, the disputes about bullock weight, but in the end he almost always got the deal he wanted. Market requirements had changed over the past few years. The smaller three-year-old beasts were in demand, not the larger five- to six-year-old bullocks. He expected he'd sell an entire paddock within the first hour. Southern Cross, crisscrossed by a maze of water channels, was a fattening paradise after the rains. The cattle were in prime condition.

Around midday he returned to the homestead, well pleased with the morning's proceedings. Emily, their part-aboriginal housemaid, was busy polishing up in the gallery, but she called to him that Mrs. M. and the twins were supervising at the Great Hall and Miss Grant was in the east wing with the painters.

He should have been organizing road trains with his overseer; instead, he found himself moving off in the direction of the old drawing room. This course of action was only deepening his involvement, but what the hell! After all, he was expected to approve everything. Roishin Grant didn't need to know his *real* reason for calling in.

As it turned out, she wasn't there, and he felt a stab of keen disappointment. Where was the legendary Mountford independence of heart? Surrendered the first moment she'd dazzled him in that magical dress. She'd probably gone down to the Great Hall where the domed ceiling was being draped with miles of rose and cream tentlike hangings. The framework had taken four of his men the best part of a week to erect, but he'd been assured by the decorator, Sydney's most famous and fussy, that the effect would be sensational. A male assistant had been left behind to stage-manage the job until the decorator returned the day before the wedding to give his all-important okay.

His own men greeted him warmly, as though they hadn't seen him for years. Ernie Powell, known to everyone as Pee Wee, had already moved his gear aside, while Bluey Reynolds, his ginger-haired nephew, was seated up on a plank finishing off a section over the double doorway.

He made a full circuit of the room before he pronounced judgment.

"Nice work, men!"

Pee Wee, who looked like a terrorist but had the mellowest of temperaments, grinned. "Real pleasure, Boss. The young lady had us mixin' away at the color until we got it just right. Celestial blue, ain't it?"

"Damned if I know, Pee Wee, but it's very effective." He glanced at the freshly painted walls, the blue perfectly matched to that of the elaborate ceiling. He could see the Persian rug from the library rolled up at the far end of the room; two matching gilt-framed mirrors with carved flowers at the corners and trails of gold leaves across the top rested against the paneling. Not only that, the enterprising Miss Grant had found a very fancy pair of armchairs, lavishly adorned with gilt scrolls and garlands, which he thought would look fine on either side of the double doorway.

"Looks beaut, don't it, Boss?" the diminutive Bluey called in a voice that would have made a deaf man jump. "Terrific idea Roishin had. A real sweetie, that one! No trouble to paint the place, either. Didn't spill a drop. We're gonna lay the rug and put up the mirrors after lunch. I believe them chairs are to go 'ere." He laid down the roller he'd been using, jerking his thumb vigorously downward. Just at that moment Roishin came back into the room, a charming smile on her face.

It was too much for Bluey, always a disaster around women. Hell-bent on greeting Roishin's return with a flourish, he threw up his hands, the left catching the handle of the roller and sending the tray of paint flying.

There was barely half a second between Roishin's expression changing to that of a woman awaiting something horrendous and the paint cascading all over her.

"You bloody fool, Bluey!" Pee Wee yelled, otherwise frozen in shock, but Mountford had moved in fast, scooping up a cloth from the rung of the ladder and wrapping it around Roishin's hair.

"Don't panic, Roishin," he said in his normal crisp delivery. "Keep your eyes shut and I'll get you under a shower."

She stood perfectly still, her arms folded inward, and he gathered her up, moving to the shower room that served the pool area at the rear of the east wing.

He had the water running within moments. He kept his arms around her, steering them both into the cubicle. She'd started making little breathy sounds and he found himself murmuring encouragement in a voice that seemed to be pulsing with something far stronger than anxiety or concern. As steam billowed all around them, he cupped her face in his hands, holding it up to the wide-nozzled jet. The water-based paint began to thin out rapidly, running in blue rivulets onto the blouse that had born the brunt of the spill. He reasoned the blouse should come off. He loathed the idea of embarrassing her, but it didn't seem the time for false modesty. More paint was coming from her blouse than anywhere else.

"You need to get that blouse off, Roishin," he muttered while the water poured over them like a miniature Niagara. "Don't be embarrassed." He slipped his palm over her collarbone, finding a bra strap.

She seemed to nod her consent, still fearful, apparently, of opening her eyes. He unbuttoned her blouse down the front, peeled it off and threw it outside the cubicle onto the tiled floor. He was totally drenched, which mattered not at all. He continued to direct the water over her with his hands, relieved beyond words that her hair, face and upper body were almost washed free of paint. Now the panic was subsiding, and he started to experience a sense of excitement that was dizzying. Every nerve in his body was humming, every muscle bunched. Her breath was coming fast and he felt her give an involuntary shiver, though steam was swirling around them in clouds.

For one long moment he allowed himself to look at her. How could he not? The strength of her magnetism appalled and confounded him, yet she was beautiful enough to take his breath away. He thought he would remember forever the first sight of her breasts, the upper slopes beaded with water, the rose-colored nipples peaking cleanly against the nearly transparent fabric of her bra. It seemed a fantasy that they should be there together like this. Shock waves were running through him. Pleasure beyond imagining. They were as close as lovers. Body to body. The sinuous slither of the water only acted as a stimulant.

With her eyes closed, head bent, she seemed tremendously vulnerable. She had such graceful shoulders, a swan's neck. Instead of keeping his distance as he'd vowed, he was plunging deeper and deeper into a sensual maelstrom. It came to him that he'd never wanted anything or anyone the way he wanted her. Like it or not, she'd entered his life; now he would never be able to return to his old, cynical self-contained self.

Emotions warred in him, each struggling for supremacy. He wasn't a man to cede control and yet…and yet… He wanted to kiss her, her full tender mouth, the hollow of her throat. He wanted to bend her back over his arm and kiss the white flesh of her breasts. He had to do *something* to assuage the hunger that burned in him so fiercely. She stirred up all the old misery and pain he carried deep within him; she challenged his elemental maleness, but something about her was pure balm. Desire wasn't born out of cold reason but *need*. What he felt for her wasn't just physical.

Slowly she opened her iridescent eyes, staring up at him, surprising God-knew-what expression in his too-intimate gaze. Steam was rising around them like incense, perfumed by the boronia-scented soap that had fallen unheeded to the floor of the cubicle. Her parted lips were trembling slightly. Her slender body seemed to be racked by little tremors.

His hands seemed to be moving of their own accord, driven by a single overwhelming impulse. They skimmed her hips, her narrow waist, shaped the satin-smooth rib cage. Her eyes were still staring into his, brilliantly clear, unaffected by her ordeal, the color now pure green. There was some star in their depths that seemed to be urging him on.

Blood rushed in his ears. He lowered his head abruptly, catching her gasping mouth, sealing it brutally, tasting her sweet breath on his tongue. Her body seemed to melt into his and he tightened his grip on her.

I must have her, he thought. *I* will *have her.* She embodied everything he most feared and worshiped. She set up such longings.

It seemed to go on for a long time, their mouths fused together. He was kissing her as though she were exquisitely delicious and he a famished man. The sweetness of her mouth enslaved him.

David!

Had she moaned it softly? Was she trying to turn her head?

He was infinitely stronger, taller—the top of her head just cleared his shoulder. But whatever happened between them could only happen with her full volition.

He threw his head back almost violently, and it was over. He reached behind her and turned off the faucets, unaware that the silvery glitter of his eyes revealed he was still riding strong emotional currents. Her body was still resting against him as though she was dazed. He had to admit that what had happened *had* been devastating. He dug his fingers through his wet hair, felt it spring back in waves. He stepped outside the cubicle and hunted up towels from a cupboard, then held one out to her. She wrapped it around her like a cloak. She'd been very pale; now color was flooding her cheeks, making her eyes blaze.

"I thought you wanted no part of me?" she asked in a strained voice.

"Oh, come, Roishin! I'm only human." A cool comment to cover what had been a very passionate encounter. "I'll be amazed if you're able to wear that blouse again. We must get you another."

"No need," she said quietly. "I hope you're not going to tear strips off Bluey?"

He shrugged. "Pee Wee's bound to have done that. You must think I'm a hard boss?"

"You've shown a certain hardness to me. I'm not imagining it. It's there."

"Maybe I don't care to see myself one of your potential victims." He gave her a tightly drawn smile. "Now, if you'll wait a moment, I'll send Emily to you. She can bring some dry clothes." After the briefest pause, he added, "I'm sorry that happened, Roishin."

She bound her long dark ribbon of hair around her hand. "Your kissing me or Bluey spilling the paint? I have a feeling it's the former."

"In that case, 'sorry' doesn't cover the situation. At any rate, I'm glad you suffered no harm. I wouldn't have cared to see paint get into your beautiful eyes." He finished pressing a towel over his wet clothing, sopping up the worst of it before he threw the towel over a brass railing. "No need to worry—I won't grab you again. It must have been all that steam!"

She looked at him, a little turbulence in her eyes. "You're speaking from experience here? I understand you've had any number of women friends."

"Not in the shower, no. I do believe that's a first."

She laughed, spilling music in his ears. "Shall I tell Sasha and the twins about the . . . incident?"

He swung back toward her. "But of course! It'll be the talk of the place, anyway. Better to forget the part where things got out of hand."

"Oh, absolutely!" She coolly matched his tone. "Especially as it's not going to happen again."

Chapter Three

THREE DAYS to the wedding, and the homestead began
to fill up. The bridegroom, Michael, and his parents arrived, along with his sister, Carey, and his older brother,
Skip, who was to be best man. Red Mountford—David
Mountford's uncle—piloted his own plane in from their
central Queensland property, Sapphire Downs, bringing his wife, Emma, the two bridesmaid cousins, Leith
and Tiffany, and the madcap member of the family,
Matthew, a first-year university student on special leave.
The following day, another large Mountford contingent
flew in, picking up the three groomsmen from a domestic flight along the way. The day before the wedding, the musicians, the decorator, the floral designer,
the large consignment of flowers, the caterers and food
were scheduled to arrive midmorning by charter flight
from Sydney. Several VIPs sharing a private Learjet arrived late that afternoon.

Over the years, the homestead had extended its original ten bedrooms to sixteen to accommodate guests.
Most guests would have their own bathrooms; a few
would have to share. Temporary facilities had been set
up elsewhere in the main compound and the station staff
would stay there, vacating their dormitories and bun-
galows so they could be taken over by guests. A celebration barbecue was being held for the staff, to start
immediately after the wedding ceremony, and the sta-

tion aborigines had planned a special corroboree in honor of the bride and groom on the eve of the wedding.

Excitement was building at a tremendous rate, affecting everyone on the station. A lot of staff had been taken off their normal duties to help out where required—the homestead, the grounds, the Great Hall, which was barely recognizable draped as it was with rippling fabric.

"It's been an enormous amount of work," Sasha admitted to her stepson, "but well worth it, don't you think, darling?"

"Sure." Mountford lowered his coal black head to smile at her. "I just hope to God it all stays in place. Just how much fabric is there?"

"Enough to carpet Monaco," Vanessa joked. "Belle wants sunset, she gets it!" Sunset was Annabel's theme. It was the time of day she loved most. The vaulted ceiling of the Great Hall billowed with pleats of rose and cream interspersed with bands of gold. Ceiling-high poles, bound by more of the rose-colored fabric, had been erected around the perimeter to deepen the illusion of a great tent. It all created a very romantic roseate glow.

Even the actual ceremony in the ballroom had been timed exactly for the moment when the glory of the sky would invade the large room through its arched walls of glass. Afterward the wedding party and the guests would walk across to the Great Hall for a formal sit-down dinner. Dozens of tall glass cylinders were already in place, rising four feet above the table and capped by three-branch candelabra, which in turn held tall pink candles. The floral arrangements that were to go around the bases of the candelabra would be placed there on the morning of the wedding, along with the low display that would run the length of the great table. In keeping with Annabel's sunset theme, the four bridesmaids' beautiful shot-silk gowns were the muted colors of the sky as the scarlet blaze softened into rose pink, mellow gold, misty mauve ombréd with blue and Roishin's rich champagne, which had the faintest shimmer of green. The men's vests had been matched to the bridesmaids' gowns, as were the gold-patterned cravats. The flowers, spiked with lots of bridal white, were to continue the theme.

He would be at the official table of course. Without their father, he was to give Annabel away, so he'd be seated next to her at the reception. He would act also as master of ceremonies. The official table had been arranged at the head of the T-shaped formation, allowing their guests to see them. Sasha and the twins had completed the handwritten place cards weeks ago. They would be given to the caterers to set on the morning of the wedding. There were lots of people involved and things had to run smoothly. Even so, it was going to be a crush. But Southern Cross had hosted many a gala event—balls, New Year's parties, banquets, post-polo parties. No big wedding, though, not since his father's disastrous first marriage. His father and Sasha had been married very quietly in Sydney.

Sasha must have picked up on his thoughts. "Belle's starting to get the jitters," she said. "The big day is closing in. I was a total mess before my wedding. I knew two things. Your father, Mont, had been crazy about your mother, and I was as different from her as it was possible to be."

"You're a very sweet lady, Sasha." Mountford caught her to him and dropped a kiss on her soft springy curls. "You made Dad happy. He loved you. So do I. That's another two things."

"If only your father were here now."

"Listen, Mum, Dad will be watching," Vanessa exclaimed emotionally.

He put an arm around both of them. "He'd be very proud of his girls." His words must have held comfort because they both relaxed. "Now, if Belle's getting nervous, we have to be strong for her. Where's Roishin, by the way?" he added as though it were an afterthought.

"Now there *is* a sweet girl!" Sasha said with obvious affection. "She's been an enormous help to us. Such a pleasure to have in the house. She has the happy knack of mixing easily with everyone. Family and staff."

"Everyone except *you*, Mont!" Vanessa gave him an almost painful dig in the ribs. "Although that must have been pretty provocative stuff, the two of you taking a shower. Roishin is so alluring and you'd be a hard guy to resist."

"You think so?" he said derisively.

"Brother, I *know* so. You nearly crackle with energy and excitement."

"Dear God!" he said.

"You're not in the least vain, are you?" Sasha smiled. "You're the best son a mother could have."

A sense of anger and loss bore down on him abruptly. "So sad my mother never thought so."

"Darling, you were a perfect son to *me*. And you never did hear her side of the story."

"Actions speak louder than words, Sasha," he muttered. "So, then, where's Roishin?"

"I told her to go off and enjoy herself," Sasha said. "We've asked far too much of her, but she's so competent and willing. Last time I saw her, young Matthew was chasing after her."

"You forgot to mention he's already got a crush on her," Vanessa groaned.

"I hope he's not planning on making a nuisance of himself."

"Roishin can take care of herself," Vanessa laughed. "She's used to guys mooning after her."

"No one guy?" As soon as the words were out, he regretted the slip.

Vanessa looked at him keenly. "Why, exactly, do you want to know, big brother? You're interested in her, aren't you? Well, you two would make a terrific team, don't you think?"

"I'd think it would be a case of history repeating itself." It was a bitter remark, but he couldn't control it.

"I understand your feelings, Mont," Vanessa said simply, "but Roishin's beauty isn't just on the surface. She's a fine human being. Can't you see that? You're usually so fair-minded, too."

He put his arm around her as if in apology. "Be that as it may, Van, there's no getting away from it. Beauty exists to hurt."

HE SPENT the afternoon tracking down a notorious brumby stallion that had stolen two of the station's mares. He took Charlie, his best tracker, and two other hands. A short distance out from the Five Mile they found unmistakable signs of the mob—a waterhole with the sand all chopped up by shod and unshod hooves.

"They're here all right, Boss. Too right!" Charlie wheeled his horse around. "We oughtta make a trap."

It didn't take them all that long to assemble what was really a small holding yard with stout branches lashed together. The country around them was defined by a low semicircle of rocks strung out like giant marbles. In the afternoon light the desert landscape was glowing with the brilliance of ocher, against which the white trunks of the desert gums stood out in a curiously three-dimensional effect. As they rode on, a group of red kangaroos bolted before them before bounding back into the tangled wall of tea-tree scrub that worked effectively as an extension of the trap. Properly broken in, brumbies made good work horses, and the stallion was widely reported as a big, sleek, high-mettled beast.

Less than fifteen minutes later, they came upon the mob. The stallion led the way on what appeared to be a pleasure stroll. The mares and yearlings followed, with a few foals bunched up at the rear. About ten in all. It was time to close in on them. A stab of pity always hit Mountford at this moment. These were wild ones. They had never known bridle, saddle or hobbles. They would fight for their freedom, especially the stallion, who in no time at all seemed to sense their presence and galvanized himself for action. Mountford saw him throw his head high, snorting furiously, openly defiant of all comers and protective of his mares, two of which he'd taken from right under their noses.

Mountford and Charlie veered off to left and right, forming a rough semicircle with the other two men. He fully expected the stallion to sense the danger that lay ahead, but for once the wily animal was caught unawares. He raced straight for the entrance to the trap, mane and tail flying like pennants, his brood following him, including the foals who were running as fast as their legs could carry them. At one point the stallion broke free, and Mountford roared at Charlie to cut him off.

After that, they stayed right on the horses until the entire mob thundered into the holding yard. The mares stood shivering, giving shrill whistlelike whinnies of terror as they protected their foals.

Virtually all creatures of the wild protected their young, he thought bleakly, his mind inevitably turning to his mother's abandonment. He shrugged off the moment's introspection, and loving horses as he did, immediately began to set about calming them. After a while they seemed to listen. All but the roan stallion, who kept dashing himself against the fence.

Freedom. Precious freedom. *We all want it*, he thought.

Sometime later, he left the men to it, working his way back to the homestead. He was thinking about his mother more than he had thought about her in years. Roishin Grant had stirred it all up. She cut, yet lured him to his very heart. Women were beautiful creatures. More powerful than they knew. He wanted her to leave. Badly. Afterward, he could go back to his well-disciplined life. Or at least try to.

He reflected on Sasha's remark that he'd never allowed his mother to give *her* side of the story. He wasn't comfortable with the thought. But what could she possibly say that would exonerate her? She'd left her husband and child for another man. Not even a man she'd bothered to marry. It was only right that his father had been granted custody. His father had never failed him. Nor had he made the mistake of marrying an unsuitable woman again. Station life wasn't for everybody. Especially social butterflies.

Not that he could honestly put Roishin Grant into that category. He had watched her like a hawk, waiting for a revealing word, an action, but she appeared to be everything Vanessa said. She was charming, warm and friendly. She was efficient and methodical, with considerable organizational skills. She coped well with everyone. She was a clever independent young woman.

He was the one who felt threatened. *He* was the one who was losing his usual iron control—something to be avoided at all costs.

About a mile out from the compound, he spotted someone riding toward him on a motorbike. Probably young Matthew. He loved riding the bikes. Closer in, he saw it was one of the twins. At that distance he couldn't tell which. He started down the slope with the peculiar intuition it was some sort of alarm. Neither Annabel nor Vanessa would normally chase out here.

They met up in a red cloud of dust. He dismounted and went to help her. It was Vanessa. "What's wrong?"

She spluttered through a dry throat, "Probably nothing. But I thought I'd ride out and tell you. It'll be dark soon, and Roishin and Matthew aren't back."

"Back from where?" he exploded, feeling a pang of agitation.

"Listen, don't get angry," Vanessa appealed to him, putting a hand on his arm. "I don't *think* anything's wrong. They went for a drive, that's all. Carey was going to go with them, only Belle wanted her to do something."

"So where did they go?" he asked, his voice impatient. "Surely Matthew told someone where. He knows the rules, if Roishin doesn't."

Vanessa took off her bandanna and touched it to her perspiring face. "He told Aunt Emma the caves."

"They're pretty damned extensive." The network of caves on Southern Cross was a well-kept secret, as much to preserve them as anything else. "What time did they leave?"

Vanessa brushed a wisp of curl from her eyes. "Hours ago. They took a Jeep—"

"Damn Matt!" he interrupted roughly. "I hope to God he's not set on showing off."

"He is a bit excitable," Vanessa agreed.

"He nearly wrecked a bike the last time he was here."

"You'll locate them, Mont. Of course you will. Tell him off when you find them."

"You have my word on that. If he's managed to get them lost... This isn't a cozy little spread like Sapphire. It's vast dangerous country. Matt knows that."

"So does Roishin," Vanessa said loyally. "She's very sensible, Mont. She won't let Matt do anything stupid."

"Who was driving?" he countered, rubbing his frowning brow.

"Matt, I believe."

"Give me the bike," he said decisively. "I'll drive across country. You ride back to the homestead."

"Good idea!" Vanessa looked enormously relieved. "You'll probably see them coming in. Take it easy, Mont. You're Matt's hero. He...he probably lost track of the time."

He shrugged and walked to the motorbike. "You realize if they've got themselves lost or the Jeep's broken down, we might be stuck for the night?" He made a visible effort to curb his anger.

"You'll find them, Mont, like you find people all the time. You know every inch of Southern Cross, even in the dark. Anyway, Roishin will be fine—she's strangely at home in the wild. But Matt'll be a bundle of nerves!"

He sent the bike careering cross-country with the wind streaming alongside. No sign of them, and sunset was closing in fast. Finally he reached the hill country, riding the length of the ancient stone formations. The tracks from the Jeep's tires were easy to spot, but there was no sign of the vehicle. Where would Matt go? Never a man to panic, Mountford discovered in himself an escalating fear, a lot of it to do with Roishin's safety and frame of mind. Being lost in the never-never with its endless confusions of sand dunes and prehistoric rock formations could fill even the stoutest heart with dread. Something would have to be done about Matthew before his thirst for violent action got him into serious trouble.

At the caves an eerie howling wind was blowing through the ravines like the voices of ancient gods. Some people claimed to find it acutely disturbing, even frightening. Sasha wouldn't come near the place. The howling winds were blowing today, though there was no such wind on the open plain. Used to the phenomenon and generally unperturbed by it, he found himself taking it as some sort of omen.

Matt, outback-born, would know as well as anyone how quickly and completely night fell here—going from hot cobalt skies to inky blackness in a matter of minutes, without any comforting man-made interventions like lighting. All the bushman had to rely on was the moon and stars. The Crux, the Southern Cross after which the station had been named, Sirius, the brightest star in the heavens, Orion, the mighty hunter, Aldebaran, the follower, chasing the Pleiades across the sky. A bushman used the stars just as sea captains had used them to know their ship's position. A vast sea of stars. A vast empty earth. It could be overwhelming. Humans had a powerful atavistic fear of the dark.

Despite the thrumming heat, he broke into a cold sweat of trepidation. Where the hell were they? He raced the motorbike up dunes and down them, roared it across the plain with its good-season bounty of yellow and white bachelor's buttons. Did anyone really need this kind of scare with a wedding going on? In less than an hour, this brilliantly glowing landscape, where everything was thrown into amazingly sharp focus, would be black and desolate, infinitely vast. Matt had to be some kind of a fool to lead her into an area where, over the long years, travelers had been lost forever.

On impulse he rode toward Mountford's Pillar, an ancient butte that rose like a tombstone from the spinifex plain. At this time of day, it was glowing like a furnace, standing some hundred feet above the rippling desert floor. Matt might have continued on there. Named after the Hon. George Clifford Mountford, their ancestor, it was an important landmark on Southern Cross but too far out for a late-afternoon jaunt. He thought he would go mad if he didn't find them soon—evidence, he realized bleakly, of the depth of his emotions.

Halfway between the caves and the pillar, a call rang across the desert like a high-tempered bell.

"Coo-ee!"

Even with the wind screaming in his ears, he heard it. The sound vibrated deep inside him, filling him with tremendous relief. He knew that voice. He'd know it anywhere. It continued to call, floating across the wave-like sands with exceptional clarity and carrying power. It continued to carol for some minutes, and he headed toward it the way he would a beacon that would lead him out of the labyrinth.

"Coo-ee . . . coo-ee . . . coo-eee!" The legendary call of distress in the outback.

He thanked God she'd had the sense to use it or Matthew had told her. Why wasn't Matthew calling himself? Mountford was more than ever grateful that he knew the desert as intimately as another man might know his home city. But no city could be so fierce or so challenging. Scorching by day, the desert could be icy by night, even in summer. In the depths of winter, under certain conditions, it could kill. The same sand dunes that burned like furnaces during the day could not retain heat. They reared like frozen pyramids, pointing to a billion timeless stars.

Toward the west, deeper into the desert, he spotted four wild camels. They were probably after the fruit of the quandongs. When the bulls came into season they could be extremely dangerous. He had good reason to know. He'd been forced to shoot one a few years back. At least there was plenty of desert plant food about. Almost a bounty after the rains. He'd learned all about "bush tucker" from his early boyhood. The aborigines knew more about desert plant food than the most eminent botanist; they'd survived for sixty thousand years with bush tucker as a staple diet. It was a long education, learning to recognize which families of foods could be enjoyed and which, though apparently identical, were deadly poisonous.

Birds exploded everywhere. The ever-present flocks of budgerigar, the black cockatoos, the white sulfur-crested, the bronze-wings, the finches. A great wedge-tailed eagle was suspended over him, seemingly motionless in the infinite blue and gold air.

The calls had stopped, but now he recognized the Jeep in the distance. It appeared to be rammed against a solitary desert oak. His heart gave one tremendous painful leap. He swore violently even as he tried to formulate a prayer. Out of the corner of his eye he spotted movement, and he swung the bike toward it, skidding in a cloud of dust. There it was again. A scarred, eroded pile of rubble that had once been a hillock crouched on the stony ground like some fearsome prehistoric monster. Around its base, incongruously, was a thick ruffle of luminous green grasses.

A female figure stood up and started to race in his direction. The search was over. Matthew would never get another chance to take her on a jaunt. His anxiety for the boy contrasted sharply with his anger. He felt so exhausted, his breath coming short in gasps as he waited for her to run toward him. Seen against the savage grandeur of the landscape, she looked incredibly fragile.

Yet she could run! Like a gazelle, she was all grace and smooth coordination, her long dark hair streaming behind her.

On compulsion he left the bike and swiftly covered the ground between them, gathering her body to him.

"David!" she exclaimed. "Thank God!"

Now that he had her safe, he scarcely knew what to do. Kiss her. Question her. Berate her with harsh words. Instead, he continued to press her to his body, where she rested as though she had discovered the source of all strength.

"I knew you'd come."

"Did you? My God! From now on I won't let you out of my sight." He took her shoulders and searched her face. Every exquisite inch of it. Yet he was surprised by her toughness. She had *flown* over the stoniest ground. The Jeep had crashed into a tree, at the very least an unnerving experience, yet her eyes even as they clung to his were clear and calm.

"You're not hurt in any way?"

She shook her head vigorously. "I was lucky."

"And Matt?" His tone was both curt and concerned.

She indicated the eroded rocks. "I have him lying down in the shade. He's concussed. Not badly, I think. He hit his head on the steering wheel. He's broken his arm, as well. I've managed to get it in a splint. I've given him a couple of painkillers."

"You could suffer some delayed shock yourself. How did it happen?" He began to walk away, with Roishin half running to keep up with him.

She caught up remarkably quickly, grabbing his arm and trying to make him stop. "David, listen to me. Matt feels very bad. He was very concerned at your reaction. More so than his father's. He's overcome with guilt and shame. The fact is, we were going along quite nicely before he hit a hidden tree stump. He lost control of the wheel . . . and the rest you know."

"You mean you smashed into the only other tree in the immediate vicinity?"

She nodded wryly. "As luck would have it, yes. The radiator's been pierced. I took a look after I managed to get Matt away from the Jeep. He was pretty groggy and obviously in pain."

"It seems you're asking me to go easy on him."

She smiled and a little color came into her cheeks. "I'm confident that you will."

Matt tried to stand up as soon as he saw them, but Roishin ran to him and gently pushed him back onto the rug she'd thrown on the rough ground.

Mountford dropped to his knees, quickly making his own examination. "Hell, Matt! When are you going to learn?"

"I'm sorry, Mont. I wouldn't have had this happen for the world. I suddenly realized the time and put on a bit of speed. We hit a stump and the wheel was nearly wrenched from my hand. Roishin's been so good. I almost killed her, but she stayed as cool as a cucumber."

"Not quite!" Roishin smiled and put the back of her hand against Matthew's cheek. "I'm sure I let out a yell."

"And who could blame you?" Mountford took a closer look at a couple of tiny butterfly clips she'd used on a gash near Matthew's right temple. All station vehicles carried first-aid kits, and she'd made good use of the contents. A gauze bandage secured the neat splint she'd arranged on Matthew's left arm.

"Damn it. Damn it. Damn it!" Matt was muttering softly. "You must think I'm an awful fool, Mont."

"I guess so." But he smiled and Matthew's expression became more comfortable. "How's the pain?"

"Not so bad," Matthew said stoically. "Roishin gave me painkillers. I really think she should have something herself, even if it's only a cup of tea. It all happened so damned quickly. We'd been having a marvelous time."

"Really?" He shook his head, both relieved and exasperated. "I'm glad Vanessa thought to fill me in on your plans. I'll go take a look at the Jeep."

It was out of commission, just as Roishin had said. No rescue mission could be mounted now. What he had to do was get them to Angel Springs before the light died. They could camp there overnight. There was water, shelter, food. After the rains, Angel Springs, formed by an underflow from a major water channel, became more than a watering hole. It was an oasis with a good supply of desert fruit from the surrounding vegetation.

Everything that was useful he hunted up quickly, loading it onto the bike. He glanced at Roishin who had moved smartly to help him. "I should take Matt first, but I don't like leaving you."

She gave him a competent smile. "I'll be perfectly all right, David. Go now. I'll stay put until you return."

Matthew, when he heard, shook his head gallantly, preparing to give place to Roishin. "Women and children first, Mont."

"Listen, I'm in charge here," Mountford declared.

"Let's put that to a show of hands," Roishin said wryly.

At her surprising tongue-in-cheek remark Matthew grinned. "Mutiny, by God! You should know, Roishin, that one of Mont's most marked characteristics is having people do exactly as he says."

The two of them laughed, obviously in sympathy, and Mountford said with extreme patience, "Stop kidding around, you two. We're wasting time. There may be objections to this operation, but I don't see too many options."

"I'll be okay, Mont," Matthew assured him, pale beneath his healthy tan.

"Well, you're tough, as I've discovered." He put a hand on his cousin's shoulder. "In all probability you'll have everyone laughing about this at the wedding. Nonetheless, I'm taking you first. Roishin, if you'll get hold of that rope, we'll strap Matt to me. It'll give him extra support."

It was easier than he'd first expected. Even injured, Matt had excellent balance. They reached the oasis without incident. Secluded behind a ring of willowy acacias, spreading desert oaks and a stand of bauhinias with their radiant white butterfly flowers, the long winding pool was clear and deep, the water good to drink. He settled Matt beneath the canopy. A breeze was blowing, and it was getting much cooler now.

"No foraging for food while I'm gone, Matt. Stay put."

"Right, Mont. I'm so sorry about everything."

"Serves you right for driving so damned recklessly. And don't tell me you weren't."

"It'll never happen again, Mont."

"Well, life's all about learning," he said with a tolerance that surprised even him.

He returned to the Honda and kicked the starter pedal. The engine fired and he roared off, the snarl of the bike shaking out a great flock of little white corellas that decorated the grotesque skeleton of a ghost gum. When he reached the crash site, Roishin was still sitting there, waiting. She seemed to be contemplating the sunset, which had faded from its early bold splendor to the luminescent pastels Annabel had tried to copy for her bridesmaids' dresses.

He parked the bike and moved toward her, extraordinarily edgy, perturbed by all the things that were happening to him. He couldn't get this woman out of his mind. He longed for her, even though there was no place for her in his ordered world. Normally he kept himself on the tightest of rein, but her aura encircled him, growing stronger, more taut. Having to fight it made him moody and dangerous.

"Matthew okay?" She looked neither weary not panicked, an enchanting serenity transparent in her face.

He nodded. "You weren't nervous?"

"What's there to be nervous about? I've been admiring nature in the wild. The light out here has the most incredible crystalline quality. The colors change dramatically all through the day." She took the hand he extended, rising gracefully to her feet.

He wanted to pull her close. He wanted to bend his head and kiss her mouth. Instead, he released her abruptly, stepping back. "So you'd be happy to stay in the wilderness?"

She laughed and brushed off her hands. "I don't think you'd catch me doing that. Not alone. Not yet. But I have a...a *feeling* of belonging." She hesitated, as though reluctant for a moment to put it into words. "It's like hearing music so beautiful it reduces me to tears."

He looked back toward her face, then off to the middle distance. If it was true for her, it was true for him. He felt, however briefly, a sense of absolute communication, one that he was unable—or unwilling—to acknowledge. "Well, your musicality is apparent," he said in a near-dismissive tone. "Who told you to start up the *coo-ees?* Matt, I suppose?"

"No." She seemed surprised. "Matt needed a little time to come around. He took the brunt of the impact. You forget I've spent time on Southern Cross. I know the traditional bushman's call."

He was determined to resist her pull. "Good for you," he said crisply. "They led me to you. I could have wasted another half hour trying to track you down. You've got the best damned *coo-ee* I've ever heard."

"Can I quote you on that?" There was a dancing light of mischief in her eyes.

"Of course." Despite himself he smiled.

"Well, thank you, David. So I'm not hopelessly un-suited to your domain, after all?"

A few taut seconds ticked by as they stared at one an-other. Did she know his abrasiveness was merely a dis-guise for the way he was feeling? He frowned and turned away. "Not after today." He glanced up at the sky, which had faded to an incandescent blue shot through with burnt orange. "Ever been on a motorbike be-fore?" He began to move swiftly toward it.

"Have I ever!" She almost had to run, but she man-aged to keep pace with him. "I have a friend with a Harley-Davidson. It's his prized possession."

"Okay, so you know what to do."

"May I put my arms around you?" she teased.

He looked down on her alluring face. "Stop trying to provoke me, Roishin."

"What an exciting thought! Do you mind if I borrow your bandanna?"

"Not at all." He untied the red scarf around his neck and passed it to her, watching while she tied back her swirling hair.

Like their morning gallop, the ride to the camp brought them exhilaratingly close. When they dis-mounted, it took an actual force of will for him not to encircle her narrow waist and swing her off her feet. While he scouted up food, Roishin built a fire. By the time he got back, the billy was boiling and Matthew was busy scoffing down shortbread biscuits with some well-sugared tea. It took an enormous weight off Mountford to know that they were coping well. He walked toward the golden circle of light, pouring his haul onto the rug.

"You've found all this?" Roishin asked incredulously.

He went down on his haunches. "Contrary to what most people believe, the desert is teeming with bush tucker. How do you think the aborigines survived? You'll find these red berries delicious. They're full of vitamin C. More so, in fact, than an orange. The mulga apples are quite pleasant, as well."

"Mont's an authority on all this stuff," Matt said, beginning to munch on a desert apple. "A few years back he rescued a couple of English tourists who ran out of water only a few miles from the station's northwestern border. Kept 'em alive on bush tucker. They thought he was sent by God."

"And why not?" Roishin said simply, popping a few berries into her mouth. "You're right! These are lovely—sweet, with a little tang."

"You'll make a real bushie out of her yet, Mont," Matthew grinned. "A lot of people don't take to the wilderness like you have, Roishin. Some go into a real panic. They're frightened of snakes, lizards, those huge goannas, scorpions, feral boars, wild camels. You name it. Mostly they're frightened of the *spirit* of the place. The vastness and the silence. They find it too threatening. And, in a way, *this* place is the scariest of all—and the most beautiful. The Mountfords have stations all over, as you know, but there's nowhere like Southern Cross. This is what Mont calls the beating heart. Our ancestral home."

"I understand why you love it," Roishin said. "Its sheer size, its grandeur. It's not like anywhere else." She gave a sigh of contentment and tilted back her head.

"The stars are coming out. Aren't they marvelous? Nothing between us and them."

"There'll be no moon tonight," Mountford warned her. "Just the light from the camp fire."

"Shall I scream, David?" she asked airily. "Just so I won't disappoint you?"

"You won't throw Mountford off balance," Matt said with a roguish grin. "Women never do."

"Is he hostile toward women?"

"I've never noticed it," Matt laughed dryly. "Mont's been voted one of the sexiest men in the country, haven't you heard?"

"Shut up, Matt," Mountford said quietly.

"I did see the magazine." Roishin gave Mountford a charming smile. "Let me get you some tea, David. There should even be a shortbread biscuit if Matt hasn't wolfed the lot."

"Not me, sweetheart." Matt did his best Bogart voice and pushed what was left of the packet of biscuits onto the rug. "There's a slab of chocolate, as well, Mont."

"How's the pain?" Mountford asked, accepting a steaming mug of billy tea from Roishin.

"Hurts like hell, but I'll survive."

"That's the right attitude, Matt. Never give in. Maybe before you turn in for the night, we'll try you with a weak brandy to help you sleep. I'll be off at first light. It'll mean leaving you on your own for a few hours, but I should meet up with the rescue party about halfway."

Nothing, he observed, seemed to disconcert Roishin or shake her calm. Even when the lonely howls of the dingoes broke the silence, she seemed to find the sound just another facet of the desert environment. In the pleasant warming glow from the fire it was easy to tell stories about Southern Cross, stories of station life—the funny, the interesting, the tragic. It was a surprisingly companionable time and the hours slipped by.

Eventually he got Matt more painkillers and sometime later mixed him a weak brandy from the Jeep's flask. He had brought the Jeep's swag and a rug, and Roishin made Matt comfortable, her manner competent and comforting. Like an older sister. She settled him in his makeshift bed on the silvery white sand. It was thick and springy, not packed hard like the red sand around the claypans.

Mountford built up the fire for warmth, and it wasn't long before Matt drifted off.

Roishin checked on him and caught Mountford's eye. "Let's hope he sleeps. He must be in quite a bit of pain."

He nodded his agreement. "Matt's tough. But he has to stop taking risks. I'll bet he took you bouncing across the scrub. It simplifies matters if you try to keep to the recognized tracks. The spinifex clumps are massive after the rains, and you might expect the occasional hidden stump. The particular area where you were driving is full of hazards. You were lucky."

"Yes, I know. We both had some frightening moments when Matt lost control of the wheel. He didn't panic, though. He kept his head."

"As did you. You've behaved very coolly."

"Women *are* capable, David." She lay back on the rug, looking up at the brilliantly blossoming stars. "The night sky out here is enthralling. It must be the pure air. I've never seen so many stars. Billions of them! They're so big and bright..." She gestured toward the sky. "Tell me about them, David."

Suddenly he felt utterly relaxed. He eased his tall frame back. "The night sky is the subject for innumerable aboriginal myths and legends. There are thousands of them associated with the moon and stars. Strangely enough, the moon is the man and the sun is the woman. Birth and death are always associated with Meenka, the moon man. If a woman wishes to become pregnant, she stares up at the moon. If she doesn't want a child, she's careful not to do any moon-gazing. Aboriginal children are taught that the moon is dangerous. It doesn't like to be stared at."

"I hope the stars don't feel the same way. The Southern Cross is outstanding tonight."

He nodded and put his hands behind his head. "It always is over the station. The desert nomads believe the constellation is the footprint of the great wedge-tailed eagle. The stars of the cross, Alpha and Beta Centauri, are great ancestor figures. The Scorpio constellation originated as two lovers who broke tribal law. Orion spends most of his time making illicit advances to the Seven Sisters, the Pleiades. The Milky Way is the sea of light every spirit must travel to find its way home."

"I'd like to be married under the desert stars," she said.

"Then you'd better marry me."

"Is that a proposal, David?"

"Not to be taken seriously. For both our sakes."

"Why do you say that?" She moved when he hadn't expected her to, propping herself on one elbow and staring down at him.

"You're an exceedingly dangerous woman."

"You *want* to believe that," she accused him.

"I do."

"Can't you tell me why?"

He reached up to release his bandanna from her long hair. It fanned out immediately, spilling around her face and shoulders.

"Women like you know how to make a man suffer." His voice had dropped to a soft growl, and his fingers of their own accord encircled her slender neck.

"What are you trying to do to me, David?" she asked simply. She seemed so very direct and honest. "Are you trying to strangle me with my own hair?"

He tugged on a thick strand until her face was poised directly above his. "You have the most beautiful mouth."

She stared back at him with intensity. "There's such a contrast between what you *say* and what you *do!* It's very, very odd."

He laughed gently. "I'll tell you something odder. I want to make love to you. It's a good thing Matt's on the other side of the fire."

"You're taking it for granted I'd let you?" she challenged.

"You wouldn't?"

"You're very sure of yourself, aren't you, David Mountford?"

"This is something I can't help."

The firelight flickered on her lovely face, revealing a certain inner turmoil. "And you're finding it intolerable? This . . . attraction you feel?"

The tips of his fingers traced her jawline. "No woman is going to rule my life. I like to be in control." Easy enough to say even though his desire for her was a furious white flame. Some of it must have shown in his eyes, because she trembled visibly. "Come down here, Roishin, and relax. I'm not going to touch you."

"I think you'd do anything when the mood's on you."

"Never by force."

"Why would you need it?" she asked almost bleakly. "After all, you can have any woman you want."

"I want *you*," he said wryly. "And it's making my life hell."

His words seemed to hurt her, shot through as they were with self-derision and hostility.

"David, what you're saying doesn't make sense . . ." Her voice trailed off helplessly.

"As a matter of fact, it does. To me."

"Has it got something to do with your background? Your past?"

"Let's look at the stars, Roishin. I'm not going to lie here being psychoanalyzed." With a single movement he had her down beside him. A mistake. A flood of electricity flowed from her slender body to his. It was anguish. It was unbearable. It was madness and he didn't give a damn. "Stay here with me. It's warmer."

"My God, David!"

He moved his head so his mouth could graze her cheek. "I want to hold you in my arms." He sighed heavily. "I must be falling to pieces."

"There's a chink in your armor."

"A lot of good it'll do you, Roishin." He spoke sarcastically, but the blood was surging in his veins. "Have you ever cheated on a man?"

"I've never lived with one or told one I loved him, so the answer's no. But you, on the other hand—I've been told you've never been short of girlfriends. You must have broken quite a few hearts."

"If I have, it doesn't make me feel good. But what's to be done, Roishin? I'm a man like any other. I enjoy women. Their strength and their wisdom. I like to talk to them. I don't think I've deliberately hurt anyone. What more could you want?"

"Are you telling me you've never been in love?"

"You've just figured it out?" he asked acidly.

"You must have been a tragic child."

"How touching of you to think so."

"My mother is a divorce lawyer. Did you know that?"

"I've heard it mentioned," he said dryly, turning his head so he could gaze at her profile.

"She encounters a lot of grief in the family courts. Human beings are capable of doing tremendous damage to one another. Love turns to hate, or love and hate coexist. The most damage is done to the children. They suffer dreadfully from marriage breakups. Mostly the pain stays with them all their lives. As for the parents, there can be degrees of guilt on both sides. My mother has been discussing her cases with me for years now. Not the worst ones, the truly ugly ones, when I was younger, but I know a good deal about the subject. My own area is litigation, as you know. That can be fairly distressing at times, but nothing touches the family courts for trauma."

"Roishin, you're not telling me anything I don't know." He spoke with cool precision.

"Of course not. You've experienced it all firsthand."

He felt like a tinderbox about to explode, but he kept his tone cold. "I told you I've put the past behind me."

"I don't think that's true, David. A famous writer once said something like, 'The past isn't dead; it isn't even past.'"

"Brilliant!"

"Don't be angry." She gave him a gentle pleading look.

"That's a tall order, Roishin. I'm not about to bare my soul or disclose any long-buried secrets, if that's what you're after."

"Actually I was thinking more of myself," she said mildly. "You don't deny a certain attraction, yet you're battling an aversion to my physical type."

"You could be right." He answered with extreme irony.

"The other thing is, I've met your mother."

"*What?*" The word shot out with such a hard ring he turned his head to check that he hadn't disturbed Matt. He hadn't.

"It's a small world," Roishin was saying quietly. "Lady Vandenberg, as well as being the wife of an important man, is an important person in her own right. She's served with my mother on several committees. In fact, they've become quite friendly. I've met Lady Vandenberg many times."

"How very interesting," he drawled, aware that his expression was cold and tight. "How come Annabel or Van have never told me?"

"They know your views on the subject. I understand your mother's name is never mentioned."

"And you find that shocking?" he asked in an attacking voice. "Are you quite sure you understand what happened, counselor, or are you putting *me* on trial? My mother left Southern Cross twenty-four years ago of her own free will. There was a huge scandal that devastated my father and upset the whole Mountford clan. My mother's conduct was shameful, impossible to condone. She broke her marriage vows and she abandoned her only child. That's *my* finding. If she finally found happiness with Eric Vandenberg, well and good. I want no part of her, and I especially don't want to hear what a wonderful person she is now. So far as I'm concerned, charity begins at home."

She studied the stars in silence, then she said, "You're very bitter, David."

"So I am." He answered more mildly. "Aren't the facts good enough, lady lawyer?"

Her iridescent eyes turned toward him. "I sympathize, David. Didn't I convey that?"

"Then who are you acting for?"

"You," she breathed. "Bitterness doesn't heal wounds, David. It leaves them open and festering."

It was a 'judgment' he'd made himself, even as his emotions held sway. "So what are you saying I should do?" he asked harshly.

"End the torment. Your mother speaks of you all the time, David. To this day she agonizes about you."

"Roishin, you're breaking my heart."

She propped herself up again, looking as though she wanted to reach out for him but didn't dare. "Couldn't you meet with her?"

"No," he said in a hard emphatic voice.

"As an adult you've never heard her side of the story."

"I heard it all from my father. I had absolute trust in him."

"He was unhappy and hurting, David. He was a man of considerable power and influence, and your mother damaged his pride. Doesn't it bother you that she may have a different story to tell? She tried very hard to contact you after your father died."

The tension that had gathered in his body found expression in his voice. It sounded daunting even to his own ears. "It seems to me, Roishin, that you've decided to act on my mother's behalf."

"No, David," she protested, the movement of her head making her hair swirl around her shoulders. "It's your antagonism to *me* that's caused me to speak. I felt it rush for me the moment you laid eyes on me that first day—when I was coming down the stairs. It shocked me so much it nearly stopped my heart. It was all there in your eyes. They're wonderful eyes, David, but their expression more often than not *threatens* me."

"Stop this, Roishin. Right now."

She shook her head. "Please hear me out. I know you'd never hurt me. You're a civilized man. The women in your family adore you. What I'm talking about is more an assault on my psyche."

"Dear me!" There was a wealth of mockery in his tone.

"I don't want you to hate me, David. I don't want that at all. And I refuse to be a victim. Your victim."

"Shut up, Roishin," he said very coolly.

"And if I refuse?" She kept her voice steady, but there was a throb of emotion in her eyes.

"Look, you can argue in a thousand different ways. I'm sure you're very good, but the fact remains. I have no mother. I haven't had one for the past twenty years and more. I have a stepmother of whom I'm very fond. I have twin sisters I love. None is the sort of woman who hurts people. Annabel is getting married in a couple of days. She'll be a great wife and mother, a man's best companion. So will Van when her turn comes. As for you, I'm sure you'll make a brilliant marriage. You have everything going for you. You're beautiful, clever, you have the right connections. You're everything a man could want. Every man but me. So much for our wedding beneath the eternal desert stars!"

"I'm not sorry I spoke."

Was there the glimmer of tears in her beautiful eyes? It affected him powerfully. "And I'm not sorry for *this*, either!"

He caught her face between his strong fingers, bearing her down to him, turning her on her back. He caught her mouth beneath his own, burning with a furious frightening passion. Her mouth still bore the taste and scent of wild berries, and he explored it hungrily, mercilessly, the way a bee devours nectar. He could feel her slender body trembling as it had on their other brief encounter. He wanted her. Completely. He wanted everything she was.

It was a love that could destroy him.

Love!

It was over almost as swiftly as it had begun. He sprang to his feet while she lay back. She didn't speak. While he loomed over her, she closed her eyes.

What am I doing? he thought. *I'm punishing her because she's brought me face-to-face with myself. I've searched for her all my life and now I've found her, I treat her abominably.*

What the hell's the matter with me?

God, wasn't it clear enough?

He loved her. He had loved her at first sight.

Another Mountford tragedy to play out?

Chapter Four

HE CAME INSTANTLY AWAKE as the first lambent blue light stole through the desert oaks and moved over the still water hole in long silver wisps. He felt no hint of tiredness, though he had barely closed his eyes. He made a quick inspection of the campsite, his gaze lingering on Roishin's sleeping form. He stretched his limbs briefly, then rose to check on Matt. Matt's face bore a faint grimace as though pain was seeping into his subconscious. The sooner he got his young cousin back to the homestead, the better. Matt's condition meant a quick trip to Derby Base Hospital.

He moved back toward Roishin. Through his fragmented dreams, his mind had been full of her. She had entered his bloodstream and he didn't know what to do about it. He approached her very quietly, going down on his knees.

She was lying on her back, one arm upstretched, the other at her side. Her thick gleaming hair made a dark halo around her face. His eyes fell to her breasts. They rose and fell gently with every quiet breath. Seen asleep, her beauty had an innocence and purity that struck at his heart. It touched him with reverence, longing and—inevitably—passion. His hard body began to stir. Wanting her was coming close to physical torture. He saw that as his punishment. He continued to stare at her, fascinated. His hand moved involuntarily, touched her cheek. Her skin was like satin, lustrous, smooth, warm to the touch. Very gently, he said her name; despite himself, he touched a palm to the curve of her breast.

Immediately she opened her eyes. Her lips moved; her breath fluttered. She arched her back, then sat up with swift sinuous grace, moving almost into his arms.

"It's all right, David. I'm awake." She said it sweetly, as though ready and anxious to help and sustain him.

They were so very close he could see a pulse begin to beat at the base of her throat. He touched a finger to it, let it linger there and felt her heartbeat. His hands began to shape her delicate shoulders, then he pulled her into him, profoundly aroused.

"I don't have the strength to resist you," he muttered.

With one arm, he encircled her, bringing her even closer to him. Her mouth opened under his, her full lips so tender, so soft, surrendering to his mouth's hard pressure with startling sweetness and ardor. The moment would live in his memory, no matter what happened. She had spoken about wounds. She was healing his one by one. It was part of her power. All at once he felt it was time to be brutally honest with himself. Could he trust her? *Could* he trust her? He knew that if he let her go, he would miss her all the rest of his life.

His breathing harsh, he released her. She, too, was quiet, as though she found it difficult to speak. "What is it you want from me, David?" she whispered finally, looking up at his dark head bowed over hers.

It was obvious that she had no certainty in her heart. Why would she? He had shown her a bewildering range of emotions, from outright hostility to blind passion.

"Nothing. Everything," he answered, as if such a contradiction was perfectly normal.

"Oh, David!" Her blue-green eyes turned liquid, sparkled like jewels.

"I think we'd better stand up." He brought them to their feet, keeping an arm around her—it was so damned difficult to let her go. "Come on. Let's walk to the bike. It'll be light soon. The bike will wake Matt if the birds don't. They're starting to call."

"You do expect a search party to be out?"

"You can count on it," he reassured her. "I should meet them halfway. Matt will need more painkillers when he gets up. Make him a cup of tea."

"I'll do that," she said quietly.

"You've done very well."

"I sense that you're still waiting for me to stumble."

"That's the dilemma, Roishin." His dilemma. The contradictions of his heart.

THE HOUSEHOLD didn't settle down again until Rex Mountford flew back into Southern Cross, a chastened Matthew in tow. He'd flown his son to Derby Base Hospital, and now Matt's left arm was in plaster and a stitch had been inserted in the gash over his left eye. It had been a long worrying night for everyone. As Mountford had predicted, the search party left the main compound in the predawn, meeting up with him several miles from the caves. No one was the least surprised that Mountford had found them, but anxiety had mounted when it became apparent he hadn't been able to make the return journey by Jeep.

An unexpected fallout of the misadventure was that Annabel had had a tiff with Michael. For several hours the wedding appeared to be in jeopardy.

"What started it, for God's sake?" Mountford asked Sasha with some irritation.

"It's not serious, Mont. Really." Sasha gave a feeble laugh. "Michael wanted to go out after you, and Annabel told him not to be a fool. Ordinarily she wouldn't have said such a thing, but she was so worried that Matt might have done something foolish and she'd let Roishin go with him. Poor old Michael was mortified, so it sort of went on from there. Poor boy—he meant well, but he doesn't know the bush at all. He'd only have lost himself."

"You can say that again!" Mountford agreed. "But it's unlike Belle to be so volatile."

"It's a big thing, getting married, Mont," Sasha said, obviously thinking of her own wedding day. "A big commitment. Putting one's life and happiness into another person's hands is pretty scary. Lots of brides *and* grooms get cold feet. It's only a passing thing with Belle."

"That's good to know," he said dryly.

"You know what I mean, darling. Belle loves her Michael. He's a fine young man with a future. He wants to go into politics, I believe."

"I guess someone's got to do it."

"Don't tease, darling. And don't worry about Belle. Anxiety put her under undue pressure. She's extremely fond of Roishin. She and Van were blaming themselves dreadfully."

"I can understand that," he answered crisply. "Well, I hope the lovebirds make it up very soon. We'll have three hundred guests on Southern Cross in another forty-eight hours, all of them expecting to enjoy a wedding."

"And they will, Mont." Sasha looked up at him with myopic intensity. "This will all blow over, you'll see. Why, Roishin's having a good long talk with Belle right now. She's marvelous at calming people down. I suppose it's her legal training. I'm such a ditherer. Roishin will make some lucky man a wonderful wife."

Roishin some lucky man's *wife!* The thought appalled him. For the first time in his life he felt a great wave of sexual jealousy. He didn't take kindly to the idea of Roishin in any other man's arms, much less married to him.

"Is everything okay, Mont?" Sasha was asking in a worried voice.

"Sure." He smiled at her.

"You do look so . . . formidable at times."

"I'll try to smile more often."

"You should, darling. You have a devastating smile. The sort that makes women go weak in the knees."

He groaned and heaved himself to his feet. "Sasha, I have to be going."

"Your turn will come, darling," she taunted him smilingly. "A man like you only falls once. *Very hard!*"

He didn't answer, but threw her a quick mocking smile.

THE DAY BEFORE the wedding was sheer pandemonium. The airstrip might have been a domestic terminal with all the comings and goings. All the station Jeeps were in use, ferrying people up to the house; even the station helicopter was put into commission, landing quantities of food and the huge consignment of flowers on the rear lawn close to the kitchens and the refrigerated room that would serve as storage. Annabel and Michael were mercifully back on the best of terms, but Vanessa was more upset than she was letting on. She was going to miss her twin, Mountford thought with sympathy. They'd been inseparable from birth.

In the ballroom, where everything was in place save for the flowers, which would be arranged the following morning, the decorator and the floral designer had a serious falling out. The decorator, in particular, was flouncing around like an actor, and Mountford stood in the doorway, for once at a loss. The floral designer, a slim dapper man in informal but expensive gear, suddenly burst into tears. Mountford looked on in horror. Where were the women? He didn't want to get involved in this.

Like a miracle, Roishin and Vanessa appeared in the hallway, talking earnestly, and he put up a hand to alert them. Both young women jumped to attention.

"What is it, Mont?"

"Listen—a crisis."

"You go, Roishin," Vanessa begged as they took in the situation. "I have complete confidence in your ability to avert a war."

Even Roishin looked a little wary, but she headed for the ballroom.

"There must be some way we can thank Roishin," Vanessa said. "She's been a tower of strength."

"I'll think of something," Mountford promised, grateful himself for Roishin's communication skills. "Personally I'd like to knock those two fellows' heads together. I'm paying them a fortune. They're supposed to be top people, and I expect professionalism. Which includes good sense and good humor."

"They're nervous like the rest of us, Mont. They take their jobs very seriously and they don't like their territory invaded. You have to admit the room looks magnificent!"

"It does." His gaze swept the double-height ballroom with its balustraded gallery—projecting balconies that encircled the ballroom. The musicians would take up their positions there. He could see the gleaming ebony lid of the Steinway already up. Guests would be accommodated along the minstrel gallery, as well as on the terrazzo floor. His eyes returned to Roishin, who was chatting to the two temperamental decorators. "Good grief, will you look at that!" he said softly. "She's got them laughing."

"She really knows how to put on the charm," Vanessa smiled. "I'm glad you recognize she's a very dear and valued friend of this family."

"Whatever you say, Van."

"She's waited a long time to meet you."

"So?"

"So... I figure she's a great success."

"Okay, Van," he said equably, "you want me to say I'm madly in love with her?"

"If ever a man's capable of being madly in love, *you* are."

"What the hell does that mean?"

Vanessa didn't smile. She looked at him very seriously. "You're that rare thing, Mont. You're a man of action *and* imagination. You're strong—like tempered steel—and you're sensitive. You're tough and you're romantic. The right woman could really get to you."

"I haven't cracked yet, Van."

"You will."

They both watched as Roishin made her way back to them. She was wearing burgundy-colored slacks with a matching silk singlet that left her arms and neck bare. A bright turquoise belt was around her narrow waist; there were gold earrings on her ears, gold bangles at her wrist. A casual enough outfit, yet she made it look haute couture.

She moved beautifully, he thought—sliding her legs from the thigh like a racehorse. The muscles of his stomach tightened into a hard knot. The great Irish chandeliers, four in all, had been turned on with brilliant effect, and for a split second, as Roishin stepped under the last one, she was all glittering animation. Her long hair gleamed like some dark exotic wood, her magnolia skin glowed, her eyes with their alluring slant were dense with color, more blue than green.

She looked wonderful.

"A penny for your thoughts, Mont," Vanessa whispered.

"I was just wondering how Roishin solved the problem so quickly."

"Incredible!" she crowed. "David Mountford telling fibs!"

The second Roishin rejoined them, Vanessa asked, "So what was wrong?"

"Neither of them was prepared to give an inch to the other. I suggested a soothing cup of tea, which I'll go and organize. Colin wanted the urns filled with orchids. Darren wanted them filled with the wonderful ferns he'd flown in. I suggested the urns on stands be filled with orchids, the ones on the floor with ferns. A simple compromise."

"You mean *that's* what they were arguing about?" Mountford asked in a disbelieving tone.

Roishin nodded mildly. "A legitimate concern. Darren doesn't like the way Colin's tied the bows on the chairs, either. Actually, I think Darren might make them even more attractive. I suggested he have a go, and Annabel will make the final decision."

"So they've had a tough day?"

Roishin laughed. "It's their job, David. They're both creative people. The wedding is a big showcase for their talents."

"Another falling-out like that and the deal's off," Mountford warned.

"Rehearsal at six, Mont," Vanessa called after him. "It won't take long. The corroboree starts at nine. Roishin's never seen one, you know. It should be exciting."

THE REHEARSAL went off smoothly, and afterward a buffet dinner was served in the formal dining room. The house was humming with music and laughter, the conversation ranging over dozens of topics, all pleasant because of the occasion. The women wore pretty dresses; the men wore jackets and ties.

Looking around with satisfaction, Mountford saw the bridesmaids had paired off with their respective partners for the ceremony. It had even been suggested to him very quietly by Sasha that Vanessa had taken a shine to Skip Courtney, Michael's brother and the best man. The family resemblance was very strong. Both young men were fair, blue-eyed, medium tall, with open engaging faces. Both had ready smiles. It would be surprising if Vanessa *didn't* find Skip attractive, Mountford thought. The twins had the same taste in everything from food to men. And Skip appeared to be pulling out all the stops to entertain Vanessa.

Mountford's eyes moved past them to Annabel, in a very pretty dress the color of sunflowers. Her whole aura seemed overlaid with gold. She and Michael were standing arm in arm in conversation with their uncle, Drew Mountford, a federal senator, and Bishop Morcombe, who was to perform the ceremony. Michael must have finished some amusing story that made the others laugh, for Annabel raised her smiling face to him, her whole heart in her eyes.

Let them be happy, he thought. *God grant her a good life.* They were going to miss Annabel's sunny presence in the house.

As for Roishin, it was taking all his effort not to go and seize her up, take her away from the circle of admiring males, including Matt, who was deeper in the throes of his devastating crush. When it was time to move off to the ceremonial grounds, he made his move, his voice clipped and very decisive. "Roishin's with me."

"Who'd want to cross you, Mont?" Matt said with a grin.

"You can lighten your grip now, David," Roishin told him sweetly as they moved out onto the veranda.

He looked down at her, some expression in his eyes causing her skin to flush. "Just so you know I'm not a man to ignore."

"That, David, is a positive understatement," she answered.

Tonight on Annabel's wedding eve, Meenka the moon man held sway in the sky. He lit up the desert, drawing out all the fiery sun-baked ochers from the ancient landscape, washing it with radiant white light. Around him to the horizon glittered the attendant stars. They blossomed like water lilies, their aboriginal symbol. According to myth, when the moon man had been on earth, he'd been a great lover of women. Meenka had always featured largely in the cycle of life, the affairs of men and women. He would feature in tonight's corroboree.

Only the wedding party and a sprinkling of family had been invited to the ceremony. When they reached the dancing grounds, the didgeridoo boomed out a deep pulsing welcome. Mountford was greeted formally by Charlie Eaglehawk. Mountford, in turn, brought forward the promised bride and groom, who were presented with a splendid bark painting by the tribe's finest artist.

Greetings exchanged, Mountford and the promised couple moved back behind the wide circle of sacred fires, their smoke scented with special timbers. A big circle had been cleared in the sand, then smoothed over. The circle was defined by a ring of glittering gibbers that gave off a strange glowing light as if they were phosphorescent.

Only men took part in the dancing. Women, the musicians, sat in the shadows with their tap sticks and possum-skin drums, and the bound rolls of tree bark they used to rhythmically pound the ground. The dancers had oiled and painted themselves; they wore elaborate headdresses of white cockatoo feathers, and their wrists and ankles were wrapped with the spent feathers of smaller birds.

Mountford looked swiftly around, checking on his party. They were all seated on the rugs they'd brought with them for the occasion. Only Roishin remained standing beside him. Her face looked dazzled. When he touched her shoulder, he felt the shivers of fascination that ran through her body. The scene was riveting, powerful and primeval. It belonged perfectly to the wild desert heart.

For almost an hour, they were part of a ritual as old as time. The quality of the dancing and the mime was extraordinary. The undulating chanting of the women had scarcely less impact. All through the ceremony the women continued to beat the drums with their thin long-fingered hands until, together with the rhythmic tapping of the clap sticks, the sound became hypnotic and curiously stirring. The performance was tender and triumphant in turn, passionate to the point of erotic, in keeping with the strong love magic and the intimacy of the subject. Marriage.

Once when Roishin gave a soft involuntary shudder, he took off his jacket and slipped it around her shoulders, his hand brushing against her beautiful breasts. He wanted to cup them, take their tender weight. His thumbs ached to excite the sensitive nipples.

God help him if the dance didn't stop!

She touched his arm. He found himself linking her slender fingers with his, holding her hand tightly. It was an admission. He knew that. In such a short time she had transformed his whole world.

Yet hadn't his father felt overwhelming desire for his beautiful Charlotte? Passion of this order could be the beginning of great pain. His very soul cried out for her, but why should the depth of his feeling be reciprocated? Why would she, such a beautiful and gifted young woman, be any more suited to the loneliness and isolation of station life than his own mother? Boredom had driven his mother into a disastrous love affair that had wrecked their lives.

History could not be allowed to repeat itself. Unlike his father, he lacked the capacity to turn the other cheek. He wouldn't sit idly by if his wife spurned him. He knew he had within himself the potential for ruthless action. For vengeance.

Chapter Five

SOME THIRTY MINUTES before the ceremony was to begin, Mountford presented himself outside the bridesmaids' dressing room.

At his knock, his cousin Tiffany, a dark honey blonde, came to the door looking resplendent in her gown of mauve shot with blue. A matching coronet, embroidered, beaded and beribboned with a medieval look about it, completed the outfit. He looked briefly over her shoulder, saw the other bridesmaids scattered around like so many roses in full bloom. The light gleamed on their magical dresses. The whole atmosphere of the room was redolent of perfume, romance and excitement.

"Talk about knock-'em-dead handsome!" Tiffany went up on her toes to kiss him full on the mouth, something she'd been doing since she'd turned sixteen. "If ever a guy can wear formal gear, it's you, Mont. Boutonniere and all!"

"Thanks, Tiffany," he said wryly. "You haven't left lipstick all over me, I hope?"

"Only the normal amount." She grinned. "Just kidding, Mont."

"You look ravishing!"

She closed her eyes. "Oh, God, Mont, do you *mean* that?"

"I certainly do."

Vanessa, a vision of soft beauty in her rose pink gown, hurried over. "I love that silver gray vest and cravat."

"Whatever you do, don't tell me it matches my eyes." That had been Sasha's first comment.

"I'll only think it." She smiled.

"May I come in for a moment, Van? I have a little memento for all the bridesmaids."

"Why do you have to be my *cousin?*" Tiffany moaned.

"You've done so much already, Mont!" Vanessa, used to Tiffany's antics, ignored her.

"It's only a commemorative thing, Van, and it will give me great pleasure."

"Girls," Tiffany called over her shoulder, "gather round."

He set the box he was carrying on a table. Four smaller boxes were inside, all bearing a well-known jeweler's crest. He had commissioned these items many months ago and was pleased with the results.

He presented a box to each of the four smiling women. Three blondes and one with gleaming dark hair sliding down her back. With the small presents went a kiss on the cheek, which the irrepressible Tiffany professed to enjoy immensely.

"Mont, how beautiful!" Vanessa said with a delighted cry that was taken up by the other bridesmaids. She held a commemorative pin of the Southern Cross constellation to the light. Fashioned in eighteen-carat gold, the points of the constellation were represented by precious stones. Diamonds formed the upright of the cross, a ruby to the east, an emerald to the west, a sapphire for the smaller star tucked in under the cross beam.

"I hope you can find someplace to pin them. Annabel's gifts are exquisite." They were already around the bridesmaids' necks—circlets of fine-quality pearls with the clasps sitting perfectly in the hollow of their throats. Each clasp was a large semiprecious stone chosen to enhance their dresses. A garnet for Vanessa, a topaz for Roishin, a tourmaline for Leith and an amethyst for Tiffany.

Now, pins in hand, the four made a rush for the full-length mirrors that had been set around the room.

Mountford made a move toward Roishin, acting on the strongest compulsion. She looked up at him with stars in her eyes. "This is lovely, David. I'll treasure it all my life."

As I'll treasure the sight of you. Her beauty dazzled him like a shaft of sunlight. Where was all his precious hard-won detachment? He felt like a stranger to himself.

"Pin it on for me," she invited, and passed the small adornment to him.

He noticed Vanessa pinning hers to her headdress, but he caught the band of Roishin's low curving neckline midway between her shoulder and the cleft between her breasts.

"I think here." His fingers touched her warm skin. Desire came rushing at him like a great wave. An exquisite scent, half floral perfume, half her own essence, tantalized his nostrils. "You should be painted in that dress." He turned her so she was facing the mirror, his own tall frame reflected behind her.

"'Shall I compare thee to a summer's day,'" he recited, holding his voice to a light sardonic tone. Unaccountably he saw attached to her gleaming coronet a *veil*.

A traditional bridal veil. It fell to the floor and stood out around her in a cloud of finest tulle. An illusion, of course, created by his imagination and the quality of the light.

"David, what is it?" she asked hesitantly.

"Nothing," he said dismissively. His vision had overwhelmed him, but he knew better than to tell her what he'd seen, what he felt. The French had a term for it, as they had a term for everything. *Coup de foudre*. A lightning bolt. It had struck him with relentless force.

When he turned around, Sasha was in the room for her final inspection of the bridesmaids. She murmured aloud with pleasure, announcing that they looked as if they'd stepped from a medieval garden. Vanessa pointed to the jeweled pin in her coronet.

"I know, darling. Aren't they lovely? Mont is so thoughtful." Sasha was looking exceptionally chic herself in a stunning two-piece suit with a fitted jacket and a long straight skirt. The color was her favorite powder blue, and she was wearing a magnificent diamond-and-sapphire brooch with matching earrings, very valuable family jewelry Mountford had seen only rarely.

Sasha's small fingers fluttered. She made minute adjustments, primping a billowing sleeve here, twitching the opulent folds of a skirt there.

"We'll have to scoot back to Belle, Mum," Vanessa reminded her.

"Bye, bye, my angels!" Sasha called. "This is one of the happiest days of my life." She blinked back tears. "A little bit sad, too."

LATE AFTERNOON saw them all gathered in the ballroom, which had drawn gasps of pleasure and admiration from family and guests. Sasha had taken her place. Bishop Morcombe, Michael and his attendants were in position.

Mountford looked down at his stepsister's small beloved face. Love *was* a bloom on a woman. An illumination. Annabel looked radiant, though her blue eyes glistened with suppressed tears. Because of her small stature—she was barely five foot three—she wore a short flaring veil attached to a pearl-and-gold crown that gave her height and reflected the design on the embroidered bodice, long sleeves and hemline of her beautiful silk gown. The bridal bouquet had been scaled so as not to overwhelm her, but the flowers in it were many. Roses abounded, extraordinarily beautiful, as were the floral arrangements that had been placed all around the ballroom. He had to admit Colin and Darren had been worth every penny.

"Be happy, Belle," he murmured. "This is your big day."

She swallowed what was obviously a lump in her throat and gave him a melting smile.

The entrance music began and Annabel took his right arm. They began their slow procession with the bridesmaids walking behind them in pairs, Vanessa and Roishin, Leith and Tiffany. As many weddings as Mountford had attended over the years, as many times as he'd been best man, this wedding was very, very special. The first in the family. Everyone had expected he himself would marry long before this, that he, the elder, the brother, would be the first. He saw now his prized bachelor state hadn't been a question of not getting involved. No woman had moved him. Until Roishin. No other woman ever would. Not like this. She had possessed him from the very first moment. Did she know it? She was highly intelligent, intuitive. She knew that his curious attitude to her revolved around an old tragedy. She had made him think about his mother. She had created fleeting confusions about his parents' marriage. About the whole business.

He had to decide how to respond.

When Bishop Morcombe asked the traditional question, "Who gives this woman to this man?", he pressed his thumb against his sister's soft palm, offering her in an unspoken gesture his love and support. For life. Whatever life held in store for his sisters, they knew they could always count on him.

A full two minutes into the ceremony, with Sasha beside him trying unsuccessfully not to cry, the sunset came pouring through the soaring casements in such a rich tide of color it embellished everything it touched. Audible gasps of delight rippled around the room, as though the visitation of the sunset was a most significant and happy omen. A few feet away from Mountford, Annabel smiled ecstatically. He touched Sasha's hand, looked into her dissolving eyes. At that moment, too, he remembered his father. Neither could he escape a momentary vision of his mother, a memory of the two of them standing side by side.

Mountford lifted his head and glanced around the gallery. Every face looked serious and intent, acknowledging this as one of the greatest, most crucial and emotional moments in life. When he married, there would be no mother of the groom for him. No father. No parents. Only Sasha, who had shown herself to be a woman of great heart. He remembered he hadn't wanted his father to remarry, but Sasha had won him over. It hadn't been easy, because he'd been a wildly unsettled child. Barely a year later the twins had arrived. Amazingly he had loved them. They had become a family.

THE USE OF THE GREAT HALL for the reception was an extravagant success. In the words of one guest, it looked like "a grand romantic fantasy," which was exactly what Annabel had wanted. Guests gazed around in open-mouthed delight. With the floral arrangements all in place and the candelabra glowing, the billowy ceiling hangings were shown off to magnificent effect.

"You certainly know how to do things!" Trish Wright, the best-known society columnist, told them during the receiving line.

The bridal dinner, chosen by Annabel, was a feast of flavors, skillfully presented and served. Honey-glazed duck or roast sirloin of beef followed cornets of trout or breasts of quail on wild rice. The main course came with a variety of vegetables. There were a number of desserts, including Michael's favorites—soufflés, luscious tortes, strawberry shortcakes, chocolate-truffle tarts, all arranged on a fifty-foot-long dessert table dominated by a four-tier wedding cake, a work of art in itself.

When it came time for Mountford to open the speeches, he kept his short. He didn't need any notes. He knew what he wanted to say. From the looks on the faces turned to him he realized his simple words had struck a solemn chord, so he ended with a funny story about Annabel when she was growing up. The hall broke into laughter and he immediately proposed a toast to the health and happiness of the bride and groom.

May they live happily ever after, he thought. *I want them to be happy.* Above all, now at this moment, he wanted to be happy himself. It was time for him to catch hold of his life. Live it. He'd struggled too long with a burden.

IT WAS SEVERAL DAYS before the household could settle to anything resembling normal routines. Annabel's wedding had been a great ceremony, marking a turning point in family life, and everyone felt deflated. Though she tried her best, Vanessa couldn't hide the intensity of her feelings. She had lost her other half. The bond between the twins had been so very, very close that some of the life seemed to go out of Vanessa as she strove to make the adjustment.

"It'll take time," Sasha confided to Mountford, "because of how close they were. Annabel, happy as she is, will feel the separation, too. You know what they were like, Mont. When Annabel hurt herself, Vanessa cried."

At the family's request, Roishin had stayed on a few extra days, but it was time for her to return to her own world. "Why not let Van go back to Sydney with Roishin?" Mountford suggested. "For that matter, you could go, too, Sasha. Both of you need a little company right now. I have to admit there's a certain melancholy in the air."

And so it was arranged.

But what about him? He was a man and he was expected to manage on his own. For the first time in his life, he had doubts about his ability to do so. He'd become very used to having Roishin in his home. Her hold on him, no matter how short the time had been, was profound. Yet he had decided not to speak. Not yet.

She had come to Southern Cross for a vast celebration—hardly a typical experience of life in the outback. Annabel's wedding had been a brilliant and memorable occasion. "There's never been a wedding like it!" Trish Wright reported in her newspaper. The homestead had been filled with people. Bright, intelligent, sophisticated people, who had made the house resound with their conversation and laughter. But there were long months at a time when the family scarcely saw a soul. Unless one coped well with isolation, knew how to use one's inner resources, relationships could founder. It had happened before. It could happen again. He might glory in Roishin's beauty and grace, in the ease and delight of her companionship, but what about her needs, her interests? Running Southern Cross and supervising the chain of Mountford pastoral properties was his life. Any woman he married would have to be self-reliant to survive. Often she would be alone. And loneliness was a time bomb waiting to go off.

His thoughts made him so restless Sasha accused him of stalking around like a panther. He just hoped his eyes didn't give out the same wild glitter when they fell on Roishin. He knew she was wary of him at some level. Maybe in love with him, too, but not liking him at all. He wrestled with the whole thing for hours. It wasn't fair to Roishin, he thought. As a child he'd been infinitely betrayed. Why should he blame *her* for that? Just because she was beautiful in his mother's fashion? Yet his fears wouldn't fade.

A sense of loss bore down on him all through that last day. He knew Southern Cross was going to feel overwhelmingly empty. He knew, too, that he was at a pivotal stage in his life. He had to make a move, had to think seriously about marrying. Until he'd met Roishin, he'd considered Cate Sinclair a suitable match. At one time Sasha had taken it upon herself to promote a marriage. Cate was a charming, sensible, station-born young woman. The Sinclairs owned several sheep and cattle properties around Queensland, and he was well aware that Cate's parents would be delighted to have him for a son-in-law. All of them had been invited to the wedding, and he'd danced with Cate, spent some time with her. She'd appeared to savor his company. He liked her. He'd always liked her. Before meeting Roishin, he'd begun to grow fond enough of her to consider the future. Cate was a straightforward person, outback born and bred.

But he didn't love her. Love didn't happen to order. Still, there was safety with Cate. Station life was her world.

It was a shock to find himself in so much inner turmoil. He could never resume his life as if nothing had happened. He couldn't put Roishin Grant behind him. She existed. She had illuminated his life. It was agony to let her go. It was cruel if she felt even a little of the passion that bloomed in him. He was a man on the edge. And he looked it.

Now it was evening, and he sat in the library with Roishin almost quietly for half an hour, then held out his hand. "A walk before bed, I think." In his dreams she lay beside him, his arms capturing her. Sheltering her.

"You're going to have to relax, David," she said. "Sasha's panther analogy isn't half-bad."

"Maybe I'm trying to stave off the hour when you're gone."

"That's no comfort, David." She moved beside him, at his shoulder. "You're in pain because of me. On the one hand you want to forget me totally. On the other, you . . . rather enjoy having me around."

She was so direct it took him by surprise. "I'm not going to deny it." He clasped her hand without thinking, linking her fingers with his, feeling sensation flood through every layer of his skin.

"You won't *let* me know you," she said.

"Which direction are we walking in?" he asked, the air around them fairly crackling with static.

"I don't really know. I guess I don't care."

"Roishin, stop it. You sound upset."

"The hurt seems to be there. On both sides." She laughed a little and looked up at him. "How can you see in the dark?"

"I'm used to it." He shrugged. "Little by little your eyes will become accustomed to it. For now you can hold on to me."

"I'd like that, David." She tightened her grip. "What are you planning to do when we're gone?"

He didn't even want to think about it. "All manner of things," he said casually. "Running the station is demanding work. I have to take a trip to north Queensland to visit one of our properties. Uncle Rex will be coming along with me and so will Bob Sinclair. Bob's thinking of buying the place."

"Bob Sinclair. That's the distinguished-looking man with iron gray hair and a rather magnificent mustache."

"Come to think of it he's had that as long as I can remember. He was a close friend of my father's."

"And he's Cate's father?"

He gave her a quick glance. Even in the semidark her skin had the luminescence of a pearl. "Why should I find that a leading question, counselor?"

"I understand you and Cate are great friends?"

"I've known her all my life."

"I found her very friendly and charming. Lovely when she smiles. She's a composed and confident young woman."

"Thank you for your approval," he said in a mocking voice.

"She'd make an excellent station wife."

"I'm sure of that." He steered her away from an overhanging branch of white bougainvillea. "Is this conversation going anywhere—or are we wandering in the dark?"

"All our exchanges have an undertone, David. You know that as well as I do. I'm trying to sort a few things out. She's in love with you."

"She's never said as much."

"David, you know she is."

"Would you prefer it if she wasn't?" he asked.

She shook her head. "Why do I make you so quickly hostile?"

"Why do you make me feel things I'm not sure I want to feel?"

"So it's a question of resentment. What kind of woman am I, David? What is it you resent? Please tell me."

They had reached the old summerhouse, a Victorian folly. All around it grew a ravishing old-fashioned pillar rose. By day its petals were the finest velvet crimson; by night it was almost the fabled black rose. Only the rich sumptuous scent remained the same. He drew her inside through the perpetually draped entrance before answering.

"What kind of woman are you? Let's see. My considered opinion is . . . a witch!" Which was to say everything he loved and feared.

She moved toward the circular cushioned seat, turning her face to the starlight. She didn't smile. "Ironic, when you're so expert at casting your own spells. Let me ask you, David, do you feel a woman like me would find Southern Cross a prison?"

"All these questions, Roishin! Yes, I do. Unlike these roses, you've grown and thrived in a far different environment. I can't emphasize it strongly enough—it's something I've lived with for a very long time. You're used to the excitement and glamour of big-city life. You have a career."

"You don't think I could leave it with ease?"

"*Could* you?" he asked in a dark skeptical voice.

"You sound as though you have doubts."

He stood a little distance from her, looking out over the garden. "Yes, given that I wish to avoid a tragedy."

Her hand flew to her breast as though he had wounded her. "Your mother didn't leave Southern Cross because she found station life intolerable, David."

He actually leaned forward and pulled her to her feet. "How did my mother get into this?" he demanded, his hands on her shoulders.

"Your mother is the problem, isn't she?"

He released her abruptly. "I think we'd better finish this conversation. Your way is to dredge up the past. Mine is to leave it where it belongs."

"Deep in your psyche? Because that's where it is, David. And that's what explains your attitude to me. You demand things from me. A...a passionate involvement, yet you push me away. Not anymore. I'm not going to take your rejection without putting up some sort of fight. This is *my* life, too. Something happened to us that first day."

"Indeed it did! A kind of classic infatuation." The harshness of his tone gave him both pain and pleasure.

"Much, much more!" she said with a spirited lift of her chin. "It could be love, if you'd only let it happen."

"And then?" he challenged her. "We could both pay very heavily. Have you thought of that?"

"David, I'm *me!*" she said in a despairing voice. "Not your mother. *Me!*"

"And you're too damned good to be true!" The hint of anguish goaded and upset him. What was the dark place in him that drove him to hurt her? It was wrong, *wrong*, but he couldn't help it. He caught her in his arms as if he'd never let her go. The thought of her leaving depressed him deeply.

Hunger overpowered him. A driving need of the heart and flesh. It seemed as strong in her, because her whole body trembled, conveying a piercing sweetness and an exhaustion of conflict.

"I love you, David," she said with a depth of feeling that left him humbled and greatly aroused.

Desire burned across his skin. He found her mouth unerringly, engrossed in communicating the passion that flowed through him so turbulently it was purest anguish. He kissed her until she gasped for breath, until she cried his name in a soft frantic moan.

Kissing her wasn't enough. He wanted everything she was. Heart, mind, the incomparable pleasure of her body. She was simply the most beautiful joyous creature he'd ever seen or dreamed of or envisioned. It would be worth it to have her, no matter what the outcome. At that moment he was prepared to pay the price.

"Do you know I saw you wearing a wedding veil?" he muttered, his mouth against the silky skin of her throat.

"You imagined it." Her answer was shaken and tender.

"It was so real. I swear I saw it that afternoon of Annabel's wedding. I pinned the Southern Cross to your gown and turned you to face the mirror."

"I remember."

"The feeling inside me was so intense. You know, if you married me I'd never let you go."

"You're all I'll ever want, David. Beside you, everything else has no meaning at all."

"And nothing and no one will save you. You must understand that. I'll never let you leave me or take our child."

At last he had articulated his private profound grief. Grief toward the two people he had loved and trusted.

Roishin's head snapped back and she spoke with great seriousness. "We have to address these fears, David.

Fears that spring from your childhood. Can't you look for answers from your mother? Great rifts in a family can be many-sided."

He had an eerie sensation that he was being led where he didn't wish to go. "My mother fell in love with another man and went away. That's clear enough. I recognize it affected me, but that was a long time ago."

"I don't think either statement is true, David."

"And you have the right to question me?"

"I don't mean to make you angry, but yes. You've given me that right, whether you're prepared to admit it or not."

"My dearest Roishin," he said in an ironic voice, "what a picture you make among the roses. However, you don't know what you're talking about. So much for the legal training!"

She reached out to him, held his arms. "Your mother denies all charges against her, save one. Your father wanted a large family, yes. So did she. But she *couldn't* have more children."

For an instant he was stunned, almost deprived of speech. "What *is* this, Roishin? I won't listen."

"Please," she implored. "For me. You didn't know?"

"I'm very skeptical indeed of any story you're going to tell me. I've heard nothing about this."

"Not even the miscarriages? She had three in as many years."

He put his hand to his eyes as though shielding himself from a painful sight. "My God, Roishin, I know you believe this, but it's simply not true."

"Your father made no secret of the fact that he wanted a large family. At the very least, three children. It's easy to understand. He had a magnificent home, a huge area of land. He wanted to put his sons on it. He didn't want you to be a lonely only child. Your mother tried desperately—it must have been terrible for her—but she couldn't carry beyond six weeks. It might be hard for a man to understand properly, but words wouldn't encompass a woman's grief, the awful sense of loss and failure. That man, Alex Turner, was in the wrong place at the wrong time. He was sympathetic to your mother. Probably he fell in love with her. Your father was furious, jealous and affronted."

"Ah, so my *father* was the one in the wrong now?" There was anger, shock, disgust in his voice.

"Misery forced your mother out. Your father must have been a hard man on some issues, David. He did his very best to turn you against your mother."

"Isn't it going to be hard to check out her story?" he asked with icy calm.

"The thing is, do you *want* to?"

"It doesn't bother you what the result might be?"

"It's my only hope. Too many emotions rage in you. They've got you in their grip. You question my suitability to become your wife? I couldn't consider it while you feel this way."

"Then forget it," he rasped.

"Tragically, I'll have to," she said quietly. "I'm not going to approach marriage full of trepidation."

"I don't think I'd gotten around to asking," he said brutally.

"I know you can be cruel."

"So be warned. If you've fallen for the great spiel my mother gave you, you've shown no loyalty to me." Even as he said it he felt pain. "How can you be so clever and such a pushover for a sob story?"

Her voice was quiet, but it held great dignity. "What your mother had to say assuredly got through to me, David. But I listened with an open mind. Your tragedy is that you won't!"

Chapter Six

AFTER ABOUT A WEEK, while he tried desperately to absorb himself in the affairs of the station, Mountford felt driven to put through a call to John Morcombe. The bishop had baptized him, as he'd baptized the twins. If John Morcombe knew anything of Roishin's story, he wouldn't lie. Mountford had already sounded out his uncle Rex and drawn a blank. Now as then, the entire Mountford clan fell in with his father's line. One fact did escape: the business about "Charlotte's taking a lover" had never sounded "absolutely right" to Rex. Disturbed, Mountford had made the decision to carry his inquiries further.

Bishop Morcombe was in the depths of far-north Queensland, the deacon told him. It was four more days before Mountford was able to hold his conversation, which again yielded only a little information. Morcombe told him quite straightforwardly that he'd always been "deeply sympathetic to Charlotte's plight." Whatever that might have been. He didn't elaborate even when drawn. The bishop was being very careful. He recalled one occasion when Charlotte had been ill. He had understood at the time that she'd suffered a miscarriage.

The single piece of information struck at Mountford's defenses with tremendous force. When had he stopped believing in his mother? Why? He had a vivid memory of his father calling him into his study, sitting him down in the big leather armchair that dwarfed him, telling him his mother had left them. There had been no attempt to soften the blow. His father had given it to him straight. His mother had formed "a bad friendship" with Alex Turner, the writer, who had been staying on Southern Cross gathering background material for a book. Turner had shown himself to be a scoundrel, a man not to be trusted, although the six-year-old Mountford had quite liked him. Now, suddenly, Turner was a monster, his adored mother a traitor to the Mountfords and the proud Mountford name. All the kisses and hugs and smiles had meant absolutely nothing, he'd learned. His mother preferred a *monster* to him and to his handsome, greatly respected father. He'd decided he would never forgive her defection—something, he now saw, his father had actively encouraged. From that day in the study, he had turned into a difficult child, hiding his wounds in headstrong action. He'd only cast off that image when he went to boarding school, then university, where he'd made quite a name for himself academically and on the sports field. Not many people had divined the ache in his soul, the pain of severance that had never really gone away. Had his wonderful father done *that* to him? If so, it was a dreadful crime. Against him. Against his mother. He had no other option but to go to her and beg for her version of past events. One thing was certain: pitted against his father and the combined strength of the Mountford clan, she wouldn't have stood a chance.

HE HAD NO TROUBLE finding where Roishin lived. He paid the taxi driver, staring up at the large apartment building on Sydney's North Shore. Vanessa had given him the address, obviously agog at what was going on, which he promised to tell her when he called again. Beyond the impressive outline of the building, he could see the sparkling blue of the harbor. Vanessa had told him, too, that Roishin's parents had presented her with her own apartment as a twenty-first birthday present. They must have forked out quite a bit, he thought.

As he reached the entrance, two young women were coming out the security door. They smiled at him and allowed him through even though they should have known better. He had intended to buzz the intercom, but it suited his purpose to surprise Roishin.

When she opened her door to him, her face flooded with color. She was wearing a loose top of violet silk over patterned leggings. A violet ribbon tied back her long hair. She looked as beautiful as ever. Maybe more finely drawn, as though she'd lost weight. As though somewhere inside of her she ached. He wanted her so badly it was a wonder it didn't shine out of his eyes. She hadn't been out of his mind for one second.

"David, how extraordinary!" Her breath caught. "I was thinking of you only this minute."

Her agitation steadied him. "That's nice. May I come in?"

"Of course. Please. Come through to the living room." She led the way to a well-proportioned, highly attractive room with sliding glass doors leading to a plant-filled balcony with views of the magnificent harbor beyond. Her legs in the tights looked incredibly sexy; her high breasts pushed gently against the silk of her loose top.

"Sit down," she invited, indicating a sofa upholstered in a soft coral with a scatter of striking cushions. "Are you in Sydney on business?" She took a seat opposite him, crossing her sleek, thoroughbred legs neatly at the ankle.

Desire ran through his body like a flaming arrow, yet he managed to keep his tone conversational. "*Unfinished* business, yes." He looked around, noting how the grace and charm of her personality was reflected in the way she had decorated the room. There was artwork to transform the walls, sheer draperies at the doors, a tall glass-fronted cabinet with a collection of what looked like antique dolls, books, elegant objects and flowers. Lots of flowers. He would expect that. "I like your apartment."

A luminous smile. "A twenty-first birthday present from my parents. As I'm their only child, they tend to spoil me."

"That would be easy. How have you been?"

"Fine." She paused, moved her graceful shoulders, corrected herself. "No, not really," she admitted. Then, in a little flurry, "David, do you know your eyes actually seem to burn like ice?"

"They've missed looking at you." He sounded almost curt in his intensity.

Even so, her eyes grew misty, jewel-bright between their thick, feathery lashes. "It's worth the agony to hear you say that."

"Was it *that* bad?" Loving her, wanting her, he still couldn't seem to lower his entrenched defences.

"It was agony for me," she said simply, allowing his sardonic tone to slip by her. "Aren't I allowed to say that?"

"Certainly, if you *mean* it."

"I do." She rose in her poised fashion, perhaps stalling for time. "Would you like something. Coffee? I was about to make some."

"I'd rather you sat beside me." He held her gaze when he wanted to hold out his arms. Hell, what was the matter with him? Was he terrified of revealing his own capacity for caring? "I want to talk to you," he said finally.

"And I want to listen."

"So sit down. Why are you so nervous?"

"I always am with you around." A wry smile fanned her mouth. "In fact I go weak at the knees."

"Then sit here." He patted the other cushion on the sofa. "I can see I'll have to cultivate more charm."

"What you've got is more than enough for me." She took her place beside him, an innocent enough action yet powerfully seductive. "What did you want to talk about?"

He obeyed an uncontrollable impulse. He reached out and drew one finger along her cheek. The skin felt like rose petals.

"Important things, Roishin," he said. "I thought you should know, since you're the one who set me free." He paused. "I spent several hours with my mother yesterday."

Her eyes held surprise, joy, a trace of apprehension. "So what happened? Tell me!"

He captured her hand, held it loosely and found it wondrous, the closeness. "It went well. More than well.

It was total reconciliation. We parted at peace. For most of my life I've been conducting some sort of war with my own mother. I regret it now. *You* forced me to face the situation. Face myself. Thanks to you, it's over."

The tears that shimmered now brimmed over. "David, I'm glad. So glad! Now the old wounds can heal."

"And you can take credit for being the physician." His voice vibrated with deep feeling. "The extraordinary thing is that after the first few minutes we felt little sense of estrangement. I had my mother back as I'd known her when I was a child. She told me so many things I knew nothing about. Things my father had deliberately kept from me. No one should do that to a child. But I could see how it had all happened. My mother told me she felt that if she'd stayed on at Southern Cross she'd have gone under or even died. She spoke with complete honesty, no bitterness toward my father. She's still very beautiful. She's obviously found happiness with Vandenberg but our reconciliation had real meaning—for both of us. Not that it wasn't painful. At one stage I thought the pain would kill me, but certain things had to be said. Because of my father, my mother was made an outcast. I was supposed to be the center of his world, yet he allowed me to become . . . twisted."

"David, no!" She leaned for him swiftly, put two fingers to his lips, sealed them. "I won't let you say that. It's not true. When it comes to the things that matter, you have *heart*. Of course, you're rather good at slamming down the barriers, as well," she added, her eyes dancing wickedly.

"I'm sorry, it's become almost a way of life."

"You have to let someone else in," she suggested. So gently. "I do love you." She gave a shaky little laugh and exultation filled him.

"How will you prove that?" he demanded.

"I could kiss you for a start."

Her whole being seemed to radiate light and love, flooding him with desire that was not without anguish. "Come here to me," he begged, drawing her across him so her head rested back within his encircling arm. "Now, go ahead. Show me how much you love me, because I'm certain I love you even more!"

They were fine words, beautiful words, and they gushed up from some wellspring deep in his heart.

She arched her back, then lifted an arm and locked it around his neck. "This is one of those moments I'll remember all my life. David, I love you. It's like I—"

"Hush!" His control was shot to pieces. What he felt for her was so elemental, so inexorable in its fierce passion, he cut her off abruptly, trying to put everything he felt for her into one single, all-consuming kiss. There was pain in it, and old grief, which miraculously unknotted as her sweet, open mouth flowered and she matched him in ardor.

"I love you," he muttered, feeling that something priceless and beautiful had been given to him. "Life without you would be unimaginable!"

He could feel her body trembling in his arms. Both of them had slid down on the sofa where they lay locked together, limbs entwined. He felt pounded by emotions so great, it was like being caught up on the crest of a great wave. His hands sought her breasts through the soft, sinuous cloth. He could feel her heart pounding. Oh

God, how he wanted her! Madly...badly—yet he wanted the exquisite anticipation of their wedding night.

"David!" She sighed, a little lost cry.

He gentled his embrace, forcing himself back to control. They had all the time in the world. He could wait. "I'm here," he murmured tenderly. "No armor. No defenses."

She opened her eyes with their lovely, liquid shimmer. "You need none with me."

"No." He brought his mouth softly back to hers. "Marry me, Roishin. I promise I'll do everything in my power to make you happy."

Her gaze was steadfast. "David, I'm honored. My answer is yes."

This time, the kiss they shared was deep and reverent, promising a lifelong devotion. He cradled her to him. "You're sure you can adapt to station life?"

"I already feel a sense of *belonging*, David. I think that's crucial. And I'll have you as my perfect companion through life."

"Then I'll have to live forever!" He smiled and dropped a kiss on her dark, fragrant hair. "No need to forgo your career, either. Southern Cross will always need a good lawyer. If it's my wife, so much the better."

"You're serious?" She half lifted her head, staring at him with widened eyes.

"Of course I am! You worked hard to acquire your skills. I want you to use them. I want you to have a rich, multi-layered life. Southern Cross is a big enterprise—you might be surprised *how* big. In fact, there's quite a large investment portfolio for you to explore. With your background you're definitely going to be an asset."

"I hope that's not why you're marrying me," she teased.

"What do *you* think?" he asked quietly. It was a wonderful feeling to be able to show the full extent of his love, in his eyes and in his voice.

"I think I love you with all my heart," she answered emotionally. "I think I want us to be married under the desert stars. A vast dome of glittering, floating stars, and the Southern Cross looking down on us. I want our wedding to be so memorable it will endure in our minds forever. Is it possible, David?"

His heart soared. He was filled with a wonderful joy and pride in her. "Not only possible, my darling," he said and his voice rang with promise. "It's going to happen."

A Note from Margaret Way

Ever since I can remember—back to the time when as a small child I was given a book filled with wonderful color pictures—our legendary Outback has had an almost mystical grip on me. In my mid-twenties when I began to write, I tried to communicate this lifelong fascination to my readers, sometimes to the extent that I got quite carried away with the descriptive passages and had to rein myself in.

The type of man I like to write about is a unique and definable breed—rugged, masculine, full of vigor and humor. He's the Man from the Outback, where mateship is tremendously strong and manliness is admired above all else.

Of the pioneering men who headed into the forbidding interior, the Never Never, none contributed more to the nation's development than the hard-riding, hard-drinking Outback hero, the cattleman. The great freedom of his outdoor way of life, his communion with nature and wildlife, his superb horsemanship and his survival skills provided the spirit and character on which the Outback was forged.

The cattleman is a culture hero, a figure of romance, excitement and adventure—tough, dynamic, adaptable, sometimes hard and dangerous, sometimes violent in his thrust to achieve. In the Old World, such a man might have been frowned on, restrained in his urge to carve out his destiny. In the young colonies men like this moved beyond the law as they drove deeper and deeper into the uncompromising Wild Heart with its extremes of stark grandeur and its bleached cruelty.

Here this unique masculine character emerged and lives on. Nowhere more than in the vast open country with its very special appealing images of man and his inseparable companion, his horse, both silhouetted against a cloudless blue sky. Man and horse have always been linked with Australian folklore. There are countless deeds of great daring on horseback right down to the legendary "Man from Snowy River." The very nature of the country has bred a race of magnificent horsemen. Our rough-riding rodeo heroes are idolized. The skills of horseman, drover, and cattleman live on through rodeo, reflecting the life of the cowboy who works from daylight to dusk, mustering, droving, tailing, branding, fencing, drafting and trucking.

One of the pictures I loved most in my childhood book was that of a lone stockman, his back against a desert oak, singing his heart out to a captive audience of a huge mob of cattle. I wonder what song it was? Strong yet sensitive, courageous enough to battle all the odds to realize a dream—these are the men I like to write about. Our cattlemen, our cowboys. We need them. We always will.

CHANCE FOR A
LIFETIME

Susan Fox

Chapter One

ERIN TAYLOR stepped from the Snack 'n' Gas into the frigid Montana air and hurried to the rental car parked next to the pumps. The below-zero windchill energized her, adding a battle-ready vigor to her natural vitality. And there *would* be a battle.

"One I intend to win, Emmett 'Chance' Lafferty," she murmured as she climbed into the car and shut the door. She glanced at the map the store owner had marked for her, relieved to see that the gravel turnoff to the Lafferty Ranch was little more than two miles past the next highway junction.

Erin couldn't suppress her growing elation. If her information was correct, she and her three-year-old niece, Meredith, would be on their way back to Chicago by noon. Never again would she have to bear the six-month separations she'd reluctantly allowed. If Chance truly had violated their private agreement, he'd be legally bound to settle for a handful of weekend visits a year.

He should have been more careful, Erin thought with a marked lack of sympathy as she tucked the map under her thigh and buckled her seat belt. She started the engine, then reached for her purse, rummaging through its contents for the white business-size envelope. Satisfied it was still there, she put the car into gear and pulled out onto the snowy highway.

For more than three years now, Erin had shared custody of her late sister's child with Chance Lafferty. Little Meredith had been orphaned at eight months when Erin's sister, Kelly, and Chance's brother, Buck, had been killed in a motel fire. And because Chance had refused to acknowledge that the baby Kelly carried was his brother's, and had then opposed Buck and Kelly's marriage, Erin had disliked the man long before she'd met him. His change of heart after the fire hadn't come soon enough for him to succeed in getting sole custody of Meri, but the lady judge's sympathy for Chance as the bereaved uncle had prevented Erin from getting it, either.

Back then, she'd been working an eight-to-five job, still struggling to establish her writing career by writing at night. She'd been short of the time and money needed to properly care for baby Meri full-time, so she'd been in no position to refuse Chance's request that the baby spend six months every year with him. A year later, she'd begun to make a living from her writing, but couldn't afford to provoke an expensive court battle by limiting Chance's time with Meri. Now, however, after two more years of bestselling historical novels, Erin's bank balance was large enough to take on any legal battle Chance cared to wage. The fact that he'd violated the most important part of their private agreement meant she didn't have to wait until Meri started school to curtail the visits with Chance.

She was surprised he'd lasted this long. Chance Lafferty had a reputation as a womanizer, a gambler and a bar brawler, which was why she'd insisted on rules to keep him in line and morally upright when Meri was with him. That he'd adhered to them for more than three years had to be a record of sorts, but he'd finally stepped over the line. According to the letter she'd received two days ago, he had a woman living with him at the ranch— and while Meri was there! Erin grew agitated all over again.

If he did have one of his women at the house—and she had scant doubt that he did—Chance Lafferty was about to get his comeuppance.

CHANCE LOOKED UP from the hand he'd been dealt, his green eyes shuttered as he laid his cards facedown on the table. He leaned back in his chair, an unlit cigar clamped between his teeth. The air in the game room was thick with tobacco smoke, and the light over the poker table cast the outer reaches of the room into shadow. Nearly every available surface, including the cart that had held a veritable feast of junk food the night before, was now littered with beer bottles and snack wrappers. They'd be quitting soon.

Chance didn't give undue thought to the fact that he and his three rancher friends had been playing poker for nearly eleven hours. It was as much the male camaraderie as the thrill of the game that motivated these occasional all-nighters.

"D'you 'spose Fayrene's up yet?" Rusty asked him, his dark eyes squinting with good humor. "I was kinda lookin' forward to steak 'n' eggs for breakfast."

Chance chuckled. "The cookhouse's your best bet for that. Fayrene isn't usually out of bed until eleven."

"How's she doin', anyway?" Rusty persisted, unconcerned that he might be prying into something that was none of his business.

"Passable," Chance answered. "She still hasn't decided what she's going to do with herself."

"Maybe she should just divorce that wheat farmer and get it over with," Rusty said, then grunted. "Always was a purdy little thing. She coulda done better for herself." He raised his gaze from his cards to meet Chance's with a sly gleam. "Coulda ended your maverick ways. Might be she still could."

Chance's lips curved in a one-sided grin. "Fayrene wasn't the woman for me years ago, and she's still not."

Rusty made a sound that indicated he wasn't convinced.

"We was wonderin' about that ourselves, Chance," Bob got in, nodding to include Sam as he finished reading his cards and tossed his chips into the center of the table. "'Bout time you took your pick of one of yer lady friends and got yerself hitched."

"When the right woman comes along," Chance recited, weary of mouthing the words. But then, he'd been saying them since he was eighteen years old. "Are you boys gonna play poker?" he asked, putting an end to the direction the conversation was taking.

The talk around the table reverted to safer subjects, and they resumed their play. Chance paid little heed to the muffled thumping he thought he heard at the front of the big house. It didn't occur to him that anyone would be knocking at the front door when everyone he knew came around to the back. He merely reasoned that little Meredith was awake.

A smile touched his lips. Meri filled his home with the full range of childish noises. He enjoyed them all, just as he enjoyed having her with him. He'd go see about her in a few minutes, he decided as he selected his discard. There was no hurry since the child's aunt had taught her to make her own bed and dress herself before she came downstairs. Chance frowned at the thought. Meri's Aunt Erin expected a lot from the girl. He intended to include a few terse words on the subject in the next letter he was required to send her.

"Sounds like someone's up and about," Sam commented.

"Probably Meri," Chance murmured as he was dealt four fresh cards. "She'll be down in a while."

The thumping noise came again, more distinctly this time. Someone *had* been knocking after all, and now had come around to the back door. Chance started to get up when Rusty laid down his cards.

"I'll see to the door. My luck's played out, anyhow," he groused as he got up and stretched stiffly.

Chance settled back into the game, pleased to see his new cards had at least got him something to bet on. He'd shoved his chips into the center of the table, when the rapid tattoo of footsteps in the hall drew his attention to the open door.

His shocked gaze riveted on Erin Taylor's slim form as she stepped over the threshold and into the circle of smoke-hazed light. Blond hair, wind tossed and curling wildly about her head and shoulders, framed her delicate features. His gaze dropped fractionally to her sensual mouth, then lower, taking a thoroughly male inventory of what he could see between the open facings of her down jacket. He also noticed appreciatively how very long her denim-clad legs seemed with those fancy high-heel boots she had on.

It was a moment before he could look at her face again. When he did, he saw that her blue eyes were leveled reproachfully on him, their sparkling depths underscoring the suppressed anger that seemed to vibrate her small body and reach across the room.

Chance was too stunned to move for several seconds, captured without warning and against his will by her arresting presence. Somehow he remembered Erin Taylor as a prudish bookworm doomed to spinsterhood by lackluster looks and heavy thighs. He'd always thought nature had endowed her buckle-bunny sister with all the beauty there was to be had in the Taylor family. Chance's interested gaze made another slow sweep of her svelte, yet enticingly curved body. It shocked him to think he'd been so mistaken.

Erin stared at Chance, set to unleash her temper on him, finding herself halted practically midstride. She hadn't been prepared for the way he looked, leaning back in his chair, a cigar clamped between his teeth, his dark shirt unbuttoned partway to his lean waist. His black hair fell past his collar, impossibly thick and shiny with a rich texture that dared a woman to touch and experience.

The jolt that went through her at the sight of him preceded a feeling of déjà vu so strong she felt off center suddenly. But at just the moment she registered the deep unshakable feeling that Chance was familiar to her in some tantalizingly intimate way, her subconscious snatched the impression and left her emotions reeling.

It was enough to give her pause, but not enough to deter her from this showdown. And the appraisal he was giving her only fanned the flame of her outrage.

"Well, boys, I guess it's about time we headed out for breakfast," Rusty said, easing into the shock wave of silence. Bob and Sam got up, nodding politely to Erin, their barely restrained grins as they looked from her to Chance sending a prickle of irritation through him.

Erin spoke as soon as Chance's friends left the room. "You know what I've come for," she said, pleased that her voice revealed none of those confusing feelings of seconds ago. Chance rose slowly to his feet.

"No, I don't," he said, his voice gravelly and low as he spoke around his cigar. "You'd better explain."

Erin stiffened at his tone, and though she'd been prepared, she was nonetheless a little intimidated at the sight of Chance's broad-shouldered body straightening to a height well over six feet.

"We made an agreement concerning my niece, Mr. Lafferty." Erin paused, watching his face carefully for a telltale flicker of guilt. "I realize a good bit of time has gone by, but I haven't forgotten any point of it, nor have I changed my mind."

Chance tossed his cards to the table, never taking his eyes from Erin as the groove on the right side of his mouth deepened with satisfaction. "I haven't forgotten or changed my mind, either," he said gruffly before adding, "which means you've just violated it yourself."

"You violated it first. Mr. Lafferty," Erin stated briskly. "Besides, the minor breach I was forced to commit wouldn't restrict my access to Meredith. What you've done has.''

Chance snatched the cigar from his mouth and started around the table toward her.

"What in hell are you talking about?" he demanded, his expression dark as he towered menacingly over her. No one was about to restrict his time with Meri, not even her prissy Aunt Erin.

It was all Erin could do not to retreat to a more prudent distance as she tipped her head back to glare up at him. Chance Lafferty was a big man, all muscle and sinew and bone, as lean and tough as rawhide. He was not a man to cross. But her niece's moral development was at stake, and she was not about to let a minor thing like cowardice undermine her intention to remove Meri from this man's unwholesome influence.

"As if you didn't know," she said, then snickered, her blue eyes icy.

"Know? About what?" he demanded, placing his hands on his hips.

"Come off it, Mr. Lafferty. You agreed not to shack up with any of your girlfriends while Meri was with you. I'm here to see for myself that you've done just that." Erin hesitated, her gaze drawn to Chance's impressive pair of shoulders. Ignoring the obvious—she was physically incapable of making anything from this big man that he didn't freely give—she stated coolly, "And then I intend to take my niece away at once."

The air exploded with Chance's curse. Erin flinched, but held her ground, struggling to hold the angelic image of her tiny blue-eyed blond-haired niece in her mind for courage as Chance leaned threateningly over her.

"You just hold on there, Miss Priss," he growled, the abrupt lowering of his voice as unnerving as his shout. "You aren't taking *my* niece anywhere."

"If you've got one of your women living in this house, I certainly can," she retaliated. No one, especially this man, no matter how physically dangerous he seemed, was going to flaunt his tomcat morals in front of little Meri. For some reason quite unknown to Erin, the child practically idolized her uncle Chance. Which was all the more reason, Erin vowed, to prevent him from being a negative influence on her innocent impressionable niece.

"One of my what?" Chance demanded, an ominous glimmer in his eyes.

Erin didn't repeat herself, knowing full well he'd heard what she'd said. How could he not? He was leaning so far over her that she was bending backward. Their faces were so close that she could see every rough hair on his unshaven jaw and could detail every ruggedly male facet of his face, right down to the tiny flecks of gold in his green eyes. His warm breath was gusting like air from a bellows over her flushed cheeks, drawing her gaze to the firm line of his mouth.

The man was a virile masterpiece. No wonder women let him make fools of them. Not quite peacock handsome, Chance was nonetheless devastatingly attractive, even to a woman who was wise to him. The realization set off a sensual explosion deep inside her. She didn't recall he'd had quite this effect on her three years ago, but then she'd been grief-stricken over her sister's death and frightened of losing Meri.

"Here." Erin lifted her purse and thrust it between them, deliberately whacking it against Chance's solid middle to create a safer distance between them. Startled, Chance stepped back and she retrieved the envelope from her purse. "This explains it all," she said as she pulled the folded sheet from the envelope and held it up.

Chance studied the defiant tilt of her small face through narrowed eyes, then jabbed his cigar between his teeth before he took the letter and unfolded it with a quick shake. Once he read it through, he reached for the envelope. "Let me see that."

The envelope bore only Erin's name and mailing address, along with a postmark that indicated it had been mailed from Montana five days before. As with the letter, there was no indication of who had sent it.

"I'm assuming this is true," Erin said, "although I'm willing to give you an opportunity to prove otherwise." She was prepared to be fair. However, she'd not allow him to deceive her. Which was why she'd arrived as early in the day as possible to catch *her*—whoever she was—in the house. Erin figured Chance's women preferred to sleep late.

"That's mighty evenhanded of you," Chance said, his flashing eyes turned on her full force before he discarded his cigar. "But I don't need to prove anything," he declared, calling on his card-playing skills as he gave her what he hoped was his best poker face. God Almighty! Miss Priss Taylor would never believe there was nothing going on between him and Fayrene once she got a look at the vivacious redhead. "This letter," he bluffed as he shoved it toward her, "is hocum."

With that, Chance reached for Erin's arm and turned her toward the door, ushering her through it so quickly she was halfway down the hall to the kitchen—and the back door—before she realized what he intended.

"Wait a minute!" Erin protested, bracing her feet and jerking her arm up in a vain attempt to free herself. Chance barely noticed the resistance as he escorted her down the hall. "You can't just throw me out of your house."

"It's my house," he said ruthlessly. "It's too bad you wasted your money on a trip out here," he added when they reached the back door. "But as I'm sure you recall, one of the few rules I insisted on was to be spared any face-to-face contact with you. That's why I spent a fortune for Meri to have escorts between here and Chicago. If you leave now, I might forget that you broke your personal word of honor to me." Chance reached for the doorknob.

"I had a legitimate reason for breaking that silly little rule of yours," Erin protested, twisting from his grip to put a wary space between them. "And I have the distinct feeling I haven't wasted my money. Otherwise, you wouldn't be so eager to get me out of this house."

Chance started toward her, but Erin bolted for the other side of the kitchen table, careful to keep it between them, though she felt ridiculous doing so. Maybe not so ridiculous, she amended as Chance's stern expression became harsher.

"If you don't have anything to hide, prove it," she challenged. Her bravado was rewarded by the slight flicker of unease in his eyes as they strayed momentarily toward the open door the led to the dining room and the staircase just visible beyond. Confident that she now had Chance dead to rights, Erin relaxed a little. "It will be a lot easier on Meri if you give in graciously," she pointed out.

"Like hell," he said. "Whoever sent that letter is trying to cause trouble, and I'm not going to let you upset Meri over a damned lie."

"There's no reason to upset her if the letter is a lie," Erin agreed, "But I'm not convinced it is."

Chance released a frustrated breath as he studied the stubborn set of Erin's fair features, surprised to find himself entranced by the loveliness he saw there—and more than a little tantalized by a woman who was assertive enough to stand up to him to get what she wanted without resorting to tears or some other female ploy. A feeling of foreboding traced an icy finger around his bachelor heart. Suddenly it seemed imperative that he find a way to excise this woman from his home—and his life—as quickly and completely as possible.

"I'm sorry you're not convinced," he said grimly as he lunged around the table. Erin wasn't fast enough to escape the large hand that caught her arm. "You'll just have to take my word for it that there's no hanky-panky going on."

Erin struggled futilely as he stalked to the door with her in tow.

"I just want you out of here before Meri comes dow—" Chance sucked in his breath at the sharp pain as Erin brought the heel of her boot down on his toe. He regretted removing his boots hours earlier.

"Let go of me!" she hissed, mutiny heightening the color in her cheeks. "I will not be thrown out like a bag of gar—"

Both froze at the quick thump of small footsteps that came from the direction of the stairs. Chance's annoyed gaze flicked down to meet the triumphant gleam in Erin's before they both turned.

"Auntie Erin!" Meri's shriek of delight banished Erin's anger as the child launched herself at her, her long blond curls whipping around Erin as she made contact. Erin crouched down and caught Meri in a big hug.

"I knew it! I knew it!" Meri exclaimed, her high voice partially muffled against the neck of Erin's down jacket. Easing back only enough to gaze up adoringly at her uncle, Meri jabbered excitedly, "Oh, Uncle Chance, thank you, thank you!" She reached up a tiny hand and grabbed his fingers. "This is the best birthday surprise in the whole world!"

Silence followed as both adults slid quick glances toward each other. Oblivious to the undercurrents that flowed in a mad torrent between Chance and Erin, Meri rushed on. "You promised me a special surprise for my birthday, and I wished so hard for this. Now we can be a real family!"

Dazed, Chance allowed the child to pull him down until he was hunkered down next to Erin, eye level with both her and their niece. The tiny hand released his only long enough to loop around his neck so Meri could hug them both simultaneously. Erin tried not to react when Chance's big embrace automatically encompassed both Meri and her while the child planted a wet happy kiss on each of their cheeks. "Oh, this is gonna be the best birthday!"

Erin forced a smile, realizing that if either she or Chance didn't make some kind of response now to gently reverse Meri's assumption, her disappointment would be that much harder to deal with. But beyond a vague smile and noncommittal word or two, what could she say? Loath to be the one to crush Meri's excitement, she glanced desperately at Chance, only to encounter his dumbfounded expression.

"Uh..." Chance hesitated, clearly snared by the same reluctance to disappoint their niece as Erin was. A panicked look crossed his face before he could conceal it. "Uh, honey... sweetheart," he cajoled as he struggled to find the right words, "your aunt just stopped by." Chance paused, clearly having a hard time formulating the half-truth. Erin was surprised he wasn't smoother at it. "She has a job to get back to, you know. She's only got a short time—" he flashed Erin a warning "—a *real* short time before she has to be on her way."

Meri's radiant excitement ebbed quickly into a frown that puckered her forehead. "But Aunt Erin doesn't have a real job. She writes books."

"Well," Chance said quickly, "I'm sure she's got other things she's got to get back to Chicago for. Besides, she'll be coming to visit you in town on your birthday, just like she's always done."

Meri's lower lip trembled and tears welled in her eyes. "But I want her to stay, Uncle Chance."

"Uncle Chance is right," Erin agreed before deciding to turn things to her advantage. "I stopped by because your uncle and I had something important to discuss. How would you like to come home to Chicago and spend your birthday with me for a change? We can have a big party with a clown, all your friends—"

"Now you just hold on," Chance cut in. "This is my six months, and *this* is Meri's home."

"It is not, and you know very well why it has to be this way," Erin argued, unable to keep the shrewish tone from her voice.

"Over my dead body," he vowed with soft menace, his expression becoming severe.

The anger that snapped between them was almost tangible. The crackling seconds lasted until a sob jerked the small body between them.

"You're having a fight." Meri's pale cheeks were streaked with tears as she looked from one adult to the other in disbelief.

"Oh, honey," Erin said softly, her voice going hoarse at the look on Meri's face.

But Meri was trying to wiggle out of Chance's arms as her tears began to flow in earnest. Her tiny body was no match for Chance's strength, of course. He pulled her against his chest, snuggling her blond head beneath his chin while he glared at Erin as if he'd like to wring her neck.

"Don't cry, sweetheart," he murmured as he awkwardly patted Meri's curls, the faint desperation in his voice tugging at Erin's heart.

Suddenly Erin felt like a witch. She'd been so anxious to spare herself the long separations from the child—and so selfish—that she'd given little real thought to the depth of Meri's feelings. Or Chance's, either, she acknowledged with a pang when she saw the love on his face as he did his best to soothe Meri's tears. All her earlier outrage and suspicion melted into chagrin.

"Hey, little one," Chance was saying to Meri, "you're making an awful big deal out of something's that all over."

Meri hiccuped a couple of times, then lifted her head from Chance's chest to look up at him somberly. "I don't want to go back to Chicago for my birthday."

Erin didn't know it was possible to feel the kind of pain that tore through her heart at Meri's words. The corners of Chance's mouth turned up in a relieved—and victorious—smile, which he didn't hesitate to turn on Erin. Erin stiffened as she tried to conceal how hurt she was.

"An' I don't want Auntie Erin to go back to Chicago, neither," Meri went on, her lip quivering again. "I want her to stay an' have my birthday with us like a real family."

Chance's smile of victory wilted, and he glanced over at Erin, catching the loving, misty-eyed way she was looking at Meri.

Damn that look. He never did handle crying females well, the little ones or the big ones. That was mostly how he'd gotten himself into this situation with Fayrene when she'd shown up bawling her eyes out. Her family had sided with her husband in this latest dispute, and she'd claimed to have no one else to turn to. He'd given in to her pleas mainly to shut her up, never suspecting what hell he was courting.

His gaze wandered toward the ceiling, as he thought about Fayrene up there in one of the guest bedrooms. The fur was going to fly when prissy Aunt Erin found out about that, but somehow, the thought of tangling with her temper seemed a hell of a lot easier than deal-

ing with that about-to-cry look on her face and more of
Meri's tears. Besides, nothing was going on between him
and Fayrene, and nothing ever would. If Erin had a lick
of sense, she'd know it as soon as she heard the story.

"Well, then." He started searching awkwardly for the
words he was certain he'd regret every minute of the two
weeks between now and Meri's birthday. "How 'bout
we ask your aunt Erin to stay on with us till after your
birthday?" The smile he offered Meri had a sickly curve
to it that the child didn't notice.

"Oh! I knew it!" Meri squealed, breaking away from
Chance to do a little dance before she flung herself at
Erin for another hug.

Chance and Erin exchanged uneasy looks as Meri
started to babble about the ranch and all the things they
could do together.

"Well?" Chance's voice was gruff as he waited for an
answer from Erin. Surely she'd know he had nothing to
hide if his conscience was clear enough to ask her to stay
for the next two weeks. He reckoned he could put up
with her that long if it would prove to her he wasn't quite
the reprobate she imagined him to be.

Erin looked at Chance, absolutely stunned that he was
inviting her to stay. She looked down at Meri and hugged
her again, doing her best to keep her tears at bay. She'd
never had more of a birthday celebration with Meri than
a day at a motel in town. But Chance, however reluctant, had offered to change that with a simple invitation
to share. She felt ashamed now for stomping in and
threatening to take Meri away because of a silly letter.
And it *had* been silly, or Chance wouldn't have asked her

to stay. He really didn't have anything to hide. Erin felt a strange spurt of relief.

"I think I owe you an apology," she said softly, though the words stuck a bit in her throat. "And I would like to stay. It would mean so much to Meri." *And to me,* she added silently. "Thank you."

Chance shifted uncomfortably at the warm look Erin was giving him. For some reason, the kitchen suddenly seemed stuffy, just a touch claustrophobic. He mumbled something about getting her settled in, but he was lost for a moment in the mesmerizing blue of her eyes.

He didn't get the ball-and-chain image that usually came to him when a woman looked at him like that. A noise from upstairs distracted him. It dawned on him then that his other guest was up early and, from the sound of it, about to come downstairs.

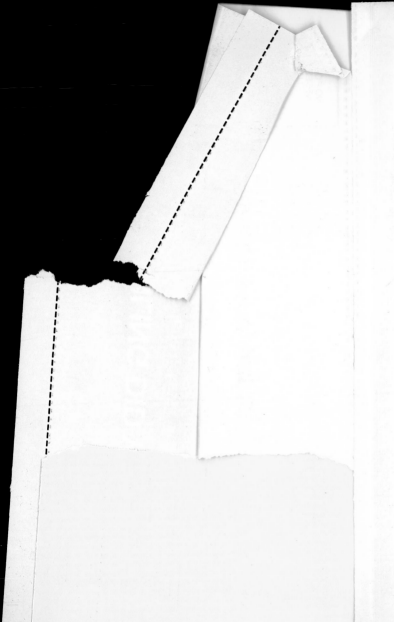

Dear Reader,

Get out a coin—kiss it for good luck—and go to work on the WIN-A-FORTUNE tickets enclosed. You could end up <u>a million dollars</u> richer!

By returning these tickets you'll also be in the running for hundreds of other cash prizes we'll be giving away. It costs nothing to play this game—there's no fee, and no purchase is necessary!

We're holding this sweepstakes to introduce you to the benefits of the Harlequin Reader Service®. Scratch off the gold boxes on the enclosed Lucky 7 Slot Machine Game and we'll send you <u>free books</u>!

How many FREE BOOKS will you get? Play the Slot Machine Game and see! These books are absolutely free, with no obligation to buy anything!

The Harlequin Reader Service is **not** like some book clubs. We charge you nothing—ZERO—for your first shipment. And you don't have to make any minimum number of purchases—not even one!

over, please

FOLD ALONG DOTTED LINE AND DETACH CAREFULLY

For example, you could accept your FREE BOOKS and cancel immediately, by writing "please cancel" on the shipping statement and returning it to us. You'll owe nothing and be under no further obligation!

But the fact is, thousands of readers enjoy receiving books by mail from the Reader Service. They look forward to getting the best new romance novels months before they arrive in bookstores. And they like our discount prices!

I'm hoping that after receiving your free books you'll want to remain a subscriber. But the choice is yours—to continue or cancel, any time at all!

Pamela Powers

Pamela Powers for Harlequin

P.S. If you're accepting free books, play the "Ace of Hearts" game for a *free MYSTERY GIFT!*

ILING DID YOU...

1. Play your Win-A-Fortune tickets? Don't forget to fill in your name and address in the space provided on the back of your game piece!

2. Play your Lucky 7 Slot Machine game for free books? If you have played your Slot Machine game, you may also play your Ace of Hearts game for a free gift.

TED LINE AND DETACH CAREFULLY ▶

Chapter Two

THE CREEK OF FLOORBOARDS overhead was unmistakable. Because he was still staring into Erin's eyes, Chance knew the exact moment she recognized the sound. Because he couldn't look away, he knew the precise second she assigned the sound significance. And because he suddenly seemed able to read the thoughts behind those incredible baby blues, he knew by the companion dip of his innards just how far her estimation of his character plummeted.

"Mice, Mr. Lafferty?" she asked softly, her light brows lifting to just the right pitch.

Chance expected an outburst of fiery temper to go with the inferno in her eyes, but her soft question threw him. Was she of that breed of shrew who used gentle sarcasm to lull a man into a false feeling of safety before she pitched a tantrum that would take his head off? He kept a wary eye on her. A tiny smile flitted over her lips as she waited for his answer. Meri, who was also watching him closely, remained unhelpfully silent.

It suddenly occurred to him that he was thinking and behaving like a guilty schoolboy. Lifesaving temper blustered up to cover his male pride, sparing him from being at the mercy of a petite female who showed signs of being a latent bitch-on-wheels.

"You got luggage?" He figured he put enough belligerence in his tone to let her know he meant to get her things from the car—however big the "mice" were.

Erin hesitated, then dug in her pocket and produced a set of car keys, which she handed over. Chance headed out the door, baffled by a relief so strong he didn't realize he'd forgotten to put on his boots until he was halfway to her car.

THE HUMOR of the situation wasn't lost on Erin. Her initial pique at the realization that Chance really did have a female houseguest had cooled the instant she'd seen the flash of horror in his eyes. That he hadn't rushed into a bumbling explanation along the lines of "I swear it's not what you think" had persuaded her to reserve judgment until she at least met the houseguest.

And houseguest was exactly what she was, Erin decided as the woman came down the living room stairs and made her way listlessly to where Erin and Meri waited in the kitchen. No mistress or live-in lover worth her salt would risk letting her man see her in such a bedraggled state. From her sleep-smashed hair to her red-rimmed eyes, ratty bathrobe and matted bunny slippers, Fayrene Hermann was too abject a vision to enslave the fickle passions of Chance Lafferty.

Fayrene responded absently as Meri made the introductions, then scraped back a chair and sat down heavily to contemplate the surface of the red-checkered tablecloth.

Chance returned with Erin's suitcase and confirmed her perception when he muttered a distracted good-morning to Fayrene. By not so much as a flicker did he

act as if Fayrene's morose appearance was anything out
of the ordinary. As Erin and Meri followed Chance upstairs to a guest room, Erin allowed herself a secret
smile—then lost it when she sensed that the feelings behind it were a little too giddy for her peace of mind.

Her first thought as she followed Chance into the guest
room was that she'd stumbled into the aftermath of an
explosion in a flower garden. From the high ceiling to
the dull golden luster of the wood floor, the room was a
faded collection of every popular floral pattern of the
Victorian era. Throw rugs, wallpaper, draperies, bedspread and upholstered chairs—not a single pattern
matched another. Gold fringe or ivory lace edged each
piece, save the flowered hurricane lamps on the tables,
yet the gold and ivory somehow managed to give the
room a semblance of harmony. Erin was so taken aback
it took her a few moments to catch sight of the pudgy
cherubs that swooped in armed glory among the pro-
fusion of hearts and flowers carved on the headboard of
the four-poster.

The room would have been an affront to the sensibil-
ities of every legitimate decorator in the country. Erin
turned in an amazed circle as she tried to take it all in.
Lord, what a screwball parody of the period it was, she
thought, then almost laughed. Until she realized that she
loved every petal and piece of fringe; something in the
creative part of her mind was applauding like a lunatic.

"There's another guest room, if you'd rather have it."

Erin came out of shock enough to hear the tinge of
embarrassment in Chance's voice.

"Is it anything like this?" she asked as she turned in
another slow circle.

"No, nothing like this," he said softly. He looked around the room, suddenly ashamed of himself for hoping she'd be so put off by the decor she'd change her mind about staying the whole two weeks. Something about Erin Taylor made him uneasy, and his initial instinct to get her out of his house and life as quickly as possible was digging him like a spur. Still, she didn't deserve a nasty trick because he didn't like the effect she was having on him. It was his problem and he'd just have to take it like a man. "Would you like to look?"

Instead of waiting for her answer, he took her arm and ushered her to the room across the hall, his haste on a level with his hope that once she saw the tastefully conservative room, she'd forget the eyesore he'd tried to stick her with.

Erin gave him a pointed glance from her much shorter height when they reached the room. Another arched brow conveyed enough reproach at his caveman tactics to make him let go of her arm and privately vow to keep his hands to himself. He *never* dragged women around, and he'd done it with her twice that morning.

Erin gave the room a brief inspection, then turned back to the other room. Chance figured she was going for her suitcase and followed to get it for her, baffled when she hefted it on top of the rose-covered bedspread to unpack. Meri bounded on the bed next to the open case to watch.

"Uh . . . Erin," he began, but she grabbed up a small stack of lingerie and turned to the dresser to put it in a drawer. "I think you might be more comfortable in the other room." That got him only marginal attention as she dispatched the frilly handful and turned for more clothes.

Something in Chance's voice made her glance his way in time to see chagrin lend a faint flush to his winter-tanned face. The flush began to blossom incongruously against the floral backdrop. "Why do you think that?" she asked.

"Well, uh... you aren't... This room's a little over-done," he got out. "I didn't realize until just now how it might look to someone who's not... used to it."

Erin glanced around, giving the room further consideration. If he'd had some goofy idea that giving her this room would either make her less eager to stay or spoil her enjoyment of the ranch, he was mistaken. He'd only just realized the room was overdone? She gave him a serene smile.

"Not at all, Mr. Lafferty. It's charming." She continued transferring her few clothes from the suitcase to the drawer she'd chosen. Her toiletries went in a drawer just as swiftly.

Meri jumped off the bed and grabbed Erin's hand. "Now come see my room, Aunt Erin." Off they went past a wary Chance, whose mind shifted to a higher gear.

She knows, he thought. *She knows I did this on purpose and that I lied about not realizing its effect.* What he didn't know was whether *she'd* lied about finding it charming. He looked around the room again to see if he could figure how the hell she could find charm in the floral riot.

"Uncle Chance!" Meri's voice floated back to him, snapping him out of his reverie. He moved thoughtfully to the hall, then toward Meri's room, more certain by the moment that nothing got by Erin Taylor's sharp eyes and instincts. And that made her the kind of woman—especially in such a pretty package—who was a threat to him in a way he couldn't quite put a finger on.

That strange stuffy feeling he'd had earlier stirred, giving him the gloomy sense that his life was about to take a drastic turn.

MERI'S ROOM was the real stunner. Done mostly in white, it was the room of a tiny princess. Soft pastel ribbons wove through yards of eyelet lace that hung at the windows and skirted the bed and the vanity table against one wall. The wood furniture was a warm honey to match the polished wood floor. The pale pink area rug was strewn with doll clothes, and the sill-high shelves beneath the windows were crammed with books, stuffed animals and dolls. Erin wondered if any toy store in Montana boasted such variety. But the focal point of the room was the large three-story dollhouse that towered at one end of the room, complete with a step stool for convenience. Erin had never seen anything like it and stared, trying to overcome her surprise at the scalloped shingle roof and the gingerbread detail of the siding, right down to the tiny silk flowers in the flower boxes.

Something painful pricked her heart. She hadn't expected Chance to have done such a spectacular job on a room for their niece. When Meri had reported on the dolls, stuffed animals and the dollhouse, Erin had imagined nothing on this scale. She recognized the loving indulgence that had gone into the design and again felt guilty for the selfish intentions that had brought her here.

"I hope I did better on this room than the other one."

Chance's voice so close behind her startled her. Erin turned to him in amazement, catching the start of another chagrined flush.

"You did all this?" She paused, but was unable to keep from adding, "*And* the other room?"

Chance's flush deepened. "That guest room was where everything that survived through the generations ended up. This room—" some of his embarrassment faded as a faint note of pride came into his voice "—started out as a picture in a catalog. I added the shelves and the dollhouse."

Meri piped up. "Uncle Chance drawed on paper first, then he sawed and builded it at the shed. He gived it to me when I was three." Meri rushed over to reach inside the door. When tiny lights came on in the rooms, Chance explained they were battery operated. Erin couldn't resist peeking inside, stepping around the structure to see the open side, further entranced by the small furnishings, complete with kitchen, bath and a lighted log blazing under battery power in the fireplace. The family of dolls included a dog, a cat and a family of fuzzy mice, and were just the right scale for the house.

Erin's assessment of Chance's character underwent a monumental change in those moments. She hoped she didn't appear too astonished. She wouldn't for the world want to offend him by showing the extent of her surprise.

"Y-you've done a spectacular job, Chance." And more likely than she wanted to think, he'd probably done just as spectacularly as an uncle to her niece. Since the surest way to Erin's heart was to treat Meri well, she was suddenly frightened she would become emotionally vulnerable to the man she'd always seen as an enemy.

He might have ceased to be the enemy concerning her niece, but as a man who would never settle for one woman, he was more dangerous to Erin herself than ever before.

AFTER A BRIEF TOUR of the ranch house, they ended up back in the kitchen, where Fayrene didn't look as if she'd moved an eyelash.

"Can we eat breakfast now, Aunt Erin?" Meri asked. "My stummy's empty."

Erin looked down in surprise. "Stummy?"

Meri patted her stomach. "I called my tummy a stummy one time, and Uncle Chance laughed, so that's what we call it now."

Suppressing a grin, Erin glanced over at Chance. The tell-tale flush was back, and it was clear that Chance's dignity was a bit ruffled by Meri's disclosure.

Meri tugged on Erin's hand, reclaiming her attention. "Can you make us a really big breakfast? Fayrene can't cook too good."

Chance spoke up at that. "Fayrene's not herself, but you don't have to cook for us, Erin. We can get something at the cookhouse."

Meri was already pulling Erin toward the refrigerator. "I don't mind," Erin assured him. "What would you like?"

Before he could do more than give a vague shrug, Meri tugged the door open. "We got lots of eggs and homemade bacon," she declared enthusiastically. "Can we make cimum rolls like we do at home?"

Chance felt an uncomfortable spurt of resentment at Meri's reference to Erin's house as home. He watched as woman and child made various selections and set them on the counter, realizing by their companionable chatter and the choreography of their movements that they'd prepared countless breakfasts together. His resentment suddenly roared into a conflagration of jealousy so strong his insides were scorched with it.

He couldn't love Meri more if she'd been his own daughter, and the tenderness he felt for her overwhelmed him. Erin Taylor could cut off his access to the one person in all the world he couldn't bear to lose. The knowledge that she had the legal right to determine how much or how little of Meri's life he could share was agony. He was literally at Erin's mercy, and any attraction he'd felt toward her earlier vanished.

Or so he thought until she at last removed her down jacket and handed it to Meri to hang at the back door. Lordy, maybe he was the reprobate she believed he was, he thought, as his gaze fell to the front of the teal sweater that emphasized more than it covered. When she turned and bent over to take a baking pan out of a lower cupboard, he was presented with a backside that reminded him of a plush heart on a valentine.

In spite of his reputation, Chance had been intimate with damned few women. He admitted he was a killer flirt, but he'd always been too fastidious and too wary of being shackled to the wrong woman to sow many wild oats. He hadn't yet met the woman who could breach the fortress of self-preservation he'd built over his thirty-five years. He wasn't even sure he believed anymore that she existed. But if the flash fire of lust he felt in his own kitchen as he watched his niece's prissy aunt cook breakfast was some kind of sign that he was ready, maybe he should start some serious looking. Someplace else.

Chance stepped over to the door, heedless of the socks that were still damp from his earlier trip outside, and shoved his feet into his boots. "I'll be back."

He welcomed the harsh sting of March wind as he shrugged into the sheepskin coat he'd snagged on his way out. He slogged down the snow-covered path to the cookhouse to say so long to his poker buddies. The sharp air was bracing, cooling him off and clearing his head.

He was certain he'd passed the test with Erin that morning. The price of passing it might be enduring the next two weeks, but when the alternative was having Meri's visit cut short, he figured he could put up with anything. He suddenly felt optimistic, that the strange thoughts and feelings he'd had about Erin were the result of being up all night and then suffering a rude surprise. The brisk walk refreshed him, so that by the time he reached the cookhouse and stepped inside, his good humor was fully restored.

"Hey there, Chance," Rusty called from the far end of the long table that had emptied of ranch hands an hour before.

Oslo, the cook, shot him his usual surly look of greeting before he turned back to the double sink to wash a skillet. Chance shucked his sheepskin, then grabbed a cup and poured himself some coffee from the server before he sat down. He took a sip, then noticed that all three of his friends were staring at him in avid expectation. His "Well, who turned out to be the big winner?" brought him a round of disgruntled looks.

"Hell, Chance, we don't give a rat's right leg about poker when somethin' like that little blonde prances in with fire in her eyes." He leaned closer, his face alive with excitement. "An' what was that she said?" He raised his voice to what was an astonishingly good falsetto, thick with sexy innuendo. "You *know* what I've come for."

All three men responded to Rusty's imitation by growling, hooting and table slapping. Chance stared in disbelief until they hushed to an expectant silence, all hunched forward as if ready to indulge in the cowboy equivalent of locker-room talk.

Chance had no explanation for the heat that surged to the tops of his ears. Or the baffling outrage he felt on Erin's behalf at being taken for one of the loose women he was reputed to have intimate knowledge of. It stunned him to think that these men, whom he'd known since childhood, who were all happily married to good women, didn't know a good woman when they saw one. Because even if Chance had never liked Erin and loathed having to share his niece with her, he'd always known she was a good woman.

"Come on, Chance," Sam goaded good-naturedly, "'fess up. You can't keep a woman as hot lookin' as that one hid under yer covers for long."

Chance's cup hit the table with a resounding crack, splattering coffee in all directions.

"She's never been under my covers," he stated, barely keeping his temper as he emphasized the words. "She never will be." He paused, frowning more fiercely at the grins his friends were suppressing so poorly. "She's Meri's Aunt Erin. From Chicago. Remember?" As much as it galled him, he felt compelled to keep talking until he banished those ever-widening grins. "Someone told her Fayrene and I were living in sin, so she rushed out here to take Meri away. Somehow, it all got twisted around, so now she's staying on till Meri's birthday."

Not a single face sobered, so he declared, "That's all," in black frustration, and got up and grabbed his coat. He slammed out of the cookhouse to the aggravating sound of laughter.

Rusty was the first to wind down after Chance was gone. "Well, boys, get yer best suits pressed."

Bob was a bit slower than Sam to catch on. "How come?"

"How come?" Rusty looked at him as if he'd lost his senses. "Are you blind? Chance Lafferty is as ripe as any man I ever seen to put his neck in the marriage noose." He elbowed Sam, who couldn't seem to stop chuckling. "When he does, he'll need his best friends there to hold him steady."

CHANCE RETURNED to the house just as Erin was pouring the last of the bacon grease into the coffee can on the back of the stove. The kitchen was fragrant with the delicious smells of eggs, bacon, hash browns and cinnamon. Hanging up his coat, he noticed the table was set for four but that Fayrene was nowhere in sight.

"Where's Fayrene?"

Meri answered. "She didn't like the smell of the bacon. She got sick."

Erin shot him an amused look as she set the platter of bacon on the table. "I think it's morning sickness. I took her some hot tea and crackers."

"Morning sickness," he repeated as if he was having trouble grasping the words. He pulled off his Stetson, then expelled a breath that sounded world-weary as he raked his fingers through his dark hair. "What next?" he grumbled as he hung his hat on a wall peg.

"Breakfast is next, Uncle Chance," Meri said helpfully, coming over to take his hand and lead him to the head of the table. "Aunt Erin said we were all too hungry to wait on cimum rolls this morning, so she's baking us a coffee cake."

He'd barely sat down before Erin placed a bowl of hash browns in the center of the table, followed in seconds by a platter fluffed high with scrambled eggs. A plate of buttered toast sat between them and the bacon platter.

"Meri said you liked your eggs scrambled," Erin explained as she and Meri sat down on either side of him.

Chance gave a halfhearted smile and mumbled something, too tired from the long night and disruption that morning to fight the unwanted notion that the three of them were sitting down to breakfast like the "real" family little Meri seemed to want.

CHANCE WENT TO BED until noon to sleep off his long night, leaving Erin and Meri to their own devices. Fayrene put in an appearance at ten o'clock. She'd showered, combed her hair and applied makeup. Dressed in a sweater and jeans, she looked far more capable of facing the world than she had earlier. That she'd blossomed from a slob into a siren didn't escape Erin's notice. Fayrene thanked Erin for the tea and crackers, but in a way that was more a dismissal than an opening for further conversation. She settled on the sofa beneath an afghan to watch the latest episode of "Days of Our Lives."

Figuring to reimburse Chance later, Erin made a long-distance call to her best friend in Chicago and gave her a list of things she'd need from home for her two-week visit. She forestalled Mitzi's none-too-subtle probe for more than a brief explanation of why she'd changed her mind about bringing Meri home by adding several more items to the list.

"You want your laptop and the stack of printout pages by the printer?" Mitzi asked incredulously. "Look, Erin, I saw Meri's picture of that cowboy hunk. With him around, I'd definitely prefer to do hands-on research for my manuscript rather than write it."

"Very funny, Mitz. You'll find some household money in an envelope by the plates in the cupboard. There should be more than enough to pay the UPS charge."

They talked a few minutes more about which house plants to water and what to do with the mail, then hung up.

Lunch was a bit more interesting than breakfast, because Fayrene joined them. She managed to eat some of the chili Erin had made, and she pounced on the cornbread. After getting out a squeeze bottle of chocolate topping, Fayrene devoured more than half the contents of the pan.

The high point of the afternoon came when Chance was about to give Erin a tour of the ranch buildings.

They were searching for Meri's mittens when they heard a car drive up. Meri scampered to the window to look out before she turned back and said sulkily, "It's just Sharon."

From the expression of Meri's face, it was obvious Sharon wasn't someone Meri looked forward to seeing. Erin realized why moments later when, without knocking, Sharon swept in, a wide smile on her face and eyes only for Chance. Quite tall, Sharon was model slim, and one of the most striking brunettes Erin had ever seen. Didn't Chance know any ordinary-looking women? she wondered. She watched as Sharon strode directly to Chance, threw her arms around his neck and kissed him flat on the mouth.

Chance froze, shocked to his toes by Sharon's very public kiss. He couldn't even close his eyes for those first stunned moments. His hands rose reflexively to get a grip on Sharon's narrow waist so that he could push her away. Unfortunately she chose that precise second to plaster herself so tightly against him that he staggered back against the counter and his arms came around her. Alarmed, he yanked his hands back to try again, but Sharon started working his mouth over so ardently that he jerked back and cracked his head on the cupboard door.

"God Almighty, woman," he wheezed, finally managing to apply enough leverage to Sharon's waist to get some space. His gaze streaked to Erin; he was not surprised that her eyes were cat-narrow. That maddening little smile coupled with the slight arch of her brow told him he'd lost whatever respectability he'd gained.

A movement from the doorway got his attention. Drawn by the commotion, Fayrene had rushed to the kitchen and stood there, the sudden dulling of her eyes telling him she'd been hoping for a different visitor.

"When are we going, Uncle Chance?" Meri whined, the puckering of her brow communicating her impatience.

Sharon still clung like a burr and Erin stood by watching. When her arched brows climbed a fraction higher, he realized she expected him to do something.

What, he didn't know. In those silent heartbeats of time, he came to the awful realization that every female in the room wanted something from him. His niece wanted to go outside, Fayrene wanted sympathy, Sharon wanted him in her bed, and Erin wanted Meri. It was a damned female conspiracy, and everything male in him bucked against it.

He looked down into Sharon's limpid dark eyes, so furious at her outrageous performance that he felt like tossing her headfirst into a snowbank.

Erin watched closely as he reached up and pried Sharon's hands from his shoulders. He set her away from him with a glare that warned her to keep her distance. Erin couldn't tell if his pique was because Sharon had embarrassed him, or if he didn't welcome that kind of greeting from her under any circumstances.

Chance's gaze shot past Sharon to Fayrene. "Call that husband of yours, or I will."

Meri fell under a less stern look, but stern nonetheless. Chance spared her two words: "Nap time."

At last his gaze sought Erin's and fixed there for several meaningful seconds. Erin met it without flinching, struck by the amusing idea that Chance Lafferty was a victim of himself somehow. She quickly surveyed the three other females whose unhappy faces registered varying degrees of what she strongly suspected was calculated hurt. That those unhappy looks had been used on Chance before with some degree of success was evident by the near-identical petulance that came to all three when Chance's attention remained stubbornly elsewhere.

Erin's amusement was cut short when she looked back at Chance and he made the quiet declaration, "Your car keys are still in my coat pocket."

With that, he stalked to the door, grabbed his coat and Stetson, then slammed out of the house, escape the only thing on his mind.

Chapter Three

ERIN PUT a small log on the fire, then resumed pacing the living room. Chance had virtually abandoned them for the entire afternoon. Though he'd called from town to assure Meri he wasn't angry with her and explained to Erin that he'd gotten tied up in town and wouldn't be back till late, Erin took a dim view of how long he'd been gone.

Business, he'd said. Meri might have been fooled, but Erin had seen Sharon race to her car and chase after him. Business probably consisted of him and Sharon having a hot time someplace. He'd seemed shocked and embarrassed by Sharon's arrival earlier that day, but he must have gotten over it quickly enough. What aggravated Erin more than anything was that she was experiencing something that felt suspiciously like envy.

At least Fayrene was gone. She'd obeyed Chance's order to call her husband, but she'd played the martyr to the hilt. The burly giant in overalls who'd pounded on the door an hour or so later, bashfully apologizing to a teary Fayrene, was her husband of ten months. Finally he'd swept her up in his big arms and carried her to his pickup, the two of them oblivious to Erin, who hurried after them and tossed Fayrene's bags into the back of the truck.

That had left her and Meri to tour the ranch buildings. Erin had been surprised that Meri knew so much about the place. It was comforting to know that Chance had restricted Meri from certain areas and that the child didn't trifle with his safety rules, not even with Erin present.

Meri's abbreviated tour consisted of several closed doors, which she pointed at, and several large animals—two bulls, a stallion and four mares—which Erin was allowed to observe only from a distance. She'd been told sternly by the child that she was not to climb to the barn loft or play on the machinery. However, Meri did take her to peek through a low crack in the wall of one of the calving barns—also off-limits without Chance—but there were no cows giving birth that afternoon.

Oslo, who reminded Erin of Oscar, the Grouch, on "Sesame Street," greeted them gruffly at the cookhouse, but got out the special cookie jar he kept for Meri and put a pitcher of milk on the table. Then he locked the door and, setting up a Candy Land game, spent the better part of an hour playing the child's game with them.

Afterward, Erin and Meri returned to the house, but not before Meri took her aunt by the shed for a supply of birdseed, suet and corn, which they used to refill the bird feeders at the side of the house. Erin was impressed by the salt blocks set out for deer, and ears of corn set on spikes for the squirrels and the little wheels studded with corn so that the squirrels could play while they foraged. The trees were hung with seed balls and fruit and vegetable peels to entice other small animals. When they'd finished refilling the feeders, Erin and Meri went into the house to view from a window the antics of the creatures who ventured out for late-afternoon snacks.

They'd eaten a supper Oslo sent over, then spent the evening watching videos. Chance had called to wish Meri good-night just as Erin was about to read her a bedtime story, but Meri had hung up the phone before Erin could talk to him.

Erin finally stopped pacing and wandered over to the sofa. She sat down, leaning tiredly against the cushions.

CHANCE SLOWED the pickup and turned off the snowy highway. Beside him on the seat was the bookstore bag containing five Erin Taylor historical-romance novels. The woman at the bookstore had told him enthusiastically that there were eight in all—she'd read every one three times—and that a ninth was due out in a month. The woman had been so excited to find a man in the romance section of the store that she'd been annoyingly helpful.

He'd slipped into the store to escape Sharon, who'd followed him to town. Because he'd gone directly to the back of the store to keep from being seen, he realized only after he'd selected a book at random off the shelf that he'd picked up one of *those* books. A harried glance around confirmed he was in the romance section.

Just as he shoved the book back on the shelf the book cover next to it caught his eye. *Nothing but Trouble*, by Erin Taylor. He picked it up. That was when the salesclerk cornered him. Recognizing that he had no chance of politely withstanding the woman's zeal, he'd given up gracefully, leaving the store several minutes later with a bag of Erin Taylor books.

In no particular rush to head home, he ended up at the small house he owned in town, careful to park his pickup out of sight in the garage. Once inside, he turned up the heat, grabbed a beer, then headed for the sofa and TV remote. He made a call to Meri and let Erin know he wouldn't be back until late, but the moment he hung up the phone, he noticed the book bag nearby. Curiosity made him haul it to the couch to look over the books in private.

Nothing but Trouble, he noted, began with a quote from Job: "Yet man is born to trouble as surely as sparks fly upward." Feeling a special affinity for that particular Bible verse, he began reading. He was barely aware of the winter gloom of afternoon dimming to full dark as he read about a cynical burned-out gunman and a hill-country woman on the run from her backwoods family and fiancé. The story was both touching and funny. He reached the end, a little stunned at how well written it was, a little proud to know the author, when he realized it was almost ten o'clock. Luckily, a few chapters back, he'd stopped to make himself a sandwich and call Meri to wish her good-night. But he'd never meant to stay away this long.

It hadn't been very hospitable of him to leave Erin to her own devices on her first day at the ranch. He cringed when he recalled that he'd kept her car keys. She must think he was holding her prisoner. Still, he felt more lighthearted than guilty. He tossed the book back into the bag and cleaned up, careful to check the house one last time and turn down the heat.

Thinking about the book on the drive home, it dawned on him that the description of the gunfighter,

Ford Harris, could just as easily have described him. Tall, overlong black hair and green eyes with tiny chips of gold up close. The wide-shouldered, lean-hipped, rawhide-tough description would be a boost to any man's ego, but Chance dismissed that. What struck him were the other descriptions—the more personal ones. The mannerisms, the thoughts and emotions. Somehow she'd managed to describe the under-the-skin man he believed himself to be.

His mind wandered back over the love scenes, sparse, tastefully done, and more emotional than physical. It had been a hell of a book. And seeing so much of himself in the hero gave him a strange rush, until he realized it had to be pure coincidence. Still, was Ford Harris Erin's idea of the perfect hero for herself, or was he simply the perfect hero for her book?

Another, more exciting thought occurred to him. If Erin had written those love scenes herself, then she wasn't quite the prissy spinster he'd always believed.

Chance let himself in the back door quietly, then pried off his boots and hung up his coat and Stetson. The only light in the house came from the fireplace in the living room, so he headed there. Erin had fallen asleep sitting on the sofa, her head resting against the cushions, her blond hair tousled. Her ivory skin was rosy from the heat of the fire. Her lips, slightly parted, were as lush and inviting as the description of rose petals from a sappy love poem.

His gaze traced the natural arch of those brows she used so effectively to chasten and followed the delicate line of her nose to her lips, but then toured on, taking account of the curves beneath her sweater and jeans.

She'd taken off her boots, and her sock-clad feet looked as small and cuddly as a child's. She was like that all over, he decided—small, delicate, cuddly.

Chance hunkered down beside her right knee, unable to take his eyes off her as the peaceful crackling of the fire soothed him. The room was warm enough to make him drowsy, and the enticing sight of Erin thickened his blood with something heavy and sweet, something more than the lust he expected. His fingers sought and gently lifted her hand before he quite realized he'd done it. As his hand closed around hers, her lashes fluttered, then floated up to reveal the slumberous blue of her eyes.

The sleepy recognition and welcome in their dreamy depths sent a shock through him. His shock deepened when her fingers tightened on his and pulled him forward.

In that instant he knew she wasn't quite awake. He also knew that he was curious enough about Ford Harris to take advantage. He let her pull him close. Time slowed to nothing when his mouth was no more than a finger space from hers. Urgency goaded him to seize those soft lips, but the tenderness he felt just as strongly compelled him to ease his mouth slowly over hers.

Lord, it was heaven to taste those lips, he thought as his arms slid around her and he lowered her until she was flat on her back beneath him on the sofa.

Erin was dreaming in technicolor. She'd never had a dream that was so starkly, so impossibly, real. The smell of wood smoke, outdoors and man filled her nostrils. She felt the pleasing weight of a hard male body, but it was his plundering mouth that went beyond anything she'd ever dared imagine. If a real man had ever kissed her like this . . .

Callused fingers, so hot they scorched her skin, prowled down her sweater and tunneled upward and under her bra to trifle with her breast. It wasn't until she realized her hands had wandered down to take a good grip of leather and belt buckle that reality began to overtake the sensual deluge that had swept her away.

Several things occurred to her. The hard male body and rapacious mouth were no erotic dream. The warm fingers that went about their business with such finesse—wonderful as they were—were also no dream. No dream, either, was the incredible fact that her mouth met the other with equal skill, or that her eager fingers had managed to unbuckle the belt and dispatch three buttons on a denim fly.

Chance felt a different tremor go through Erin. He felt the mental explosion several seconds before Erin's lips began to stiffen. Her small clever fingers, which had nearly reached their goal, clenched, as if she'd lost track of them and was testing to see where they were by what they were doing. He heard the small helpless sound, worlds different from the helpless sounds she had been making moments ago.

Tides of near-pain washed over him. Disappointment for sure, considering the state of his body. Dread was also there, expanding exponentially as he forced himself to tear his mouth from hers and, with no small effort, slide his hand away from the delectable place it had been. His blood was roaring so loudly in his ears he was nearly deafened by it.

A volcano was about to erupt, he was certain. He could tell by the harsh little gusts of breath heaving the small body beneath him. He could also tell, as those little gusts got deeper and faster, that he'd been selected as this night's sacrifice to appease the volcano gods.

He turned his face toward hers, seeing her crimson-stained profile as she stared at the ceiling as if in shock. Her ongoing silence made his gut churn. What was she thinking? Her eyes closed, then wrinkled in spasm. She started to speak, paused to swallow, then tried again.

"Would you mind?" Her prim voice was a hoarse whisper. The slight movement of her trapped hands gave him a clue to what she wanted but hadn't—or couldn't—put to words.

Hoping he guessed right, he started to shift his weight off her, but found she had such a death grip on his jeans that he gained her little more than an inch of space. He watched with a kind of morbid fascination as the crimson stain darkened to deep red. She was completely still now, barely breathing, though her eyes were still scrunched tightly.

He noted her teeth were clenched just as tightly when she said in a strangled voice, "My...ring seems to be...caught."

Sure enough, he remembered that ring on her right hand. Because he'd shifted his weight to the outside edge of the sofa, the ringless left hand and the elbow above it were pinned beneath him. She should have been able to pull her right hand free since that arm was no longer under him. But a tiny experimental tug assured them both that the ring had indeed caught on something. And because that hand had been the more adventurous of the two, it had snagged on either a button hole or the soft cotton knit of his BVDs.

Erin was mortified. Since she could move her ringed hand in no more than a limited way because of the sensitive nature of its placement, she concentrated on easing it upward. Chance's swift intake of breath stopped her. Her ring was evidently caught on Chance's most personal article of clothing.

Brazening it out, she opened her eyes and glared up at Chance's guarded expression. Humor at her predicament lit the gold chips in his eyes, spearing through her humiliation to her temper. The shallow curve of lips she gave him was anything but lighthearted.

"Well, Mr. Lafferty, you're the expert in these matters."

Her sarcasm doused his amusement. "Expert, huh?" He was all set to respond to the insult when a tremor quaked through her.

Her temper blazed higher and she gritted through clenched teeth, *"Do something!"*

Before he could untangle his fingers from her hair to do anything, she expelled a huffy breath. With more strength than he thought possible, her slender body heaved upward, bucking against him. His balance—his body was half on her, half on the edge of the sofa—was thrown off. His hand was barely clear of her hair when she bucked more forcefully. The added thrust of her trapped hand sent him backward.

Like fresh-cut timber rolling off a semi, Chance went over the edge of the sofa, unable to break his fall before he hit the floor. Still snagged by her ring and the forearm Chance had behind her neck, Erin was yanked off to land inelegantly atop him. The center sofa cushion went with them, wedging their hips against the thick base of the coffee table.

Frantic to extricate herself from her ignominious position, Erin braced one knee on the floor and managed to lift herself enough to unhook her ring. Her escape was thwarted by the big hands that suddenly lashed her hips against the hard cradle of his.

Anger and something a bit more unsettling was communicated by the grip on her backside. Erin stilled. She lifted her head, her wide gaze traveling up Chance's shirtfront to his face. His fingers flexed, hauling her up his body until her face was directly over the unyielding set of his.

Without missing a beat, he seized the back of her head and pulled her face down to his. There was no tenderness in his kiss this time, just mindless hunger that took charge as he devoured her soft mouth as quickly and efficiently as he devoured her resistance. Any pride or pretense was cast away as Erin pushed her hands up to his head and found fistfuls of luxurious black hair to gain more leverage. She was on fire, and so far gone that she didn't understand why Chance broke off the kiss and held her away as they both gasped for air.

Chance's eyes opened, their green a forest fire as they blazed up into hers. The anger in them was baffling.

"I don't want to hear any self-righteous wisecracks about *my* vast experience," he said grimly.

Still immersed in a sea of sensuality, Erin nodded stupidly, though she was still too fogged to grasp what he was saying. Her gaze was drawn to those fantastic lips; she felt like a famished diner partway through a sumptuous meal who'd been cruelly yanked from the table. Her will long gone, she'd have agreed to anything he said to keep him happy and get back to the feast.

But it didn't happen. Her world spun. Erin found herself thrust aside, abandoned on the strip of carpet between the sofa and coffee table. Her gasp of dismay as she realized Chance had deserted her couldn't be heard above the purposeful sound of his footsteps as he crossed the living room and ascended the stairs.

Erin watched him go, sagging back against the sofa cushion, frustrated to the point of tears.

Chapter Four

ONE THING Chance knew for sure. Erin Taylor was trouble. Never before had he come across a woman with the potential for calamity that she had. Their ill-fated tangle on the sofa merely underscored the high level of personal danger she posed for him.

He'd never been kissed down to the bare wires before, and his body still sizzled. Common sense was elusive. He couldn't seem to forget that there was a hot-tempered, hot-blooded blonde in the cherub bed. Alone. How in hell he was going to keep her there, alone, for the next two weeks was beyond the limit of his suddenly overactive imagination.

Chance lay in his own bed, listening to the familiar creaking of the old house as he tried to sort out his thoughts. For all her passion, Erin wasn't the kind of woman a man dallied with. It was his bad luck that her kind was for marrying. The idea wasn't as scary as it should have been, and that didn't bode well.

He sat up, pummeled his pillow, then flopped back down, determined to sleep. No fancy little blonde was going to sashay into his comfortable life, upset his hormones and instantly qualify for a marriage proposal.

Restless, he grabbed a fat corner of pillow to position his head, then froze. His hand had closed over something just as soft little more than an hour before and his senses hadn't forgotten.

Chance let out a frustrated sigh that ended on a heart-felt curse.

BREAKFAST THE NEXT morning was an ordeal. Erin was evidently an early riser. She was also a great cook, and when she set a pan of homemade cinnamon rolls next to his steak and eggs, Chance's bad mood went black. His first full look into her glacial blue eyes warned him that despite the feast she'd placed before him, her mood was just as dark. It was a good thing Meri wasn't up yet.

Erin hadn't slept well. Mortification was too mild a word for what she felt about her part in their romp on the sofa. Her pique at being deserted so cold-bloodedly was just as strong. He had some nerve, ignoring her now while he stuffed himself with her rolls like a surly bear. She picked up her knife and fork and attacked her own breakfast steak.

"You don't have to get up early and cook for me," Chance grumbled, for the life of him unable to sound even remotely pleasant. When he added, "You're a guest," he'd meant to soften his tone, but that came out just as bad.

Erin hacked at her steak, unaware she was reducing it to half-inch squares. "I don't mind, Mr. Lafferty. I can hardly accept your gracious invitation to visit without making some effort to show my appreciation for your hospitality." The brittle smile she gave him was received with ill grace.

He fixed her with a suspicious glare. "I don't care much for poison politeness this early in the morning. If you're unhappy about last night, I'd rather you said so straight out." He watched the anger in her eyes flare higher and felt a surge of his own temper.

"Very well. I'm unhappy about last night."

Her prim tone nettled him. "Which part?" he shot back, then could have kicked himself when he saw her anger give way to a magnificent blush. Hellfire! She was as worked up over him as he was over her. Moments ticked by. He sensed she wouldn't berate him for taking advantage of her when she'd been half-asleep. That left the part where he'd started something he'd not finished.

The tiny flash of helplessness in those baby blues told him he'd guessed correctly. He might have been more upset were it not for the savage male pride that stormed over him.

Which she deflated. "I'd appreciate it if Cowboy Casanova looked elsewhere for his late-night entertainment."

The remark stung. Cussedness made him give her a slow arrogant smile. "As I recall, Cowboy Casanova was gallant enough to leave Miss Priss's virtue intact." He paused, then added, "Maybe that was his mistake."

For a precarious moment, he was sure she would explode. That grand blush was now a scarlet mask. The steak knife trembled in her hand and her eyes blazed an ominous blue. He could tell the effort it took to get her temper under control and admired the hell out of her for it. Particularly since he kept the steak knives sharp. The stormy seconds passed, but the electricity between them was high voltage.

One elegant brow winged upward and froze into an arch of disapproval. "Be careful, Mr. Lafferty, that you don't choke on all that male pride."

It was a poor time to get tickled over her priggish tone of voice and the faint pucker of her lips that made him think of sour pickles. Something way past ornery in his nature shoved him over the line. He leaned toward her and said in a low drawl, "It's not male pride that's chokin' me."

Her silverware hit the table. "You may be right. Especially if I can get a dish towel around your neck."

Chance chuckled, pleased at the tiny tremble at the corner of her mouth that indicated she was trying not to smile. There was still plenty of fire in her eyes, but her sense of humor was winning out.

Which made her more appealing than ever. His appetite, even for those tasty rolls, suddenly vanished. If he didn't pull back now and get out of the house, he'd do something simpleminded. The idea that she'd been here only twenty-four hours and there were still thirteen long days until Meri's birthday was the sobering reminder he needed.

He drew back, gulped the last of his coffee and stood. His abrupt "You're a damned fine cook, Erin, thanks" sounded gruff, but there was no help for it. Erin Taylor, temper and all, was just more temptation than he could trust himself to resist.

ERIN COULDN'T UNDERSTAND why she was disappointed by Chance's remote manner during the next days. She didn't want any replays of the sofa incident, so she should have been pleased that he spent so much time away from the house.

On the second day, her things arrived from Chicago, but the big UPS truck left more boxes than she'd expected. She lugged them from the kitchen, hurrying to get them out of sight and into her room before Chance saw them and got the idea she was moving in on him. She'd felt bad enough when she'd realized he wouldn't have stayed away from the house so much with Meri there if she wasn't around. So she tried to absent herself when he came in, giving him as much time alone with Meri as she could. After all, this was his time with their niece.

Things went as smoothly as could be expected until the third day. Chance was somewhere outside, and Meri had just settled for her nap. Erin got out the first half of her new manuscript to go over at the kitchen table when a car pulled in. A few moments later, the back door swung open.

Sharon swept in, the wide smile she gave Erin so phony it was laughable. Certain she was in for some kind of up-close reconnaissance, Erin set aside the stack of pages.

"Got any coffee?" Sharon asked, then pulled out a chair and sat down as if she expected to be waited on.

Erin got up to fetch a cup. But not before she caught the superior lift of Sharon's chin as the leggy brunette gave her the once-over.

"Your name is Sharon?" she asked brightly, deciding to do some up-close reconnaissance of her own.

"Sharon McCandless," she said with a pretentious purr that suggested she considered herself a woman of no small consequence in the state of Montana. Erin turned around to look suitably impressed.

"Cream and sugar?" she asked. Sharon nodded and she delivered them with the coffee and sat down.

"I hear Fayrene went back to her farmer," Sharon remarked.

Surprised she would bring up a subject that would remind Erin of the way Chance had fended Sharon off in front of them all, Erin nodded, opening her eyes wide and looking as awestruck as she could. "Chance is certainly impressive when he's irritated."

Sharon tipped her head back. "Oooh, he sure is," she cooed, then gave a fond chuckle.

It was time to move things along, Erin decided. Sharon was definitely irritating her. "You sound like you know him pretty well."

Sharon pounced on that. "We've been neighbors and close friends since I was a baby. Everyone's always assumed that . . . well, you know, we'd someday . . ."

Erin noted she hadn't dared use the word "marry." She forged ahead. "Well, I imagine you know that Chance and I share custody of our niece. If you and Chance do marry, it might be better if Meri spends more time here," she lied, thinking, *over my dead body,* as she gave an unhappy sigh. "I would miss Meri terribly, of course, but every child is better off with two parents in the same household."

Erin didn't believe that was true in every case, but it wouldn't hurt Sharon to think so. Meri normally disliked no one, but she clearly disliked and resented Sharon. Erin had to know if there was a reason.

"Weeell," Sharon started, "we wouldn't be her *real* parents anyway, so there wouldn't be much cause to drag ou—I mean, extend her visits. Besides, once Chance has children of his own, other people's kids won't be as fascinating. He might see her from time to time, but . . ." She shook her head with a try at regret that fell flat.

Erin's blood pressure shot skyward, so she took a calming sip of coffee. Meri didn't like Sharon because Sharon didn't like her. As far as Erin was concerned, that made Sharon a selfish coldhearted witch.

Feeling a little witchy herself now, Erin forced a smile and concocted an outright lie to get rid of the woman quickly. "Oh, that's too bad, but I'm sure you're right. By the way, would you mind keeping an eye on Meri while I dash off to town? I need to pick up a few essentials. It shouldn't take longer than an hour or two."

From the abrupt sobering of Sharon's remarkable features, Erin could tell she was appalled at the idea of watching Meri. Sharon did manage to fake an admirable look of disappointment.

"Oh, I've got to get back home. I didn't really have much time to stop, but I just had to see how you were doing. I imagine it's awfully lonely and boring out here for a city girl like you." She got up as if her chair was spring-loaded and hurried toward the door. "Tell Chance I stopped by and that I said he needs to call me today about Saturday night."

With that, Sharon was off. Erin set her cup down, residual anger making her drum her fingers on the tabletop.

CHANCE WATCHED from the kitchen end of the hall that led to the game room and his office. He could tell by Erin's rigid posture and the drumming of her fingers that her temper was hot. Because he'd heard every word of her conversation with Sharon, his temper was running a little hot, too. Sharon had finally revealed what he'd suspected for a long time, but it had taken Erin to get it out of her.

"I wonder if Sharon would have any ideas on who sent you that letter."

Erin was so startled by Chance's voice behind her that she shot to her feet and spun around.

"I thought you were outside," she said, unnerved by his sudden appearance.

Chance entered the kitchen and walked to the counter to pour himself some coffee. "You were upstairs with Meri when I came in to do paperwork."

"Then you heard," she said as he turned toward her and leaned back against the counter. His level gaze revealed nothing, and her chin lifted defiantly. "If you marry that selfish little—" Erin cut herself off, alarmed at what she almost said. If Chance married Sharon, she'd have Meri to herself, but it stunned her to realize she'd be as heartbroken as Meri not to have Chance in her life. The thought of Chance Lafferty marrying anyone—of *looking* at any other woman with lust in those fabulous green eyes—suddenly made her sick at heart.

Chance watched her calmly. "It's never been my plan to marry Sharon. And even if I did, she couldn't come between Meri and me." He decided to bring up the subject that had troubled him all morning, ever since the foreman mentioned that his five-year-old son was being enrolled in the kindergarten class that would start in the fall. "You're the only one who could come between Meri and me."

There was no anger in Chance's voice, just a quiet declaration that sent tender pain through her heart. She'd seen how deeply he loved Meri, and it hurt to know that he seemed to think she was as oblivious to it as she'd been when she'd first arrived. Chance wasn't quite the man her sister had led her to believe—at least when it came to Meri, he wasn't. Perhaps it was time to let him know.

"I wouldn't do that, Chance."

His "You might not mean to" baffled her.

"How?"

"Next year, Meri will turn five. Old enough for kindergarten. I assume you plan for her to go to school in Chicago. That leaves summers with me out here, if you allow it."

"I think that sounds . . . reasonable." It was hard to say in the face of Chance's calm expression. Particularly since she sensed right away that he was covering pain.

"It's a long time between summers," was all he said, and Erin didn't know how to respond. The alternative—allowing Meri to attend school here and shortening her Chicago visits to the summer months and winter holidays—wasn't something she wanted for herself, either.

Silence dominated the kitchen for several moments.

"Will you let things go on as they have for another year?"

Erin wanted to tell him that she really did regret what would have to happen. She nodded her agreement to his request, but her "I'm sorry" seemed inadequate.

Chance took it well, if wordlessly, as he headed for his office. Erin watched him go, wishing she could think of a realistic way to give them both what they wanted.

HE COULD DRAG Erin back to court. But he'd have to prove she was despicable before a judge would take away her primary custody and give it to him.

He could get her to move to Montana. Hell, she could write her books anywhere, couldn't she? Chance warmed to the idea until he considered how citified she was. She probably thrived on the noise, traffic and human hoards in Chicago. Small-town Montana with its sparse population and small-scale entertainments would likely bore bright sophisticated Erin to tears in a week. No, he decided, she'd never consider moving here.

That also spared him from sacrificing his freedom by offering her marriage. If she would hate small-town Montana, she'd detest living the rest of her life on a working ranch, miles from shopping and big-city attractions. A delicate little thing like Erin, with her peaches-and-cream complexion and salon manicure, would loathe the great outdoors. Ranch chores would be out of the question. Besides, he was no prize catch for a city girl, not when most times of the year he came in stinking of sweat, horses and cow manure, regularly tracked in dirt or worse and had been known to fall asleep in a chair or the bathtub after a particularly grueling day.

The image of Erin's face, lit by firelight and passion, invaded his dismal thoughts. The wave of desire that flowed hotly through him made him close his eyes. She'd felt so right, her lips so lush and willing, that he craved the taste and feel of her again. But no matter how often he tried to dismiss his feelings for her as lust, the denial that clamored in his heart grew louder.

He lusted after Erin Taylor, but he wanted her in deeper ways, more high-minded ways. He liked that she was smart and perceptive, that she was a good mother to Meri and was no-nonsense about the things a good woman ought to be. She'd made a success of herself with her writing, and he found the mystery of how she thought up her stories—he'd read another of her books—intriguing. Erin was more than he'd thought to look for or require in a woman, but as the days went by, she was fast establishing the standard for his ideal mate.

Chance slumped lower in the desk chair, deep in thought. The bad part about finally getting straight in his mind how his ideal woman would be was that the ideal woman would likely not see him and what he had to offer as *her* ideal.

ERIN COULDN'T concentrate on the manuscript, so she decided on a walk in the snow-bright afternoon sun. The air was frigid, but inhaling it was like catching a breath of heaven after the smog of Chicago. Curiosity drew her to the stable where a few of the new foals were. Once inside, she lingered at a stall, admiring the spindly-legged baby with the charcoal face and speckled rump. Unable to coax the youngster close enough to touch, she rested her arms on the top rail and quietly watched the little one eye her from the other side of its mother.

The barn door opened, the sound spooking the foal. Chance strode down the long aisle, a corner of his mouth curving.

"I hope it's all right to visit the foals," she said, easing away from the stall as he walked up.

"As long as his mama doesn't get riled, there's no harm." Chance reached over the top rail to rub the mare's cheek, then unlatched the stall door. "Want to get acquainted?"

Erin's face lit up. "Can I?" Her response pleased him—until he reminded himself that even city slickers weren't immune to the appeal of cute baby animals. He opened the door and stepped inside, nudging the mare back. Recognizing him, the colt ventured forward, butting his head against Chance's outstretched hand.

"Just step in slow and don't make any sudden moves."

Erin was careful to do as he said, allowing the colt to inspect her jacket and knit scarf until she dared to put out her hand and touch his neck. The soft fuzzy texture of his coat delighted her, and when she trailed her fingers along his cheek to his velvety muzzle, she couldn't suppress a soft "You little sweetheart." She leaned down and rubbed her check against his, but the foal promptly nabbed her scarf and jerked away. Erin came up laughing.

Chance watched as Erin gently reclaimed her scarf and scolded the foal in the silliest spate of baby talk he'd ever heard. The colt actually submitted to a hug as he pressed close for more attention. Clearly approving the stranger who treated her baby so adoringly, the mare ambled close for her share.

Chance looked on, feeling every touch of those small gentle hands as if she'd been touching him, instead of his horses. Every silly word sent talons of pleasure through him, and when Erin turned her delighted smile on him, his emotions got the better of him.

Erin was stunned by the raw heat in Chance's eyes. She was suddenly in his arms, with time for no more than a startled breath before his mouth descended to hers. The fire ignited by Chance's lips was as hot as it was welcome, and Erin responded wholeheartedly until Chance's mouth slid off hers and he buried his face in her hair. They clung to each other tightly, almost painfully.

"I don't want to be just another of your women." Erin was stunned she'd voiced the thought. When Chance stiffened, an awful suspicion stirred to life. She sensed his withdrawal and the suspicion defined itself in her mind. "But I'm not just another of your women, am I, Chance?"

Erin's frigid tone banished the offense he'd taken at her reference to his reputation. He realized he had a much bigger problem when she pushed him away and he saw her flushed face.

She answered her question before he could. "Of course I'm not another of your women. None of them get to decide how much or how little of Meri's time you can share."

"What the hell does sharing Meri's time have to do with us?" he asked, his gut jumping with alarm. Could she really have mistaken his move on her?

"Us?" she hissed. "You wouldn't know how to have an 'us' with a woman if you were permanently glued to her. Was that kiss supposed to make me think about moving to Montana?"

Erin could have bitten her tongue. She'd let slip what she'd been thinking about since their talk in the kitchen. She'd always wanted to live in the country, and Montana was about as country as you could get. She tried not to dwell on the thought that having an excuse to live in Chance Lafferty's vicinity made the idea irresistible.

Chance was still stuck on the "us" part. Forgetting the mare and foal, his voice was a shade too loud. "It's damned hard to have an 'us' with a hotheaded harpy—"

He was cut off when the mare, startled by his harsh tone, suddenly whirled and lashed out. His quick reflexes saved Erin from a nasty kick. He wasn't able to save himself, however, and the hoof connected with his thigh like a sledgehammer.

Erin grabbed him when he staggered against her, managing to yank him out of the stall and shut the door. Chance sagged against the rails, his face rigid with pain.

Erin hovered anxiously. "Are you all right?"

"I'll live," he said through gritted teeth.

"What can I do?"

Because his head was tipped down, his Stetson shielded his expression from her for several moments. His breathing slowly became less tortured and he cautiously massaged his leg.

"Chance?"

"I'm all right," he muttered, then carefully leaned some of his weight on his injured leg.

Erin was at his side, yanking his arm up and around her shoulder before he could get his balance, and he almost fell. Fresh pain made him suck in his breath, but he clamped down on his irritation. He was too big for petite Erin to be any kind of support, but if her eagerness to help meant a truce, he wasn't about to discourage her.

Getting to the house was painful. But by the time they stepped into the kitchen he could walk alone. He gingerly lowered himself on the nearest chair and was forced to submit to Erin's ministrations as she yanked off his hat and peeled him out of his coat. She loaded a dish towel with ice cubes from the freezer and had it pressed on his leg in record time.

"If I wanted you to move to Montana, I'd ask you straight out."

Erin's startled gaze met his.

"It would uncomplicate things for me if you would, but with you being a city girl, you'd be the one making the sacrifice." His look was intense. "Any shady intention in that damned kiss and the one the other night exists only in the suspicious imagination of a sexy little blonde who has no idea how irresistible she is," he grumbled, then added darkly, "And I *do* know what an 'us' is."

Erin suddenly found his disgruntled look vastly amusing, and she couldn't quite suppress the smile that bubbled up in response to his backhanded compliment. "Oh, yeah? What is an 'us'?" she challenged, then stepped back to lean against the counter to hear what he had to say.

"Damn it, woman." He adjusted the ice pack and paused to flex his leg before he muttered another curse. His gaze met hers. "An 'us' is what happens when two people take up space together and pay too much attention to a reckless kiss or two."

Erin's smile widened. "Paying too much attention to a reckless kiss or two, are you?" She gave him a sympathetic look. "Poor baby."

A dull flush tinted his features. "Step on over here and we'll see who's the poor baby."

Erin shook her head. "Not on a bet, cowboy. How's the leg doing?"

Chance cautiously flexed it again. "Better."

"How about an aspirin?"

"In the cupboard behind you."

Erin turned to get it and suddenly regretted teasing him. Despite his words, she could tell his leg still hurt. "Thanks for pushing me out of the way. I'm sorry the mare kicked you."

Chance grunted, apparently satisfied that she was, indeed, sorry. Erin filled a glass with water and carried it and the aspirin to him.

"Should you see a doctor?" she asked when he'd downed the aspirin.

"It's just bruised good, not broken."

Erin started to step away, but he caught her hand. The glint in his eyes was her only warning. Suddenly she was sitting across his good thigh, his big hands clamped on her waist. She braced her palms against his chest.

"This isn't a good idea," she said, but her insides were gyrating with excitement. Chance Lafferty was more compellingly handsome every time she looked at him, and the hot look in his eyes was about to burn her up. The feel of his hard-muscled thigh beneath her backside was giving her palpitations.

"I agree."

"Good. Let me up."

Chance ignored the order, which ended a little breathlessly. "I'd like to take you out to dinner Saturday night."

Her agreement was instant. Then she remembered Sharon's request to remind Chance to call her about Saturday night. "But I think Sharon McCandless has plans for you that evening."

"Sharon can get her own date."

"What about Meri?"

"Trudy Brooks, my foreman's daughter, already said she'd watch Meri. No reason to say no."

"Don't you think it would be a mistake?" she asked softly.

"We're way past mistake, lady." It was clear Chance was not too happy about it, and Erin liked that. A true predator wouldn't be bothered by how far things went or how fast. It occurred to her that both times Chance had kissed her he'd been cranky afterward. Most of the heroes in her books initially reacted to their heroines in much the same way. But was that just a plot device, or did real flesh-and-blood men act like that? For the first time, she wondered if she had too many fictitious notions about love.

"So, if we're past mistake, where are we now?" she wanted to know.

Chance glared at her. "Running damned close to out of hand."

In spite of that dark declaration, Chance still held her on his lap. The conflict she sensed in him made her bold.

"What happens after out of hand?"

His low "insanity, most likely" made her smile.

"You're such a flirt, Chance Lafferty." It amused her to tease him when he was out of sorts.

"And most times, that's all it's been. Simple flirting." The tightening of his fingers on her waist punctuated the words. "That bedpost up in my room doesn't have half the notches you think, Erin."

The utter seriousness in his eyes was convincing. God help her, she believed him. But whether it was because he was telling the truth, or because she didn't want him to be a Cowboy Casanova, she didn't know.

"Are you saying you're more the Celibate Sam type?"

He frowned mightily at the name. "Most times. But I'm no trembling virgin."

The high childish voice that intruded startled them both. "What's a tumbling virgin, Uncle Chance?"

Erin couldn't get off his lap fast enough. It helped that he practically shoved her off. As though seeing her aunt sitting on her uncle's lap was not at all remarkable, Meri came up and wrapped an arm around Chance's neck.

Ignoring Meri's question, Chance asked, "Have a nice nap, squirt?"

"Yup. But what's a tumbling virgin?" Meri repeated, determined to have an answer. She leaned over to force eye contact with Chance, blocking the silent appeal he was trying to send Erin.

Enjoying his predicament, Erin leaned back against the counter with her arms crossed and waited.

His desperate "Uh . . . honey, I don't think you heard tumbling virgin" amused Erin, but she nearly burst out laughing at Meri's stubbornly insistent, "Yup, I did."

Chance all but squirmed and Erin took pity on him. "I think he said tumbleweed version," she offered, earning a quick look of gratitude from Chance."

"Oh." Meri considered it. "What's that?"

"Something we were discussing," Chance informed her, rallying. "Grown-up stuff." He managed a stern look.

"Not for nosy ears?" the child asked, obviously repeating words Chance had used before.

Chance nodded. "How about letting your banged-up uncle go sit in the recliner a while?"

Meri obligingly stepped back, and Erin reached for the ice pack Chance handed her.

"How did you get banged up?" was the next question.

"One of the mama mares kicked me. I just need to sit someplace with some ice. Nothing too bad."

Meri seemed impressed and looked on sympathetically as Chance slowly stood and moved stiffly toward the living room. Erin followed, touched at the sight of Meri latching onto Chance's hand to give him support.

Chapter Five

CHANCE SPENT the rest of the day in the house. Erin was glad he was on hand, because it wasn't long after she'd made him a second ice pack before Rusty, one of the ranchers from the poker game, and his wife, Bess, stopped by.

"Thought you might be ready to meet some of the neighbors," Rusty said, introducing his dark-haired wife. They spent the next hour getting acquainted over the apple pie Bess brought.

Erin liked them both and was sorry when they left to get back to the twelve-year-old twin sons they predicted had been home alone long enough to get into mischief.

Their visit turned out to be the start of a steady stream of neighbors and townsfolk who stopped by. Erin didn't realize this was anything out of the ordinary until the third day. Chance had recovered from the mare's kick and had just come in from the calving sheds when they heard a pickup pull in.

"I didn't think there was anyone left who hadn't found some damn fool excuse to stop by," he grumbled as he yanked aside the curtain to look out. "Good. It's Oslo back from town."

Erin turned from where she stood at the counter, shredding lettuce for tacos. "Am I to understand that all this company is more than usual?" She felt the start of a smile when Chance scowled.

"Hell, we go the better part of the winter without seeing half of them," he informed her.

"You don't sound happy. Don't you like these people?" She knew this wasn't the case. Chance was very sociable. She'd been impressed to find he had so many close friends—most of them happily married.

"I like them fine when they mind their own business."

Erin flashed him a smile and his scowl deepened.

"Don't tell me you haven't caught on?" he said.

Erin saw the familiar hint of color along his cheekbones and glanced away to hide her amusement. She'd caught on all right. Chance's friends and neighbors were dying of curiosity about what might be going on between them. If his scowl was any indication, there might even be some matchmaking afoot.

"And the men are worse than the women," Chance declared, then stopped abruptly when the remark got Erin's full attention.

"Is that so? How?"

Chance pressed his lips into a stern line. Damned if he'd repeat to Erin the dozen or so variations on "When's the wedding?" Each of his friends had found some opportunity during their visits to ask him, from Rusty, who'd mouthed the words from across the room, to old man Hardy, who'd dragged him out to the porch. The Methodist minister hadn't said a word on the subject, but the beatific smile he'd bestowed on them both said it all.

"Chance?" Erin's gentle prompting jarred him from his reverie. "Why are the men worse than the women?"

When his brows snapped together and swooped low, she giggled.

The feminine sound slipped past Chance's defenses. He'd felt harassed by the not-so-subtle pressure of his friends and had made what he'd considered a successful effort to squelch his raging attraction to Erin. But looking at her now, seeing the laughter in her eyes, unraveled his resolve. And damn, he loved that smile of hers. It amazed him that something that small could give him such a deep-down good feeling.

He wanted the two weeks to be over so she'd go home; he never wanted her to leave. His gaze fell to her lips, and a craving came over him that made his knees quake.

"I'm going out," he announced.

Erin watched as he grabbed his coat and hat and fled the kitchen. Her good humor vanished. Clearly Chance's friends' matchmaking jokes had agitated the die-hard bachelor. It was equally clear that he didn't like being paired with her.

Troubled, she turned back to her meal preparations. She'd written about heroes and heroines who were perfect for each other, who at first glance experienced a mutual recognition of their mate for life. Erin had always hoped she would recognize her man in that elemental way, and he, her. But now that it seemed to have happened to her, it appeared to be a one-sided phenomenon.

SATURDAY NIGHT ARRIVED. Chance was eager to get to the restaurant. The sooner they got there and had their meal, the sooner it would be over. The heavy cows were about to overrun the calving sheds with deliveries, and he had a perfect excuse to spend as many hours away from Erin as he needed until Meri's birthday. Then Erin could go back to Chicago and leave him to enjoy Meri's visit in peace.

The thought sent his jittery insides into a slump. The peaceful days he'd convinced himself he wanted suddenly seemed lifeless and unappealing. Chance stopped fiddling with his string tie and glared at his reflection. He'd had a good life until Erin had barged in.

He repeated the thought like a litany. But he couldn't dispel the notion that after Erin, the good life he'd been so fond of would never again be enough.

ERIN LOVED the quaint restaurant Chance took her to. The menu at Lucy's boasted everything from Italian to seafood to Mexican, but the desserts were home-style pies and cakes. The lasagna Erin ordered was the best she'd ever had, better than anything she'd tasted at some of the top Chicago restaurants. Chance chose the spaghetti. Erin admired his skill with the pasta. Not one wayward spot of sauce ended up on his shirt.

They had a pleasant time, and lingered over coffee and dessert, talking about everything from the Montana cattle kings of the late 1800s to current state and national politics. Chance was a wonderful dinner partner. Erin couldn't help but feel disappointed when it was time to go. It was barely ten o'clock, but the only other nighttime entertainment she knew of was the movie house at the corner of the square. The last show had already started.

They'd reached Chance's car when Erin heard the distant thump of a bass guitar. A live band was playing somewhere, she realized.

"Where's that music coming from?" she asked Chance, then turned from the car to listen again. Chance heard the music, then stiffened.

"It's just the Bull Shoe," he mumbled as he glanced off in the direction of the music. Erin wasn't certain she'd heard right.

"Did you say the Bull Shoe?" Somehow, the name was familiar. Chance didn't answer until she tugged his sleeve, prompting a low "yes" from him. Erin cocked her head and listened again, now able to distinguish the notes of a country tune she'd heard before. Faintly humming along for a moment, she recognized the melody.

"Hey, that's a Garth Brooks song," she said, suddenly enthused.

"It's not Garth Brooks," he informed her brusquely.

"Well, of course it wouldn't be Garth himself, but it's a live country band. Could we go listen a while?"

The discomfort that crossed Chance's features puzzled Erin. Though his Stetson shaded most of his face from the streetlight, there was no mistaking the reluctant twist of his lips.

She suddenly remembered where she'd heard the name. "Kelly told me about the Bull Shoe. It's a bar," she said, and Chance relaxed a bit. Only to go tense again when she added, "She said it was authentic Montana, not just a cowboy bar for tourists." Erin's enthusiasm grew and her smile brightened. "Come on, Chance. It's too early to go home."

"Authentic Montana, huh? Your sister told you that?" Chance was incredulous. Perhaps if they drove past the bar, Erin would be able to see the kind of place it was and would change her mind about going in. Chance liked to go to the Bull Shoe himself, but he'd never taken a date to the place. The idea of taking very proper Erin anywhere near the rough-and-tumble bar was unthinkable.

Chance opened her car door and waited for her to get in, distracted momentarily by her graceful elegance as she did so. All that graceful elegance would be sorely out of place at the Bull Shoe. Hoping to dissuade her, he rounded the car and got behind the wheel. They were on the outskirts of the small town in front of the Bull Shoe in minutes.

The nightclub was a one-story building, built in the 1950s and originally little bigger than a shack. With haphazard additions built on over the years, its size now rivaled the strip mall near the highway. Short on appeal to more aesthetic architectural tastes, it was probably in violation of more than one building code. That those violations were overlooked was due to the bar's popularity and the fact that the owner was on the town council.

The huge parking lot was filled to capacity when they arrived. Chance found a spot to park on the street and turned to Erin without switching off the engine. But there was no evidence that her enthusiasm had dimmed. She was peering out her window, taking everything in.

"I didn't realize so many people lived around here," she remarked, then turned to him, her face aglow with excitement. "Shall we go?"

Chance reluctantly switched off the engine, trying to think of a way to discourage her. His gaze skimmed the above-the-knee hemline of her smart little flared skirt, her short leather vest and red silk shirt. She'd dressed Western tonight, casual for Lucy's as he'd suggested, but that outfit on her petite form might be trouble in the bar. As he looked from her shapely knees to her face and the riot of blond curls that haloed her head, he realized that if Erin Taylor wore an ankle-length tent tarp her presence would be just as disruptive.

He heaved a sigh and reached for her hand. "Are you sure you want to go in there?"

"Why wouldn't I be sure? The band sounds good. Kelly mentioned in her letters that of all the night spots she and Buck went to on the rodeo circuit, the Bull Shoe was her favorite."

Chance usually avoided bringing up the subject of Erin's younger sister, particularly when he'd realized that Erin seemed to be unaware of how wild her buckle-bunny sister had been. The sisters' tastes and behavior seemed as different to him as night and day, but it was probably a poor time to mention that.

He tried another tack. "The Bull Shoe is pretty notorious, and it's popular in these parts mostly because it has live bands and no competition." Seeing he'd made no impression, he went on, "The decor made the local taxidermist a big name in the state, and the spittoons aren't just for show...." Chance hesitated, noticing that she was more amused than repelled. He persevered. "This isn't some posh city night spot, Erin. It's loud and rowdy and rides the edge between disreputable and raunchy."

Chance was appalled when Erin burst out laughing. "And you go there regularly," she guessed, then laughed again when he gave a disgruntled nod. "Come on, Chance," she said as she gave his hand a prompting squeeze, "don't be stuffy. I'd really like to see what it's like. If it's too loud or gets too rowdy, we can always leave." She reached for the door handle, too eager to take no for an answer. Chance released her hand and got out to go around to her side of the car and open the door, certain he was making a big mistake.

CHANCE WAS WRONG. He'd made a *huge* mistake, he realized later. It hadn't been apparent at first. Their luck held until a little past midnight, in fact. Erin had been animated and entertaining in the large crowd. He'd gone through the motions of introducing her to the people he knew, but the loud band made name exchanges difficult. It was a larger crowd than usual, the rising popularity of the band drawing more people. Winter had been hard and long, and the crowd was the blowing-off-steam kind he usually avoided. A photographer from the *Sprig Gazette* was there to cover the band, but having heard that romance writer Erin Taylor was present, he'd sought her out and got her to consent to a photo for the visitors' section of the small-town paper.

Chance and Erin had spent a lot of time on the dance floor. To his delight, she knew most of the dances, particularly the line dances so popular now across the country. And slow dancing with Erin turned out to be nothing less than sweet torture. He'd finally had to maneuver her off the dance floor before he lost his head completely.

They'd ended up toward the west end of the place, where the band wasn't as loud and half a dozen pool tables were in use. He and Erin had joined the crowd around one table where a grudge match between two players had begun to gain momentum. Chance intercepted a waitress on her way to deliver someone else's beer and slipped her a bill to let him have two of the frosty mugs.

Erin stood just a bit ahead of Chance so she could see the game better. The crowd was pressed so close behind them that she hardly noticed the tug on her skirt. She'd just gone up on her toes to see over the couple in front of her when a hand slipped under her skirt. The pinch on the back of her thigh startled a yelp from her that was lost in the noise of the bar.

Outraged, she turned, her first thought being that Chance had gotten fresh with her since he'd been standing closest. She was all set to set him straight when she saw he had a mug of beer in each hand. She immediately glanced around for another culprit, her brows drawing together in displeasure. Everyone behind her seemed intent on the players. Ruffled, she took the mug of beer Chance offered and turned back to the game, angry and embarrassed.

The place was as rowdy and loud as Chance had said it would be. But it wasn't until the pinch that the atmosphere of the Bull Shoe seemed as raunchy as he'd warned. Eventually she relaxed, drawn back into the tension of the game.

The second pinch came almost as unexpectedly as the first. Incensed, her temper launching like a rocket, she spun around. Peripherally, she could see that Chance had his beer mug in one hand and that the thumb of his other hand was hooked in his belt. She caught a quick flicker of movement from a man behind her—a big florid-faced oaf with rough features—and knew he was the offender. He'd been standing behind her before with that same simpleminded look of innocence on his face, but this time, the two men standing off to his right had poorly suppressed grins on their faces.

When she turned back to the game, she first passed her mug to Chance, not trusting her temper with the chunky glassware in her hand. Not being a person who drank beer often enough to realize it had lowered her inhibitions, and never one to tolerate crude behavior, Erin fumed, alert to the slightest brush against her skirt.

The length of the wait almost caught her off guard. The third pinch was harder and more daringly high than the other two, and Erin's fist curled tight. She swung around so fast that her attacker was taken by surprise. With more force than Erin thought herself capable of, her fist connected squarely with the big man's nose.

Chance had seen the blur of motion when Erin pivoted. He hadn't realized the significance of her quick action until he'd felt the jolt to the floorboards beneath his feet. He glanced down, shocked to see the burly brute flat on his back. He looked up at Erin and his jaw went slack when it dawned on him that she was responsible. The band was on a break, so when the crowd around them quieted and pushed back to form a circle around the felled patron, the hush spread through the bar like ripples on a pond.

Speechless himself, Chance stared at the anger on Erin's face, heard as clearly as anyone else in the place when she said, "Next time, keep your hands to yourself," then continued to stare as she looked up at him, her mouth curving into a smile that was part victory, part chagrin.

He'd known what was going to happen next. He would have warned Erin, but there hadn't been time to open his mouth before they'd heard the inevitable shout ring out from halfway across the bar.

"Fight!"

The bar had erupted.

ERIN SAT at the breakfast table at three a.m., a towel-wrapped ice pack over her left eye. Chance sat across from her with a similar towel pressed against his split lower lip. The kitchen smelled like a brewery, their clothes were grungy and disheveled, and Erin was so miserable that it took what remained of her energy to keep her tears at bay.

Her voice was barely a croak when she asked, "What will we tell Meri?"

Chance's gravelly "Trudy won't be bringing her home until after church," reminded Erin that Meri had insisted she wanted to stay all night at Trudy's in the company of the foreman's other children and go to Sunday school with them. Erin had initially thought it might be an imposition on Trudy's family, but the teenager had assured her that they'd done the same thing earlier in Meri's visit and that all the kids had had fun.

Now Erin was grateful for Meri's absence. It gave her extra time to rid herself of the swelling around her eye so she could conceal the bruise with cosmetics. She still wasn't certain whose elbow had jabbed her, but from the look of her eye, it might as well have been a fist.

The sick feeling in her middle reminded her that her black eye and Chance's split lip and skinned knuckles weren't the only evidence of their visit to the Bull Shoe.

"Do you think that reporter will really print all those pictures?" she asked, her open eye blurring with moisture.

"If he and his camera made it out the door in one piece," Chance mumbled, then gave a humorless chuckle. "The *Gazette* has been trying to boost circulation."

Erin felt worse than ever. She set the ice pack aside and, propping her arms on the table, put her head down. She closed her aching eyes, but scenes from the bar fight played vividly behind her closed lids. It still shocked her how suddenly the brawl had broken out and how completely the patrons had participated, even the women. Whether actively involved in a fist fight or dodging blows, everyone in the bar had been in motion, and the melee prevented anyone from making a quick or easy exit from the building.

But it hadn't kept the enthusiastic little photographer from taking his darned pictures. It seemed that at every turn, that camera flash had gone off in her face. She couldn't bear to imagine the poses he'd caught her in, from her trying to retrieve what was left of her silk sleeve to her climbing on top of the bar in her short skirt and crawling on her hands and knees to get past a knot of brawlers. She hoped to heaven he hadn't caught her smashing that heavy tray over the brute who'd been about to kick Chance in the ribs after he'd been knocked to the floor.

She moaned, partly because her cheek and eye hurt, mostly because she was miserable with shame. How could she face herself in the mirror, and worse, how could she face Meri?

Meri, whom she'd been so determined to protect from seedy elements. Meri, whom she'd thought threatened by her uncle's immoral life-style. But Chance Lafferty didn't have an immoral life-style. He really wasn't a womanizer, and according to Rusty's wife, Bess, he only played an occasional game of poker with his friends. And after tonight even his reputation as a bar brawler seemed greatly exaggerated.

He'd tried to discourage her from going into the Bull Shoe, hinting it was no place for a lady. But she hadn't listened. Instead, he'd gallantly catered to her wishes, suffering the consequences right along with her when the brawl had broken out—the brawl *she'd* started— which would probably end up a headline with pictures on the front page of the *Sprig Gazette*.

She raised her head and gave Chance a teary look. "I'm sorry, Chance. It was all my fault."

Chance gave her a lopsided smile that made him wince and pulled his right hand from the bowl of ice water he'd been soaking his knuckles in. "Don't tell me you regret getting a taste of 'authentic Montana'?" he joked. "It won't turn out all bad, Erin." His grin widened and he winced again, but his eyes twinkled with orneriness. "Consider its research value. You wrote a good fight scene in *Penny Lace*, but if you'll pardon my saying so, it was obviously written by a city woman who'd never experienced a saloon brawl. You ought to be able to write one now that'll make your fans shudder when they read it."

Erin stared at Chance in disbelief. How could he make light of the whole thing? He started to chuckle, then flinched and pushed the towel-wrapped ice chunk to his split lip as he tried to control his mirth.

Miffed that he was laughing at her and unsure about whether he was making fun of her book, she grumbled, "I should have let that brute stomp you."

Chance shook his head at that and tried to wind down. "I'm grateful for your quick action there—those work boots had to be size thirteen—but I didn't really need that pitcher of cold beer dumped in my face."

"You were flat on your back, out cold," she reminded him.

"I've never been knocked out in my life. I was getting my breath back."

Erin gave him a skeptical look. "Sure. That's why your eyes rolled back in your head as you fell."

Chance's humor faded and they exchanged surly expressions. Erin was the first to glance away, again overcome with embarrassment. She tried to make a heartfelt statement, but it came out on a sob. "I'm so ashamed."

She heard Chance's chair scrape back as he came around to her side of the kitchen table. She turned her flushed face away when he hunkered down beside her.

For some reason, Erin's tears didn't panic him. Instead, they made him ache to comfort her and lift her spirits.

"Hey there," he said in a low voice, "look at me."

She almost couldn't bring herself to do so. Chance grabbed hold of her chair and angled it toward him, then took her hands. The consoling feel of those warm hard calluses brought more tears squeezing from between her lashes. She finally mustered enough control to turn her head and gaze into his fabulous green eyes, blinking rapidly to stave off more tears when she saw the tenderness there.

"Chance, your friends and neighbors will all hear about tonight. What will they think of me?"

Chance gave her a gentle smile. "They all like you, darlin'. They're bound to admire a woman spunky enough to punch a guy for assaulting her dignity."

Erin groaned, touched that he was trying to soft-peddle it. "But the fight wouldn't have happened if I hadn't insisted you take me there. You were right, the place was rowdy and raunchy. And I started a brawl."

"That most people there were itching to have start," he insisted. "Believe me, brawls that start over a woman defending her honor are a whole lot nobler than what usually starts them."

Erin squeezed his hands, careful of his sore knuckles. "You don't understand," she said in frustration. "I wouldn't have had to defend my honor, as you put it, if I hadn't insisted that you take me into a place that a respectable woman wouldn't be caught dead in."

Chance laughed. "Everybody, including most of the female population hereabouts, has been to the Bull Shoe at least once. You were a city girl out to see the local sights. No real harm was done beyond the usual damage to glassware and fixtures, Erin. This is no big black splotch on your character like you seem to think."

Erin lowered her head and said in a small voice, "Well, it is to me. It was stupid to hit the guy. I should have just asked you to take me home." Chance rubbed his thumbs over her knuckles a moment, sending a charge along her nerve endings that lifted some of her gloom. She looked up into the watchful depths of his eyes in time to see a smile start there.

"Never thought I'd end up trying to save the reputation of a lady who starts brawls at the local saloon," he said softly. "Particularly one with a mean right and a lethal gift for swinging drink trays."

Erin's emotions rushed up and filled her eyes with fresh tears as she felt herself smile at Chance's teasing. He leaned forward and placed a feathery kiss on her trembling mouth.

With that kiss, he reckoned he'd sealed his fate. His brain was finally getting in line with the tender but fierce emotions in his heart. He opened his eyes and drew back, sorry for the dark little mouse beneath Erin's left eye that must hurt, but taken again by her heart-stopping beauty. The woman could be hellfire hot with temper, and rose-petal soft and sweet. Erin Taylor was a miracle to him, and finally, she was more than he wanted to resist.

"As I see it," he began, "there's probably only half a dozen ways to restore the respectability you imagine you lost tonight."

Erin, catching the odd seriousness beneath his playful tone of voice, went along. "Oh, yeah? A whole half a dozen?"

"At least," he confirmed. "But the one I have in mind is a surefire way to straighten halos and patch reputations."

Erin stared at Chance, a thrill starting in her heart at his words. She watched in near disbelief as his smile slowly faded to solemnity and she sensed what was coming.

"It would be a hardship for a city woman like you, a pretty big adjustment, and that'd just be the relocating part. For this idea to work you'd have to live on a ranch." He paused and his voice lowered. "But the really hard part, and incidentally the only guaranteed way to mend your reputation, would be that—" he had to get in a quick breath "—you'd have to marry me."

Erin was so overcome with love that her throat closed and tears fairly spurted from her eyes. At last she was able to get out "Y-you don't have to make the supreme sacrifice, Chance. I'll live through this embarrassment and be on my way home in a week."

Chance's grip on her hands tightened.

"I—I know you don't want to get married," she said.

Chance waited until she opened her eyes and looked at him. "Didn't used to want to get married," he acknowledged. "Couldn't imagine wanting or loving any woman enough to take those dreaded vows. But after a few days with you, I'm damned glad I held out."

Erin reached up to lay her palm fondly on his cheek. "Oh, Chance." Her love for him overwhelmed her, but she hadn't heard the right words from those battered, but magically skilled lips.

This wasn't going exactly as he'd hoped, Chance realized, a trickle of panic assailing him. Though he saw what he was sure could only be love shining from those baby blues, the glimmer of sadness in their depths confused him a moment. Until a sudden thought struck him.

The final scenes from *Nothing But Trouble, Penny Lace,* and *Darling Clem*—the Erin Taylor books he'd secretly read—came back to him. Hell, he'd left out—or at least hadn't made clear—what was probably the most important part of any marriage proposal that Erin Taylor would accept. If she was anything like her heroines, she would settle for nothing less from him than her fictional women settled for from their fictional men.

He wished he could say the words with the finesse that Erin's heroes always managed, the way a woman like her deserved. Instead, he had to settle for what Chance Lafferty would say, however lackluster. Anyway, his heart was about to burst with it, and he was suddenly afraid this moment would slip away and she'd end up turning him down.

"I'm probably no prize to you, Erin. I live out here miles from nowhere in a state without most of what you're used to. I get dirty and smelly and tired enough to get sore-tempered. I clean up good and know my table manners, but—"

Erin stopped him with a finger gently placed on his lips. Chance reached up and caught her hand, kissing her finger before he went on. "But the instant you barged in on my poker game, you changed my life. Forever. Nothing will ever be the same after you. I love you, and I'd consider it the nearest thing to heaven on earth if you'll give me the right to spend the rest of my days loving you. Will you marry me, Erin?"

Erin let out a shaky breath of profound relief.

"Oh, I love you, Chance." She practically fell into his arms, showering his face with kisses before he took control and kissed her as meaningfully as his injured lip would allow. Sometime in those next fevered moments—just in case she hadn't made her response clear enough—Erin managed to get out a simple breathless yes.

THE PICTURES of the bar brawl didn't make the front page of the *Sprig Gazette*. Instead, the negatives arrived with a set of developed eight-by-tens—mostly of Erin in the poses she'd imagined. The note that accompanied them was a cut-and-paste job addressed to Chance that read, "Take heed. If you get silver trays and glass pitchers for wedding presents, send them back." There was no signature, but Chance swore Rusty was responsible.

The wedding was held four days later, on a weekday evening, at the Methodist church. Nearly everyone in the county turned out. Rusty stood up with Chance, Erin's best friend, Mitzi, flew in from Chicago for her, and Meri was the flower girl. A teary-eyed Sharon McCandless caught the bride's bouquet and suddenly noticed that Clive Peavy, the owner of the Snack 'n' Gas on the highway, looked quite dashing in a three-piece suit.

Erin made it all the way to their wedding night before she realized that Chance had been the model for every one of her romance heroes. However, by the next morning, even her favorite, Ford Harris, seemed a pale imitation of his real-life counterpart.

Meri had her best birthday yet. Not only did she get the real family she'd wished for, but a rascally palomino pony named Ringo. . . .

Which was eventually passed down to five other Lafferty children, all of them rough-and-tumble boys who loved to tease their older sister. Practically from birth, the Lafferty boys had a penchant for hair-raising misadventures that gave their proud daddy gray hair and provided their adoring mother with many challenges in her efforts to civilize them. That their children's antics provided Erin with an occasional story idea was merely part and parcel of happily-ever-after in the Lafferty household.

A Note from Susan Fox

Remember those great Doris Day movies? The feisty, virtuous blonde with a heart as tender as her temper was hot? A romantic heroine who was both wise to the ways of men and naive? Whose discovery of true love was fraught with goofy situations and charming high jinks, with a healthy dose of fun underlying it all. I didn't realize the similarities between Erin and those Doris Day heroines until the manuscript for "Chance For a Lifetime" was complete and I happened to watch a Doris Day movie.

I had written the first chapter years ago, but could never seem to get past that betraying creak of floorboards at the end of Chapter One. When asked to do a story for *Marry Me, Cowboy!*, I remembered Chance and Erin, reread that chapter, and the story suddenly took off. I had no idea what would happen on the way to their happy ending—particularly since writing a light romance was foreign territory for me. Chance and Erin simply lived the story that seemed the natural outgrowth of their personalities and motivations. I was reduced to following along, putting into words what I witnessed.

I hope you enjoy "Chance For a Lifetime," whether it seems like Doris Day Lassoes Montana Rancher to you or not. That said, I'll let you get back to reading. Turn that page, get a look at that sexy cowboy and fall in love! May your lives be filled with happily-ever-afters!

HITCHED IN TIME

Anne McAllister

Chapter One

Dodge City, Kansas
July 1878

IT WAS JUDSON BLACK'S lucky day.

Of course there were prob'ly a dozen cowboys hittin' Dodge today and thinkin' the same thing. Difference was, Judson knew it was true.

Hadn't he been first in line to get his hundred-dollar wages from O'Leary, the trail boss, on the stroke of noon? Hadn't he found himself a room south of the "deadline" in the Great Western Hotel for a buck and a half? A room with a real feather bed and blankets that didn't smell like he did—as if they'd been dragged through hundreds a miles of Texas dust and good red Oklahoma dirt? Hadn't he even got one with a window that looked out over the street and with a basin and pitcher that weren't even chipped?

Not that he cared. After two months' driving cattle from south of Amarillo up to the rail line at Dodge City, water in anything other than a river or bog hole was a luxury.

And speakin' of luxuries, what about that bath and shave and haircut he'd got at George Dieter's Tonsorial Palace? By the time he'd swabbed off months' worth of dust and grime and George had shaved him as close as a polished apple and cropped his shaggy dark brown hair so short he felt like a sheared sheep, he came pretty close to resembling that good-lookin' feller who was his poor dead sainted mother's son.

'Course there were plenty of other bathed and shaved, sainted mother's sons out prowling Dodge looking for new duds and a high old time, too. But wasn't it Judson who got the last pair of fancy boots in Mueller and Straeter's Boot and Shoe Shop, while his best pal, Mert McGee, had to settle for plain old brown ones?

"I swear you are the luckiest son of a buck goin'," Mert had grumbled that evening as they made their way into the Lady Gay Saloon.

And judging from the looks he'd been getting from the dance-hall girls and sporting women since they'd walked in, Judson reckoned his luck was just beginning.

One of them, a saucy little gal with wide blue eyes, short curly hair and a dimple in her left cheek, caught his fancy right off. He walked right past the click and rattle of the poker chips, the dice, the roulette wheel, the patter of the dealers and even the song-and-dance routine on the stage at the end of the room.

Instead, he propped himself up against the bar, tipped his hat, bought her a drink and set about doin' a little flirting. Not that he had to. Everybody knew what sporting women were there for, and it sure as shootin' wasn't box-lunch socials.

But Judson did it, anyway, because it made her smile and giggle and bat her lashes at him and, hell, he hadn't seen a woman in so long he figured he might've forgotten how.

Apparently he hadn't, for she cozied right up to him, told him her name was Celestine and invited him out back for a "little visit" to her crib.

It was tempting. But Judson had other things to do before he settled down for a "little visit" with Celestine. A few whiskeys and a bit of poker for starters. And if his luck turned bad, well, the thought of solacing himself in Celestine's arms afterward wasn't too hard to take.

But his luck held all evening long. While Mert and a redheaded cowboy Judson didn't know were having the devil's own time keeping a stack of ivories settin' in front of 'em, Judson was doing fine.

Doing better even than the wheeler-dealer in the shiny black eleven-dollar suit who was dealin' the cards.

Judson had spotted him when they first came in.

"Take a look at the dandy," Mert had said, jerking his head toward one of the far tables. "Cain't hardly miss 'im, can ya? All duded up, public as a zebra."

He sure wasn't a cowboy. His starched collar was so high he damn near couldn't turn his head. He wore a bowler hat balanced just so on top of his oiled black hair. His mustache was waxed so the ends curled, and when he dealt and shuffled Judson could see his hands were fine and white as a girl's.

"That there's Amos Stout," the bartender offered as he set them up with whiskeys. "A gentleman and a scholar."

Judson grinned. "That what he's doin' here, gettin' schoolin'?"

"Doin' a bit of it himself actually. Per-fesser of Higher Mathematics, he calls himself." The bartender grinned. "Di-rect from Concord, Massachusetts, or so he says. Him an' his sister. Been here 'bout a month or so."

"Sister?" Mert lifted a skeptical brow.

"Reckon she must be. No man in his right mind'd have her otherwise. Not Marvela." The bartender shook his head. "Ugly as galvanized sin, that woman. Not to mention she's got the disposition of a sidewinder and the voice of a screech owl. Boys here'bout call her Amos's Albatross." He chuckled. "Reckon his life'd be pretty fine if he weren't hobbled with her."

"Mebbe," Mert said. "Be a damn sight finer if he'd shed those duds 'n' look like a real person."

"That buryin' suit he's wearin' gets him noticed. You fellers see that and think he's a tenderfoot fit for the fleecing. Well, Lord, lemme tell ya, it ain't so. I seen him often enough teach 'em otherwise."

Mert leaned an elbow on the bar. "You sayin' he's a cardsharp?"

"Sayin' I seen Amos outhold a warehouse when he's a mind to."

"He cain't beat me," Mert had snorted, knocking back his whiskey and heading for Amos Stout's table.

In the next four hours Amos Stout took most of Mert's wages and most of the redheaded cowboy's, too.

The only man he hadn't beaten consistently was Judson. The growing pile of chips in front of Judson seemed to irritate the starch right out of his collar. He shot his cuffs, shuffled and dealt again.

Judson had three times as many ivories as Stout did, and from the looks of those four handsome kings Stout had just dealt him, not to mention that slightly tilted ace of spades, it looked like things were going to keep going his way.

The only hand that could beat him was four aces, and since he was holdin' one of 'em . . .

Celestine hovered behind him, brushing her breasts against his back, then bent down and nibbled his ear. "You won't be long now, will you, darlin'?" she breathed.

"Not long," Judson promised.

"You just come and get me," she whispered, then sashayed toward the bar where she commenced chatting with a tipsy cowboy Judson didn't know. Every once in a while she'd bat her lashes at Judson or run her tongue over her lips and mouth kisses and pretty words at him. Judson's anticipation rose.

And that wasn't all, he thought with a private grin. He'd had enough luck at cards tonight. It was about time to move on to Celestine.

"I'm out," Mert said, and tossed his cards facedown on the table in disgust. He shoved back his chair and scowled. "Y'all are playin' too deep for me."

"And me," said the carrot-topped cowboy, tossing his in, as well.

Amos Stout smiled. "And you, sir?" He lifted an arrogant brow in Judson's direction.

Judson hadn't spent hours on his poker-playing daddy's knee without learning a little about the odds and how to read a man's moves. Amos Stout wasn't half as amused as he pretended to be. In fact, the way he ran his tongue along his upper lip and cracked his knuckles time and again told Judson he was gettin' nervous.

"Don't reckon I'll be bowin' out quite yet," Judson said easily as he shoved a stack of ivories out into the middle of the table. "I'll see you and go you fifty better."

"Fifty?" There was a sudden faint edge of panic in Stout's voice. He cleared his throat quickly. "My, my, our boy must have a good hand, eh?'' He gave Mert and the red-haired cowboy and the others who'd come to stand and watch a mocking smile. Then he turned that same smile on Judson. ''By heaven, it seems you've had a lot of good hands tonight.''

Judson ignored the insinuation. ''Reckon ol' lady luck must be ridin' on my shirttail,'' he said mildly, his gaze level and unblinking as it met Stout's. ''So, mister, you in or out?''

Stout ran his tongue along his lip again, ran a finger inside his high collar and shot his cuffs again. ''Oh, I'm in, laddie.'' A muscle ticked in his jaw as he pushed a matching number of chips into the pot, then met Judson's eyes and deliberately added another fifty.

One of the dance-hall girls sucked in her breath. The red-haired cowboy coughed. Around them the chatter and clatter from a half dozen other tables, the clink and slosh of whiskey at the bar, and the tinkle and warble of the pianist went on unheeded.

''Reckon you must have a pretty good hand, too,'' Judson said. ''Or,'' he added with a grin, ''you're one hell of a bluffer.''

He considered his hand, then the pile of chips. It looked to be about triple the wages O'Leary'd handed him no more than twelve hours before. Not a bad night's work.

Celestine pursed her lips and blew him a kiss. Judson shifted in his chair.

''Well, my man?'' Stout prompted with an oily smile. ''We haven't got all night, you know.''

Judson nodded. He looked at his hand, then at Stout's dwindling pile of chips. Coolly and deliberately he shoved all of his into the center of the table. A gasp went up around the room.

Stout's face was implacable. The only thing that moved was his Adam's apple against his high collar. His thin lips pressed into an almighty tight line.

Then, "Deke," he called to the bartender. "My revolver, if you please."

It was an unwritten—and frequently unobserved— rule in Dodge that firearms stayed in the hands of the bartenders while their owners were imbibing. Saved a few lives and more than a few lamps, mirrors and panes of glass. At Stout's request there was another gasp.

"Don't worry, my good man, I have no intention of shooting anyone," Stout said. "I'm merely upping the ante."

The bartender brought a Colt with a carved ivory handle and laid it on the table. Stout shoved it toward Judson, who picked up the gun and weighed it in his palm, tested it in his grip. Then he put it back down. "No, thanks. I got me a better gun than that already."

Clearly Stout hadn't been expecting the refusal. His teeth came together. "Well, what will you take?"

"What've you got?"

"Very little that would interest the likes of you." Stout looked down the considerable length of his nose. "A wealth of mathematics books. Have you an interest in numbers, sir?"

"Only in the ones on cards. What else?"

"A family Bible. My wardrobe."

"What about the saddle?" Deke, the bartender, suggested. "Won him a saddle just last week, he did."

"What kind of saddle?"

"A Gallatin."

"Let's see it."

Amos Stout frowned. "My dear man, do you honestly expect me to drag a saddle in here?"

Judson shrugged equably. "Only if you want to put it in the pot."

Stout was lookin' like he got weaned on a pickle. "Deke, have someone fetch my saddle."

It was indeed a Gallatin saddle—a half-seat, square-skirted rimfire beauty with Sam Stagg rigging, Visalia stirrups and a hand-stamped cantle. Almost perfect except for a gouge in the near side fender. A saddle like this would cost Judson more months' wages than he wanted to think about. He looked it over carefully, lettin' Stout snort with impatience while he tried to control his eagerness. Hell, in a million years he'd never get enough silver together to own a saddle like this. But now . . . He smiled at his four kings, then shrugged with as much nonchalance as possible. "Fair enough. You can put it in the pot."

Stout's knuckles whitened against the backs of his cards. "It's worth too much."

"So fold." Judson gave him a level stare.

The tips of Stout's ears turned red beneath the brim of his bowler hat. "The saddle is on the table. Match it. Or is it time for you to fold, perhaps?"

Fold? Like hell. Not with a Gallatin saddle and every goldarned nickel he'd earned in the past three months sitting in the middle of the table! Not with the best damned hand he'd had in his entire life!

Still, what the hell did he have left to bet?

A slow smile curved Amos Stout's lips. "Shoe on the other foot, cowboy?" he taunted.

Judson looked hopefully at Mert. Mert gulped and cleared his throat, then looked away. Judson glanced around to see if any of his other trail buddies might come through. None did. He ran his tongue over suddenly dry lips. One glance at Celestine showed him that she was talking a mile a minute to that drunken cowpuncher she'd latched onto just minutes before.

"Don't have much, do you, cowboy?" Stout was still smiling, but it wasn't a pleasant smile. "Well, no matter. Maybe we can make a deal."

Judson's eyes narrowed. "What kind of deal?"

Stout shrugged expansively. "Perhaps you have something more valuable than you think."

"Like what?"

"You're a single man, I take it?"

Judson nodded. "So?"

"So I think you might have something I can use."

Judson's gaze grew suspicious. "What's that?"

"Your hand in marriage."

Judson's eyes bugged. He half rose from the table. *"What the hell are you—"*

Stout raised his arms and spread his palms toward Judson. "Relax, my good man. I make no untoward suggestions. I don't want you for myself, I assure you. I want you for my sister."

The one the bartender had talked about? The one as ugly as galvanized sin? *That* sister? "Ho, no! I ain't gettin' married to no sister of yours!"

Stout lifted one shoulder negligently. "Very well." He reached out an arm to rake in the pile of chips.

Judson's teeth came together with a snap. "Just a damn minute."

Stout waited, his mouth still curved in that taunting smile.

Judson looked at his hand, his four wonderful kings. What was he worrying about? He had a sure thing. He lifted his gaze to meet Stout's. "You're on."

Stout's smile widened. Judson smiled, too, and laid out his cards, saving the ace for last.

There was a titter, then a murmur, then a mumble from the crowd. Mert chortled. The carrot-top grinned.

"Ah, what a shame. Reckon you won't be my brother-in-law, after all," Judson said, and reached out an arm to rake in the pot.

"Not so fast," Stout said. With great deliberation he laid his cards out on the table. Four aces.

Judson's brows came together. "Now, hang on there, fella. I ain't never seen a deck with five aces."

"Nor have I, cowboy," Stout said mildly. "Yours isn't an ace."

Judson stood up. "What the hell does that mean?"

"It's the cuter!" Deke shouted all at once. "The cowboy got the cuter, just like Carney!"

"What the hell are you talking about?" Judson demanded over the growing noise of the muttering and grinning crowd of spectators.

"You been playin' with a fifty-three-card deck, you know that," Deke said. He picked up Judson's ace. "See? This here ain't really an ace, just sorta looks like it. It's the cuter."

Judson's slightly titled ace of spades. The cuter. What they called the wild card.

Judson stared at it, then at Stout's cards. They were all perfect. His wasn't. It was the joker.

And the joke was on him.

Deke slapped him on the back. "Same thing happened to ol' Governor Carney right here just last year. Thought he had the top hand, same as you. Four kings and an ace. But Charlie Norton, he had four real aces. Ol' Carney lost his shirt and damn near ever'thing else. Knocked him on his rear, I can tell you."

Judson had no trouble imagining.

"Ho-leeee," Mert murmured.

Judson watched numbly as Amos Stout, still smiling that smug smile, reached out an arm and raked in all the ivories. "If you'll change these for me, my good man..." he said to Deke. Then he stood up and picked up his saddle. "It's been a pleasure, cowboy. What'd you say your name was?"

Judson hadn't. He wished he could lie now. But when a man's word was all he had, he didn't trifle with it. "Judson Black."

"And where might you be staying, Mr. Black."

Judson told him that, too.

Amos Stout nodded, clearly pleased with his evening's work. "I'll be by in the morning to take you to meet your bride."

"YOU AIN'T REALLY GONNA marry 'er, are ya?" Mert asked.

Judson lifted the arm from across his face and peered at Mert through one bleary eye. He groaned. He'd been awake for maybe half an hour—or as awake as he could manage, considering the amount of booze he'd consumed after his card game with Amos Stout.

He still couldn't fathom it. He'd been telling himself it was all a bad dream, the delusions of a hungover cowpoke after a night of end-of-the-drive revelry. But the fact that Mert seemed to be having the same delusion made it hard to maintain. And that made him even sicker, if possible.

He rolled to a sitting position and clenched his teeth together, holding his head. The pain in it like to killed him, and he wondered if dying might not be such a bad idea, after all.

"I been talkin' around town," Mert went on, "and what that bartender said about her, about Marvela—" Judson winced at the sound of the name "—well . . . it's all true."

"Great," Judson managed before clamping his jaw shut again. A sour whiskey bile rose in the back of his throat.

Mert shook his head pityingly. "Surprised you didn't remember 'bout the cuter. Musta been the heat of the moment. Reckon that's what made you forget, don't you?" He went on, determinedly trying to fill in what was clearly an uncomfortable silence.

Judson wondered if being hung for murdering his friend would be any worse than marrying Marvela Stout.

Of course he should've remembered about the cuter. But hell, when a fella has four kings and a pretty girl makin' kissy faces at him . . .

He groaned again.

"I was thinkin' you could maybe skip town," Mert said. "I mean, what're they gonna do, get the Mastersons and Earp and send out a posse?" He grinned, but at the look Judson gave him the grin vanished immediately. "Just a thought," he said hastily. "You ain't gonna run, then?"

"What do you think?"

"I think you're a damn fool not to. But—" Mert shrugged "—I reckon you'd be thought a coward if you did."

Judson nodded grimly. "Maybe she won't want me. After all, it ain't exactly flatterin' being raffled off in a card game."

"To the loser, at that," Mert said cheerfully.

Judson's hands strangled each other. He wished it was Mert's neck. He shut his eyes, trying to think straight. The whiskey still gurgling around his insides didn't help. Nor did Mert changing the subject to say, "That little brown-haired gal, the one you was eyein' last night, my, she sure was somethin'!" He rolled his eyes and rubbed his hands together.

"I don't want to know," Judson muttered. Of course he hadn't got to enjoy the pleasure of Celestine's company, either. What woman would wait around for a cowboy who'd obviously lost his last nickel before her very eyes? But he could've lived a long time without knowin' it was Mert who'd replaced him in her bed.

There was a knock on the door. "Mr. Black?" said a female voice. "There's a man downstairs to see you. A Mr. Stout."

"Tell him I ain't up yet." He raised his voice to make himself heard, and the echo in his own head nearly did him in.

"He says he'll wait," the disembodied voice reported. "He says don't think about going out the back door." There was a hint of laughter in the voice. Clearly his predicament was well-known.

"Tell Mr. Stout to go to—" He bit off the word and sighed, rubbing his hands over his face. "Tell him I'll be down directly," he said heavily.

The woman's footsteps disappeared down the hall.
Mert looked at him, awed. "You're gonna do it?"

"What choice have I got?"

"Well, if you wasn't so damned honorable. . . ."

"Honorable. Yeah, that's me." Judson grimaced as
he grabbed the bedpost and hauled himself to a standing position. The room reeled. He hung on.

"Reckon you're gonna puke?" Mert asked cheerfully. "Mebbe you oughta wait'll you see ol' Marvela.
Save some for her."

If it hadn't hurt his head and caused his stomach to
roil, Judson might've laughed. As it was he said, "Shut
up or get out of here."

"Not me. I'm stayin'. I wouldn't miss this for the
world."

Apparently most of Dodge City felt the same way.
When he and Mert came downstairs twenty minutes
later, it seemed to Judson there was an uncommon lot of
people milling around the lobby looking useless as a
cow's tail on a pump.

Amos Stout was seated in an armchair by the window, reading yesterday's copy of *The Dodge City Times*.
When he saw Judson, he folded up the newspaper, stuck
it under his arm and stood up.

"Well," he said briskly, "if it isn't my prospective
brother-in-law. Come along then. Marvela is waiting."
He took Judson's arm and led him out of the hotel and
onto the board sidewalk. Mert and a dozen or so spectators followed.

Judson glowered over his shoulder at them.

"The people of Dodge are in awe of Marvela," Amos
Stout said, leading Judson north across the railroad
tracks and up one of the streets that rose behind the

businesses on Front Street. The gaggle of spectators followed.

Judson shot them another equally useless hard glare. Stout talked on, expounding on Marvela's accomplishments. She could play the organ like Bach, the piano like Beethoven. She could make ambrosia out of bog water and trail dust.

"If she's so wonderful, how come you're saddlin' me with her?" Judson asked when at last Stout stopped for breath. His mother would've switched him for askin' such a rude question. But Judson had been a long time away from a mother's proprieties, and he didn't reckon Marvela Stout, for all her accomplishments, was going to be any bargain.

"Because Marvela is never happier than when she is saving a man from himself. I think you'll do admirably," Stout said dryly.

He gave Judson time to digest that, then added, "Besides, I promised her she'd be able to settle down once we came to Dodge. Her fondest desire is to marry and have a family."

"Mine ain't," Judson muttered. "I reckon there's lotsa other fellers more suitable for her."

"No doubt," Amos Stout said cheerfully. "But you are the man of the hour."

Like bein' told you were gonna be hung at dawn. "What if she won't have me?"

"She will. In fact, she's delighted."

"She is?"

"Indeed." Amos turned up a narrow walk and bounded up the narrow wooden steps that led to a tiny unpainted one-story wood house. "She says she'll have you shaped up in no time."

He opened the door, hauled Judson inside, then shut it again in the faces of the still-curious swarm of onlookers.

Marvela Stout was everything Judson had heard and imagined and feared—and more.

She came into the tiny parlor with her black hair skinned up into a knot at the back of her head and lookin' like she'd spent a lifetime sucking lemons. The only thing Stout about her was her name. She was narrower even than her brother, all elbows and angles, and so prickly looking she put Judson in mind of that new-fangled barbed wire all them Kansas farmers were jabberin' about. And about as much fun to run afoul of, too.

"My dear," Stout said to her, "look who's here. Your fiancé, Mr. Black. Mr. Black, your bride."

"Mr. Black," she said, eyeing him carefully. By damn if she didn't have eyes like a weasel! Judson swallowed against another attack of bile and ducked his head. "Ma'am," he muttered in a low tone.

She studied him like he was a freak in a sideshow, walking clear around him, then moving in close and peering up into his face.

He bared his teeth at her.

It didn't even faze her. "Have you been having trouble with your teeth? I believe Doc Holliday is seeing patients at the Dodge House right now if—"

"My teeth are fine, damn it!"

"Which is more than I can say for your manners," she said tartly. "Clearly we'll need to do some work in that area. And we'll need to find you a suitable occupation of course. Amos said you were a cowboy?" Her nose wrinkled as she said the word.

Judson straightened. "I am."

"You were," his future bride corrected. "I'm not having you off gallivanting around for months at a time. There'll be no more card playing, either. Plumb foolish waste of money." She gave him a hard look that told him she sure as heaven wasn't simply making a suggestion. Judson gritted his teeth.

"Perhaps Mr. Wright will hire you. Or Mr. Collar."

"You mean Bob Wright at the provisions store?"

"That's correct. Or Jacob Collar. He runs the grocery, furniture and undertaking parlor."

"You expect me to bury folks?"

"I was thinking more along the lines of selling coffins—among other things."

"Stay in a store all day?" Judson could almost feel the noose tightening around his neck.

"How else do you expect to support me?"

The only ideas that came to mind would have Marvela breakin' crockery over his head, so he swallowed them and shifted from one foot to the other. "I reckon I'll think of somethin', ma'am."

"I reckon you'd better." She turned to her brother. "He'll need a suit," she told him. "And a dress shirt and a tie. I suppose we'll just have to hope that Morris has something in stock that will fit him as there's no time for tailoring. Go along now and have him try it on. You can put the announcement in the paper while you're out. I'll have dinner on the table by one-thirty. See you're not late. I don't abide tardiness," she said with her gaze fixed on Judson. It didn't surprise him.

"What's the hurry? What's she mean, there isn't time for tailoring?" he demanded as Amos hauled him back outside. He felt as if he was caught in a whirlwind. It wasn't doing his head any good at all.

"Just what she said. Wednesday's only four days away."

"What happens Wednesday?"

"You're getting married."

"I COULD BE your best man," Mert said.

Judson didn't answer. He just lay on his bed and didn't say a word. He didn't move except to carry his cigarette to his lips and take one long desperate drag after another. Inwardly he moaned. Outwardly he didn't bother. Bellyachin' wouldn't solve his problem.

Nothing—apparently—would solve his problem. Short of a blessed miracle, he couldn't think of a thing that would keep him from saying wedding vows with Marvela Stout tomorrow evening at seven o'clock.

Mert smiled down at him from the foot of the bed. "I ain't never been a best man before, and if you want somebody else more experienced, well, heck, I reckon I'd understand. But seein's how you're my best pal, I'd really be really happy if you was to say I could be your—"

"Sufferin' saints, all right! You want to be the best man, by God, you can be best man." Might as well make someone happy tomorrow night. Sure as hell wasn't gonna be him. Judson took a deep drag on his cigarette and exhaled once more.

"You ain't got yourself talked around to it, have you?" Mert said with a rare burst of insight.

"No, I sure as hell ain't." Though with every passing hour his fate seemed to become more certain and more appalling. Judson stubbed out the cigarette and scrubbed at his face with both hands.

Even as Morris had been purt near chokin' him to death with one of those high-collared shirts that Marvela insisted on and even while he had his circulation cut off by shiny black shoes that sure as shootin' weren't his size, he'd expected a reprieve, some force of nature—hailstones, a buffalo stampede, an Indian attack, hell, he didn't care what—that would send Marvela Stout skedaddlin' back to Concord, Massachusetts, and give him back his freedom.

But the sky stayed blue, the buffalo stayed dead, and though he heard rumors of Indians making a run for the Dakotas, so far they, too, had stayed right where they were.

And now here was Mert wantin' to be his best man and waving a fresh-off-the-press issue of *The Ford County Globe* complete with an announcement of his impending wedlock the following day.

Wedlock. Why was it the word conjured up prison cells with thick walls, stale air and a prune-faced woman holding all the keys?

"I need a drink," he said.

Mert brightened perceptibly. "'Course you do. Gotta celebrate, right?" One look at Judson and he hastily changed it to, "Wrong. Er, well, drinkin' can dull a man's mind to tomorrow, too."

Judson desperately hoped so.

There wasn't any shortage of gents in Dodge City that evening willing to buy the prospective bridegroom a drink.

"Least we can do," the faro dealer at the Varieties said.

"Have one on me," said O'Leary, the trail boss, who was watching Foy and Thompson perform at the Comique. "Have another," he said when Judson downed the first in one gulp.

"I'll buy this one," said the redheaded cowboy, giving Judson a commiserating look. "I reckon it coulda been me," he added sympathetically.

"Wish it had been," Judson muttered, already well on his way to bein' roostered. He banged his glass on the bar. "Gimme another."

"Reckon you oughta slow down a little?" Mert suggested after the first dozen shots. "Miss Marvela ain't gonna think too kindly on a husband who cain't walk a straight line tomorrow."

"That's her problem," Judson growled. "Tonight I'm free, and I'm damn well gonna do what I want."

"But—"

"You wanta spend the rest of your life bein' preached at? You wanta wear starched collars and sell coffins the live-long day and go home ever' night an' eat weasel?"

"She don't cook weasel!"

"Tastes like it. An' then she sings hymns and plays the organ! Every night and twice on Sunday!" The memories of what he'd endured in the three days of his "engagement" made him shudder. A lifetime spent married to Marvela Stout was too awful to contemplate. "Shut up and pass the bottle."

Mert shook his head. He passed the bottle.

He also dragged Judson back up to his room at the Great Western when they'd finished the rounds of every saloon in Dodge, nigh onto five the next morning.

"Lea'me in the street," Judson begged. "Mebbe a coach'll run over me."

But Mert hauled him up the stairs and into his room, giving him a shove in the direction of the bed. "See ya in the mornin'." He shut the door, leaving Judson alone.

Judson wove his way unsteadily toward the bed. He considered simply collapsing on it fully clothed. But he knew he stood less chance of being able to cope with boots and buttons in the morning than he did right now.

He stripped down to the buff, letting his clothes lay where they fell. Then he put out the light and fell onto the bed.

Tomorrow night he would be going to bed with Marvela.

"Oh, God," he groaned.

It wasn't blasphemy. It was prayer, the first prayer he'd uttered since he was no higher'n a grasshopper. He'd always figured God had enough to do without bein' bothered by the likes of him. Now, as fuzzy-minded and helpless as he felt, there wasn't anyone else to turn to.

"I know You reckon I prob'ly deserve this," he said to Whoever might be listening. "But lemme tell Ya, it ain't gonna work. You gotta do something. I mean, You're God, right? You can do hailstorms and locust plagues and all that stuff. So, this oughta be easy. Just fix it. Call it off. Do somethin'. Hell, er, I mean, heck, God, You got to! We're gonna make each other miserable every day of our lives. I'd sooner marry a cross-eyed librarian from Topeka than get hitched to Marvela Stout!"

Chapter Two

Dodge City, Kansas
September 1994

"SARA JANE! You'll never guess!" Her mother's voice was the last thing Sara Jane Jones expected to hear when she answered the phone that bright breezy morning in September. Evangeline Jones was a firm believer in nighttime and weekend rates except in emergencies or when one of her seven daughters snagged a husband.

This morning she didn't have the hysterical edge that went with family emergencies, and Sara Jane felt as if a tiny dark cloud had drifted over the sun.

"Heather is engaged!" her mother went on without bothering to let Sara Jane guess at all.

"Damn," she muttered under her breath as she pivoted to move yet another stack of the ancient newspapers she was sorting. "How nice," she said dutifully. She even meant it more or less.

Sara Jane had met her youngest sister's boyfriend when she'd gone to her parents' house on Chicago's North Shore for the Fourth of July right before she'd moved to Dodge to open her rare-books-and-antique store. His name was Philip, he was half a year away from finishing his residency in neurology from Northwestern, and Heather had dragged him to the family gathering, telling him, "If you can survive my parents, all of my sisters, all their husbands and children, and still want to see me tomorrow, I'll know you're for real."

Apparently Philip was for real.

And he'd just given Heather "the most lovely diamond," Evangeline was saying now. "Quite the prettiest I've seen. Philip has wonderful taste."

"Of course he does, Mother," Sara Jane said. "He picked Heather."

Sara Jane was truly fond of her youngest sister. She wanted Heather to get married, to be happy. She just didn't want her to be engaged. Not now.

Maybe not ever, she admitted to herself. Because once Heather was well and truly wed, all Evangeline Jones's considerable matrimonial efforts would be concentrated on her one as yet unmarried daughter—Sara Jane.

It wasn't that Sara Jane didn't think matrimony was a worthwhile goal—it just wasn't her goal. She liked men. Heavens, some of her best friends were men. But she'd never met the man yet who thought of her romantically. She was their pal.

Sara Jane prided herself on being a realist. There was no point at all in having goals that weren't attainable, and to her way of thinking, her getting married seemed about as likely as a duck climbing trees.

But try telling Evangeline that. Her mother would never believe it. Not for a minute. And she would spend the rest of her life making herself—and Sara Jane—miserable trying to prove that somewhere out there, if they could but find him, was the right man.

"You'll be one of the bridesmaids of course," Evangeline went on. "You know, dear, Philip has a brother.... I'm sure he'll be one of the ushers. He's a lawyer in Evanston. Not too well established yet, but..."

There. It had begun already.

"Ma," Sara protested. They'd done this countless times before.

"Don't call me 'ma.' It makes me sound like some backwoods woman in a poke bonnet," Evangeline said, just as she had countless times, as well.

"Heaven forbid," Sara Jane chided softly. "We know nothing could be further from the truth."

"Well, I do try to keep myself together." Which was something of an understatement. Evangeline worked out more often than Jane Fonda. She was fit and vigorous and determined. She was caring and kind and solicitous—exactly what one ought to prize in a mother. And ordinarily Sara Jane did.

She just didn't want her mother trying to work her matrimonial machinations on her. As long as Heather had been available and unattached, there hadn't been much to worry about.

But now...

Sara shuddered to think, glad that nearly a thousand miles separated her from her mother's determination.

"I really ought to go, Ma, er, Mother," she said now. "I bought a bunch of old books and newspapers at an estate auction this past weekend, and I'm going through them this morning trying to see what I have and figuring out how to market it."

As she spoke she unfolded one of the musty copies of *The Ford County Globe* on the oak library table in front of the window of her fledgling shop and ran a loving hand over the yellowed newsprint.

"Well," Evangeline harrumphed, well versed in Sara Jane's diversionary tactics, "if old newspapers are more important than talking to your mother..."

"Oh, Mom." Sara laughed. "You know better."

"I know you too well. You don't want me to start on you. And don't try to deny it," she added before Sara could do just that. "You have no concept of how attractive you really are. You think you're that same bespectacled little girl with the scabby knees and the pointed chin that you were when you were eight."

"Don't forget the chipped front tooth and the eyepatch." Sara Jane added dryly. There were reasons none of the boys ever felt romantic.

"It's not your fault you had amblyopia," Evangeline said sharply. "Lots of children do."

"It was my fault I fell out of the tree and knocked half my tooth off."

"Well, I trust you're not still climbing trees."

Sara Jane smiled. "Only occasionally."

"You're trying to irritate me, but it won't work."

"Damn," Sara Jane said mildly. "What will?"

"I should think that would be obvious," her mother said lightly.

"Huh?" Sara Jane was squinting, trying to read about how they celebrated the Fourth of July in Dodge City back in 1878. There had been horse races and parades and roaring cannons and beating drums. Sara Jane could almost picture it.

"Stop reading and listen to me, Sara Jane."

Guiltily Sara turned away from the newspaper. How did her mother know these things? Could she see through telephone wires?

"If you don't want me to help you, do it yourself."

"What?"

"Find yourself a man."

The simplicity of it was startling. Sara Jane wondered why she hadn't thought of it before. If she already had a man, her mother wouldn't be stuffing Philip's brother or anyone else down her throat!

"As a matter of fact, I have," she said before she could stop herself.

There was a moment's silence on the other end of the telephone line. Then, *"You have?"*

She supposed she should deny it, say she'd misspoken, hadn't heard her mother right. But there was such a wealth of hope in her mother's voice, and such a possibility of peace, that she couldn't bring herself to do it.

"Well, I didn't want to mention anything until we were sure," she waffled, "but—"

"Who? Who is it? You sly child." Evangeline's enthusiasm was growing by the second. "And you never let anyone know! Tell me! Tell me all about him."

Sara Jane swallowed. She cleared her throat. "Well, there's not much to tell, actually. He's, um, not quite in Philip's league. No MD from Northwestern, I mean." She gave a small nervous giggle at her daring. She'd never lied in her life. Now she felt guilty and exhilarated at the same time.

"He doesn't have to be a doctor," her mother said quickly. Besides Philip, only three of Sara Jane's brothers-in-law were doctors. The other two were lawyers.

"He's not a lawyer, either."

"What does he do?"

"Er, he's…um…a cowboy." Why not? Sara thought, slightly hysterical. This was Dodge City, after all.

"A *cowboy?*"

"A cowboy." If she was going to lie, why not tell a whopper? "They still exist, you know, Mother."

"Do they?" Evangeline sounded doubtful. "Well, I'm sure he's very nice," she said warily. She paused, then went on with renewed determination, "And it doesn't matter, anyway, just so long as you'll be happy."

Sara Jane felt a stab of guilt. But now was not the time to back out. "I'll be happy," she promised. "I already am."

And she realized as she spoke that in fact she was, because, guilty or not, a plan was forming in her mind, a way to subvert her mother's matchmaking once and for all.

She didn't really know if she had the guts to carry it off. But if she dared . . . Oh, if she dared . . . !

"I'm so glad," Evangeline said. "I always knew there was a man out there for you." She still sounded slightly dazed, as if this double good fortune of getting both Heather *and* Sara Jane engaged was too hard to believe. "When can we meet him?"

"At the wedding."

"At the wedding? You mean Heather's?"

"No. Ours. We'll come back to Chicago for it," Sara Jane said quickly, pushing forward her plan while she still had the courage. "We only want a small one. Just family."

"But, Sara—"

"You can plan it."

The words that would get Evangeline to swallow all her objections. Sara Jane's mother loved to plan weddings. It was, she said, why God had given her seven daughters. "You want . . . me . . . to plan it?"

"Yes. Please. Over Thanksgiving."

"That's less than two months!"

"We don't want a production. Only a small wedding."

"But the church! The reception!"

"You can do it. You're so good at it. It must be all that experience," Sara Jane added teasingly.

"Must be," Evangeline said, and Sara Jane thought her voice sounded choked with emotion. Then, mustering all her aplomb, Evangeline said, "Oh, Sara, I had no idea. I never thought you'd . . . I mean, I'm so . . . so pleased."

And Sara Jane, knowing her mother and knowing she was telling the truth, swallowed hard. "Thanks, Mom. I . . . really have to go now."

"Is he waiting for you?"

"Who? Oh, er, *him*. No. Not exactly."

"But you'll be seeing him soon?"

"Sure. Of course."

"Well, tell him we're thrilled. Tell him we're dying to meet him."

"I'll do that," Sara Jane promised. "Bye."

"Wait. You haven't told me his name. What's his name?"

His name? Oh, God.

Sara scanned the ceiling, the walls, the floor, the windows, the yellowed newspaper lying open on the table.

A small announcement caught her eye. An announcement of an upcoming wedding. The wedding of Miss Marvela Stout and—

"Judson Black," she told her mother. "His name is Judson Black."

SHE SHOULD HAVE FELT even guiltier than she did. She should have called her mother back and confessed that

Judson Black was a figment of her imagination, a masculine construct invented solely to protect her from her mother's best intentions.

But she couldn't.

Because she was a coward. She knew her mother had been worrying about her for years. All the Jones girls were beautiful. And if Sara Jane wasn't, well, she was simply the exception that proved the rule.

And while her mother might be right in insisting that she had outgrown some of her youthful ugly-duckling tendencies—Sara Jane had in fact traded her eye patch and later horn rims for contact lenses, and now had orthodontically aligned adult teeth to replace her chipped, snaggly baby ones—she still knew who she was behind the contacts and the nice even white teeth.

She was the gawky weedy tomboy who'd spent her childhood swinging from trees or holed up in her bedroom reading books. She was never going to get the doctor or lawyer or CEO that her mother was sure would make her life happy.

Her life was happy, thank you very much.

The trouble was, she'd never been able to convince her mother of that.

But now, thanks to one small lie and a wedding announcement, she thought she could. As deceitful as her pretense was, in the long run it was going to save both her and her mother a world of trouble.

Of course Evangeline would have to plan a wedding, and that would be a world of trouble in many people's eyes—but not in Evangeline's.

And when the wedding came and Sara Jane's cowboy stood her up at the altar, well, she wouldn't be happy about that. But truth to tell, Sara Jane didn't think any-one would be especially surprised.

Her mother would feel awful for her. So awful that she wouldn't be quick to find Sara a replacement.

And that was the whole point. Sara was quite certain that her sensitive empathetic mother would be so dis-mayed by the fictitious Judson Black's defection that she would allow her daughter to lick her wounds forever unbothered by potential suitors.

Yes, Sara thought now, rubbing her hands together eagerly. Once she had been jilted, she would be safe. It was perfect.

She sang her way through the rest of the morning, fil-ing away the newspapers in acid-free folders, then be-ginning to catalog and sort the books.

She'd only had her shop open for a little over a month, though she'd been in Dodge since July gathering her merchandise, going to auctions and estate sales, haunt-ing garage sales and following up rumors of antiques that had led her to meet some of southwestern Kansas's more interesting old codgers.

Now she had a little bit of everything in her small an-tique shop, though her particular emphasis was on books, especially books on the West, in particular, on Dodge City's colorful history.

That was why she was so happy to have found this cache of newspapers. And she could thank Kyle Arm-strong for that. She could thank Kyle that she was here at all.

A woodworker and antique-restoration expert she'd met two years ago while she was working at the State Historical Society and he had come in looking for old pamphlets on early Kansas furniture makers, Kyle was the closest thing Sara Jane had to a real man in her life at the moment.

She'd dated him for a time. But like all the others, whatever chemistry was supposed to exist between a man and a woman didn't exist between her and Kyle. They were good friends. Nothing more.

But they were good enough friends that when she complained that she didn't want to work in the State Historical Society for the rest of her life, he'd said, "Well, what do you want to do?"

And when she'd said, "I want to buy old books," he'd actually encouraged her to do it.

Her corporate-executive father had shaken his head and told her she would lose her financial shirt. But with Kyle's encouragement, Sara had found the nerve to quit her job, move to Dodge near where Kyle lived on the old family farm outside of town and try her hand at the old-book business. He even found her a place to set up shop in an old brick building with a vacant apartment right upstairs.

"What more can you ask?" He'd grinned at her.

He'd helped her build her inventory, too. He knew of possible sales before anyone else even heard rumors.

"Goes with bein' a native," he told her. Last Sunday he'd taken her out to an old ranch where she'd bought the newspapers and a couple of dozen boxes of old books and hymnals, a surprising collection of dusty cut glass and a stack of piano music.

Kyle had bought the bigger stuff—an old buckboard, half a dozen mismatched oak chairs, a commode with the towel bar missing, a .50 caliber Sharps buffalo rifle, lots of cracked and split tack, an old saddle and saddlebags, and some of the mustiest old saddle blankets Sara Jane had ever had the misfortune to smell.

"Better you than me," she'd told him, holding her nose.

"I can clean 'em up," Kyle assured her. She knew he could. Kyle was a genius at bringing out the best in things that Sara Jane couldn't imagine would ever be useful, let alone beautiful again. All the same she was glad the books and newspapers and cut glass were hers.

Her stomach growled and she glanced up at the clock. It was already well past one. She'd stayed open over the lunch hour because often on weekdays that was when most of her customers appeared. But now, just as she was going to close and go upstairs to grab a sandwich, a woman came in and began looking at the cut glass. Sara Jane smiled at her encouragingly and went back to sorting papers.

"Have you got any more cut glass?" the woman asked.

"In the back. I haven't washed it yet. Would you like to see it?"

She led the woman into the back and unwrapped several pieces she'd bought at the auction. "Take your time," she said, and went back to the papers.

The woman reappeared a few minutes later and went back to the glass Sara Jane already had displayed, lingering over an ornately cut celery dish that Sara Jane had washed until it sparkled.

"It's lovely, isn't it?"

"Beautiful. I've got to think about it, though," the woman said ruefully. "No impulse buying."

"Of course not," Sara Jane said, crossing her fingers under the table.

"You'll be open all afternoon?"

"I'm just going to run upstairs for a minute and make myself a sandwich. Then I'll be back."

"I work at the bank," the woman said. "I may be back after four. Three hours isn't an impulse, is it?" She smiled.

"Not at all." Sara Jane smiled, too.

When the woman left, Sara Jane followed her to the door and flipped the sign over to CLOSED. Then, humming to herself, relatively certain that the celery dish was sold and that her morning's work was justified, she climbed the narrow staircase and opened the door to her tiny efficiency apartment.

There was a naked man asleep on her bed.

By nature Sara Jane was not a screamer. She did not put her hand over her mouth and gasp in horror. She didn't even dial 911. In fact she hadn't been in Dodge long enough to find out if they had 911.

What she did was blink, then blink again.

But whatever else he was, a mirage he was not. No matter how many times she blinked, he was still there.

He was lying prone, his arms splayed, his face buried in her pillow. He looked for all the world like he'd been shot, but she took a cautious step closer and examined all that she could see of him; there were no bullet holes anywhere.

What she did see was a lot of pale skin over extremely well-developed muscles. Only his forearms and the back of his neck were deeply tanned. His dark hair had been cropped close to his head, and rather recently, too, since she could see another pale line of flesh where it brushed his nape. She couldn't tell how old he was, but it looked like a young man's body. Except for an inordinate number of nicks and scratches and scars. But then, she wasn't very knowledgeable about men. Perhaps that was the way they came.

At least he had.

And that brought her right back to where she'd started, wondering where he'd come from.

She reached out and tugged on his foot, feeling rather like Papa Bear confronting Goldilocks.

He didn't move.

"Excuse me! Mister!"

That, too, got no response. She opened the door and slammed it as hard as she could. At that he jerked and emitted a muffled groan. Then he rolled his head to the side, still sound asleep, and began to snore.

Sara Jane edged around to get a better look. Whoever he was, his face was tanned and lean and gorgeous. Even the faint stubble on his cheeks and jaw was attractive. And the thick dark crescents of his lashes were to die for. She was curious about what the rest of him looked like.

Coloring at the direction of her thoughts, Sara Jane stepped back quickly. The man snored on. He sounded like a pig. He smelled like a still. Obviously he'd come up here to sleep off a stupendous drunk. But how had he got in?

Maybe when she'd taken the celery-dish lady into the back room. But she hadn't heard the chime on the door and . . .

There was absolutely no sense in speculating. She'd just have to wake him up and find out.

What if he was dangerous? A criminal? A murderer? *Don't be silly, Sara Jane,* she admonished herself.

But there was no sense being imprudent, either. Her gaze lit on the Sharps rifle Kyle had left leaning against her kitchen counter the night before. It didn't work, and

Kyle had no intention of fixing it. Wood and leather were his passions—not guns. But he bought them to sell to collectors.

He'd left it with her, saying, "You show it here. You'll be able to sell it in a minute. It's the real thing, after all."

And as such, even if it didn't work, it still made her nervous.

But so did the naked stranger in her bed. She picked up the rifle—the damn thing weighed a ton—and, bracing it against her stomach, she aimed it at his butt.

"Hey!" she said loudly. "You! Get up!" And when he still didn't move, she prodded one firm buttock with the end of the rifle.

A groan. A muffled moan. A twitch.

She prodded him once more. "Up and out, buddy."

The groan grew louder. "The hell?"

And damned if he didn't roll over!

He had a fair number of nicks and cuts and scars on the front of him, too, including one nasty one just below his rib cage on the left. But it wasn't his nicks and cuts and scars that captured her attention.

Just as Sara Jane wasn't extremely conversant in men's nicks, cuts and scars, neither was she overly well versed in, well, men's equipment, either. Even so, whoever this man was, he looked very well equipped indeed.

Face flaming, Sara Jane jerked her gaze from his masculine endowments to his face.

He frowned fiercely at her. His face was as tanned as the rest of him was white, and deep blue eyes were trying their best to focus on her. When they had, they moved from her face to the gun, and he spoke at last.

"Th'hell you doin' with that?" His voice was rough and slightly hoarse. He sounded as if he'd spent the day yelling for his favorite team and the night celebrating their victory in a smoke-filled bar—which he probably had.

"I'm pro-protecting myself," Sara Jane said, the barrel wobbling even as she tried to hold it up.

"You're gonna have an almighty big mess to clean up if you figure on blowing a hole in me with that." He started to move toward her.

"Don't!" Sara Jane commanded. "Or I'll shoot." The barrel wavered between his crotch and at his head.

"Put that damned thing down before you hurt someone. You drunk or somethin'?"

"Me? Drunk?" Sara Jane stared at him, outraged. "You're the one who's drunk!"

"Ain't drunk, 'm hung over." He looked at her, his expression curious and a bit perplexed. He gave his head a small shake. "Ain't never seen a sportin' woman in a get-up like yours."

"I beg your pardon!"

"I reckon some fellas'd like a woman in trousers. Takes all kinds, I guess. But I ain't one of 'em, an',' he added almost ruefully, "I couldn't sport with ya right now if I tried, so put the damned rifle down."

Sara Jane was torn between outrage and bafflement. She leaned in to peer at him closely trying to see if his pupils were the same size. Maybe he was concussed.
' But it was hard to tell and the rifle was getting heavier by the minute. "I'll lower the barrel if you stay right where you are."

"May God strike me dead if I move a muscle."

Sara Jane's eyes narrowed even as she cautiously lowered the barrel toward the floor. "All right. Now, talk.

I want to know what you're doing here and how you got into my bed."

"Your bed?" He started to ease himself up against the headboard, but when Sara Jane lifted the rifle barrel again he stayed where he was. She lowered it.

His gaze flicked around the room, then came back to focus—or to try to focus—on her. "Where's Mert?" he mumbled.

"Who's Mert?" A far better question as far as Sara Jane was concerned.

"You don't know? Don't tell me that son of a dog left me in your crib and took off!"

Sara Jane stared at him, still baffled.

He groaned and rubbed his palms down his face. "Hell an' damnation. I can't believe he'd do this to me." Worried blue eyes peered at her from above his hands. "What time is it?"

"One o'clock. Thursday afternoon," she added, in case he might not know the day, either.

He practically jumped off the bed. "*Thursday?* God A'mighty, now I've done it!"

Sara Jane stepped back hastily, raising the rifle again. "Done what?"

He was looking about, wild-eyed. "Missed the weddin'!"

"Wedding? What wedding?"

"You don't know?" He gave an almost incredulous laugh. "You ain't heard? Hell, you must be th'only one in town who don't."

Sara Jane looked at him blankly. "What *are* you talking about? Just exactly who are you, anyway?"

He gave her a weary smile. "My name's Judson Black."

Chapter Three

"IT IS NOT!"

The man calling himself Judson Black blinked, then stared at her.

"It's not. It...it can't be," Sara Jane said fiercely. Her eyes narrowed in suspicion. "You heard me," she accused. "You were spying on me! Don't try to deny it."

The stranger pinched the bridge of his nose, then gave his head a small shake as if trying to clear it. "You wanta maybe ride down that trail again?"

"What trail?"

"What you said."

"I don't understand a thing you're saying."

The man shoved a hand through his short dark hair. "Reckon that makes two of us," he mumbled. He was still naked as a jaybird and distracting in the extreme.

Sara Jane reached out and snagged an afghan off her rocking chair and tossed it to him. "Would you mind?" she said frostily.

He draped it across his lap. She felt slightly better. "Now then, let's try again. Your name, please." She enunciated each word separately as if that would help.

"Jud-son Black." He enunciated, too, and it didn't help at all. She shook her head. "Don't see why you don't believe me," he said plaintively. "It ain't like a lotta other fellas'd be dyin' to step into my boots."

"I don't believe you because...because..." But how was she going to explain what had just happened between her and her mother to a perfect stranger? And why should she?

She raised the rifle again. "Well, whatever your name is, you'll have to leave."

"I'd be happy to oblige you, ma'am," he said, "soon's you give me my clothes."

"Clothes?" Sara Jane echoed faintly. She followed his gaze around the room. There didn't seem to be any obvious helpful piles of men's clothes. She started to bend to look under the bed, then thought better of it. She gestured with the rifle toward the coverlet. "You look," she commanded.

He moved to the edge of the bed, began to bend over, then just as quickly straightened back up again. "I'll puke."

And from the fast-fading color in his face, she was fairly sure he wasn't lying about that.

"All right. Don't move. I'll look." She bent and snatched the coverlet out of the way, but there was nothing under the bed, save her moccasins and her inky black cat.

"I don't get it." Sara straightened, scowling. "I don't know how you got in here in the first place, but I'm damn sure you didn't get in here naked."

"Glad you're sure," the man called Judson Black muttered under his breath. "Damn Mert, anyway."

Whoever Mert was, if this man's presence in her apartment was his fault, Sara Jane was quite ready to damn him, too. "Who's Mert?" she demanded again. It seemed like a safer place to start.

"Mert's m'friend. Leastways I thought he was." The man grimaced. "Hell of a friend, doin' this to me." He looked at her consideringly. "You sure you don't know 'im? He kinda likes skinny women. Though I don't know as he likes 'em in trousers,'' he added as an afterthought.

"I can assure you, I don't know your friend. And whether he or anyone else likes women in trousers doesn't interest me a bit!"

"Oughta," the stranger said mildly. "Y'ain't gonna get much business if the men don't like 'em."

Sara Jane stared at him, nonplussed. "Are we just a little bit sexist or what?"

The man blinked. "Huh?"

Sara sighed. "Never mind. I will do business in whatever clothes I want."

He shrugged. "Guess you're right. It don't matter anyhow once you get outa 'em."

"What!"

"Sorry," he said quickly, and she thought his face reddened slightly. "I reckon I shouldn't a done so much plain speakin'."

"I don't think plain speaking is the problem here," Sara Jane said flatly, planting her hands on her hips and facing him squarely. "Just exactly what do you think I do for a living?"

Good heavens, that was a flush of color creeping up his neck and into his cheeks! Sara Jane stared, astonished.

"Well, I thought you was ... Hell, mebbe I made a mistake," he mumbled, refusing to look at her.

"Maybe you did. In fact I think you may have made more than one. You and this Mert person."

"Yeah, well, it ain't the first, believe me," he said fervently, propping his elbows on his thighs and resting his head in his hands. "My whole life's goin' t'hell in a handbasket."

"Let's get back to your friend Mert. Presuming for the moment that you didn't get up here under your own power, why would he have brought you?"

"Mebbe he was tryin' to save me."

"Save you? From what?"

"I tol' you. Gettin' married. God, I reckon ol' Stout'll be out lookin' for me with a shotgun."

"Stout?" Sara Jane frowned.

"Her brother."

"Whose brother?" Sara Jane was beginning to think she'd stumbled into an Abbott and Costello routine.

"Marvela's," the stranger said irritably.

An icy finger slid down Sara Jane's spine. "You were going to marry someone named Marvela Stout?"

He nodded gloomily. "That's what I been tellin' you."

"And your name is Judson Black?"

He nodded again, slanting her a glance.

"No," she murmured. She took a step back. No. It wasn't possible.

She screwed her eyes shut, told herself to be sensible. Maybe she was just light-headed from missing lunch. She took a deep breath. Maybe he was the product of a guilt trip.

Whatever he was, when she opened her eyes, he was still there.

"No?" he said, echoing her. For the first time he brightened. "Don't tell me she didn't show up!"

Sara Jane ran her tongue over suddenly parched lips. "I—I don't know," she said hastily, stepping backward toward the door. "I, uh… Could you just, um, wait here for a second?"

"I ain't goin' nowhere," he said. "Not dressed like this."

Sara Jane practically fell down the stairs. Her heart was pounding as she stumbled through her shop, almost knocking over the secretary with all the cut glass as she hurried to the cabinet where she'd filed the old newspapers. Frantically she thumbed through the folders, trying to remember which one she'd seen the article in.

"The Fourth of July," she muttered. "It was close to the Fourth of July." She snatched out two—a *Dodge City Times* of July sixth, and a *Ford County Globe* of July ninth. With trembling fingers she spread them on the library table, scanning them furiously, looking for the announcement she'd spied when she'd tossed Judson Black's name at her mother.

It wasn't much. It was far more than Sara Jane wanted to see.

Barely three lines stated only that Professor Amos Stout was pleased to announce the upcoming wedding of his sister, Marvela, tomorrow evening at seven to Judson Black, cowboy.

Sara Jane sat down.

She understood now exactly why her mother and twelve years' worth of catechism teachers preached, "Thou shalt not lie." Because, if you did, you suffered divine retribution in the form of instant hallucinations.

"I'm sorry, okay?" she said in a shaky voice to Whomever she had offended. "I'll call her right back now and tell her I made it all up."

And she tried, too, really she did. The line was busy.

No big surprise. Her mother was probably on the phone to Heather or Diana or Marcia or Victoria or Elizabeth or Cecelia—any or all of the above—passing on the news that their ugly-duckling sister was getting married. To a cowboy named Judson Black.

Sara Jane groaned and buried her face in her hands.

"Excuse me . . . ma'am?" a hoarse masculine voice sounded right behind her.

Sara Jane jumped a foot. She might not have been a screamer before, but then she hadn't been visited by her lie personified. Swallowing a yelp, she spun around.

Judson Black, afghan wrapped around his middle, stood beside the secretary. "Didn't mean to scare you," he apologized.

Sara Jane licked her lips. "Didn't you?" she muttered. Then, "Look at this." She pointed at the announcement in the newspaper.

He glanced at it, then away at once. "Believe me, I already seen it."

"This is you?" Sara Jane persisted. "This Judson Black?"

"How many Judson Blacks you reckon there are gettin' married in Dodge City?"

"I just . . . need to be sure."

He shrugged. Then he took another look at the newspaper. "Why's it all yellow? Your cat pee on it?"

Sara Jane almost laughed. She would have if she hadn't thought she might be losing her mind. "What year is it?" she asked him.

His gaze narrowed. "You sure you ain't been drinkin'?"

"Just answer me. Please!"

Another shrug. "It's 1878."

Slowly Sara Jane shook her head. Her knees felt rubbery and her palms were damp. "This is 1994."

"What?"

"It's 1994."

"Ma'am, I don't know who you are or why you're wearin' men's trousers or whether you been drinkin' or not, but if you think it's 1994 you're nuttier than my sainted dead mother's Christmas fruitcake."

Sara Jane cast a glance around for evidence. "Look!" She flipped the light switch. Immediately the overhead fluorescent lights flickered on.

Judson Black's gaze flickered, too, from her to the lights, then back again. She flipped the switch off again, then on. His jaw tightened, but he didn't say a word.

Sara Jane reached out and grasped his hand to pull him toward the window. She wouldn't have been surprised if her hand had gone right through him. It didn't. He was solid, firm and clearly warm-blooded, which was not something she should be thinking about.

She gestured out the window toward the parking lot between her shop and the cars whizzing along Wyatt Earp Boulevard. "Does that look like 1878 to you?"

He looked. The color drained from his face. His jaw sagged. "Son of a two-fisted Jehoshaphat, what the hell's goin' on?"

"It's 1994. You must be the . . . the victim of a time warp or something." Even saying such a thing made her feel like a fool.

Judson Black shook his head, disbelieving. "What I am victim of is the goldangedest hangover I ever had. I been hung over before, I admit it. But I ain't never seen pink elephants or dancin' bears or . . . or—" he shook his head "—whatever's goin' on out there."

"Life, Mr. Black," Sara Jane said, oddly comforted by the fact that now he was more disoriented than she. "Late twentieth-century American life."

"God A'mighty," he breathed. Then, still clutching the afghan around him, he stumbled toward the stairs. "I need some more sleep."

Sara Jane watched him go, heard him bang his head on the ceiling where the stairs turned to enter the apartment, heard him swear, kick something, then stumble onto her creaky old bed.

Then there was silence. Or a sort of silence. There were still the sounds of cars passing, of the muffled rumble of trucks, the nearby clatter of skateboard wheels bumping along the boardwalk and the chatter of shoppers moving past. But still, it was twentieth-century silence and Sara Jane basked in it.

There was a tap on the door. She turned to see the celery-dish lady smiling at her. With nerveless fingers, Sara Jane unlocked the door.

"I couldn't wait. I'm here on my break. The impulse has outlasted the hour at least," the woman said. "I'll take it."

Numb, Sara Jane wrapped it up for her and put it in a bag.

"I'll be back," the woman promised. "You have such a marvelous collection here," she added as she took the dish and looked around, pleased. "Books, china, glassware, silver. It's amazing. Everything's so old and yet so well preserved."

"Thank you," Sara Jane said. She thought, *You ought to see the man I've got upstairs.*

"NINETEEN NINETY-FOUR?" Judson tasted the words as he said them. They tasted off, sorta foreign, like that Chinaman's swill he and Mert had eaten last year in Abilene.

"You're sure?" he said to the girl in trousers looking down at him. He felt slightly less like he'd been trampled by a herd of stampeding longhorns the next time he woke up, but it didn't seem to be helping much. He was still here—wherever here was—in her bed.

In other circumstances he could see where that mightn't be a bad thing. She was pretty, this gal in trousers. Prettier than any gal he'd ever seen. Sure as heck prettier than, what was her name, the sporting lady. Celestine. Yeah, Celestine.

This girl had real long glossy dark hair about the same color as his chestnut horse and a damn sight softer lookin'. She had kissable lips, too. Prob'ly at least as kissable as Celestine's would've been. And a hell of a lot more kissable than he reckoned Marvela Stout's would ever be.

He felt a faint flicker of relief that, strange as it was, it was keepin' him from findin' out more about Marvela's.

"I'm sure," the girl said solemnly. "It's 1994."

"So what does that make me? Rip van Winkle?"

"Something like that." She didn't look a hell of a lot happier about it than he was. The way she was twistin' her hands and wrinklin' her nose, she looked like she might start bawlin' any second.

"For Lord's sake, don't cry," he snapped. "If anyone oughta be cryin' around here, it's me."

"I'm sorry," she mumbled, still sniffling. "It's just that... it's my fault."

He stared at her. "Oh, yeah? You God or somethin' that you can just sorta whip people from century to century?"

She opened her mouth, then closed it into a tight line. Her hands strangled each other, and at last she ducked her head and said, "I lied."

"Chew it a little finer."

"What?"

He sighed. "Don't you speak English? I said, come again. You lied and I ended up in 1994? Sorry, ma'am, but it don't tally."

The look she gave him would've singed the hair off a hog. "Fine. Have it your way. It's all your fault then. And stop calling me ma'am!"

She had red spots on her cheeks now, the sort like painted women had. But these weren't painted. They were real—and he'd caused them.

Damn, but she was even prettier when she was angry. Whatever nonsense was goin' on with time, he could still get hot for a pretty woman. Judson was surprised—and pleased—despite bein' confused as hell. "What do you want me to call you?"

"My name. I'm Sara Jane Jones."

Sounded like a snooty schoolmarm to him. "How 'bout I call you Sadie? So, tell me, what'd you lie about, Sadie?"

She pursed her lips. "Sadie isn't much better," she muttered under her breath. "And it's none of your business what I lied about." She turned away, fussin' with the doodads on the bureau.

"The hell it ain't!" Judson said, bounding up so fast that his head was likely to come off, and the afghan almost did.

Sara Jane jumped a foot. "Be careful," she snapped.

He got a firmer grip on the afghan. "Listen here, Sadie, my girl, if you reckon you are responsible for this—" he shook the afghan and poked his own bare chest as he spoke "—then you better believe it's my business. Now, what in hell could you possibly have lied about that would get me into a fix like this?"

Sara Jane turned away and for a long time he didn't think she was going to give him an answer. Then finally he heard, "I said I was going to marry you." She said the words to the window and so softly he had to strain to hear them.

"You said *what?*" he bellowed.

She spun around, glaring at him again. "I didn't mean you! Not really. I meant . . . well, I guess it was you, in a way. I was talking to my mother. She was telling me my sister'd got engaged and I just knew she was going to start in on me next, so I needed a man. To stop her, you see. Or rather, I needed a man's name," she corrected herself. "And, well . . . I saw the announcement in the paper and I just sort of . . . borrowed yours."

Judson reckoned if he could sort all that out he might find a kernel of sense in it somewhere. At the moment, though, it was a little like lookin' for a sunbeam in a blizzard. Also, it seemed to him that all of a sudden there was a heck of a lot of women wantin' to marry him.

"An' you think that did it?"

"You're here, aren't you?"

He grunted. That was indisputable.

"And you seem real enough," Sara Jane went on. "And you sure don't act normal."

"What's that supposed to mean?"

"That you're not . . . not exactly . . . contemporary. Not even for Dodge. Granted, I wasn't born here. I grew up in Chicago and until two months ago I was working in Topeka, but—"

Judson's head snapped up. "What? Where? *Where were you working?*"

"I was working at the State Historical Society in Topeka. I just started my own business in July."

"Is that a library?"

"It has lots of the state records and—"

"*Is it a library?* Are you a librarian?"

"I have my MLS."

"Damn it, lady, can't you answer a blinkin' question?"

"I have my degree in library science."

Judson slumped onto the bed and held his head in his hands. "A librarian," he said, a leaden feeling settlin' on top of what was left of the whiskey in his stomach. He lifted his gaze and regarded her narrowly. "You ain't cross-eyed, though."

"I beg your pardon."

"I said I'd marry a cross-eyed librarian." He wasn't even really talking to her. He was talking to God, or Whoever it was Who'd pulled this cosmic parlor trick.

"I was," he heard Sara Jane say.

His gaze jerked up. "What're you talkin' about?"

"Amblyopia. I had amblyopia as a child. A lazy eye," she explained when he frowned at her. "It was turning in, crossing, my eye. I had to wear a patch over the strong eye. All the kids thought I looked like a pirate."

He stared at her. "A pirate." The leaden feeling was getting heavier by the minute. He couldn't believe it.

But then he looked at this woman—this woman in narrow denim trousers that looked like they was glued to her and some thin blouse that showed him a hell of a lot more woman than he was used to seein'—and he looked at her lamps, which sure as hell weren't kerosene, and he listened to the rattle of some machine in her window, which seemed to be blowin' cold air at him, and he remembered talkin' to God and suggestin' a deal, a deal involving a cross-eyed librarian from Topeka.

And he believed.

And he was furious. Who'd've thought God was so flamin' literal minded? Had He searched through every blinkin' year till He found a cross-eyed librarian, for mercy's sake?

He raised his eyes heavenward. "I s'pose You think this is a heck of a joke," he said to the Almighty.

"I beg your pardon?" said Sara Jane.

"YOU WON A WOMAN in a poker game?"

It was past suppertime, but Sara Jane hadn't spared a thought for eating. She was still trying to make sense out of what Judson Black had been telling her.

He was still wrapped in the afghan, still sitting on the bed, and Sara Jane was sitting in her rocking chair, watching him, trying to keep her mind on what he was saying when her eyes kept wanting to pay more attention to the physical Judson Black.

"Didn't win," Judson said flatly now. "I lost. If I'd won, I'd've had me more'n three hundred dollars and a damn fine saddle."

Sara Jane couldn't believe her ears. On the other hand, she didn't think it was a lie. She couldn't imagine anyone being able to make something like that up. "You preferred a saddle and three hundred dollars to a woman?"

"This woman," Judson corrected her. "If you'd've seen 'er, you'd savvy quick enough."

"All right," Sara Jane said hastily at his belligerent tone. "Fair enough." Maybe it made sense. "But I don't understand why she wanted to marry you."

"*You* wanted to marry me," he pointed out.

Sara Jane flushed. "Not you," she assured him. "Just someone. And I wasn't going to marry you, er, him. I was going to let him stand me up."

He looked so totally confused that she found herself smiling and saying, "Don't tell me. You want me to ride down that trail again."

He grinned.

It was the first time she had seen Judson Black grin. It almost stopped her heart. She who had lived twenty-six years in disdain of heart-stopping smiles had met her first. She took a desperate gulp of air.

The grin vanished. "S'matter? Swallow a fly?"

"N-no."

But when she still didn't speak, he prompted her. "Why was I—he—s'posed to stand you up?"

She felt foolish admitting to such a good-looking man anything about her ugly-duckling childhood. She felt idiotic explaining that she couldn't bear having her mother try to set her up with a man. But since it was at least half her fault he'd so abruptly been jerked into her life, she owed it to him. She took a deep breath and began. He listened, eyes wide, absolutely amazed.

"So, anyway," she finished finally, staring at her fingers knotting in her lap, "that's the gist of it. Maybe it was stupid. No, it *was* stupid, but it's nothing that I can't correct. I'll just call her up tonight and tell her...tell her I lied."

"The hell you will!"

The force of his voice startled her. She stared at him.

"You said you were marryin' me," Judson said firmly. "And so you will."

"But why? I mean, I don't— Why should you want to? You don't even know me!"

"Nope. But I know Marvela, an' that's enough. God gave me an out. If I don't marry you, He'll make me marry her. You just see if He don't!"

It was an indication of how substantially her world-view had shifted in the last few hours that Sara Jane had the sinking feeling that he was right.

SHE WENT OUT to Gibson's and bought him some clothes. She would've preferred to take him with her since she had no idea what an 1878 cowboy—or any man for that matter—wanted to wear. But she couldn't see dragging him through the store in her afghan, so she went by herself, promising to come right back.

"You'll stay right here?" she asked.

Judson glanced downward in an unnecessary reminder of his nakedness beneath the afghan. "Don't reckon I'm goin' anywhere. Not unless God gets another bee in his bonnet."

Sara Jane sincerely hoped not. She'd had enough divine meddling for one day.

She got him T-shirts and briefs, threw in a couple of pairs of boxer shorts just in case he preferred them. She bought a pair of pajamas, picked out three long-sleeved shirts that looked like an 1878 cowboy might be caught dead—or alive—in, added three pairs of Wranglers— "boot cut"—and a belt to hold them up in case she got the waist size wrong. Then she added several pairs of socks, picked out a pair of boots and, because this was

1994, not 1878, she tossed in a pair of white leather athletic shoes.

She wondered what he'd think of them!

HE THOUGHT they were the most amazing things he'd ever seen. He held them up, still clutching the afghan around his middle with one hand, and looked over them, his eyes widening. "People wear these? In public?"

Sara Jane fished her own pair out of the closet.

Judson frowned. "Women's shoes? You got me women's shoes?"

"Everybody wears them."

But Judson wouldn't. He went into her bathroom and put on his new underwear and jeans and one of the shirts. He put on the socks and the boots, but the athletic shoes stayed in the box they came in.

He came out again in his new clothes, walking like the Tin Man in *The Wizard of Oz* and looking embarrassed. "I feel like a Monkey Ward cowboy that ain't never been west of St. Louie."

"The jeans need to be washed. They'll be more comfortable when they're washed. We can take the others to the Laundromat tonight."

"Laundromat?"

"You'll see. You hungry?"

"I could eat six bobcats single-handed."

She was fresh out of bobcats, so she opened two cans of soup, then made toasted peanut-butter sandwiches, and tore up lettuce and chopped green pepper and carrots for a salad.

It wasn't much, but she hadn't been expecting company. She was afraid to feed him fast food, not sure if all those additives might upset his stomach. Still, if getting teleported 116 years hadn't played havoc with his indigestion, she didn't suppose a Big Mac or a Whopper would.

He didn't say a word all the time she was cooking or while he was eating. He watched every move she made with avid fascination, and when he finished eating he got up and prowled around the kitchen.

He fiddled with the can opener, turned the burners on and off, watching the blue gas flame grow and shrink, then he peered into the refrigerator and freezer and poked at the ice crystals she needed to defrost. "This how it keeps cool?"

"No, that makes it work, harder, actually. Electricity cools it."

He looked perplexed.

"I'll buy you a book," Sara Jane promised. She piled the dishes in the sink and began washing them. Judson picked up a dish towel and started to dry.

She gaped at him.

"Don't men dry dishes in 1994?"

She nodded. "Some of them. I just didn't think they did in 1878."

"Any cowpuncher eats supper at some outfit's fire, he earns his keep." Judson set down one plate and picked up another. "I don't know any cook don't think more kindly of a man when he dries a dish or two."

Clearly there was something to the etiquette of the Old West that ought to have been preserved. "Thank you," said Sara Jane.

Judson nodded. "My pleasure."

After they finished the dishes, she took him to the Laundromat. She dumped his new clothes in with her dirty ones and picked up the basket. Judson took it out of her hands.

"You lead," he said. "I'll just follow along."

Bemused, Sara Jane led, but she had to reach out and grab him a couple of times or he would've gawked himself right into a telephone post or stepped out in front of a truck.

"What's it called?" he asked, when she opened the door of her Jeep Cherokee.

"A car. An automobile. Right after they were first made they called them horseless carriages." She patted the hood. "There's an engine under here that has the power of 190 horses."

"No."

She grinned. "Don't believe me? Come on, get in."

Shaking his head, Judson climbed in. Sara Jane went around and got into the driver's side. She put the key in the ignition and turned it. The engine surged to life. Judson's hands clenched on the tops of his thighs. His breathing came fast and hard.

Tempted to gun it, she took pity on him, instead, backing slowly out of her parking place and heading for the Laundromat at a snail's pace. It was nearly dark now and the neon lights from all the businesses along Wyatt Earp shone brightly. Cars and trucks whizzed past. Judson gaped, his head swiveling this way and that as he muttered under his breath.

She never went over thirty-five, but when Sara Jane finally pulled up to the Laundromat, Judson's knuckles were white.

"Surely horses run that fast?"

"'Course. We call it a stampede."

The Laundromat was another source of amazement. Sara Jane showed him how to sort the clothes, putting his new dark indigo jeans in with her dark colors, adding his new shirts and pajamas to her colorful T-shirts and blouses, then doing a separate load of his new white briefs and T-shirts and her underwear.

He picked up one of her lacy white bras and studied it openly. He did the same with a pair of her skimpy bikini briefs.

"You don't have to show my underwear to the world," she snapped at him.

He turned to gaze on her. "That's underwear? *Your* underwear? Well, I'll be damned." He grinned again.

"I haven't a doubt that you will," Sara Jane said, snatching them out of his hand and tossing them into the washing machine. "Here. Put in the soap."

He did what she told him, measuring it carefully, scowling as he poured it into the machine, then setting the dial where she showed him.

"Makin' a modern man out of him?" the woman at the next machine asked, grinning at Judson's concentration.

"You have no idea," said Sara Jane.

"WHAT'RE THESE?" Judson stared at the clothes she handed him later that night. He'd seen them in the wash. He'd thought they looked too big for her.

"Pajamas. You sleep in them."

"I don't," he said, which was the absolute truth.

She blushed. Lord, but she was gorgeous when she blushed. But for all her blushes, she was as dogged as a collie on the heels of a balky steer. "You do if you're sleeping in my bed," she said flatly.

That was news to him. "I am?" He couldn't help grinning.

Sara Jane slapped her hands on her hips. "Unless you'd like to get a motel room?"

"Motel?"

She sighed and thrust the pajamas at him again. "Never mind. Do you want a shower? You do know what a shower is?"

"I got an idea," he said. He'd checked it out while he was changing his clothes. "Amazin' all the things you can do in a privy these days."

"Isn't it?" Sara Jane said tightly. "Do you want a shower or not?"

He shrugged. "Guess not. Had me a bath the day I got into town."

"And that was when?"

"Oh, mebbe four, five days ago."

"Give or take 116 years," Sara Jane said dryly.

"You sayin' I stink?"

"Actually," she told him, "you don't smell nearly as bad as I imagined you would."

"You'd smell, too, if you was to spend two months drivin' cattle from dang near Mexico!"

"Without a doubt," Sara Jane said. "So, I repeat, do you want a shower?"

He got the point. "I reckon," he grumbled. He started for the bathroom, those ridiculous pajama things in hand, when a thought occurred to him. "Don't suppose you'd want to wash my back? Didn't think so," he said quickly at the expression on her face.

Showers were interestin' things. Judson enjoyed his. But he could well imagine how he might enjoy it a sight more with a little female companionship. Hell, this twentieth century was givin' him fantasies he didn't even know he was capable of!

When he came out at last he hoped to heaven Sara Jane thought the flush on his skin was from all that hot water pourin' over him and not what he reckoned they could've been doin'. Or maybe she thought it was from his embarrassment at bein' seen in these floppy blue pajamas.

"I feel like the blinkin' Sheik of Araby," he grumbled.

"You look, um, fine." Sara Jane slipped past him into the bathroom without, as far as he could tell, looking at him at all. "You go ahead and go to sleep. I'll be out shortly." She shut the door behind her.

Judson stretched out on the bed, but he didn't go to sleep. He lay there thinking that the world was a very strange place, a heck of a lot stranger even than it had been the night before. Or 42,400 nights before, more or less.

He looked up at the ceiling. "You sure You know what You're doin', God?" he asked. "I mean, I reckon You got this all figured out, You bein' so smart and knowin' everything. But lemme tell Ya, this ain't gonna be no Sunday-school picnic You got me into. Automobiles! Electric lights! High-falutin' indoor privies! Ever'-thing's changed."

No. That wasn't true. One thing had stayed the same.

Every time Judson thought about Sara Jane Jones naked in the shower he felt an urge that hadn't changed at all.

Chapter Four

THEY WERE ON EITHER SIDE of Sara Jane's bed with a space the size of Nebraska between them, lyin' there stiff as a couple a cigar-store Injuns. On Sara Jane's part, Judson reckoned it was on accounta her bein' nervous an' proper an' not quite sure what to do.

Well, the same could be said for his stiffness—except it owed some to lust, too.

"I missed my weddin' night," he realized suddenly.

Sara Jane's gaze snapped around to meet his. "Well, don't expect me to take her place!"

He grinned. "Thought you was takin' her place," he said mildly.

"Don't be ridiculous."

"I ain't."

"You're not."

"That's what I said."

She groaned. Then she squirmed in the bed, folding her hands behind her head, which lifted her breasts so they stood up straight as the Tetons, dark shadows against the light that filtered in from the lights still on outside.

Judson did his own bit of squirming.

"I mean that I think we need to take our time and think about this," Sara Jane said slowly. "You might think I'm a better deal than your Marvela, but—"

"She ain't *my* Marvela!"

"—than a woman you won by losing a poker game, but you might change your mind," Sara Jane went on right over his interruption. "After all, we've only known each other a few hours."

"It's enough for me," Judson said flatly.

"Yes, well, we have a pretty good idea of your judgment, don't we?"

"Meaning?"

"Meaning you might just possibly be considered a bit headstrong and impetuous."

He squirmed again. "It ain't like you never did a foolhardy thing in your life. Who said they was married to me?"

"Obviously the biggest mistake I ever made." But she didn't sound actually annoyed.

"Most interestin', anyhow," Judson said. He turned his head and grinned at her. "Reckon we could make it more interestin'."

She rolled onto her back again. "Go to sleep, Judson."

"Aw, Sadie—"

"Sleep." She turned away from him and snuggled into her pillow. "It's been a long day."

Judson lay on his back and stared first at her, watching her until her breath came slow and even. Then his gaze shifted to the ceiling where he could see the ghostly reflections of things called headlights moving against the cracked plaster.

"A long day?" he murmured. "You don't know the half of it."

A PART OF SARA JANE expected she'd wake up in the morning and find she'd dreamed it all.

And it was with a tiny tingle of excitement that she rolled over to discover that Judson Black's appearance in her life had lasted longer than a day. He was sprawled on his back, one arm flung above his head, the other on his stomach, as he slept.

Carefully, so she wouldn't wake him, Sara Jane eased herself to a sitting position. It was seven—past time for her to get going—but she didn't get up. She didn't even move.

She sat very quietly and looked at Judson Black.

Yesterday afternoon when she had found him asleep naked in her bed, she'd been too astonished to do much more than notice his lean strong body and the nicks and scars that marred it. This morning the body with its nicks and scars was mostly hidden beneath the pajamas she'd bought for him. The buttons on the shirt were undone, however, and she allowed herself a leisurely perusal of a hard-muscled chest, lightly furred with dark hair. It was very nice. So was his face.

It was a strong face, not classically handsome perhaps. The nose was a bit too pronounced—or had been broken a few too many times. The cheekbones were strong, set off by the dusting of dark stubble in the hollows of his cheeks. There was just the faintest hint of a cleft in his chin to soften its uncompromising firmness. Once more she marveled at his beautiful lashes. They lay like night-dark half-moons shielding his eyes. Sara Jane would have died to have lashes like his. She wondered if the women in 1878 had appreciated them.

Probably. The lashes, the eyes, the body. Every bit of him.

She didn't think it would matter when Judson Black lived; women would fall all over him. He was the sort of deeply masculine, confidently sexy man that she'd never aspire to call her own in a million years.

A woman knew her limitations, after all. And in a million years Sara Jane wouldn't have imagined someone like Judson Black wanting to marry a girl like her.

Well, it hadn't happened in a million years. It had happened in 116.

But it wasn't that he wanted to. Not really. She was simply the less awful of two bad alternatives. Hardly a comforting thought. Still, she couldn't help thinking that he hadn't seemed exactly repelled by her. He'd even teased her a little bit.

Sara Jane's cheeks felt somewhat warm as she remembered the insinuation in his tone last night as they'd lain here side by side. Another man—heavens, plenty of other men—would have pressed their advantage much more than Judson had. He was obviously a cowboy and a gentleman.

A tiny furrow appeared between his brows now as she smiled down at him. His mouth drew into a hard frown. Then his expression slowly softened and he smiled.

Sara Jane could have melted at the smile. Instead, she steeled herself against it, got up, made breakfast and went down to work.

She was hanging up some old tools that she and Kyle had found at a farm auction a couple of weeks back when she heard the sound of boots on the stairs and turned around.

"Mornin'." Judson was wearing another of the new shirts, a pale blue chambray, and a pair of jeans that, having been washed, had softened and fitted him like a glove. Sara Jane swallowed and managed a smile.

Judson ducked his head. "Reckon I slept in. Sorry."

"I'm sure you needed it. Did you have some breakfast?" She gave him a quick smile and edged away.

"I don't need it." He followed her.

"I don't have to open for another twenty minutes. Come on. I'll show you where everything is. Teach you how to use things. Then tomorrow you can do it yourself."

"I don't want to trouble you none."

"No trouble." Sara Jane ducked past him and hurried up the stairs. Damn it, she felt like a star-struck schoolgirl. If she hadn't had something to keep her occupied, she probably would have drooled on the tops of his brand-new boots!

She showed him the bread and the toaster. He thought the bread was spongy, but the toaster impressed him a lot. She fried him two eggs and some turkey bacon and, at his amazement, did her best to explain about cholesterol. If he was out of his depth, he didn't say so. He simply nodded his head.

He liked the milk, saying he'd never had it that cold before. He thought her coffee was for sissies.

"I'll show you how to make coffee sometime," he promised her. But he was smiling as he sat at the small oak table in front of the window. And Sara Jane knew he wasn't really complaining. She smiled at him in return, pleased.

Then guiltily she glanced at her watch. "I have to open in a couple of minutes. I've got to go."

It was too much to hope that he would simply stay upstairs. She barely had the door open and was hanging the tools again when he came down.

"Can I help?"

"No, that's all right. I'm fine. I'm used to working on my own." She knew she sounded abrupt, but somehow she couldn't help it.

He nodded. "Reckon I'm in your way."

"Well, not really."

"I'll leave."

"Leave?" She felt a sudden panic.

"Go out and have me a look around," Judson explained. "See what I recognize."

"Oh." She felt unaccountably relieved. "I don't think there's anything much left," she said apologetically. "There was a big fire in 1886 and one a couple of years later. Most of the town burned down."

"Was anyone killed?"

Sara Jane was taken aback by the urgency in his tone, then realized that the people killed were people he might have known. "I—I don't know. I don't think I've ever heard anyone say. I have old newspapers, though. That's where I got you, remember," she added wryly. "We could look."

But just as she suggested it, a couple came into the store and the woman asked about the pressed-back rocking chair in the window.

Judson headed for the door. "Adios, then," he said.

"I'll be right with you," Sara Jane said to the woman, and dashed out after Judson. "Wait!"

He stopped on the sidewalk and looked at her expectantly.

She felt suddenly awkward. "I—I thought you might need some money." She fumbled in her pocket, then pressed some bills into his hand. He took them reluctantly, making a wry face as he did so.

"I'll pay you back."

"Don't worry about it." She reached out and caught his arm as he turned away. "I also wanted to remind you about . . . about stoplights and crosswalks." She felt like an absolute fool. She couldn't help herself.

"Green is for go, red is for stop." He grinned. "I got that figured out. What're crosswalks?"

She explained, hoping he'd use them, since he had a tendency to gawk.

"You folks sure got a lot of rules."

"For safety's sake."

"I was reading the newspaper before I came downstairs. Your world don't look a whole lot safer to me."

"Probably not." Sara Jane smiled. "But think how much worse things would be without crosswalks."

He grinned. "I'll keep that in mind." He gave her a wink and headed off down the street.

Sara Jane watched him go, feeling like a young mother sending her child off to school by himself for the first time.

"Er, miss, about that rocker?"

Sara Jane went back to work.

She told herself Judson was a grown man, a capable man. He'd be fine. All the same, she worried.

It wouldn't have been so bad if he'd come back at noon. She expected him for lunch. He didn't come. She dawdled around downstairs, instead of going up for lunch. She dusted and rearranged her books. Then she redid her window because the couple in the morning had taken the rocker, but mostly because while she was doing it she could keep scanning the street for signs of Judson.

He never came.

Finally at quarter to two, she put a note on the door telling him to ring the doorbell and went upstairs to grab a sandwich. She thought she heard the bell twice and came skittering down the stairs to let him in. Both times there was no one there.

Where was he?

Had he stepped in front of a truck? Got hit by a train? Got disoriented and lost his way?

She opened again at two-fifteen, peering out the door to look both ways down the walk. No Judson.

Should she call the police?

Oh, yes, definitely, she mocked herself. And tell them what? That she was worried about a one hundred and forty-four-year-old missing cowboy?

Well, what other alternative did she have?

Waiting.

She waited.

Three o'clock came. Then three-thirty. And four. Finally she stopped peeking outside every few minutes and, on the proverbial corollary that a watched door never opens, retreated into the back room to unbox some goodies Kyle had brought over.

At last, at quarter past four just when she was about to scream from frustration, the door chimed as it was opened. Sara Jane hurried from the back room.

It was the celery-dish lady. "Just me, back again," she said cheerfully.

Sara Jane's stomach had dropped like lead. Now she mustered a smile. "How nice to have you come back."

"I'm just looking today. I love the celery dish so much. It may seem silly to be that fond of a trivial piece, but it's cut so beautifully, and when I put it on the table last night the evening sun hit it and you should have seen the prisms of color that splashed across the tablecloth. Even my husband was impressed."

"I'm so glad," Sara Jane said, edging past her and craning her neck to look out the window and down the street. *Where on earth was he?*

"So I thought I'd see what else you had. I'm not in the market for any more right now. Can't really afford it. But I love to look. I was telling my husband about some of the old tools you have here. He's interested in that sort of thing—not exactly a cut-glass man, if you know what I mean." The woman laughed.

Sara Jane nodded. "I don't know many cut-glass men." She opened the door and leaned out. No Judson anywhere.

"He'd be fascinated by these things," the woman went on, nodding at the tools Sara Jane had hung up that morning. "I don't have the vaguest notion what most of them are for."

Sara Jane glanced distractedly at her customer who was taking down a wooden racklike object with long handles on each end.

"What's this?"

"A curd strainer." Sara Jane was glad she'd done a fair bit of reading about household tools over the past few months. "They used it in the making of cheese. And that," she said as the woman picked up a hand-size squared-off wooden scoop, "is a butter scoop. After the butter came it was worked to get the excess water squeezed out. Then they dug it out with the scoops and formed it into blocks or rounds or pressed it in molds like those." She pointed at the several wooden molds on the wall across the room.

"What about the machete?" The woman pointed to a lethal-looking tool that Kyle had hung up on Sara Jane's wall the weekend before.

"I'm not sure," Sara Jane began as the bells chimed.

"It's a hay saw," Judson said.

Sara Jane spun around, her knees rubbery with relief. She took a deep shuddering breath and for the first time realized how little breathing she seemed to have done in the last hour or so.

"Where've you been?" she asked him, unable to mask the worry that still lingered in her voice.

"Walkin'," he said. There was a dark brooding look in his eyes she hadn't seen before. "There ain't no water in the river!" He sounded outraged.

The woman gaped at him.

"Judson's been away quite a while," Sara Jane said quickly. "They dammed it up in Colorado," she told him.

"They did *what?* How the hell can they do that?"

"Believe me, a number of people have asked the same question. The case is being decided in the courts right now."

He shook his head, muttering under his breath. He'd bought a black felt cowboy hat, Sara Jane noticed, and he gave it an irritated tug. Then he looked at the tools on the wall again. "Where'd you get the hay saw?"

"A friend of mine brought it in. I didn't know what it was."

"That's what it is," Judson said. "Used 'em back in Iowa where I grew up. When they stack the hay in the barns for winter, they pack it in so tight you need one of these to cut out slabs to feed the stock." He took it down and demonstrated.

"Amazing," Sara Jane's customer said. "And you say they're still using them in Iowa?"

"Well, I don't 'zactly know about now. They did when I grew up." He looked at Sara Jane and gave her a wink.

She hoped to heaven the woman didn't ask how long ago that had been. Fortunately she had moved on to a piece of forged iron rod with one end in a flattened U-shape. A wrench, Kyle had guessed, but he wasn't sure for what.

"What's this?" she asked.

"That there does double duty," Judson said. "They use em for loosenin' the nuts on covered wagon-wheel axles. They stick it down in the hub like so." He showed both Sara Jane and her customer how it worked, taking the wagon wheel that was hanging on the opposite wall and demonstrating. "An' when they ain't usin' it for that, it's the reach pin."

"Reach pin?" Sara Jane echoed.

"The piece that runs from the front axle to the back, the reach pin holds it together, so." He showed them with his hands. "An' that's a splicer," he said, pointing to something that reminded Sara Jane of a crimping iron for hair. "It's for splicin' telegraph wires. An' those there are sheep shears."

Sara Jane winced, grateful she hadn't been asked since she'd assumed they were some sort of primitive pruning shears.

"You wanta be careful hangin' those out in plain sight," Judson told Sara Jane with a grin. "This here's cattle country. And that there's the blade of a field hoe," he said when the woman picked up something that looked like a heavy-duty croquet wicket with a rounded opening at the top. "The handle's gone. Reckon it rotted or split. It fit in here, then you stuck the tines in the ground and levered it up."

The woman looked at him admiringly. "My goodness, you certainly know your antiques."

"I reckon I'm something of an antique man," Judson said with a faint smile. Then he turned to Sara Jane. "I'm goin' upstairs," he said. He tipped his hat to the other woman. "Ma'am."

"Is that your husband?" The woman asked as they watched him disappear up the steps.

Sara Jane hesitated. "My fiancé?" she said, then hearing the question in her own voice, said more firmly, "My fiancé."

The woman let out an appreciative sigh. "I didn't know they made men like him anymore."

Sara Jane smiled. "They don't."

"YOU CAN TURN ON the lights, you know," Sara Jane said when she went upstairs. She was surprised to find Judson sitting on the bed in the waning light. He was leaning against the headboard, his knees bent and his hands loosely clasped between them. She flipped the switch and smiled at him.

The smile he gave her in return was almost imperceptible.

She cocked her head, crossing the room so that she stood beside the bed looking down at him. "Something wrong?"

He shrugged, but didn't say anything.

"Are you hungry? How about a bobcat?" She gave him a grin, hoping to get an answering one in return, but all she got was another halfhearted smile.

"Whatever you want," he said so softly she could barely hear him.

"Judson?" She reached out a hand and touched his knee. His fingers came up and wrapped around hers. He looked up and met her eyes and she saw pain in them that she wanted to understand. She turned her fingers in his grasp so that their hands clasped, then she gave them a gentle squeeze.

He sighed. "I feel like I been drug through a quicksand bog."

"I was worried about you. You were gone so long."

He shifted, letting go of her hand and getting up off the bed. He went to stand by the window and looked out over the parking lot, Wyatt Earp Boulevard and the train tracks. "Had a lot to see."

"Where'd you go?" Sara Jane asked, beginning to hunt through the cupboards for something to fix, deciding on a tuna casserole. She didn't ask Judson if he'd like it. She didn't imagine he'd ever had one.

"Down by the tracks. Over to the river." He shook his head, turning to face her. "Thought I was seein' things. Tell me 'bout that dam business."

Sara Jane did while she prepared the casserole and put it in the oven to cook. Then she set the table and made a lettuce-and-tomato salad. Judson leaned against the counter, listening, scowling, shaking his head.

"I reckon all them folks I know would be spinnin' in their graves if they knew. They'd be pleased with them new buildings that look like the old ones, though." He jerked his head in the direction of the Front Street reconstruction. A whole set of buildings based on photos of the earliest businesses had been reconstructed near the site of Boot Hill.

"You liked it?"

"Like to scared me to death."

She glanced at him. "What do you mean?"

"It was like I could see where I come from, but I couldn't reach it. Like it was there, but if I tried to touch it, it wasn't real. A mirage." He shook his head and gave her a dazed look. "Don't make much sense, does it?"

"Actually, it does." And it made sense of his pain.

He grinned suddenly. "Y'know that little ol' hoose-gow they got up there?"

"The jail, you mean?"

He nodded, still grinning. "I got throwed in it once."

"You got thrown in that jail?"

"Well, I think it was that one. Looked like it. Sure 'nuff sounded like it—full of pukin' fightin' cowpokes who drunk too much, that tour fella said."

"And you were one of them?"

Her consternation must have registered just then, because Judson suddenly looked slightly sheepish.

"Well, as a rule I'm as dry as that ol' Arkansas river-bed you got out there. But at the end a the trail, well, hell, Sadie, I been known to h'ist one or two. An' if a fella was to take a swing at me, well—" the corner of his mouth lifted "—I reckon I might swing back now an' again. In defense of a good cause an' all."

"Oh, of course," Sara Jane said. She should have been appalled. She should have been appalled that she wasn't appalled. But somehow she could well imagine Judson, fists swinging, in the midst of a barroom melee, and the image only made her shake her head in bemusement. "We'll have to keep you out of bars, then, won't we?"

He shoved a hand through his hair. "I went in a cou-ple this afternoon," he confessed. "They ain't the same at all. No dealers. No fancy women. Whiskey's not bad, though," he reflected.

"How comforting."

"Hey, don't fret yourself. You ain't gettin' yourself hitched to no drunkard. I was just testin' the waters, so to speak. I needed a little fortification after what I seen at the river."

Sara Jane put the casserole on the table and they ate in silence. Judson seemed trapped in thoughts of what he had seen that afternoon, things that must have jolted him to the very core.

It was more than just no water in the river, and Sara Jane sensed that meaningless small talk would only make things worse, so she finished her meal without speaking, then cleared the table. She washed the dishes and Judson dried them as they had the night before.

It wasn't until the last dish was dried and put away and Judson went to stand once more to stare down toward the river that was no longer there that he spoke again.

"You know the worst thing?" he said. His back was to her and his voice was so low Sara Jane had to strain to hear him.

She came to stand close behind him, but didn't touch him. "What was that?" she asked softly.

"Listenin' to the guide fella talk about Bat an' Wyatt, an' Prairie Dog Dave like they was history. Hell, they *are* history. But I knew 'em! I knew ol' Prairie Dog Dave. I won fifty bucks off him in three-card monte once. An' Wyatt? Hell, he wasn't no saint. Nor Bat, either. I reckon people know that, but they ain't never seen 'em drunk, an' I have. An' they ain't never seen 'em pull a gun, an' I have. They ain't never heard 'em laugh nor yell nor nothin'. An' they never will, 'cause they're dead, Sadie! They're dead."

He braced his hands in front of him on the windowsill and stared down, seeing what Sara Jane could only guess. "Ever' single one of 'em is dead." His voice was hollow and ragged now, and Sara Jane saw a shudder run through him.

She reached out and laid a hand against his back and felt him tremble. Moving closer, she wrapped her arms around him, hugging his waist and laying her cheek against his back. And he turned in her arms and his own came around her, pulling her into his embrace, holding her hard and fast against his lean body. He looked down into her eyes. His own seemed to her to be deeper and bluer than the clear autumn sky, as fathomless as the depths of the sea. His breath came quick and shallow and warm against her cheek. And then his lips touched hers.

Sara Jane had, since her earliest days, wondered about what it would be like to kiss the man of her dreams. She'd never admitted it. What tomboy would?

But late at night, curled up in her narrow bed, when the chatter between her sisters about their dreams and loves and real live boyfriends had subsided into the soft sounds of sleep, Sara Jane, who hadn't shared her dreams and had no real live boyfriend, would imagine the man who would someday be hers.

He kissed like Judson Black. Like he was hungry for her. Like he couldn't get enough of her. Like she was his lifeline in a stormswept sea. Oh, Sara Jane had dreamed exactly how it would be. And then she'd forgotten.

Until now.

Now the memories flooded back, swamped her, swept her away on a tide of longing that was so sudden and so fierce she couldn't have fought it if she'd wanted to.

And nothing in Sara Jane wanted to.

On the contrary, it seemed to her the very thing she'd been living for, waiting for, hoping for. It wasn't realistic. God knew it wasn't sensible. It was entirely irrational—and absolutely right.

Sara Jane pressed her mouth eagerly to his and kissed him back. She didn't even stop to think—as she'd always imagined she would—that she might not be doing it right. She *was* doing it right, and she knew it. And if she hadn't known it instinctively, Judson's eager response would have told her what she needed to know in order to believe.

He backed her toward the bed, and when she felt it against her legs, she leaned back and drew him down with her until they lay tangled together, their hands stroking, touching, caressing, their tongues teasing, tempting, tormenting. She felt a tremor run through him and knew her own heart was pounding frantically within her chest.

Judson's hands tugged up her T-shirt and slid under it, his fingers, rough with calluses, gentle against her soft skin. He reached behind her, fumbling with her bra. It unhooked at once, and Judson skimmed both her shirt and her bra away. Then he tore his own shirt off.

Sara Jane watched him, then reached out her hands and ran them lightly across his chest, ruffling the hairs, brushing the tiny points of his nipples. He shivered as he knelt straddling her, looking down into her eyes, then dropping his gaze to her breasts, watching as his hands slowly caressed them, cupped them, teased them to aching fullness. He was serious, intent, his sun-darkened skin taut across his cheekbones, his jaw tense. He ran his tongue along the line of his lips.

"My heaven, you are beautiful, Sadie girl," he said, and his voice sounded as if he had something caught in his throat.

"No more than you are," Sara Jane said, and meant every word. She'd never touched a man like this, never spoken to a man like this.

Before she'd met Judson she might have doubted that she ever would. Now it seemed unthinkable that she wouldn't say exactly what she felt.

He was the man she'd always dreamed of—the man she'd never believed existed. That he did was magic, a miracle. But she had no doubt that he was hers. Somehow, as different as they were, she felt as if she'd known him forever, as if they'd belonged together since the beginning of time.

What Judson thought shone in his eyes. They were alive now, where they'd been lifeless before. They shone now, where they'd been haunted before.

With a fine tremor in his fingers, he eased open the fastener at the waist of her jeans. Then, frowning slightly, he pulled the zipper down. It came easily. He smiled. His hands caught fabric on either side of her waist and tugged. Sara Jane lifted her hips and felt the jeans slide away. Judson moved back as his fingers skimmed down her legs and pulled off her jeans, taking her skimpy cotton panties with them. Then he fumbled with his own buttons, muttering as his fingers refused to cooperate.

"May I?" Sara Jane offered hesitantly.

He looked at her, stricken almost, then he swallowed and nodded jerkily. He dropped his hands to his sides, his fingers clenching and unclenching lightly, his breathing shallow and fast.

Sara Jane sat up and reached for him, her fingers trembling now, too, as they slipped inside the rough denim of his jeans. She could feel him hot and hard against the back of her hand as she eased the zipper down. Then slowly she peeled the jeans down his hips. He kicked them away as quickly as he could, shed his shorts, as well, and came down on top of her on the bed.

Yesterday she'd felt the space between them as if it were as wide and frozen as the Arctic reaches. Tonight there was no space, no space at all, and she burned.

Judson was burning, too, his skin hot and moist against hers. His hands were everywhere, setting off tiny fires wherever they touched.

She squirmed beneath him and he started to ease away. She shook her head and pulled him back, settling him between her thighs. He came willingly, eagerly. His fingers found her ready, and his intimate touch made her shiver and dig her fingers into his back.

"Judson!"

And he was no proof against her urging. Tense and trembling, Judson surged between her thighs. He looked for an instant startled at her body's resistance. But his own body was beyond control by then. He shut his eyes and kissed her with a fierce hungry desperation.

And then his body joined with hers. His spirit met hers. Past and present mingled. Time really wasn't a line, but a circle.

And Sara Jane, lying in Judson's embrace and filled with a peace and a completeness she had never known, kissed Judson gently and stroked his hair. And all the while she thanked God for this incredible gift—this man who was both separate and yet a part of her, this man whose lovemaking had showed her at last how two could really become one.

Chapter Five

HE SHOULD'VE KNOWED she was a virgin. Sure she wore skinny pants that showed off more curves than the tightest dress of any soiled dove he'd ever seen. And sure she wore the skimpiest unmentionables he'd ever seen, and sure they came off in a breeze.

But she talked like a lady. And she'd made him wear pajamas!

But had he noticed? Hell, no. He'd seen exactly what he wanted to see and done exactly what he wanted to do. He'd plowed her weeds under just like she was some grass widow come abeggin'. Judson rolled away from her and lay on his back with his hand over his eyes.

"You coulda tol' me," he said to God.

"Told you what?" Sara Jane asked softly. She was so close her breath was teasing his ear, sending shudders right down through him. He edged away, feeling guiltier than ever.

"Sorry," he muttered.

"You are?"

He pulled his arm away from his eyes and blinked up at her, then frowned. "You're not?"

She shook her head. "Should I be?"

"Well, hell!" Judson exploded. "If you don't know... I mean, you gave... I took... You're a lady, for mercy's sake!" He shoved himself to a sitting position, yanked the sheet up over his hips and sat there glowering at her.

Sara Jane eased herself up and sat curled against the headboard facing him. "And ladies don't sleep with cowboys?"

He could feel his face burning at her plain speaking. "No, they damned well don't! Not if they want to keep on bein' ladies and make respectable marriages," he muttered.

"I thought I was marrying you."

Judson shoved a hand through his hair. "An' I thought you wanted to wait and see."

"So you don't want to marry me," she said stiffly. "I thought I was marginally better than Marvela Stout." He could hear hurt in her voice even as she tried gamefully to hide it.

"You are a dozen an' fifty times better'n Marvela Stout, an' I am marryin' you—unless God decides otherwise! But you an' I both know He's got a mind of His own. I'm just saying I shouldn't ought to've done . . . what I did, just in case He gets a notion to jerk me outa here. I mean, who's gonna marry you if you . . . if you're . . ."

Hell, he couldn't believe he was talkin' like this to a lady!

"If I'm a fallen woman?" Sara Jane finished for him. She was smiling at him, making his insides quiver.

"You think it's funny?" Judson growled.

"No, I think it's lovely. Don't worry," she told him, and she reached out and touched his knee through the sheet. "Someone will marry me if I want to get married."

"Oh, sure. Someone will." Judson could well imagine plenty of men who'd take advantage of a woman like her. "But what woman would want him?"

"It isn't as big a deal now," Sara Jane assured him. "Women don't always guard their virginity the way they did in the 1870s."

"You had," he pointed out.

"Maybe no one wanted it."

He stared at her, shocked.

And she went on hastily, "Just kidding. But really, Judson, women are valued for other things besides that nowadays. And truly, there are perfectly respectable men who would have me. Don't worry." She gave him an earnest determined smile.

Judson grunted. He supposed he oughta be relieved. She was tellin' him he didn't have to regret what he was havin' the devil's own time regrettin'.

But somehow, knowin' that there were good men out there who'd have Sara Jane even deflowered didn't make him feel all that much better.

KYLE LOOKED from Sara Jane through the doorway to the man sitting at the table in her back room studiously dismantling the Sharps rifle and then back at Sara Jane again. "You're kidding, of course."

"I'm not," Sara Jane said. Though she could certainly understand how Kyle might not believe her. "I know it sounds weird—I know it *is* weird—but believe me, it's true."

She'd debated about what to tell Kyle about Judson when he'd said he was coming by to drop off a few things and to invite her to go with him to an auction near Hays. She knew she would have to tell him something. They'd been friends far too long for her to pretend that Judson was someone she'd known before.

While she waited for Kyle to drop by, she'd tried out several stories, had managed to get herself totally tangled up in them and knew ultimately that if she told no one else, she would have to tell Kyle the truth. So she had.

And now he was shaking his head. "God just dropped him out of heaven into your bed?"

"Someone did," Sara Jane said. "God's getting the blame. Come on. I'll introduce you." She grabbed his hand and hauled him toward the table where Judson sat. "Judson. This is Kyle. I've told him all about you."

Judson looked startled. He eyed Kyle narrowly. "An' he believed you?" he asked.

"No," Sara Jane said.

Judson nodded, satisfied. "I wouldn't, either," he said, shaking Kyle's hand. But Sara Jane didn't think he sounded very friendly. He set the rifle aside and got to his feet, studying the other man closely. Kyle eyed him with equal wariness in return.

Like gunfighters weighing each other up. Not an analogy Sara Jane particularly wanted to pursue.

"1878, huh?" Kyle said finally under his breath. "We'll see about that. How 'bout I take him with me to Hays?" To the farm auction, he meant.

"Oh, Kyle, you don't need—"

"Why not? We can see how much he knows."

"There's no one to watch the store."

"You watch it. You don't need to come. Does she, cowboy?" Kyle glanced at Judson. "Unless maybe you need to hide behind a lady's skirts." The challenge was as obvious as it was age old. Sara Jane groaned.

Judson straightened. His shoulders squared. His chin jutted. "Lead on, greener."

"Oh, for heaven's sake," Sara Jane said, stepping between them. "You don't have to go," she told Judson.

"The hell I don't," he shot back. "You oughta be glad I'm goin' when he as much as called you a liar!"

"He thinks I'm confused."

Judson shook his head. "He thinks I'm suckerin' you."

"Not really." Then, "Well, sort of," she admitted when he gave her a look of frank disbelief.

Judson snorted. "I ain't. And I aim to make him eat every last one a them words."

Visions of Judson and Kyle playing High Noon at opposite ends of Front Street danced once more through her head.

"Don't be rash," Sara Jane said, touching his arm. "This isn't 1878, you know."

Judson just stared at her, then jammed his hat down on his head. "Mebbe not, but some things don't change, Sadie."

Apparently not. Men of every generation must take on the appearance of horses' rear ends whenever they thought their territory was threatened, Sara Jane thought irritably. She turned her sights on Kyle.

"You're being ridiculous," she told him.

"I'm not the one trying to swindle you, *Sadie*." He twisted Judson's nickname for her with obvious relish.

"Judson's not trying to swindle me. I told you, God sent—"

Kyle rolled his eyes. "God sent him to you. Fine. Then let God prove it to me."

"I doubt He'll feel the need."

Kyle shrugged. "Then I guess it will be up to your hotshot cowpoke, Mr. Black." He gave Judson a look that was half challenge, half sneer. Judson's hands balled into fists.

Sara Jane gave up. "Fine, go on, both of you. Kill each other. I don't care. Just get out of here and leave me in peace."

Judson looked at Kyle. Kyle jerked his head toward the truck and started walking. Judson began to follow, then stopped, turned and came back to Sara Jane.

"Is he one a the ones'd marry you no matter what?"

Sara Jane blinked. "What?"

Judson didn't answer, just wrapped his arms around her, hauled her against him and kissed her with a thoroughness that left her stunned. Then he stepped back and tugged his hat down and sauntered back to the pickup. On his way he looked at Kyle, and Sara Jane could have sworn she saw him smirk.

JUDSON RECKONED that this Kyle Armstrong fella trusted him about as much as he'd trust a polecat at a picnic. Well, the feeling was mutual.

He might be a friend of Sara Jane's, but that didn't mean Judson had to like him. In fact Judson didn't like anybody who thought Sara Jane owed him more allegiance than she owed Judson. Sara Jane was *his*.

Judson wasn't quite sure when he'd started thinkin' about her that way. It didn't much matter really, as long as it was the truth—and as long as fellas like Kyle Armstrong understood it to be so.

Meanwhile he was doin' his damnedest not to let Armstrong know he was unnerved. But God A'mighty, the fella was drivin' like a bat outa hell!

Judson's knuckles went white against his thighs as they sped along. Didn't matter that it was sort of a smooth paved road that had a number and not a name. Judson had never gone so fast in his life. And he couldn't help suckin' air when Kyle slipped out and passed right around a truck half the length of Front Street before cuttin' back in an' just missin' a truck comin' the other way.

"Jeez," Judson muttered under his breath.

Kyle shot him a quick look and noted his clenched fists. Carefully, consciously Judson eased open his hands and looked right at Kyle. Kyle kept frowning.

"I don't know what your game is," he said to Judson finally. "But it better not hurt Sara Jane."

"I'd kill anybody who hurt her," Judson said flatly.

Kyle's eyes widened as he digested that. Finally he nodded. "Just so it's understood."

They didn't speak again until they were at the auction at a farm near Hays. "You see anything good, you let me know," Kyle said to Judson. His tone was neutral, as if he wasn't wholly convinced but was willing at least for the moment to give Judson the benefit of the doubt.

Judson wandered among the tables of tools and household items. He saw some whose uses were familiar to him, and more that he hadn't a clue about. Kyle went straight to the furniture and began examining it. He seemed to know what he was doing, Judson thought, watching him with grudging respect.

Judson picked through a box of tools and useless old farm gear. He might know what it was all for, but he didn't have the slightest interest in any of it. Hell, that was why he left Iowa when he was barely fifteen. Farmin' held not a speck of interest for him.

In the middle of one of the tables, though, he found something that did. A gun. A single-action army revolver, a Colt .45. He carried—*had* carried, he corrected himself—a .44-caliber rimfire himself, but he was familiar enough with this gun.

It looked just like the one Mert had won off Ed Masterson in that poker game back in '77, last time they'd been in Dodge.

"Ain't worth a plug nickel," Judson had argued. "Don't let him put it in the pot. You already got a gun."

"This one shoots straighter," Ed had argued.

At the time Judson hadn't known what he meant.

Afterward Mert had explained. "Belonged to his brother. See here." He'd tipped the gun to show Judson the initials W.B.M. scored into the metal of the butt.

Judson tilted his gun. The metal was tarnished and scratched. He spat on his thumb and rubbed at the butt. A moment later he shook his head and smiled. "Well, I'll be damned."

"BID ON THE GUN," he told Kyle.

"I don't do guns."

"You got a Sharps."

"That one was special. A little bit of history."

"Like that brass spittoon you just bought for fifty bucks 'cause you thought Wyatt Earp mighta spit in it?" Judson was still disgusted at the thought.

"I bought it because it's dovetailed," Kyle said huffily. "And Earp was a name."

"Masterson a name?"

"Huh?"

"Bid on the gun."

"Guns cost a mint," Kyle grumbled as the auctioneer held up the gun and began his patter.

"Bid on the gun."

Kyle looked at him. Judson looked back. Kyle bid on the gun.

"HE BELIEVES YOU NOW?" Sara Jane asked.

"Yep," Judson grinned.

"You convinced him?"

"I reckon." He pushed himself up against the headboard of the bed and looked smug.

Sara Jane shook her head in wonderment. "You must have. He trusts you. He even let you drive his truck." And that more than anything Sara Jane found amazing.

She, too, lay in bed, looking at Judson with more than a little awe. Kyle never let her drive his truck, and she even had a driver's license, which was more than Judson had.

But there was no doubt that Kyle had undergone a complete conversion where Judson was concerned. She'd sensed it the minute they got back.

When they'd left Kyle had been surly and stiff as a branding iron; when they got back he was whistling and clapping Judson on the back and telling him he'd see him in the morning.

Now Judson, propped against the headboard and wearing pajama pants but no shirt, grinned at her.

"What'd you do?" she asked when he didn't volunteer. "Tell me."

Judson reached down and hauled her up in his arms so that she sprawled on top of him. "I found him a gun that belonged to Bat Masterson."

"You didn't!"

He shrugged modestly. "Well, Someone did."

SARA JANE BEGAN to think that God was busy as a beaver over the next few weeks. There was the matter of getting Judson a driver's license, for example. She didn't see how he could do it without a birth certificate.

"What's a birth certificate?" he wanted to know.

"A piece of paper that says you were born."

"Hell, I'm here, ain't I?"

She acceded that point, but insisted, "You have to have one if you want a license."

"I don't want a license. I just want to drive."

Kyle had created a monster by letting him take the wheel of the truck. Judson was worse than any teenager just after his sixteenth birthday.

"You have to have one to drive," Sara Jane said.

"I drove Kyle's truck without one."

"Yes, well, Kyle might be a desperado, but I'm not. So we have to get you a birth certificate if you're going to drive my Jeep. And—" she sighed and shook her head "—I don't know how we're going to do that."

"Send for one," Kyle said. He was sitting at the kitchen table cleaning the Masterson gun under Judson's supervision. "Where were you born?" he asked Judson.

"Iowa."

"And how old were you when you were—" Kyle waved his hand "—when you were . . . you know."

"Twenty-eight."

"When's your birthday?"

"March 7."

"So, write the Iowa Bureau of Vital Records or wherever they keep those things and tell 'em you were born March 7, twenty-eight years ago."

"Oh, Kyle, that's ridiculous. They won't have one," Sara Jane protested.

"How do you know?" Kyle said with the conviction of the converted. "Who did you say was running this show? You figure God ever let a little bit of paperwork stop Him?"

THE SCARY THING WAS, Kyle was right. Within two weeks of writing, Judson had a birth certificate—and a driver's license.

The next day he got a job.

The lady who'd bought the celery dish appeared one lunch hour and introduced herself as Emmalynn Foster. She and her husband, Wilf, were ranchers from west of town. Wilf needed a foreman, she said. A man who did things the old way. Emmalynn, smiling, said she'd told Wilf she knew just the man.

Would Judson be interested in coming out and talking about the job? she suggested hopefully.

Judson would. Judson did.

He started work the next afternoon.

Everything happened so quickly and so smoothly that Sara Jane began to get more worried by the minute.

"It shouldn't be like this," she told Judson one night in early November when she lay in his arms in bed.

"No? Why not?"

"It's like...I don't know...like getting rewarded for having been bad."

He grinned. "Don't sound so awful to me."

She dug her fingers into his ribs. "That's what I mean. I lied! And you...you were no example of sterling virtue, either! And yet...and yet..."

A corner of his mouth tipped up. "You feel blessed to have me?"

She thumped him on the head. "See. You have no modesty at all."

He looked down at her. She was lying naked alongside him. "You ain't exactly hidin' your light under a bushel, either, darlin'." He grinned, leaning over to kiss her nose. "Reckon God prob'ly thinks we deserve each other."

"But—"

"And I reckon He's right."

"But—"

"Shh." He touched his lips to hers. "Just shush now and kiss me, Sadie, girl."

Heaven help her, Sara Jane did.

"YOUR FATHER THINKS I should make a career of planning weddings," Evangeline said when Sara Jane picked up the phone the second Saturday in November. "And I'm beginning to think he's right. It's all set."

The wedding, she meant. Sara Jane's wedding. The one she had tossed like a hand grenade into her mother's lap six weeks before. The wedding with the imaginary groom, Judson Black.

Judson Black, the man who was at this very moment lying on top of her naked in her bed, nibbling on her ear and doing other wickedly delightful things to her body that six weeks ago she couldn't even have imagined.

"It is?" Sara Jane's voice went from a squeak to a gasp as Judson's hand moved provocatively between her thighs. "Er, how, um, cleaver of you, Mother."

At the word "Mother," Judson pulled his hand away and rolled off her.

"She can't see you," Sara Jane mouthed at him, but he stayed resolutely away, sitting up, arms folded across his chest.

"She can sure as shootin hear you," Judson retorted in a gruff whisper.

"Oh, is that Judson? Is Judson there?" Evangeline asked eagerly. "Do let me speak to him, Sara Jane."

"He's busy, Mother," Sara Jane lied.

"I'm not busy," Judson said.

"He's not busy, Sara Jane. I heard him say so," Evangeline said. "I don't know what's the matter with you! All the other girls brought their young men home first thing. We've never even met your Judson."

"He's not my—" Sara Jane began, then stopped because whatever else Judson was or wasn't, in this life he was certainly hers.

Before she could think of something else to say, Judson took the phone out of her hand. "How d'you do, Mrs. Jones," he said with as little of his cowboy drawl as Sara Jane had ever heard. "It's a real pleasure to talk to you."

"Lovely to talk to you, too, Judson. Richard and I are so looking forward to meeting you. We can't wait to meet the man who had the wisdom to pick our little Sara Jane to be his bride!"

"That'd be God, ma'am," Judson said solemnly. "He's the one that did the picking."

"Judson!" Sara Jane poked him in the ribs.

"God? I don't—" Evangeline began, bewildered.

"S'truth," Judson said to Sara Jane, then to her mother, "An' I have to say, ma'am, I'm mighty happy He did."

Sara Jane, who knew his fervency had a lot more to do with Marvela Stout than with her, thumped him hard on the head with her knuckles.

"Ouch!"

"Ouch?" Evangeline echoed.

Crimson, Sara Jane snatched the receiver out of Judson's hand. "Ma, we have to go, really! Shop's going to open in twenty minutes."

"But I want to talk to you about the wedding, Sara Jane!"

"I'm sure it's fine. I'll call you later," Sara Jane promised, "when Judson's at work. We can talk about it then."

"Well, if you think that's best, dear," Evangeline said doubtfully.

"It is." She had the phone halfway down when her mother spoke again.

"You know, Sara Jane," Evangeline said almost wistfully, "I thought you were foolish to want things so simple, but I begin to think you might be right. This wedding will be truly lovely, and the focus will be right where it belongs—on the two of you. I'm so happy for you, darling."

Sara Jane swallowed, her throat suddenly dry as Kansas dust. "Thanks, Mother. I . . . I'll talk to you later." And she hung up.

She looked at Judson lying beside her, his eyes dark and smiling at her. A brief smile touched her lips, then she blinked rapidly and looked away.

"What's wrong? Did I embarrass you, Sadie?"

She shook her head and gave an awkward little shrug. "It's not that."

He cocked his head. "What is it?"

Sara Jane curled up tight and held her head in her hands. "She thinks the wedding's going to be wonderful, that it will focus on the right thing. Us."

"An' that's bad?"

"It's a lie," she said desperately, hoping against hope that he would contradict her, that he would tell her that Marvela Stout be damned, he'd marry her even if he didn't have to, that he'd fallen in love with her just the way she'd fallen in love with him.

Because, fool that she was, she had.

She didn't know exactly when or how and sometimes she was sure she would wonder why, but she was in love with Judson Black.

But Judson Black didn't seem to be in love with her.

At least he didn't contradict her. On the contrary he was as silent as a stone. He lay back down again and stared at the ceiling. Outside she heard the whistle and rumble of a freight train and the windowpanes rattle with the perennial Kansas wind. Inside she heard Judson swallow.

He shoved himself down and turned onto his side and reached for her. Slowly he drew her into his arms and kissed her. His kiss was long and fierce and hungry. It stoked the fires he'd set earlier. Then, with all the skill of which she knew he was capable, Judson made her want him, need him, love him. Like a fire, he consumed her.

Still he never said a word.

JUDSON LIKED AUTOMOBILES. He liked having all those horses under one little bitty tin hood, and once he'd stopped white knucklin' and got his bearings, he liked makin' 'em go damn fast. It wasn't quite the thrill that riding hell-bent-for-leather on the back of a good horse was, but it was somethin', all right.

Airplanes was somethin' else.

"I ain't gettin' on one a those," he told Sara Jane when Kyle dropped them off at the Wichita airport the Wednesday before Thanksgiving. "No, sir."

"They're quite safe," she told him. "Honestly, Judson, they're safer than cars."

Judson didn't believe it for a minute, even though Kyle said, "She's right, you know," as he wrestled Sara Jane's luggage out of the back of the truck.

"How can it be?" Judson wanted to know. "And don't tell me you'll buy me a book," he said to Sara Jane. Most of the advances of the twentieth century suited him right down to the ground, but flyin' through the air seemed more'n a little risky.

"We have to," Sara Jane said to him. "We don't have time to drive. It would take close to eighteen hours."

"Eighteen hours?" Judson stopped and stared at her, incredulous. "You know how long it takes—took—to get to Chicago in 1878? Eighteen hours? Holy Moses."

Sara Jane stopped, too. She looked at him, then she looked at Kyle, who was unloading a huge box. She looked back at Judson and shrugged.

"All right. Don't come." And then damned if she didn't turn and walk into the building without him!

"Hey!" Judson grabbed his bag and shot after her. "What're you doin'?"

She took a deep breath. "I'm going to Chicago," she said. "I'm going to have Thanksgiving with my parents and my sisters and their families. I'm going to do my best to enjoy myself. And then Saturday I'm going to show up at my wedding."

Without him.

She didn't say it; she didn't have to. He knew damned well what she meant.

And he knew damned well where that would leave him. At another wedding with another bride.

A shudder ran through him. He shut his eyes, sent a message in God's direction, then he opened them again, looked at the shiny silver monster that was going to bear him where sensible, God-fearin' men knew they damned well shouldn't be, then met Sara Jane's gaze grimly and squared his shoulders.

"Lead on," he said.

"SEE?" SARA JANE SAID when they'd landed at last. "That wasn't so bad, was it?"

Judson blinked, still dazed, still not quite convinced those little bitty houses he'd been lookin' down on were real. But hell, they sure weren't in Kansas anymore. "Weirder than travelin' a hundred an' some years, if you ask me."

All those people jammin' themselves into a metal tube with wings and not even payin' attention when it like roared loud enough to stampede a million cattle? All of 'em listening to little things on their heads and eatin' food that came wrapped in clear stuff while solid ground was so far down Judson had to swallow and look away.

Nope, travelin' across time made more sense than that.

He looked down to see Sara Jane watching him. "But you're all right?" She sounded worried.

He looked at her more closely and thought she looked worried, as well—a lot more worried than she'd looked when they were getting on the plane.

"I'm right as rain now," he assured her. "What about you?"

She gave a quick nod and about the phoniest damn smile he'd ever seen. "I'm fine." She started to lead him down the walkway again, but he dug in his heels.

"You ain't," he said, hauling her to a stop. "What's troublin' you, Sadie?"

"I don't know," she said with another faint smile as she shoved a hand through her hair. "I'm just... nervous, I guess. I've never taken a man home to Mother before." She gave a small slightly nervous laugh.

"You reckon they ain't gonna like me?"

"Of course they'll like you," she said, but she didn't meet his eyes. She started to move again. He held her back.

"Sadie?"

She looked up at him.

"Do you want to call it off?"

"Of course not! You need to marry me. I need to marry you. Don't be stupid, Judson. I'm just a little skittish is all. You don't know my mother."

Judson wasn't sure he wanted to, but this time he let her drag him onward, only saying once more, "You're sure?"

"Trust me, Judson. It'll be fine." She gave him another smile then, and in this one he caught a glimpse at last of the real Sara Jane.

He smiled back.

"There they are!" Her fingers tightened like a death grip on his wrist and Judson looked to where she was pointing. He saw a lady—there was no other word for her, so elegant and proper did she look, even in one of those short dresses of 1994—and a stern-looking man in a business suit.

His future in-laws.

Amos Stout suddenly didn't seem so threatening, after all. As Sara Jane's parents descended upon him, Judson raised his gaze to heaven and wondered belatedly if perhaps he shoulda been doin' this when he'd been a few miles farther up. "I hope You know what You're doing," he said.

Chapter Six

THEY LOVED HIM.

Her father, the CEO; her mother, the grande dame; her sisters, the society belles; and her brothers-in-law, the pillars of the North Shore establishment. Her goggle-eyed nieces and nephews. Her aunts and uncles and cousins.

All of them. Every one was smitten with Judson Black.

"He's got his feet on the ground, your young man," Sara Jane's father said after he'd spent an hour talking to Judson in the privacy of his study. "Not a know-it-all like some of those young fellows nowadays. I like that."

"He's so polite. So respectful," said her mother. "So refreshing."

"Gorgeous blue eyes," said Marcia.

"Yummy dimple," said Cecelia.

"Cheekbones to die for," said Heather.

"And a grin to match," said Diana.

"Great butt," all six of her sisters agreed, and gave her a sextet of grins and thumbs-ups.

Sara Jane blushed mightily.

"Always knew our Sara was a dark horse," cackled her ancient aunt Abigail.

"Where'd you find him?" asked her cousin Melissa.

Wouldn't you like to know? thought Sara Jane.

"He really is a very nice man," Evangeline said to her as she and Sara Jane sat in the den on a blustery Thanksgiving afternoon, watching out the window as the brothers-in-law and the nephews and nieces taught Judson the rudiments of Jones-family football. He was wearing the athletic shoes she'd bought him.

"Yes," Sara Jane said softly, watching him go out for one of Philip's passes. He bobbled it, then made a last-minute grab only to be tackled by two of her nephews. He crashed to the grass, face first, and came up grinning, still holding the football. The little boys cheered. Philip slapped him on the back. And Sara Jane's heart brimmed over with love for him. "Yes, he is."

Evangeline picked up her needlepoint. "I wondered when I met him last night," she went on, "if he would . . . fit in."

Sara Jane cocked her head. "Oh?"

Evangeline gave her an apologetic smile. "He seemed so . . . so Western."

Sara Jane laughed.

"Not quite what we expected for you." Her father looked at her over the top of his newspaper.

Sara Jane smiled. "No. Life is full of surprises."

SARA JANE CALLED IT "information overload." To Judson it just seemed like a hell of a lot of new stuff to learn.

Flyin' had taken the starch out of him. And then ridin' in her father's Lincoln along those roads she called expressways. They sure didn't seem like express to him. He could go a damn sight faster in Kansas with Kyle's truck. Hell, a puddin'-footed horse in a rainstorm could go faster'n these six lanes of backed-up traffic.

He didn't say so, of course. Much as he could, he kept his mouth shut. Didn't catch any flies, didn't stick his foot where his teeth oughta be.

And didn't—he hoped—embarrass Sara Jane.

But still he had to do some augurin'. Like when Sara Jane's father had taken him into his study for "a little man-to-man talk."

If he felt like a fish outa water in small-town Dodge, it was nothin' compared to the way he felt penned up in Richard Jones's walnut-paneled study bein' asked about his prospects.

He tried not to say he didn't have any. Even in 1994 where women were liberated and had jobs of their own, he didn't reckon their fathers wanted to hear that their prospective bridegrooms didn't have a feather to fly with, not to mention no horse an' no saddle—even if it was true.

So he augured on about Wilf's spread, about the price of cattle and the responsibilities of his job. An' he felt like he'd sweated off ten pounds before Richard Jones finally clapped him on the back and told him he was pleased to welcome him into the family.

Fittin' in with the rest of 'em wasn't much easier. They were friendly as a litter of lop-eared pups at feedin' time, even those pill-pushin' fellas who were married to Sara Jane's sisters. But they talked about things he hadn't a clue about—video games and football scores, knee replacements and laser surgery, IRAs an' whether the stock market was bear or bull. Hell, even when he thought he knew somethin'—like about what a stock market was—it turned out he still didn't have a clue.

He felt like a prairie dog tryin' to swim with swans. He splashed too much and it tired the hell out of him. And he reckoned just watchin' him must be makin' Sara Jane squirm.

But every time he shot her a worried look, she smiled at him, and that smile was enough to make him plunge back in an' try to swim again.

He didn't do too bad at the football business. Catchin' a little ol' ball was a damn sight easier than wrestlin' a steer. An' keepin' away from everybody else while he ran with it wasn't too hard, either, when you'd spent as many hours as he had dodgin' mad bulls.

Still he was glad when it was over and they came back inside and Sara Jane came up and put her arms around him. He winked at her, and she kissed him, and the room got a whole lot brighter when she gave him a real honest-to-goodness Sara Jane smile.

He felt a tug on his arm. "Wanta play my new video game, Uncle Judson?" Timothy asked him. Sara Jane had half a dozen nephews, and Judson still had trouble keepin' 'em straight, but he knew which was Timothy 'cause he didn't have any front teeth.

"No, he wants to see my magic tricks," said another of the nephews.

"Does not, Benji," said two of the nieces. "He's going to tell us all about his horse, aren'tcha, Uncle Judson?"

"Er," Judson said, feelin' like the prairie dog again, about to go down for the third time.

"I think," Sara Jane said quickly, "that Uncle Judson might like a little rest from all this attention. How about going for a walk with me?"

He gave her a grateful grin. "I'd be plumb tickled."

But before they could get out the door, Evangeline said, "Not now, Sara Jane. We need to have you try on the wedding dress."

"Now?"

"Now," Evangeline said firmly. "I'm sure Judson will understand."

"It was my mother's dress," Sara Jane told him. "And her mother's before her. And three of my sisters have worn it. There's a lot of tradition in this dress."

He could see that.

"I thought it would be easiest," she went on. "We're all pretty much the same size, but I probably should try it on." She was looking at him worriedly again.

"You go right ahead."

"You're sure?"

"Don't matter to me. I reckon I'll take a little walk by myself." He wanted to kiss her, to soothe away some of that worry he saw in her eyes. Instead, he rubbed a knuckle against her cheek and let himself out the door before any of her relatives could offer to come with him.

He walked quickly, heading down the rocky path that led to the narrow beach bordering the lake. The night was as quiet as the house had been noisy, and he relished it, stopping at last to breathe deeply and let the air out real slow.

Out over the lake a wedge of silvery moon cast a reflection across the water. The same moon he'd seen scatter silver across the Red River. Overhead he saw stars. The North Star. The Big Dipper. The same stars. In not quite the same places they'd been back in '78. Had it really been 116 years ago?

Seemed like yesterday, he thought wryly. He sat down on the sand and leaned back against a log, staring up at them. Was yesterday, he thought. Or damn near.

And yet it wasn't.

He thought about Sara Jane's family, their mansion—she said it wasn't, but it seemed that way to him—their television and their stereos, their videos and CDs, and the fifty thousand other things that all the books in the world couldn't make him understand. He thought about the way they took airplanes and expressways and some damned things they called space shuttles for granted, the way they just "ran down to the grocery" for some ice cream or called Paris without even thinkin' about it.

He thought about Mert and wondered what had happened to him. He thought about O'Leary and the cattle. He thought about Amos and about Marvela. Had anybody ever married her? He knew what had happened to Bat and to Wyatt and his brothers. He read that Doc Holliday had died in bed.

From what he remembered about Doc, that seemed pretty unlikely. But it didn't surprise him. Stranger things had happened.

Look what had happened to him.

His insides kinda squeezed together when he thought about it.

"Judson?"

Sara Jane's voice, soft and tentative behind him, made him jerk his head around. He sat up quickly when he picked her out of the darkness coming toward him across the sand.

"Are you all right?" she asked, her hair blowing in the evening breeze.

He caught her hand and pulled her down into his arms, kissing her hard, needing her warmth, her substance, to fend off the questions, the memories. "I'm fine," he muttered against her lips. "Now."

He shouldn't do it. Not now. Not here. What if her father came along? Her mother appeared?

But he couldn't help himself. He was beyond every ounce of common sense the good Lord had given him. He needed Sara Jane. He needed her now, needed her desperately, with everything that was in him.

And so he fumbled open the buttons, he bungled the zippers until Sara Jane undid them for him. He pulled off his jacket and spread it under her, then pushed down his jeans and hers, settling himself between her thighs, and with one urgent thrust, slid into her warmth.

"Sadie," he muttered. "God, Sadie, I need you." And then he took her—and himself—beyond the moon and the stars and the past and the present. He took them to a land of bliss and warmth and love, to a time out of mind.

"Sadie," he murmured against her neck, replete, peaceful at last. His hand stroked her cheek. He lifted his eyes and gazed down into her wide dark ones. Sadie. He kissed her lightly on the lips and smiled faintly. Sadie. The only thing that kept him from feelin' like he really was one hundred and forty-four.

SHE SENSED the pain in him. It didn't surprise her. If Dodge City 116 years later had been hard to cope with, urban fast-paced Chicago and a skillion relatives must be nearly impossible.

He did well. But she could feel his strain, saw his determined smile, his desperate casting about for the right words, the suitable thing to do or say.

"You can back out," she wanted to tell him. "You don't have to do this. You can say forget it. I'll understand."

"No." He said with his arm around her, the two of them huddled against the night, staring first out across the water, then into each other's eyes. "No," he said. "I'm marryin' you."

She swallowed. She willed him to say, "I love you," the words that would make the marriage all right, no matter how it had come about.

But he didn't.

Because he didn't love her. She knew that. Had always known it. He was marrying her not for love, but because if he didn't marry her, he'd have to go back and marry Marvela.

Nothing had changed. Not for him.

Only for her.

Well, all right. So she'd make the best of it. It was, in fact, more than she'd ever hoped for. And if she couldn't have it all, she was still enough of a realist to be grateful for what she did have.

She hoped it would be enough for Judson. Still, somehow she wanted to make it up to him, to offer him some sort of consolation for his existence having been totally uprooted and transplanted. She didn't really know how.

There was only one thing she could think of, and now, on this cold November night, barely twelve hours before they would become man and wife, she was worried that he would think it was silly.

Still, as they were going up the stairs to their separate bedrooms, she said to him, "Will you come in with me for a minute?"

He looked startled, as if she'd suggested something improper. "Reckon I'd better not—"

She shook her head. "Don't worry. I'm not asking you to…to make love. I just…have something I want to give you. A wedding present," she added awkwardly.

Color washed his cheekbones. "Wedding present?" he muttered, dismayed. "Damn. I didn't get you nothin'." He shook his head a little desperately. "I ain't any good at this."

Sara Jane touched his cheek. "You're fine. Better than fine," she said firmly. She took his hand and drew him down the hall and into her room, shutting the door behind them.

On the top of her dresser she had wrapped the very large box that Kyle had struggled up to the ticket counter with in Wichita and that her brother-in-law Tom had wrestled all the way home.

"For you," she told Judson now.

He swallowed. "What is it?"

"Open it."

He looked dubious, approaching it warily as if it might spring to life and attack him. "I…" He cleared his throat and scratched the back of his head.

"What's wrong?" Sara Jane asked, worried that she'd offended him without even knowing it.

"Nothin'. It's just… ain't nobody ever give me nothin' before."

"Never?" She was aghast.

He gave an awkward shrug. "Nothin' that I remember. My folks died when I was fryin' size. Never had nobody after them that give two cents about me." He spoke matter-of-factly as if it hadn't ever really bothered him. It bothered Sara Jane. Terribly.

He plucked at the wide white ribbon, testing it with his fingers, then studying the knot.

"Cut it," Sara Jane said.

He shook his head and worked it off slowly. "Don't want to ruin it. It's beautiful." With equal care he picked open each piece of tape and finally, slowly, eased the box out and set it on the bed. Then he stood back and considered it for more than a minute. At last he fished his knife out of his pocket and slit the tape along the top of the box, then opened the flaps to expose her gift to him.

He stared. She saw his throat work, saw him blink. But he didn't speak. He didn't move. He simply stared.

Sara Jane licked her lips nervously. "I—I know it's not great," she said quickly. "But I thought...I thought...well, it was because of a saddle that all this—" she gave a vague wave of her hand "—that all this happened. And I remembered what you said about it being a Gallatin. That saddle Kyle got at the same sale where I got those newspapers, well, it was a Gallatin, too. I know it's not the same but—"

"It is."

She was babbling so much she almost didn't hear him. She stopped. "What did you say?"

But Judson didn't answer. He had reached into the box and was pulling out the saddle and saddlebags that she had got Kyle to do his best to clean up and restore.

Sara Jane cringed when she looked at them now in the full glare of the lamplight. Even cleaned up they looked pretty grim. Certainly they were nowhere near new-looking. Old leather simply couldn't survive what this saddle and bags must have undergone for many years and come out looking good.

Judson was examining them intently, running his fingers over the saddle, squinting at it, turning it this way and that, scowling all the time he did so, his brows drawn together in a grim line.

"I should have got you a new one," Sara Jane said a little desperately. "Kyle will take it back—"

"No." He looked at her, his expression dazed. "This is it."

"Is what?"

"Stout's saddle." He sounded dazed, too, his voice a little shaky. "I'm sure of it. It's a Gallatin, of course. The *same* Gallatin. Same riggin', same stirrups, same ever'-thing."

"But there must have been lots—"

"And here," Judson went right on. He was rubbing his finger along the fender. "See this gouge? There was one like it on Stout's saddle. I was wonderin' how it got there." He shook his head. "Well, I'll be damned. Who'd a guessed?"

Certainly not Sara Jane. Her knees felt rubbery and her head light. She sat down on the edge of the bed and picked up the saddlebags, running her fingers over them, shaking her head, while Judson continued his study of the saddle.

She opened one of the saddlebags that had come with it. There was an old crumpled white cloth still in it. She was thinking she'd have to chide Kyle for leaving a rag behind, when she opened it up and saw that it wasn't a cleaning rag, but an old handkerchief wadded around something. She opened it up. Inside it was a deck of cards.

"Where'd you get those?"

"In the saddlebag. In this." She showed him the handkerchief and at the same time looked at it more closely herself. If she'd doubted Judson's memory, she did so no longer as, with her fingers, she traced the embroidered initials—A.S.

Judson took the cards out of her hand and weighed them in his. He fanned the deck out.

Sara Jane had never seen such an old deck of cards. "Is it a full deck? All there?" she asked.

"More'n all there," Judson said. His voice sounded hollow.

"What do you mean?"

He flipped several cards out onto the bedspread. The ace of hearts. The ace of spades. The ace of diamonds. The ace of spades. The ace of clubs. The ace of diamonds.

Sara Jane stared at them. "*Six* aces?"

Judson flipped one more card onto the bed. "And a cuter. The joker," he explained at her blank look. He sat down suddenly beside her, his face pale.

Sara Jane remembered the hand he'd told her he'd held. She remembered Stout's four aces. She remembered the cuter. She looked at the aces on the bed.

"He *cheated?*"

Judson ran his tongue along his upper lip. "He used to shoot his cuffs. It was a habit. At first I wondered if he had somethin' up his sleeve, but he didn't seem to win enough. And then—" he shook his head "—then I reckon I got a little high on my own hand and my own luck and maybe a little whiskey and I didn't pay attention."

"He cheated," Sara Jane said, and her voice sounded hollow now, too. "You didn't have to marry her," she said.

They looked at each other.

"And that means," she went on, "that you don't have to marry me, either."

He stared at her.

"You don't," she said. "You can go back now. You can call him on it. You can leave. Be free." Her throat was tightening even as she spoke, and she was afraid she might cry.

She couldn't cry! Wouldn't let herself! But she almost didn't get the words out past the sudden thick ache. She met Judson's gaze and dug down deep to find a determined smile. "You don't have to get married at all," she said with as much cheerfulness as she could manage.

Judson didn't smile in return. He looked down at the cards, then back at her again.

"Jilt you, you mean?" he said slowly, comprehension dawning. His voice was gruff.

"Right. Just don't show up." She smiled again, making her voice deliberately bright.

"The way you'd planned it?"

"Exactly." It was killing her, but what else could she do? She couldn't beg him to stay. It wouldn't be right. It wouldn't be fair. If he'd loved her it would be different, but he didn't. Besides, she'd planned on being jilted, getting her mother to back off the matchmaking. Now she could get her wish.

It was what she'd wanted all along, wasn't it?

Of course it was.

She knew it. Judson knew it, too.

She mustered another smile. She tried to laugh, but when it sounded more like a sob, she ducked her head and cleared her throat. "You know God," she said lightly. "Always a little unpredictable."

One corner of Judson's mouth lifted ruefully. "I guess," he said softly.

They just looked at each other then, deep blue eyes locking with Sara Jane's dark brown ones. Hers swam with tears. She prayed he wouldn't notice.

Out in the hall she heard two of her sisters pass, giggling as they went. Her father said something to her mother about getting to church tomorrow. Her brother-in-law Tom said he was glad there wouldn't be a receiving line because his feet hurt. They moved past. It was quiet again.

"You're sure?" Judson asked, his gaze intent.

Sara Jane thought about how willingly he'd struggled to deal with her father, her family, her world. She thought of making him cope with airplanes and televisions, with expressways and video games for the rest of his life. She thought of him riding fences at Wilf's, and at the way he'd sit tall in the saddle and stare off toward Texas and the faraway look she'd see in his face. She thought of the way she'd seen him last night on the lakefront—the strain on his face, the wistfulness, the memories of the life that was rightfully his. The life he could reclaim now that he knew he didn't have to marry Marvela. Or her. She wanted him with her forever because she loved him. But because she loved him, she had to let him go.

She smiled. "I'm sure."

Judson bent his head. His hands clenched lightly on the tops of his thighs. Then he gave a slow nod, drew a breath and stood up. Sara Jane stood, too. They faced each other.

"How'll I get back?" Judson asked.

"God will figure something out." No doubt about that.

"Guess so."

She picked up the cards and handed them to him. "You'd better take these along for evidence."

"You think I'll need it?"

"Probably not. I think knowing the truth will set you free." She almost reached out and touched him then. She balled her hands at her sides, afraid that if she didn't she would make a fool of herself, would grab him and refuse to let him go.

"Guess so," Judson said again, his voice ragged. His gaze flicked toward the door and he started toward it, then stopped and looked back at her. He swallowed. "Sadie?"

She looked at him mutely, not trusting her voice.

"Kiss me goodbye?"

It was the easiest—and the hardest—thing Sara Jane had ever done.

She took two steps and faced him squarely. She lifted her hands and laid them lightly on the soft cotton of his shirt. Then she tilted her face up and gently, carefully touched her lips to his.

Judson didn't move. He stood absolutely rigid and didn't reach for her at all. He touched her with nothing other than his lips and his eyes—and his heart.

Sara Jane shut her eyes, still kissing him, and willed the moment to last forever. *You can do it, God! Please, God, You can do anything!*

But his lips left hers. He stepped back. She heard him swallow and take a breath. Then the door opened. And closed.

He was gone.

"WHERE'S JUDSON?" Cecelia asked the next morning.

"Haven't seen him," said brother-in-law John.

"Maybe he went for a walk," said Marcia.

"Or for a run," said fitness-freak brother-in-law Jeff.

"Where's Judson?" asked her father when it was time to go to the church.

"Haven't seen him," said her mother. "Wasn't Ralph going to bring him?"

"No, Eric was," said Heather.

"I thought you and Philip were," said Aunt Abigail.

"Oh, well," said Evangeline, brushing a lock of hair out of Sara Jane's face, "we don't really want him here right now, anyway. It's bad luck if he sees the bride. Right, darling?" she said, giving Sara Jane a squeeze.

Sara Jane felt like she was going to throw up.

Why had she ever thought this was a good idea, anyway? It seemed to her now the stupidest, most presumptuous notion she could ever have come up with.

"Because I'm the stupidest, most presumptuous person in the world," she muttered under her breath as her father bundled her into the back seat of the car, her mother into the front and headed toward the church.

"What's that you're saying, dear?" Evangeline looked back at her, concerned.

Sara Jane shook her head numbly. She would just have to go through with it now. There was no way she could possibly explain. She would have to pretend to be surprised when Judson didn't show up. But she wouldn't have to pretend her pain.

God had seen to that.

He'd given her what she'd thought she wanted, and it was exactly what she deserved.

She hoped He was pleased that at last she understood that she had acted precipitously. She hoped He was glad that she realized now that love was a possibility. She hoped He was pleased that His cosmic shuffle had opened her eyes. She supposed she should hope that someday He would see fit to provide her with another man she could love.

But not any time soon. Please God, not any time soon. She wasn't ready for that yet.

She might not be ready ever.

Not as long as she loved Judson Black.

"Where's Judson?"

"I haven't seen him."

"He's late."

"Probably caught in traffic."

"Somebody should have ridden with him."

"I didn't see him this morning or I would have."

"It's almost time. Where is he?"

"He's late."

"Where's Judson?"

Sara Jane stood shaking in the small anteroom off the back of the church and listened to them talk—her mother, her father, her sisters and brothers-in-law.

He isn't coming, she wanted to tell them. *He's gone. Gone back. Gone home.*

She couldn't say a word.

They milled. They muttered. Finally they filed out.

"Have to take our places," Evangeline poked her head in and said. "Reverend says so. Come along. It's time."

Heather handed Sara Jane her bouquet. Martha lifted her veil and settled it once more on her head.

"Smile," Cecelia urged her.

"All set," her father said and took her arm, drawing her out of the waiting room at the back of the church and into the vestibule.

Sara Jane heard the organ in the loft begin to play.

She hadn't counted on this.

Surely someone would have noticed by now that Judson still wasn't there. Surely they would call it off now. They wouldn't make her walk down the aisle to no one.

Would they?

The door opened. Her father put his hand over hers. Please God, enough is enough, Sara Jane pleaded.

But Cecelia had already started down the aisle. Moments later she was followed by Victoria. Then Heather.

"Our turn," her father said softly and took the first measured step.

Woodenly, eyes cast down, aching to the depths of her soul, Sara Jane went with him on the long walk down the aisle to her humiliation.

It was the worst experience of her life, and she knew she deserved every second of it. She wanted to run, to hide, to disappear and never be seen again. She wished that when she got there the ground would open and swallow her up. She lifted her gaze just enough to look hopefully for an opening chasm.

She saw a pair of shiny black cowboy boots.

Her head jerked up.

She stared, amazed, at Judson Black.

He looked grave and nervous, every bit the apprehensive groom even as he gave her a tentative smile.

Her father was smiling, too, as he put her hand in Judson's.

The minister took over from there. He led them through the prayers, the vows, the responses. Sara Jane could hardly form the words. Judson's were strong and loud and clear.

She trembled when he put the ring on her finger. Her eyes brimmed when she looked at him. His hands felt real and solid and warm under her shaking fingers.

But she didn't believe it was true until the minister said, "God bless you," and Judson looked into her eyes.

"He already has," he said.

IT WAS A WINGDING of a party. The Lady Gay Saloon on the first night after they brought the herd in couldn't've been louder. There was toastin' and music and dancin', and Judson could always hold his own in that. He did, too, toastin' and grinnin' and dancin', holdin' Sara Jane in his arms.

But he couldn't put his whole heart into it, not until he got Sara Jane alone.

And when at last he did, when finally he managed to dance her out on her parents' deck and they faced each other in the silence, he felt panic in full measure, for her smile had vanished.

She looked right at him and demanded, "What are you doing here?"

"Marryin' you?" he said, and he couldn't quite keep the question out of his voice.

"But . . . but why?" There was anguish in hers.

And he knew he'd kept his lip buttoned long enough. "Because I love you, Sadie."

They were words he never reckoned he'd say. But there was no question at all when he said 'em. When he gave her the words, he gave her his hopes, he gave her his heart.

And he prayed that Sadie would give him hers.

"Judson?" Her voice was a whisper. The anguish was gone. There was a kind of breathless disbelief that had replaced it.

He shook his head. "I didn't want to go back. I could have. I didn't want to. I wanted to stay with you."

She pressed her hands to her face. Her shoulders were shaking. Was she laughing? Or crying?

He was frantic. "Don't be mad, Sadie. Please, don't be mad! I'll go if you want me to!"

She opened her arms and fell into his. "Oh, Judson, no! I love you! I wanted you to stay! I just didn't want you to feel you had to."

He smiled. "But I do have to, Sadie," he said softly, cradling her face in his hands. "There ain't no life for me anywhere, anytime without you."

And then he kissed her, gently at first, savoring the moment, then hungrily, getting a taste of what the future promised them, and thanking God for it. For her.

But there was only so far a fella could go with his wife on her parents' porch in any day and age. Reluctantly Judson pulled back.

Sara Jane wiped her eyes with her fists, then blotted them again with the sleeve of his coat.

"I didn't believe it when I saw you there," she said, smiling at him. "I was sure you were gone."

Judson shook his head. "I won't leave you, Sadie. Not ever."

"But this morning— They said you were late. They couldn't find you. *You weren't here!*"

Judson eased open the neck of his starched shirt and squirmed just a little. "That didn't have nothin' to do with the weddin', Sadie. I borrowed Ralph's car. Wanted to drive myself, prove I was a modern man, you know?" He shrugged and gave her a sheepish grin. "I reckon I got a little more to learn. Leastways about some things." The grin widened. "Like flat tires."

A Note from Anne McAllister

There is a group of bestselling authors who learned all they really needed to know from kindergarten, from their cats or even from watching "Star Trek." I say, more power to them, but it didn't happen to me. From kindergarten I learned that I hated taking naps. From my cat I learned that litter boxes must be changed daily—or else. From "Star Trek" I learned nothing because I never watched it. I watched Westerns.

And it occurs to me now that all I really needed to know in life I've learned from cowboys—the televised, the fictionalized and the oh-so-very-real. From cowboys I learned that independence and self-reliance can be coupled with caring and generosity. I learned that gentleness and toughness can coexist in the same man, that it is possible to be dependable yet flexible, reliable yet still spontaneous. I learned the virtue of keeping my mouth shut and my eyes open, and to do what needed to be done without waiting to be told.

I learned to leave gates the way I found them, to do the best I could with what I had, to keep my sense of humor and to always live up to my word. Most of all I learned that power and money are less important measures of a man than strength and tenderness, courage and compassion. And as I've grown up, I've learned, too, that, as measures, these traits weren't valuable only in one particular century. They stand the test of time.

While I knew all these things before I started writing "Hitched in Time," I found the truth of them again in Judson Black. He might have been a little rough around the edges, but he was—and is—a good man to ride the river with, a man to count on wherever—and whenever—he was. I certainly didn't want him to ride off into the sunset when the story was over.

I fell in love with him. So did Sara Jane. I hope you will, too, and that if you do, you'll find your own Judson Black somewhere, somehow…sometime.

Take 4 bestselling love stories FREE

Plus get a FREE surprise gift!

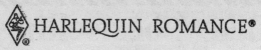
HARLEQUIN ROMANCE®

celebrates

FAMILY TIES!

**Join us in June for our brand-new miniseries—
Family Ties!**

Family... What does it bring to mind? The trials and
pleasures of children and grandchildren, loving parents
and close bonds with brothers and sisters—that special
joy a close family can bring. Whatever meaning it has for
you, we know you'll enjoy these heartwarming love stories
in which we celebrate family—and in which you can
meet some fascinating members of our
heroes' and heroines' families.

The first title to look out for is...
Simply the Best
by Catherine Spencer

followed by...

Make Believe Marriage
by Renee Roszel in July

FT-G-R

HARLEQUIN SANDALS SWEEPSTAKES
HERE'S HOW THE SWEEPSTAKES WORKS
NO PURCHASE NECESSARY

To enter, complete Official Entry Form or 3" x 5" card (mechanical repro-
ductions are not acceptable) by hand-printing your name and address and
mailing it to: Harlequin Sandals Sweepstakes, P.O. Box 9076, Buffalo, NY
14269-9076, or P.O. Box 637, Fort Erie, Ontario L2A 5X3. Limit: One entry
per envelope. Entries must be sent via First Class Mail and be received no
later than 5/31/95. No liability is assumed for lost, late, misdirected or non-
delivered mail. Some prize restrictions apply.

Sweepstakes is open to residents of the U.S. (except Puerto Rico) and
Canada, 21 years of age or older. For complete rules and prize restrictions,
send a self-addressed, stamped envelope (WA residents need not affix
return postage) to: Harlequin Sandals Sweepstakes, P.O. Box 4798, Blair,
NE 68009.

HSAN-RLR

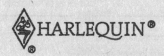

WIN A DREAM VACATION FROM

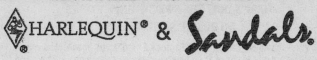

HARLEQUIN® & *Sandals.*

Harlequin Books and Sandals Resorts are offering you a vacation of a lifetime—FREE!

You could win your choice of a 1-week vacation at any of Sandals Caribbean resorts. Just fill in the Official Entry Form immediately and you could be on your way to a DREAM VACATION from Harlequin and Sandals.

HARLEQUIN BOOKS/SANDALS RESORTS SWEEPSTAKES
OFFICIAL ENTRY FORM

Name: _____

Address: _____

City: _____ State/Prov: _____

Zip/Postal Code: _____ R-KAQ

Entries must be received by May 31, 1995.

Return entries to:

In the U.S.	In Canada
Harlequin Sandals Sweepstakes P.O. Box 9076 Buffalo, NY 14269-9076	Harlequin Sandals Sweepstakes P.O. Box 637 Fort Erie, Ontario L2A 5X3

HSAN-ENT-R